Of Shadows, Stars, and Sabers

an anthology
edited by

Jendia Gammon & Gareth L. Powell

Copyright © 2025 Stars and Sabers Publishing

All rights reserved. No part of this book may be used or reproduced by any means, graphic, electronic, or mechanical, including photocopying, recording, taping or by any information storage retrieval system without the written permission of the publisher except in the case of brief quotations embodied in critical articles and reviews.

This is a work of fiction. All of the characters, names, incidents, organizations, and dialogue in this novel are either the products of the authors' imaginations or are used fictitiously.

The views expressed in this work are solely those of the authors and do not necessarily reflect the views of the publisher, and the publisher hereby disclaims any responsibility for them.

No part of this anthology, including the works herein or any cover artwork or interior illustrations, was created through the use of artificial intelligence ("AI") technologies or systems, and no part of this anthology will be used by the publisher nor may be used or reproduced in any manner by other parties for the purpose of training artificial intelligence technologies or systems.

ISBN: 979-8-9907055-1-7 (hardcover)
ISBN: 979-8-9907055-0-0 (trade paper)
ISBN: 979-8-9907055-2-4 (ebook)
Library of Congress Control Number: 2024951858

First printing edition: February 11, 2025
Published by Stars and Sabers Publishing in the United States of America.
Cover Artwork: Niall C. Grant | Cover Design and Layout: Dash Creative
Edited by Jendia Gammon and Gareth L. Powell
Proofreading and Interior Layout by Scarlett R. Algee

Stars and Sabers Publishing is an imprint of Roaring Spring Productions, LLC.
Los Angeles, California

https://www.starsandsabers.com/

For all those who love to be transported by words, whether through shadow or light, into realms both possible and impossible.

And for our beloved families.

Table of Contents

INTRODUCTION
9

Of the Shadows

THE SHADOW EATER OF ÓRINO-RIN
Eugen Bacon
15

MORGEN'S COTTAGE
Helen Glynn Jones
27

UNDERLAND
Gemma Amor
37

EXISTENCE: A THOUGHT EXPERIMENT
Greg van Eekhout
53

SING YOURSELF BACK TO SLEEP
Laurel Hightower
57

THE MAGIC WOOD
Jonathan L. Howard
67

An Earth So Strange

'THE DREAMBUG INFESTATION OF HALF MOON OAKS
KC Grifant
83

CRUEL MACHINATIONS
Pedro Iniguez
93

THE FIRE TOWER
D.K. Stone
105

To the Moon and Stars

LAST GASP
Stark Holborn
121

UNREMARKABLE
Alice James
131

WHO'S AFRAID OF LITTLE OLD ME?
Sarah L. Miles
141

A HUNDRED THOUSAND EYES GAZE UPON
THE CORE OF YOU
Khan Wong
153

DONHAGORE
T.L. Huchu
167

GREY
Ren Hutchings
179

By the Saber and the Spell

HOLY FOOLS
Adrian Tchaikovsky
193

HUNGER AND THE LADY
Peter McLean
207

HIS LORD RECALCITRANT
J.L. Worrad
219

SHADOW WRAITH
Dennis K. Crosby
229

THE BIKE
Mya Duong
243

AN ASEXUAL SUCCUBUS
John Wiswell
253

TO THE RESCUE
David Quantick
263

WISH YOU WERE HERE
Renan Bernardo
269

LONG LAST ALICE
Cynthia Pelayo
281

Toward the Light

OUTRIDER
Antony Johnston
289

GLITTER TOWN
Kali Wallace
299

ALICE STREET
Paul Cornell
313

THE COMPANIONSHIP OF LIGHTHOUSES
Lizbeth Myles
319

A SPECIES CALLED HOPE
Ai Jiang
331

Acknowledgments
337

Publication Credits
339

About the Authors
343

About the Editors
353

Upcoming Releases
355

Introduction

The power of story to connect the world is limitless. Our minds grow when we can dream, and when we read of the fantastic, we read dreams made real upon the page.

Jendia's note
I am the child of a storyteller and indie author, my father, and of a keen editor and proofreader who worked in a small city press, my mother. I have written since early childhood, and it is no wonder growing up in a home of vibrant siblings and word-loving parents that I should end up a published author and now, a publisher of other authors. My parents instilled in us the love for story, whether written, on the screen, or on the radio. So I am instilling that love in my children, and sending it out into the universe for everyone.

We believe we're living in a golden age of speculative fiction. Never before have there been so many diverse and interesting voices writing across such a wide range of genres. However, the industry is experiencing a turbulent time with the closure of some magazines and publishers and the rise of generative AI. In response to this, we think that now seems to be the perfect time to lift up and celebrate the best human writers working in our favorite genres.

At Stars and Sabers Publishing, we have made it our mission to champion and celebrate human creativity, and bring you original and powerful stories from new and established writers.

Introduction

This book is our first release, and as editors, it has been an absolute privilege and delight to work with so many fantastic authors to produce such a fabulous collection of tales. Each one is a masterclass in short form world creation, and together they add up to something truly special. In fact, we love this book so much that as writers ourselves, we can't help feeling a little envious we haven't included stories of our own.

We hope you enjoy reading this book as much as we have enjoyed making it, and that it stands as a beacon of quality writing and art in a world where both are being increasingly devalued.

Of Shadows, Stars, and Sabers

Of the Shadows

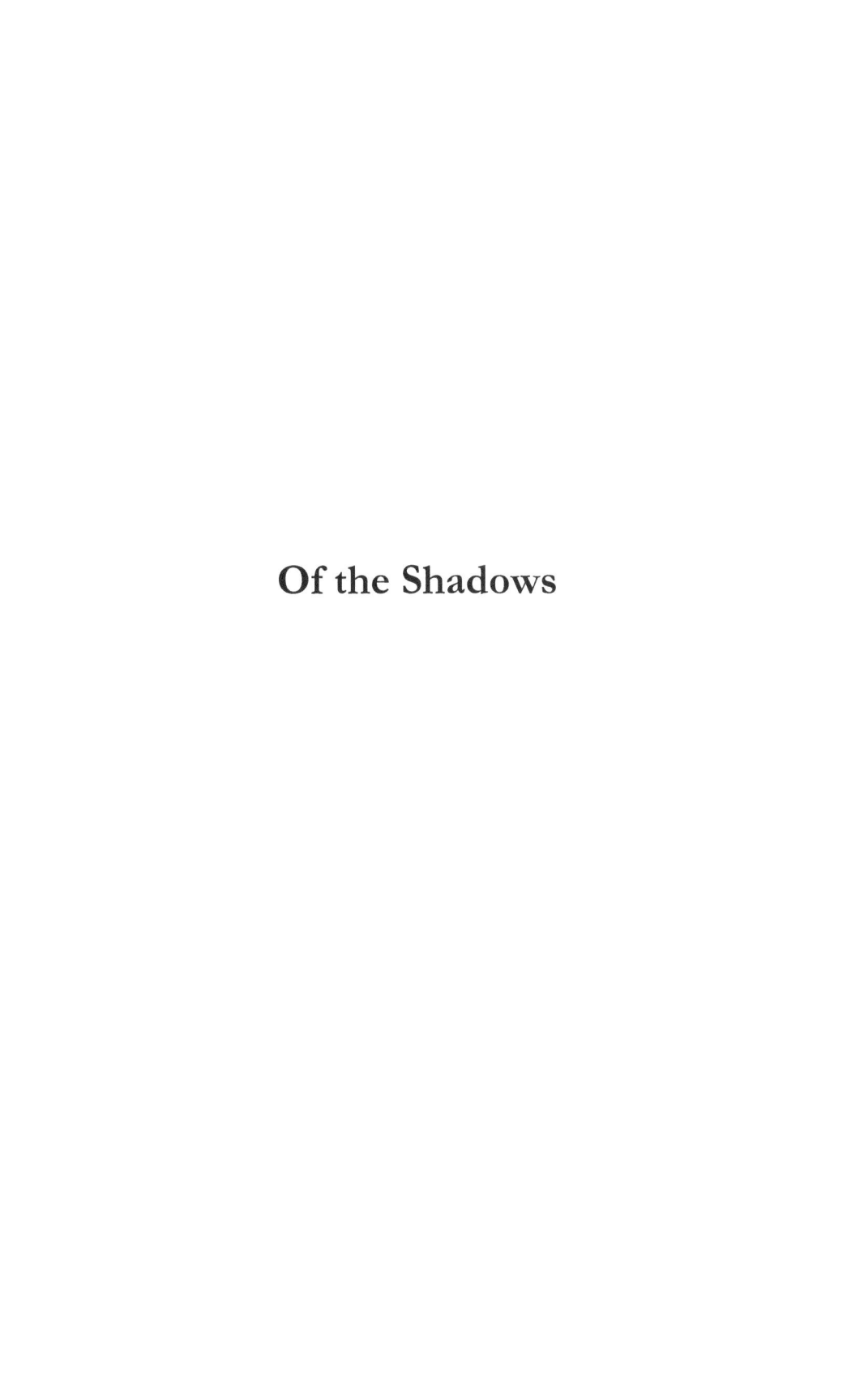

The Shadow Eater of Órino-Rin
(A Sauútiverse story)

Eugen Bacon

ALL HER LIFE, rather than living normally and being human, Ng'wa was exercising how to contain her hunger, whose very uncontainable nature was inhuman. The ravenousness was a disease. The uroh-ogi, the healer her parents summoned to perform the curing, suggested all sorts of remedies: octopus ink, cured egg yolk, bird's nest soup, mummified mushrooms, black ant larvae, guinea fowl liver, even rotten t'apiapia fish, the freshwater one. Echo cupping, magicked ululations, or implanting a vibrating chip just inside the skin of her stomach was no good. So that was that for sound-based cures—already exorbitant for folk living hand-to-mouth. After an intense round of maggot casseroles, broiled spiders, live marula worms, horned nguwe'we brains served raw, the barefooted uroh-ogi, dressed in nothing but loin cloth, had all but bankrupted Ng'wa's parents. He threw his hands in the air, called it an incurable sickness of the bottomless stomach.

Ng'wa had the deepest craving. She felt as if a v'hushalele—such a ruthless spear!—was piercing her throat and she needed food to assuage the torment. She desired to eat perpetually. It was a compulsion that clawed at her throat, and she needed to gobble something to push it down. Eating anything else felt like dreaming. It did not disturb her tongue or her teeth or her gut. Chewing cassava was a blur. Swallowing chicken all happened in a haze. She never remembered what food tasted like. If someone asked, "Was it leafy or earthy or coppery or fruity?" she blinked at them. Ingesting was for her light and space and darkness, and all the in-betweens. Dining was color: magenta, char, jungle, raw, blood. The doing was no better than slumbering because, at the end of it, she looked at her hands and the empty plate and felt groggy. Just like she did each dawn. Eating or dreaming messed up her head—they hummed in her mind a shredding chant. Her life was chaos and she wanted simplicity. She yearned for a song that would know her fears—and one of them was consumption. Then one bés something happened. She ate a shadow and felt full.

Maé said Ng'wa was born screaming. Her tiny face was all scrunched up, her fists and legs pumping as if she was boxing and stamping the universe, nearly shaking with her cries the whole of Songea'aa in the Kigo'Kigo Province north of planet Órino-Rin. When Maé pushed her face into a teat, Ng'wa snatched at it and sucked until the milk was spent and blood flowed out, but she was still hungry. Her maé first sweated and then cried out, her joy at the birthing permanently stifled.

Folk never missed a detail—a woman wearing a tiered head-wrap and a loosely-tied waist sash around a voluptuously-shouldered bark dress peered closer. She saw the blood dripping down the greedily-sucking baby's cheeks, and blurted out loud what everybody was thinking: "You have birthed a shai'tan!"

At the mention of a bad spirit, the gleeful ululations of friends and relatives all at once died—it would have been better if they had just petered out. It didn't stop folk digging with keen hands into platters and platters of clove rice garnished with roasted groundnut sauce and crispy with freshly-fried mopane worms. The food some good people had donated was still going round despite the unfortunate birth. Gourds of hoguro also didn't stop. They continued to pass from hand to hand, and everyone was properly inebriated. They were adorned in a bright array of color, as flamboyancy always accompanied a birth, a marriage or a death.

Her da, weighed by the significance of expectations, stared, shellshocked, at the truth. He didn't like it. The bub they had brought into the world was not so much a miracle but was rather an omen. Ng'wa had turned their already poverty-stricken lives to rubble.

"Who vibrated the wrong sound?" he cried.

Then they started blaming each other. He spoke harshly to Ng'wa's maé. "You insisted on the uroh-ogi remedies for our childlessness. Now look what we've got!"

"Aiiiii, so it's my fault. Your people would not stop asking if there were little feet on the way, each time they came to visit. It was only a matter of time before they gave me the bad sound and got you a new woman!"

"You made the choice to carry this child incorrectly. Were you reciting the right words to your stomach?"

Behind their accusations was their fear, everyone's fear. That the bub would grow too many limbs and glow at midnight. That it would metamorphosize into a winged monster and, by dawn, the hut where they lived below the cloud-line, the meridian, because of their poverty, well devoid of sunlight and more susceptible to the malevolence of sonic storms, would be left with cadavers and husks.

But, of course, that didn't happen.

Midnight came and went, and the baby was still a baby. And the reprieve was nothing to do with the paid trio of masked musos who sang an exorcizing wail:

"Jebelelele! Ng'ong'o jali bowa! Ng'wa. Ng'wa!"

They played the k'hora'aa, slapped a ngonini drum and it went *Doombadoodoodoombadoo*! They scratched and clacked a shekere-re, and plucked the luhte-te.

"Jebelelele! Ng'ong'o jali bowa! Ng'wa. Ng'wa!"

The uroh-ogi who invigorated all who were in attendance to chant prayer-filled recitals to Our Mother, the Creator, also determined that the best discourse to protect the child from the evil eye was to name her by the last sound of the exorcizing hymn: Ng'wa.

And so everyone danced and sang the curse-removing chant:

"Jebelelele! Ng'ong'o jali bowa! Ng'wa. Ng'wa!"

After they had all left, most of them to similar meagre huts below the meridian, but one or two of the wealthier fork up to their elevated homes in the promenade of light, Ng'wa's maé tried something different, away from judging eyes. She mixed breast milk with kudu-kudu milk from the market of barter, and even took the unusual measure of draining the milk of the single horned nguwe'we they owned into a pail, because it was thick and wild, and turned out to be rather sweet. If she felt any pity for the suckling nguwe'wes in the backyard that squealed at the deprivation of their mother's milk, it quickly ebbed because they just as swiftly adapted to maize husks, soaked beans and hoguro residue from the winery in the promenade of lights where the rich went to discuss business, and where Ng'wa's maé was a part-time cleaner. The sucklings also took a great liking to the mash of anything that had died in a manner that prohibited any human from eating it.

In time, Maé supplemented the mixed-up milks with crushed durian and red peas, mashed bananas and avocados, ground oatmeal and nuts, pureed amaranth and eggplant, blended wild mango and marula, millet porridge stirred with lard… to no avail.

Ng'wa was still hungry, so hungry, the hunger was a clawing, a v'hushalele in her throat and she couldn't satiate its rage.

This is how it happened.

It was a bés just like any other, and Ng'wa was helping Maé with the chores. This time, they were cooking a hot meal for Ng'wa to deliver to her da above the cloud-line, where he worked in a crystal factory, supervising the vibration panels that swallowed energy from whirling proto-storms to convert it into ririni crystals. The pay was a pittance, but it was a pay—as the nomad who owned it often reminded them, which was better than sitting with a begging cup in the streets.

The hot meals were Maé's way of perpetually making up to her husband for the anomaly of their gluttonous child.

"We will never get dowry with that one," Ng'wa once heard him say. "No one will be foolish enough to marry her."

"Yes," said Maé. "We're stuck with her."

Sometimes, her maé showed kindness, but, often, she jammed it down Ng'wa's already famished throat how much she inconvenienced them. Maé was particularly more vicious with her choice of words when flooding from the sonic storms washed out food gardens, yanking out and floating whole potato vines. They had recently lost an entire crop out the back.

"You're eating all this much and what good is it doing you? Look. Your skin is just as tight around those bones, no meat in them."

"But Maé—"

"It's not raining yams. Go and catch some lizards."

And Ng'wa had become adept at it. She would brave the most malevolent of sonic tempests, the most vicious ones flashing the bluest licks of potentially fatal energy, duck from rockslides to find the precipices where critters took refuge, and piripiri locusts and lizard tenders had become her specialty. She learned to settle her stomach with the nutty, warming goo of larvae, but for her da, she understood the wholesomeness of smoked toad. It had to be the right kind—not the warty ones. She skewered two of them, a male and a female, chargrilled them over a smoke pit with paprika and chili oil, and packed them close to the klalabash tagine lathered in groundnut curry.

She wrapped herself best she could with sonic storm gear that included galoshes and a helmet, guarded the hot meal in its special flask and took to the skies. Well, not really, but that was how it felt when she reached the promenade of light, where the added protection was completely unnecessary. Carrying the food made her hungry, so hungry, she thought she might eat her toes. But she delivered the food intact, through a duty guard at the gate because her da was still on shift.

On the way back, the whiteness of the horizon heartened her to peel off her storm paraphernalia, and feel some sunshine on her skin. She was standing there in a frock that felt like nakedness—because she'd always wrapped it in something weather protective—and the kiss of the suns was tender as silk. She closed her eyes, relishing good weather, when something fragrant arrested her nostrils. She opened her eyes and there was nothing there—just a man moving away, but his scent beckoned her with its toastiness mingled with something earthy that made her hungry, so hungry. She forgot her storm gear, and ran after him. He was short but with a long shadow following him on the ground. His pungent aroma was also astonishingly mouthwatering. Her galoshes made her advance ungainly.

Perhaps she was reacting to the weather, because she felt the itch of a sneeze coming, and she opened her mouth. To her astonishment, the man's shadow peeled from the ground and leapt onto her tongue. It was like her jaws were a magnet and the shadow metal. Something about her mouth attracted the shadow. She gobbled it and found it toasty and nutty. But what astounded her was the unexpected absence of the clawing need in her core, as soon as she swallowed the shadow.

The flavor was as pretty as sight. How magical was it? It was one of a kind. It was an aurora, and it dazzled her. The v'hushalele in her throat went lifeless and, suddenly, she was free from starvation. The man continued his journey, ignorant that he had lost his shadow to the stomach of a once very hungry Ng'wa.

Ng'wa returned home with a skip, despite the weight of the storm gear she had to wear again below the cloud-line. The world trembled with an intense thunder that rippled and groaned. Still, she felt ecstatic!

"There is nothing to laugh about," her maé said. "I need you to clean the nguwe'we sty—must I ask you to do everything, can't you do it for yourself?"

"Yes, Maé."

"Make yourself useful. Life is not all about your hungry stomach."

Ng'wa still ate cassava and beet and kale, all those things normal people ate, but it was out of necessity for nutritional sustenance. It was shadows that she craved. She started finding more and more excuses to take hot food to her da, or help her maé cleaning toilets at the hoguro winery, sometimes cleaning after customers inside commuter spacebuses at the sky port—anything that would take her to the promenade of light where she ate them all. It didn't matter if it was the shadow of a man or a woman or an old person or a child. There were two benefits to her excursions. 1) She was no longer hungry. 2) It pleased her to see a glimmer of pleasure in Maé's eye each time Ng'wa lifted the lid of the treasure pot and added a few owo or ririni crystals that were instant payment for her casual work.

"Be careful," her maé would say as Ng'wa prepared to set out. "All this news we've been hearing is a bit scary. There's a pandemic going around. People getting sick and losing their immunity." Still, she didn't protest too much, and was keen for Ng'wa to keep making herself more beneficial by bringing in earnings.

Sometimes Ng'wa felt like she was followed. Something at the edge of her vision, but she understood it was her nervousness at being caught. No one said eating shadows was anything illegal, but life was awkward enough as it was, with people thinking she was half-shai'tan, part-inhabited by a bad spirit. Imagine how complicated it would get if they found her gobbling shadows!

Life without a v'hushalele in her throat was immediately optimistic, but her merry disposition attracted unwelcome suitors, one of them with a bad dishwater smell. She preferred to lick the bottom of nguwe'we rather than be hastily wed to men she felt no attraction to. She was her parents' bitter disappointment, but she was satisfied with herself. She figured—who but her best understood her needs? She was perfectly capable on her own to find a partner, if she did *at all* need a spouse, and she could very well do it without the coordinated efforts of her parents' interventions, thank you very much! She was self-efficient. What she needed other people to give her was dignity and self-respect, but she wasn't going to get it here.

So, one bés Ng'wa stole into the treasure pot, pulled out some of her earnings—surely, they were also hers—and pushed her way through an especially vicious squall whose caerulean energy sparked her protective wear. It was bitterly cold, and she hugged herself as a lashing rain whirled and switched patterns of pelting. She saw in the horizon the swirl of a soundless storm—those were the most deadly. She began to run in those stupid shoes and fell splat in the torrent. A terrible wind pushed at her face.

She reached the sky port and fell into the lift.

Higher up, she paid at the entry point with her hard-earned owo and climbed into a spacebus. It was distracting to be there sitting in the commuter shuttle, rather than cleaning it. The vessel whistled and whirred skyward from the docking port, lifting Ng'wa and fellow passengers who paid her no mind.

Ng'wa was astounded how careless people were with their shadows. And each shadow tasted different. Some were sweet, others juicy. Some were lemony, others honeyed. Some were pillowy in texture, others nutty—all crunch. Some were fruity, others full of spice.

She didn't mind the short nights of Zezépfeni—how could she if it meant more sunlight, more edible glooms? She would leap onto a mobile scooter that anticipated her commuting, and she would utter a destination on a whim. Za'anzi, the beachcomber town, had the best shadows, most of them tropical flavored. Ba'bati in central city was hit and miss. The structural angles of the metropolis and its aesthetic workplaces meant that, sometimes, it was hard to get the right natural light. Lindi was the worst. It had eco-friendly skyscrapers and clusters of steel and mirrors in parametric design—everything was megastructured and imposing, she could never get a decent feed. Imagine catching a shadow on a vertical garden!

She kept moving around, planet to planet, led by her stomach. Kijito-Mawe in Pinaa had an astonishing menu with its clusters of non-augmented humans who separated themselves in "green" villages, away from the AI or augmented humans. But a good part of the planet held sparse vegetation, and citizens spent most of their lives in multidimensional technobuildings.

Wiimb-ó with its bays and embankments, archipelagoes, boulevards and paramikules—chiefdom-based villages rife with hospitable folk—was a degustation! Having relished such plenty, and not once missing her parents, Ng'wa did not think twice about an odyssey to Ekwukwe.

It took half a bés to travel from one planet to another. Sometimes she allowed herself to doze, but this time she felt restless. The overhead screen inside the spacebus vibrated with an ad about a new hair pomade, Curls 2.0. Pictures of children, men and women modelling the fluffiest curls on their heads floated on holo around the spacecraft. She went to the restroom. She looked at herself in the bathroom mirror or the space shuttle, and loved what she saw. Her cheeks were soft with health and her golden eyes shimmered with the brightest future that could never be Órino-Rin.

On the way back to her berth, the news was running:

"Fears are growing of a widely-spreading pandemic, as uroh-ogi across the planets report a strange malady that weakens those suffering from it, and they have a growing susceptibility to formerly non-fatal conditions. A man in Inku'lulu, Zezépfeni, is reported to have died after losing his eyelashes. Scholars in mahadums and scientist maadiregi everywhere are now investigating what a number of victims appear to exhibit: a loss of shadows."

Ng'wa felt momentary panic, and walked faster and away from the overhead screen as if it was onto her. She saw a young man with tribal marks on his face, a set of two parallel scars across each cheek, and he was looking at her.

She discharged him from her mind and thought of the longest shadows the stark, hollow grounds of Ekwukwe would cast. She imagined basking on a hot crag hosting a cave where she would find rest at dusk. She saw herself stretching her body in all that freedom, feeling lethargic and replete from a decent crunch. She worried for a moment: what if an impudu-pudu showed? That cast a bit of gloom. The planet was renowned for its beasts, and the lightning bird was a fierce one. But what if she came across a lost baby one that cast a shadow whose taste was as sweet as an oasis? She was mostly starved for human shadows, but who knew what a beast might taste like?

She met him again one sunny bés in a cave bar that had attracted her for its 'menu'. It was a popular place and folk visited it for its in-house hoguro brewery. Inside was stark and hollow, but it bustled with patrons. Ng'wa was more interested in the woman behind the bar than the young man tailing her, for whom she had no romantic interest. She wondered if her parents had put him to it, but quickly dismissed the thought because they could never afford it. She allowed the distraction of the woman at the bar, how she smiled like she knew a secret, how she tilted her head for Ng'wa.

"Do you have a name?" asked Ng'wa.

"Upe'ndo," the woman said. "It means love." There was something in her eyes as she said it.

"Good to know," said Ng'wa.

"So… what would you like?"

"You—come wrapped as a gift?"

Upe'ndo laughed. "What *else* would you like? In many words, what's your poison?" She nodded at the taps of hoguro.

"How does it come?"

"Soft, hard, frozen, warm. Red, black, the color of watered blood. Cherry, raspberry, peppery, mushroom. Root vegetable hoguro is always the best. We have cassava, sweet potato, yam, even beet. The cloudy hoguro is barrel fermented, comes with precipitate."

"What? Do I look like I need plumping?"

"Something like that," said Upe'ndo.

"Choose for me," said Ng'wa. She felt a little bit behind on the dating game, and was keen to catch up.

"You're a long way from home," Upe'ndo said, and placed a carafe of cloudy hoguro in front of Ng'wa.

She would have a pleasant shadow, Ng'wa surmised, but she favored to eat Upe'ndo in other ways. To do so, she needed to satiate her other hunger.

The young man was wearing an unbuttoned shirt, chest hair sprouting from it. He slid into a barstool next to her.

"I'll have the same," he said to Upe'ndo, nodding with his chin at her cloudy hoguro.

Ng'wa decided to take the bull by the horns. She would confront him about his interest in her when he faced her. She stared hard at him, but he never looked at her once.

As he downed hoguro after hoguro, she wondered how he would taste. When he reached for the reader and settled his bill with a chip in his hand, Ng'wa smiled at Upe'ndo, said, "Be right back," and slipped from the bar.

She stumbled into the sunlight and trailed the young man. She was thrilled to see the length of his shadow in the hot white suns. That would teach him to follow people. She wondered if he'd know when she took his shadow.

He walked hurriedly, almost in a trot. She half-walked, half-ran after him, past a corridor of thorn trees. When she emerged into a clearing, he was gone. She looked about her. A bit further stood a giant mopane tree that had shed all its leaves. She heard movement like the snap of a twig in that vicinity, aha, then saw his cast on the sunlit ground. She beamed. After all that hoguro, of course, he was relieving himself.

Normally, she could smell a shadow. But not his.

She saw it stretching from the foot of the tree, elongating toward her, and this startled Ng'wa a little. But she was famished! The clawing was at its worst and the v'hushalele in her throat was doing something she didn't like.

The shadow reached her, and she didn't hesitate to open her mouth.

It rushed down her throat and she gagged. It tasted of unwash. It smelled in her throat like the fecal matter of a diseased nguwe'we. She clutched at her neck and tried to pull out the shadow. It was solid like a rope. The more she pulled, the more of it swept down her gut. She heaved, hoped her whole stomach would fall out. But the shadow clutched greedily to her intestines. She was gagging and crying when the scarred man emerged from behind the tree, clean of his shadow.

"So you're the shadow eater," he said nonchalantly.

"Who are you?" she managed through her suffocating. His was the most dreadful shadow she had ever ingested, and eating it gave her no relief. She was starved in a way she had never felt before.

"Once upon a time, I was born with a curse a little different from yours. I had a terrible urge to gulp shadows, but each swallow left me wretched. An uroh-ogi told me how to rid myself of it, and he was right."

"What… What?" She looked up at him, confused. His scarring was more visible now. It was the skillful art of a tribal knife or a thorn on a cheek—markings that sometimes came with cultural rites of transition to adulthood.

He was still talking, but she couldn't listen to one more word. What she needed was to eat, to eat, to eat!

Somewhere in the distance, her famishment eating her inside out, she heard him say: "The uroh-ogi said I needed someone to eat my own shadow. That the curse would pass on to the shadow eater."

"How…" she gasped. "How did you find me?"

"You're a hard one to find. But you leave quite the trail. I needed to be sure. Can you feel it—that horrible craving? It slashes at your throat and bellows for appeasement. You will eat a shadow and another and another, and the hunger will never go away."

The hunger was an attic, a river of tears. It was everything she had grown to forget. She had never climbed on her da's knees to stop her from falling. She had never heard her maé's sound fresh and soft like morning dew. The hunger was simultaneous. It was light and dark in a way she couldn't explain. It was a birth. It was a funeral.

She tottered to her feet, fell back to her knees. She felt ruin. She was ruin, and yet not. Her shadow smelled of broiled cockerel and she wanted to eat herself. She ached that this was different. She ached for more.

She cried and lunged at him, but was too weak from starvation to cause injury, and collapsed back to the ground. She thought of Upe'ndo at the cave bar, and drooled at the anticipation of consuming her shadow.

The scarred man stepped over her.

"I guess, like me," he said, "you'll just have to find your own shadow eater."

Morgen's Cottage

Helen Glynn Jones

PETER'S SHOULDERS CLEAVED the water, muscular arms working as he swam, his dark hair plastered flat against his head. He turned onto his back, arms and legs wide like a starfish as he floated, his skin pale against the nightshade depths. Mountains rose green around him, mist on their summits, an occasional *baa* of a sheep the only sound apart from the gentle lapping of water on the shore. His family had been on this land for so long it was beyond memory, but Peter was the last of them. Bending his body he let himself sink, watching the light above him ripple across the water, his hair and beard like clouds as he descended towards tangled green weeds, his fingers brushing their soft tendrils. Then he turned, silver bubbles catching around him as he swam towards the rising pebbled shore. The lake reflected the sky above, mist lifting from the mountains. He felt the deep stillness of the hills lying heavy around him and breathed it in, knowing himself to be in one of the old places, where the land told a story if you just cared to listen.

"Oh, for goodness' sake!"

Beverly Farnshaw stood with blonde head tilted back, hands on her hips as she looked up at yet another damp patch spreading across her hallway ceiling. Heading for the kitchen, she dodged several bowls and buckets already on the floor, the sound of dripping a constant monotonous noise. Rummaging through cardboard boxes piled haphazardly on the scrubbed pine table, she pulled out another plastic bowl, still half-wrapped in paper. It would have to do, she thought, but really, she needed to get some more buckets if this continued. They'd only been in the house a few weeks and already the builder was refusing to take her calls. And now her husband was away on yet another of his interminable business trips, leaving her to deal with it all. Tutting, she pulled the paper from the bowl and went to place it under the leak spattering the new carpet, darkening the beige pile.

They had thought it so exciting when they bought the house. A life change, selling up in the south and moving west to the misty mountains of Beverly's childhood holidays, to a small town nestled in the folds of the Welsh hills. The house was a new build but the old wall and gate, still bearing the legend "Morgen's Cottage," indicated theirs was not the first home on the site. Set into a natural bowl in the hillside, trees in a semi-circle around it, the house had resembled something out of a fairytale, local grey stone and white painted trim adding to the fantasy. She had reveled in her new life at first, walking the narrow streets lined with grey stone cottages, past green slopes rising to distant summits. But a week or so after they'd moved in, the first leaks had started.

A short while later, Beverly pulled into a parking space near to the hardware shop. The high street was quiet, stone facades reflecting pale sunshine. Getting out, she slammed the door harder than she needed to, then blew out a breath, manicured nails tapping on the roof of the Mercedes. Pulling herself together, she marched along the pavement to the shop. A little bell rang above the door as she entered, and a man behind the painted wooden desk turned, rubbing his hands together.

"Can I help you there?" he asked. His salt and pepper hair was unruly, his dungarees marked with paint, but his smile was welcoming.

"Um, right, yes." Beverly pulled her Barbour jacket a little more tightly around her. "That is, I need some buckets. And a plumber, please, if you know one."

"Oh, you're in the new place, aren't you?" said another voice. Beverly turned to see an older woman, full figured with dark red magenta hair, meaty arms crossed under her copious bosom as she nodded at Beverly. Her brown eyes were shrewd, and Beverly drew herself up to her full height, braced against the usual onslaught of questions for the newcomer.

"Yes, that's right," she started. Then her face crumpled and to her horror she began to cry. The other woman came over, laying a plump hand festooned with rings on her arm.

"Come on now," she soothed. "A nice cuppa is what you need." She steered Beverly into a small room at the back of the store. Painted white, it held a small table and two chairs next to a window. Kitchen cabinets lined one wall, and a kettle and mugs waited on the spotless blue countertop. Beverly sat down, pulling a tissue from her pocket and dabbing her eyes.

"Oh, I'm sorry," she said. "I really am. It's just the new house, and all the stupid leaks, and now I'm alone and the builder won't take my calls, and I don't know anyone here…" She stopped again, trying not to cry as the other woman boiled the kettle and filled two mugs, stirring in the teabags.

"Sugar?" she asked, turning to Beverly.

"What? Oh no, thank you, just a little milk. Please." She took the proffered mug with thanks, watching as her host liberally sugared her own mug before coming to sit opposite her, the chair squeaking under her weight.

"Right then. Tell me all about it."

Peter emerged from the dark water, his hands dislodging pebbles and clouds of sand as he pushed himself up and out of the lake. He stood naked on the shore, water streaming down his body. Shivering, he gasped as the cold air touched his skin, swinging his arms, then shook himself like a dog, droplets spraying everywhere. He picked up his towel from where he'd left it lying on a rock, wrapping it around himself before sitting down. Something was coming, he could feel it: a deep shiver in the fabric of the land.

"It's just, my husband's always away and it's been one leak after another…" Beverly carefully blotted her eyes so as not to smudge her mascara, sniffling a little. She looked up as the man from the counter stuck his head round the door.

"Gwen, my love, I need you in the store. It's gettin' busy out here."

"Oh, right, Bryan. We're just comin'," replied Gwen. She leaned on the table as she got to her feet, the wood bending slightly. "Come on." She beckoned to Beverly. "Let's see what we can do."

Beverly put down her mug and followed Gwen out into the store. There were several other customers there, all of whom turned to look at her. Straightening her scarf, she put her shoulders back, feeling her mouth settle into its usual tight lines.

"Righto," said Gwen, who'd moved around to the other side of the counter and was writing something down. "Here you go." She handed Beverly a piece of paper, which had a name and number printed neatly on it. "David's a good man, he won't let you down. Give him a call, right?"

"What about Peter—"

"No." Gwen frowned at Bryan, who was now on a small stepladder reaching something down for a customer. "No, David will be fine." She stared hard at him for a moment until he looked away, going back to his shelves. Beverly twiddled the piece of paper, hoping the house would still be there when she got home, rather than washed down the hillside. Then she shook her head, wondering where that thought had come from. She was overwrought, she decided. All the stress of moving, Gerald being away so often, and now this. It was all too much. When he got back, she would book a weekend away, perhaps to that spa she liked. And she would get him to chase that builder, see if he could sort out all the problems they'd been having. She came back to herself, startled out of her musing by someone patting her hand. It was Gwen.

"You all right now, then?" she said, her eyes and face kind.

"Oh yes, thank you, you've been great." Nodding, Beverly backed out of the shop, trying to ignore the stares, hating how flustered she felt. When she got to the car, she realized she'd forgotten to buy plastic buckets. Her mouth twisted, but something in her didn't want to go back to the store, to bother them with any more of her problems. She pulled her mobile phone from her pocket, tutting when she saw she had no reception, and waved it around above her head to see if anything would change. But the little bars didn't appear, the carrier message still stubbornly stating "No Service." Stifling a sigh, she got in her car and headed for home.

The house looked so peaceful, set at the end of the long drive, hills rising around like arms cradling the house. She parked the car and got out, trying to remember how she'd felt when she first came back, how the land had seemed to be speaking to her. She shook her head. It was all fantasy, a leftover from long ago holidays when she and her siblings would storm the ramparts of imaginary castles, fighting monsters from myth and legend, before she grew up and had no time for such nonsense anymore.

But as she stood next to her car, the mist starting to descend from above, deep damp silence all around, it came back to her, the idea that such things could be real. Folding her lips tight she put her head down and marched for the front door, fumbling with her key until she got it open, closing and locking it behind her as though to keep such thoughts at bay.

Peter sat by the lake, watching the sky change color, cloud reflections rippling across the water. The nearby trees were patched orange and grey with lichen, branches bent and twisted. Sheep dotted the nearby hills like cotton balls caught in folds of green velvet. He breathed in the scent of sheep dung and grass, of water and stone. The ripples in the lake increased as though something were moving, deep below the surface. Peter nodded. It was almost time. Standing, he stretched, letting the towel fall. Then he picked up his clothes and started slowly, methodically, to get dressed.

Thank God we decided to put in a landline, Beverly thought as she checked her mobile again. Still no reception. The engineer she'd called in to connect the Wi-Fi had taken one look at the water dripping everywhere and left, telling her to call him once she got the leaks sorted out. She picked up the phone from its cradle on the hall table, an antique she'd picked up for a song in a local charity shop. She dug the piece of paper with the plumber's number out of her pocket and dialed, waiting for someone to answer. As she did so she realised the house was strangely quiet, the constant dripping noise almost gone. She looked up in bemusement to see that most of the leaks seemed to have stopped. There was a click in her ear, and she opened her mouth to speak but a recorded voice spoke:

"This is David, please leave a message and I'll call you back."

Damn! Huffing out a sigh, Beverly hung up and headed into the kitchen. The damp patches were still there, wallpaper peeling off in one spot in the corner, but the water seemed to have stopped flowing for the time being. Still, she needed to have the pipes checked. It was completely ridiculous, really it was. She hit redial and waited, but once again she got the answering machine and hung up without leaving a message.

She shrugged off her jacket, leaving it over the back of a chair, then flicked the switch on the shiny chrome kettle. She got herself a mug and teabag from the cupboard while she waited for it to boil. There was a small pile of post on the table, including what looked like a local phone directory still wrapped in plastic. She picked the pile up and started to go through it, feeling more relaxed than she had in weeks. There were a couple of bills, a postcard from friends in Spain and a local fast-food menu—she put them aside to look at once her tea was made. Then, as she turned back towards the counter, there was a rumble and gurgle and the house seemed to shift on its foundations.

"Oh!" Beverly reached out to steady herself, fear rushing over her. *What the hell was that?* There was another rumble and the cupboard door under the sink flew open. Water gushed out, spreading rapidly across the kitchen floor and heading for her newly carpeted hallway.

"Oh God oh God oh God!" She tried to close the door, but it flew out of her hand, banging against the cabinet, the volume of water too strong. She stood there a moment, her head darting frantically as she watched it bubble and foam. Then she grabbed the phone and dialled again.

"Hello, hello!" she cried, but all she got was David's message. "Please, call me at once," she said, her voice trembling. "It's an emergency!" The water was already up to her ankles, the flow showing no sign of abating. The hallway carpet was soaked, water seeping into the living and dining room. Frantic, she ran into each room, rolling up the rugs and carrying them out into the hall, at which point she remembered she'd locked the front door. Groaning in frustration, tears prickling at her eyes, she finally wrestled it open, heaving the rugs outside to lean up against the side of the house. *Oh God, the cupboard under the stairs!* She ran back in, opening the cupboard door to reveal a pile of boxes, the bottom ones already damp. Gerald's files! He'd kill her if they got ruined. Struggling under their weight, she ferried the boxes outside, piling them on the lawn. Water was trickling out through the front door, rivulets meandering along the path. Kicking off her soaked shoes, she went back inside, fighting the burgeoning flow as she headed back to the kitchen. Grabbing the phone book on the kitchen table she tore off the plastic, flipping through the newsprint pages until she found the Plumbers listings. For god's sake, there couldn't be just two in the area! What had that man in the shop said? Peter something. She moved her finger down the list until she found it. Peter's Water Works. Punching the numbers into her phone, water rising around her, she made the call.

A loud buzzing intruded on the silent hills. Peter frowned, patting at the breast pocket of his padded vest, reaching in to pull out his phone.

"Peter's Water Works."

Squawking came down the line, and he pulled his phone away from his ear.

"I'm sorry, what did you say? Really? And you've had no luck with them? All right, I'll be over as soon as I can."

Morgen's Cottage. So that was what he'd felt. He heaved a sigh as he disconnected the call. Still, it had to be done. And he was the only one left who could do it.

Getting to his feet, he started up the slope towards an ancient grey stone cottage surrounded by a snaking network of stone walls. His mud-splashed Range Rover was parked outside, filled with the tools of his trade. Wellington boots, several pairs. A large pile of old towels. Waders, for extreme situations. And a small piece of wood, wrapped in a soft felt cloth, polished and darkened with age. It had been in his family for years, for so long that Peter couldn't say, really, how old it was. Opening the car door, he climbed in, his hair still damp from the lake. He turned on the ignition and roared out of the driveway towards Morgen's Cottage.

He arrived to a scene of devastation: several damp boxes piled on the front lawn along with a couple of rolled up rugs, water flowing out of the front door. He paused for a moment, hands on hips as he watched it ripple through the grass, before his eyes moved to the hills beyond, and he nodded to himself.

Knocking on the open door, he went inside, taking in the stains and damp patches on the walls and ceilings, the water rushing along the hallway. She'd been right to call him, he reflected. Really, he was the only one who could deal with something like this. He followed the flow through to the kitchen, where a slight blonde woman waded through several inches of water, a phone tucked under her ear as she opened the lower cupboards, taking out crockery and putting it on the worktops.

"…can't take this anymore. Honestly, Gerald, I thought you were going to wind down the business when we moved here…"

Peter knocked on the doorframe and she turned, smiling briefly, though her eyes were dark with worry.

"You have to call the builder and that's it." There was a pause. "Sorry, I've got to go, I'll call you back." She hung up the phone with one hand while beckoning Peter in with the other.

"Mrs. Farnshaw?"

She nodded.

"Right then," he said, rubbing his hands together. "Under there, is it?"

"Yes, under the sink." Her voice was trembling, dark circles under her eyes. "It won't stop. And my husband's away again, and the other plumber just isn't answering his phone. Can you help?"

He nodded, squatting down to peer into the dark cavity of the cupboard. Reaching into his pocket he took out the small piece of wood—a stick, forked at one end. Rubbing it with his hands as though to warm it, he stuck it into the space and closed his eyes, breathing deep.

Oh yes.

Beverly watched hopefully as Peter bent down to look under the sink. But then he started waving what looked like an old stick around, closing his eyes. She frowned. Oh, that was all she needed, some sort of hippie nonsense…

Peter opened his eyes and turned to her, still crouched down by the cupboard. "I'm sorry, there's really nothing I can do. You must let it run its course."

"Wh-what?"

He stood up, still smiling. His eyes, Beverly noticed, were a curious shade of blue-green. Water droplets seemed to be falling from him, running from under his beard and the sleeves of his shirt as he waded towards her through the deepening water.

"Did you not wonder, Mrs. Farnshaw, about the name of this house? About the Morgen?" His voice was pleasant, but as he came closer, she could smell dampness around him, the cool green of waterweed and deep pools. She felt the coldness of the mountains again, the mists starting to fall, this ancient land with its secrets taking hold of her.

"W-well, I mean, I just thought it was an old superstition—"

Peter shook his head, though his eyes were kind. "Those are usually the truest ones of all, the old ones."

Beverly started to back away. The hall table floated past and she grabbed at it, but it slipped from her grasp. She was so cold now, the water almost at her hips, pulling at her legs like tangled weed.

"The ancient springs will not be denied," Peter went on, moving with the current towards her. "You can build over them, box them in, but they'll find a way. Water always does."

"B-but, what am I—"

"Supposed to do? Well, Mrs. Farnshaw, there's one more thing you need to know about the old springs. Once woken, they require a sacrifice."

She tried to hold onto him as he went past her, but her hands slid on his wet clothes as she fell with a splash into the bubbling torrent. As the waters closed over her face she thought of her childhood, of days running on golden beaches, carefree. She tried to find her feet, her head breaking the surface as she shrieked, gasping for air. Then another surge took her.

Peter Fontus, last of the water gods, followed the flow of water outside. The doorframe cracked as he passed beneath it, stone cladding starting to fall from the exterior walls. The waters roared as they breached the windowsills, drowning the last of Mrs. Farnshaw's cries. His hand caressed the small piece of wood in his pocket as the power of the Morgen eddied around him. He turned to watch, waiting for what was to come. This wasn't the first home on this land, nor would it be the last. But, as he'd told the woman, the springs would not be denied, nor could they be held back. With a rumbling sigh the house collapsed, the sacrifice made and accepted.

And the ancient spring returned to the land once more.

Underland

Gemma Amor

IN THE GLOOM of the early morning, I am woken: a small, hot, elbows-and-knees boy slips under the covers of our bed, worms his way between our sleeping forms. I curl an arm around his middle, and we arrange ourselves into the usual family sandwich. He sighs happily. My husband mutters and shifts to make room without waking.

"Mummy," my boy whispers.

"Mmmm?"

"You are the bread. Daddy is the ham. I am the cheese. Okay?"

"Yes darling," I mumble, drifting back to sleep.

When I wake, they are gone. I am a single slice of lonely bread. There are no quiet snuffling noises, no heavy breathing, no boyish heat, no curls brushing against my nose. No delicious small boy smell, no cold toes poking into my belly, asking to be warmed up.

There is only silence.

I am without.

It is the same every day.

After my third drink, the monotony of loneliness gets a little easier to bear. As it's Tuesday, today's poison of choice is whisky, single malt, no ice, sip it slow. Tomorrow is Wednesday, which of course is vodka day.

Vodka is not meant to be sipped slow unless it's the really good stuff. Vodka is meant to be slammed, and so slam I will, until Thursday rolls in. Thursday is kind of a freestyle day, so who knows what I'll fancy by then. That's Thursday's problem, not mine. All I have to think about is Tuesday.

One day at a time, they tell me. *It'll get better.*

It makes them feel useful when they say it. Like they've made a difference.

I don't have the heart to tell them it doesn't get better. It only gets worse. Some cruel force of nature keeps moving the goalposts of grief farther away from me. The only thing that seems to stop the ground getting eaten up beneath my feet as I slog towards them is the drink. So drink I do, with enthusiasm. With dedication. I always was good at things I put my mind to.

By midday, I am comfortably numb. And then, disaster strikes.

The whisky runs dry.

I rummage through the assorted bottles in my drinks cabinet. I've got a drink for every letter of the alphabet, but no more whisky. And yet Tuesday is whisky day, so I am faced with only one real option: leave the house. Shop or bar, doesn't matter which. As long as there is a bottle of the W. There are rules, you see. A person has to have rules, to survive.

I put on my coat, drag trainers onto my feet, and head to the local supermarket, stumbling a little as I go, but doing a decent job of hiding my inebriation. Or so I think. Perhaps not. A woman and her child give me a wide berth: the mother's face is hard with disapproval and apprehension. I want to tell her why I am like this, rail-thin and greasy-haired and tripping over my own feet, a zombie woman, I want to tell her this is what it's like when you give birth to a boy, a golden boy, and he is ripped away from you before you've barely had time to understand what sort of person he really is. But I don't tell her that. I let her think what she wants to think, because she still has her child, and I can't hate her for that, much as I want to. She's just doing what mothers do when they're out with their offspring: looking for potential threats, assessing likely dangers. I avoid eye contact with her, partly out of shame, partly so she knows I'm not going to be a problem. The woman lets out a sigh of relief as I pass. The child, a little girl, asks: "Mummy, what's wrong with that lady? Why was she walking all funny?"

The mother hushes her. They disappear around a corner.

The tiny supermarket I frequent is dry too; it's the day before restock day. That settles it: bar. There's one right along the street, imaginatively named The Cave, set partway into a small limestone shelf that runs along the train tracks near my house. The Cave lives up to its name: it's cool, dark, and smells of damp rock and mildew. It's also quiet. If I drink there, I know I'll be left alone.

Except today, I'm not left alone.

Today, the Emperor finds me.

By the time he gets to me, I am slumped on a bar stool, trying and failing to roll a cigarette with a soggy clump of Rizla papers that have stuck together.

He sits down beside me. He smells strange, like ash. His skin has a greyish tint to it. He has thick red hair, waist-length, shiny. I think there are small bones woven into it. His fingernails are long, polished, sharp-tipped. His two front teeth, when he smiles, are capped with gold. He would be odd-looking to me if I cared about that sort of thing anymore.

I don't. All I care about is rolling the fucking cigarette.

"Let me help with that," the man says, taking the green packet out of my hands.

"The fuck?" I mumble, snatching the papers back. "Leave me alone."

"I can't do that," he replies, flashing those golden pegs. "We have things to do."

I can feel a headache building. "Just go away," I say, wearily. "I'm not in the mood."

"Don't be too quick to throw away a new start," the man says, and then he levers me up out of my seat, hooking his arm through mine. His hands and wrists are covered in tattoos, a network of geometric patterns and lines, triangles, other swirling shapes that all interlock. These tessellating marks appear to be moving on his skin, like a screensaver, like he is asleep, but his hardware is still running.

I blink, realizing I am far more drunk than I'd accounted for.

He continues to try and steer me away from the bar, away from my half-empty glass.

"Get off me!" I lurch out of his grip. The man is slippery and strong. His hand threads back through the crook of my arm as if he has known me all his life.

"Shh," he says, calmly, like I'm an animal, feral, in need of feeding. "Relax."

And bizarrely, I find myself doing exactly as he says: relaxing, almost as if hypnotized. I can't stop staring at his tattoos. They *are* moving, pulsing, shifting; his skin is a live canvas. The part of my brain still active and sensible looks around desperately for some help, but the barman is on break. There is no one available to jump to my rescue.

Rescue from what, anyway? A voice whispers in my head. *You can't be in any real danger if you have nothing left to live for.*

"No danger," the man says, reading my mind. "Only new beginnings."

His voice is weird and soft and slurred, distorted. His eyes glow with a faint purple light. He flicks on a bulb in my head. I decide, with a sudden two-and-two coming together to form four, that I must still be asleep, and still dreaming.

I never left the house at all, never made it to the bar.

Thank fuck, I think to myself. *A different dream, for once.*

And I find it enormous comfort to not dream of the boys I lost, or the accident, the mangled iron, the beeping hospital bed sounds, the funeral, two holes in the turf, plates of finger food eaten around bouts of weeping, or worse, to dream of all the things now denied to me: the early morning cuddles, the walks through the woods near my house, the games of hide and seek, the tantrums, the laughter, the mess, the smells. I find it immense relief to dream of someone entirely new and strange, someone not wrapped up in pain and longing, so I let the Emperor wrap his thin arm around my shoulder, and we walk towards the back of The Cave, where a door leads to a cellar. Steel barrels of beer are stacked alongside packets of soda, juice, bottles of wine and boxes of salted peanuts, and there is another door behind a pile of stools. That door leads into a tunnel, and the Emperor draws me along it into darkness, where, for a while, the dream leaves me.

But that is okay, because I have had quite enough dreams for a while. To sleep and *not* dream is a precious gift, one I accept greedily.

I have a brief period of lucidity that coincides with our arrival into a vast chamber formed of stone. Clusters of milky-white stalactites dangle down. A cave, I understand.

In the middle of the cave stands an enormous bed.

My subconscious, I assume, is telling me how damn tired I am.

Grief is exhausting, I hear people say all the time. *It's okay to be tired.* As if they know. As if any of them could possibly know.

The Emperor says none of these things. He leads me to the middle of the chamber, and we stop before the bed.

The frame is crystalline, the headboard two giant ammonites fused together. The bedding is silk, black, dozens of pillows carefully arranged on it. Candles on massive iron stands are positioned to either side of the bed.

The Emperor motions.

Lie down, his hand gesture says.

Oh no, I think. *No, I don't want this kind of dream.*

I baulk, pulling out of the Emperor's grasp, heart skipping in my chest.

But the bed looks comfortable. Inviting.

My eyelids droop.

Can you sleep within sleep?

Dream within a dream?

I don't know, but I do know it's been a very long time since I've slept properly. Without dreams, or nightmares, or the weird, sticky states in between. Without tossing and turning, snoring drunkenly, waking myself up scratching or crying. I am tired, tired to my bones, tired beyond my bones, tired right down to the last fiber, the last cell, the last atom. Perhaps if I sleep properly, maybe I can begin to heal, to process what my life has become, to acknowledge my loss.

"Come," the Emperor says out loud, but still I hesitate. I don't know what dark spell he has me under, I don't know what this place is or why it is down here, beneath the city, beneath my grief, deep in my imagination, but I am fairly sure I don't need to know to understand how vulnerable I am.

I look behind me. The tunnel down which I was led has disappeared. Of course. Things do that, in dreams. This is not one I am in control of. All that stretches around me is rock, leaping shadows. The tunnel is sealed. I am trapped.

Panic grips me. I spin, almost falling over as my unreliable body tries and fails to keep up with the swiftness of the motion, but the Emperor catches me, hands me a chalice carved from quartz.

Inside, a dark black liquid sparkles.

"Who are you?" I mumble, fearful, exhausted, confused.

"One last drink," the man replies, lifting the chalice to my lips.

It smells sweet, tastes bitter, a little like aniseed, a little like chocolate. The aftertaste reminds me of hot coffee, acrid yet satisfying. The liquid trickles down my throat and my body starts to relax, *truly* relax, for the first time since my son and my husband died. My fists, always clenched, unfold. My shoulders, up by my ears, drop. My spine stretches out. My arms flop down from where they usually rest, perpetually gripping my belly. My head lifts, chin rescuing itself from the folds of my neck, where it has lived long enough to make deep creases in my pale skin.

A deep and incredible sense of peace floods through my veins, spreads into my extremities. I am soft, malleable, cotton candy, warm taffy, ready to be pulled every which way, worked into any shape, just so long as it doesn't resemble the wretched person I've been for three long years.

I exhale. The first breath where I don't feel like I am starved of air.

"What magic is this?" I whisper.

"Sleep first," the Emperor commands.

He leads me to the bed, which swallows me. The sheets are cool, gliding like water across my skin as I roll, find a comfortable position. The Emperor holds me like it is the most natural thing in the world for a complete stranger to do, arms encircling me with strange, intoxicating familiarity, and I surrender myself to whatever is happening, for it feels more peaceful than I could ever imagine, and peace, after all, is a vastly underrated state of being.

I dream-sleep for days. How many, I cannot tell. Upon waking, I have a raging thirst. My clothes feel loose, my skin and joints sore from being in bed too long. For a second, I imagine I've woken back at home, in my own bed. No satin sheets. My husband next to me, snoring. I have missed him so much.

Here is love, I think.

Memory Husband groans, puts out his hands to feel my body, always the first thing he used to do, before he decided to die on me.

"How are you feeling?" he asks. I wish I had better categorized every detail of his appearance, his voice, his movements, memorized every second of the encounters we had, knowing it would soon be over, that I would never see him again.

I press my face into the back of his neck.

"I miss you. I miss you so much."

"But why?"

The Emperor's face hovers above mine, grey, long, serious. His eyes are massive, those deep purple irises huge. "I never left."

He kisses me, dissolves. I am left holding onto smoke; it pours into my lungs and stings my eyes. Faintly, in the distance, I can hear my son crying.

And then I am alone in the black satin bed, a thousand stone daggers suspended above me. I think there are bats up there amongst the stalactites, I can hear them chittering, hear the rustle of wings folding and stretching.

"Welcome back," the Emperor says, farther away now.

I prop myself up on an elbow. He is nowhere to be seen.

The bed dips behind me. Weight, movement.

I feel strong hands on my body again, but these do not belong to my husband. Long nails scrape gently across my shoulders. I respond. The Emperor is gentle. His kisses are soft, insistent, and quickly become urgent, with a current of control rushing beneath us. I decide I like relinquishing control. I like being powerless. No decisions to make. No burdens to bear. After such a long time battling, trying to hold everything together, trying to bind the universe to me, trying to hold onto smoke. And now, I'm here, where my body no longer feels like my responsibility. The decisions belong to someone else. It's like getting drunk without the vomiting, without the hair loss, without the gut ache, without falling over every five minutes.

I let the Emperor do as he wants.

☙

Time passes. I dream-sleep and suffer. I dream-wake and the Emperor fills my tender mind and body. Always, he stares intently. I start to dread eye contact, like staring into the heart of a volcano. I feel moored to the heart of some tremendous power about to erupt forth into the world above and destroy everything in its path.

Occasionally, the Emperor feeds me, holds my head while I drink from the chalice. Once he bathes me, right there on the bed, with water and a cloth. I wonder if this is how people feel when they are baptized. Cleansing as a form of rapture. Candles flicker. The bed, stoic, anchoring. This chamber, my new country. This man, my new regent.

I am clever enough to realize that what the Emperor is doing is not solely for my benefit. Rather, he ties me to him with these extravagant acts of service. I know this because I encounter others bound to him thus. They appear periodically, dressed in black. They deliver food or water, replenish the candles that gutter out, rearrange the sheets around us, then vanish discreetly, but not without an appraising look in my direction.

The Emperor uses his body as a tool, which is fine, because really, I wasn't living before I met him. He has begun to fashion a new version of me that feels raw, unformed but alive somehow. I am being molded, prepared. For what, I don't know. But I begin to feel restless. The cave chamber starts to bore me.

It is then that he brings me a gown.

☙

The fabric is soft, velvety, dark, embroidered with pinpoint knots of brilliant thread woven into tiny stars that give off their own light. It fits me perfectly: I do not question this. In dreams, all things are possible.

He helps me climb into it, draws the laces tight in the back. It is no surprise I cannot breathe well: this is a soft type of prison, an elegant straitjacket masquerading as a ballgown.

"What is this for?" I ask as he attends to my hem, arranging the folds of it just so.

"It's time you met the Family," he replies. Then he kneels before me, presses his face into my skirts. He holds me like a child holding his mother's legs, and I wonder if grief will ever leave my side, or if I am about to marry it, marry him, for I think that the Emperor is sorrow made solid, or as solid as an ash and smoke man can be.

˜

The Family are gathered in a neighboring cave with a high, domed ceiling carved out of the rock and polished smooth. There are more candles, hundreds more. There is a table too, oval, ten feet long, also carved from stone. Around the table the Family are seated, talking quietly to each other. As a group, they are strikingly homogenous. Everyone dressed in black, everyone doused in shadows and hunched into their chairs. They look like a murder of crows waiting for someone to die so they can peck at the bones.

Murmuring subsides as we walk into the cavern. I am suddenly self-conscious. My gown pools around me, a velvet waterfall.

The Family stare, rising from their seats in unison. I sense I am approaching a point of no return. I clear my throat.

"I'm Eve." My voice carries across the cave.

"Eve," the Family confirms. It is not my real name, but my chosen dream name.

"What would you know of us, Eve?"

The question feels like a test, or an opportunity. I treat it as both.

"Is this all of you?"

"No, we are more, but the rest have other duties to perform."

More. Like a community, living down under the city, in the shadows of my mind. Have they always been here? What is my brain trying to tell me? Show me? What lesson is this?

"How old are you?"

"Old enough."

Whoever they are, I find I am desperate to belong to a family again.

"What are the rules? Of acceptance?" I am almost afraid to ask, for fear I won't qualify.

"Citizenship is only granted when we say so."

A subconscious collective, buried down with all the thoughts, feelings and fears I have been so terrified of.

I tried to drown them all with alcohol, but they are impervious.

The Family Endures.

The Emperor has taken his own seat at the long table. He is wearing a crown now. I think it is made of rock needles, crystals, feldspar, quartz, pyrite.

I see there is a spare chair beside him, set aside for me.

I swallow. My head is spinning. None of this makes any sense, and yet, it sort of does. I think I can detect what my brain is trying to tell me, via the Family mouthpiece. I feel darkness rising in my gullet, an urgent need to vomit. The poison will never be sucked from the wound, I realize. It fills me up and seeps out through the holes in my skin and dims the stars on my sweat-soaked gown, and...

"Mummy?"

"Yes darling?"

There is no voice like that of your first born, no smell, no touch.

"Do you want to know a secret?"

Conspirators. Best friends. Teammates. Family.

"Tell me."

"I don't love you."

"Oh. Alright then. I don't love you either."

We grin at each other, revel in our shared joke.

Smoke, and ash, and poison, and sodden velvet, and...

The cave comes back into focus. I swallow the rising bile. The chair sits, empty.

I walk to it, take my place.

Acceptance, they said, can only be given, not taken.

I wait, heart in my mouth.

The Emperor's nails tap on the tabletop. His tattoos are shifting in a wild, anguished kaleidoscope of emotional patterns. I place my hand atop his. The patterns slip from his skin, crawl onto mine, wrapping themselves around my wrists and arms like snakes.

The Family sit. Their long black garments sigh loudly.

"Welcome," they say.

I blink.

This feels too easy.

Surely there is some further test, some challenge, some proof of worthiness?

My face betrays my thoughts.

"Don't worry," the Emperor says. "All that is left now is the small matter of your death."

Thank god, I think.

At last.

⁓

They place a crown on my head. Made of broken glass, jagged shards of all colors mounted upon a silver circlet. Heavy, cumbersome, I fear it will slip off, so I cram it farther down my skull to keep it secure, scraping the delicate skin of my scalp. Blood trickles down my forehead.

Coronation complete, the Emperor leads me from the main cathedral-sized space into an adjoining cave, and then another, and another. I begin to grasp how vast this subterranean network is.

Is this really the size of my mind? The scale?

I have only explored such a small, pedestrian part of myself.

I wonder how he will kill me. I think it will be violent, painful, with elements of ritualism—a knife, maybe. A stone dagger. The others might join in. They trail behind us, a shuffling silent column, except for the swishing robes dragging across the polished stone floors. There will be more candles, incense, weird chanting. My palms sweat. My stomach lurches. I don't bother to ask him where we are going. Knowing will blunt the edge of anticipation.

In my previous life, when I had been married, had a home, a son, a job, a heart—back then, I always hated surprises. Control, or the idea of it, was the glue that held my existence together.

But when the rain came, when the car skidded on the road, when the glue dissolved...

∽

It seems I am always being led by the hand of the Emperor.

When he first brought me to Underland, I presumed, in my distressed state, that, at most, there were one or two caves under the jurisdiction of his gloomy Kingdom.

But as we walk towards my end, I piece together the fragments of local history I didn't realize I knew until now. These fragments have coalesced into an alternate environment, one that's been lurking at the back of my consciousness for some time.

I have simply never needed this dream terrain until now.

Underland is chiseled out of all the local history I absorbed, and furnished with my loss. An upside-down city, designed solely to wander and feel things, to seek solace and acceptance. The architect: me, I think. The Emperor may consider himself sovereign, but I understand differently.

There has always been a network of tunnels under the real-world city I live in, spreading like a root system. Almost every part of the up-side world had a subterranean mirror: tunnels and caves winding under train stations, hotels, tower blocks, pubs, parks; airshafts, culverts, caves, fissures, service tunnels, underpasses, cellars, mines, sewers... All of it unclaimed, until now. A dank playground empty of patrons. Smugglers, they say, ran freely down here in the old days, as did hermits, even giants. Some of the caves were used to house French and Dutch prisoners. Ghosts are rumored to drift forlornly through the tunnels, trailing their woes, as I am now doing.

I'd had friends before who renovated houses. Friends who did not cope well with my losses. Grief didn't suit dinner party conversations, where candles and cut-glass crystal wine glasses sparkled. Some of these "friends" uncovered tunnels leading into the dark from their basements. Once the novelty had worn off, the open wounds in the earth had been quietly cemented or boarded up. No one could quite stand the idea of their house being so insidiously open to the world beneath. *Because of the rats*, those friends would say.

Now I am here, a velveteen rat, scuttling under the pavements. The darkness and all-pervasive smell of damp stone is a comfort. Sometimes, thin roots tickle the back of my neck as I pass remarkable sights: vast, empty towers, great, deep chasms, bridges, chambers, altars, even a forest, each tree meticulously fashioned from limestone, individual leaves carved with incredible skill and artistry. A river, flowing red. A temple. The windows in its facade glow a deep purple. Chanting comes from inside. A cemetery, only the headstones are weird little pyramids, hundreds of them. A stone horse. A waterfall, only crystals pour from a hole, not water. They tinkle and shatter as they land in a great pit below.

And still we walk. The Emperor leads me along, around, down, through, never pausing, never correcting himself. This is part of his power; he knows how to navigate the darkness. Without him, I would be lost.

~

I am crying. I do not like being lost inside my own dreams. I hate the anticipation.

"Can't we move faster?" My feet bleed from the distance we've walked. A trail of bloody prints marks the stone behind us.

"No need," the Emperor says. 'We are here.'

He halts abruptly before a door seemingly made of thick, opaque glass, with a brightly polished crystal doorknob set in the centre.

"Ready?" the Emperor says, taloned hand on the knob.

"Finally," I sob, stepping through the door he yanks open for me anyway.

I yearn for my old dream.

I yearn to wake in bed, a piece of bread once again, with my boy the ham, and my husband the cheese.

I yearn for death, so I can join them.

The Emperor closes the door behind me. I feel the wind on my back as it shuts. No goodbyes from him, for he lives inside me, always. He knows this.

It's taken me a while to understand, is all.

Beyond, no cave as I expected. No more Underland.

Only the light of day, traffic. A bus, pumping brakes. A seagull shrieking in fury overhead. Voices, laughter. The clatter of rubbish being thrown into a bin. A train distantly rattling along its tracks.

And a woman, thin, sweat-drenched, face down on a bubble-gum caked pavement on a busy street.

She is unconscious. A large gash has opened on her forehead. A piece of glass is stuck in her skin. Blood pools around her. She has tripped, fallen, landed on a broken bottle. Drunk, no doubt.

A woman on her way to a bar, for it is Whisky Tuesday.

A little girl stands over her, thumb in mouth. Her mother hovers protectively behind, on her phone, calling for an ambulance. She tells the operator the address, crouches over the prone woman, who slowly rouses.

Caught between compassion and disgust, the woman on the phone holds out her free hand to help me sit. I refuse to accept the offered hand. I have pissed myself. A damp patch spreads across my crotch. My face is hot with shame, especially when I see the little girl.

"You had an accident," the child says, around her thumb.

"What a state you've gotten yourself into," her mother says, not unkindly.

The woman who is not called Eve sits up, painfully. I look up into the confused faces above me.

"I wasn't always like this." Blood leaks down my chin. "I was like you. I had a husband. A little boy, the same age." I nod at the child.

The other woman's face shifts into slow understanding.

"Oh," she says, softly. "They…?"

Not-Eve nods. Plucks the glass shard from her head. An ambulance siren wails in the distance. *Too fast, it can't be for me.*

"Died."

"I'm sorry."

"Me too." Behind the woman, I sense shadows, watching. The Emperor lurks.

I have no time for him now. My little pavement death has to mean something, I have to use it to start afresh. Ascend, and descend, concurrently. I will never be the bread in a sandwich again, but this does not mean I cannot honor my family, chosen or otherwise.

The woman's entire demeanor has changed. She is benevolent, kind. Her eyes sparkle with a purple glint, a brief flash of amethyst. Shared grief, a gift from below.

I wonder suddenly where her own husband is.

"Would you like a cup of tea?" she asks, softly. "I don't live far from here."

She holds out a hand again.

But it's *Whisky Tuesday*, I think.

But maybe, Eve replies, *you can try tea, just for today, and see how you go.*

And beneath her, the city stretches, shudders. Great halls tremble far down below.

But that is okay.

Underland will be there, waiting, when the time is ripe. The Emperor, she knows, will keep it in good stead.

Existence: A Thought Experiment

Greg van Eekhout

I THINK, THEREFORE I am.

I don't know how old I was when I first heard René Descartes's statement, but I probably didn't know what a philosopher was, and if I knew that France was a country, it was only because of a Richard Scarry book.

Still, the words changed me.

My parents and church and kindergarten poured out contradictory knowledge nuggets like Cap'n Crunch into a cereal bowl, but thanks to Descartes, my own existence was the one thing I knew was true. I didn't know what I was—an insect, or a microbe in a test tube, or a smart wad of algae—but I knew I existed.

I sort of believed in some other things, as well. UFOs and the Loch Ness Monster were probably bullshit, though fun to think about, while Bigfoot was a real guy. I also believed I *might* have telekinesis.

When Papa was working a lot of overtime, the family could afford to go out for Saturday breakfast. The four of us would pile into the Chrysler Valiant and make the short trip from Venice to Santa Monica to go to Norm's, a family restaurant. Papa would get bacon, sausage, hash browns, and fried eggs over-medium-soft. I can't remember Mama's order. Her presence at Saturday breakfast wasn't as strong an imposition on my reality as Papa's. I know she liked cantaloupe.

I'd always get a waffle and a glass of milk, and I painstakingly tried to fill every square pocket with butter. Papa would tell me I was using too much butter as he demonstrated health consciousness with his oil-fried plate, but it wasn't really about the butter for me. It was about filling the absences in the waffle's fabric.

The light fixtures over the booths were stamped aluminum cylinders suspended from long wires, and they became a small obsession. If I stared long enough, I thought I could make them sway, just the tiniest much. So breakfast became an exercise in attempted psychic phenomena.

When I was six, we moved to Culver City and the Saturday breakfasts moved to Denny's, and then money was tighter and the experiments ended.

I used to write children's books. My decision to do so largely came about because I remember how flexible and expansive my brain was when I was a kid. Weird thoughts came easily to me back then. Children's lit is a good space for a speculative fiction author to work in. Kids have obsessions that may not be evident through observation to adults. I had several.

For instance.

The bloody Jesus on all the crucifixes I ever saw wore a loin cloth that reminded me of my tighty whities, so I rushed through getting dressed and undressed because I was pretty sure getting caught in only my underwear put me at risk of gory execution. I was also told God sees all, which I interpreted as Him having me on closed-circuit television, which tied in nicely to the whole crucifixion fear.

And then there was the whole universe. For reasons, I'd put "Classical Gas" on the record player, climb up the top bunk, and swoosh around my AMT model of a Klingon battle cruiser. And then my brain would start to burn. If all of space was contained within the bedroom, then what existed beyond the ceiling? I was so frustrated by how close I could come to grasping infinity without being able to break through the barrier.

Again, I was young when I realized that my own existence was the only thing I could ever be one-hundred percent certain of. I was still young when I realized other people might be thinking the same thing.

Maybe a kid's mind is like a loaded gun. It's too powerful a thing for them to responsibly possess.

Just like the infinity beyond my bedroom ceiling, the idea that other people existed inside their own heads deeply troubled me. As I grew into adulthood, it became less troubling but more annoying. The person talking on the phone, blocking the supermarket aisle with their cart, acts like they're the only person in the world, and how I wish that I, God in the form of the microbe in the test tube, could think them out of existence so I could get to my box of multi-grain cereal.

It can be hard to think of them as a real person, to put the microbe thoughts back in a safe, proper place.

Mama died in January 2015, and Papa followed in May. We all grieve differently, they say, and that's okay.

I didn't grieve my parents' deaths at all. Is that okay?

There was little sense of loss. It wasn't numbness. It wasn't pain so great I couldn't process.

My parents were beyond the ceiling, which I had learned was just a crawlspace with insulation. Empty waffle squares.

Mama and Papa were dead and could no longer think. They were not am.

Vincent Samuel Roth, twenty-four, was a human-shaped thought I came upon while we were both waiting to cross the street on the corner of Lincoln and Colorado where the Norm's once was. It's now a Denny's, but so are a lot of places. He was holding his take-out food in a plastic bag. I never found out what his order was. For reasons that I could spend the rest of my life trying to uncover, the microbe decided to perform the experiment.

"Are you real?"

He turned his head with a side glance. "What?"

I stretched out my arm a short distance to brush my fingers against the bounds of infinity and shove Vincent Samuel Roth in the back.

The bus.

The desperate wail of a horn.

The squeal of brakes, the shriek of voices.

The bitter stench of burnt rubber.

The wet crack of a saturated sponge with a bone in the middle striking a hard surface at speed.

"Oh," I kept saying, not long after, when cops had me on the ground, my teeth grinding against the pavement. "Oh. Oh."

Oh.

Oh.
Oh.
Let there be light.

Sing Yourself Back to Sleep

Laurel Hightower

THE LAST NOTE of a song she doesn't remember singing hangs heavy in the air, the melody snapped in the middle, filling her chest with an aching need to hear how it ends.

The song came from her throat, there's no doubt about that—her vocal cords still vibrate with the noise of it. She waits for the tune to return, for the memory to burst forth in the way it does when she's entered a room and forgotten why. She hangs in the countless seconds of uncertainty, coaxing her mind and the sense memory of her voice, but nothing comes. Where the song should be is a blank wall, and as she stares at it, she comes to the knowledge that more than the song is hidden from her.

She frowns, looks down at her feet and sees only an unfamiliar dark wood floor. For a second, it's so dark she can't find her body—she feels unmoored, a limitless mind floating in the ether, seconds away from splitting apart, her consciousness abandoning her for the four corners of the universe. With effort, she reels in her panic and finds she can move her arms, lightly pats her sides and thighs with shaking hands. She doesn't know what they're supposed to feel like, as she can't find any memories of this sort of touch, but she's relieved to feel *something* at least. Rough fabric soaked through with something warm, stiffening in its exposure to air. Her fingers sting where she makes contact, her thighs answering with a pain all their own. Easing up on the pressure of her touch, she explores further, and discovers her pants are sticky and stiff with blood.

Her heart speeds up, an uneven kick to its gallop. She tries to reach back through the last few seconds, to before she woke in this place. It made sense then, she's sure of it, so the wisest move is to turn, face back in the direction she came from. Retrace her steps, emerge from wherever this place is with an unanswerable wall and pain wherever she touches. She waits still for a rush of recognition, the feeling of landing back within herself, the snug fit of her life after a short foray into space. Any second, she'll remember who she is and what she's doing here.

At first, she can't make sense of what she sees. So certain she'd find her way back, find herself on familiar ground, she can't process what lies across the path she must have traveled. She squeezes her eyes closed and faces front again, that blank wall beyond her eyelids preferable to the impossible scene she's turned her back on, even as her heart quickens. But it's too late—connections form in her brain, the truth of her reality battering at the walls of her sanity. She doesn't want to look again— doesn't want to confirm what a small, shrieking part of her mind already knows. That it is *her* spread across the path behind. Bits of her, anyway.

Her breath coming short and fast, she turns once more and opens her eyes. As her gaze alights on each shred of bloody flesh, the corresponding part of her body flares with red hot pain. The flesh of a de-gloved hand lies several feet before her, the fingers deflated yet graceful. She can't tell which one it is, but it doesn't matter as every nerve ending in all ten fingers and both palms lights up like a Christmas tree. A strip from the front of her right shin—she can tell by the deep scar running down where it used to cover bone. Relic of slipping on a ladder, the metal sharp enough to shave the flesh almost to the tibia. Why can she remember the cause of the scar, but not who she is? Both legs sing in anguish and she knows if she keeps looking, she will find every scrap of who she used to be. She refuses to look down at her body, her chest locked against the notion of seeing herself flayed as she must be. Her cheeks sting with tears and her dread rises— does she have a face anymore? In her current fog she might not recognize it, but the concept of it being gone, no chance to get reacquainted, stirs a panic she fights with everything she has.

How is she alive? Skinned as she is, gobs and bits and shreds strewn before her and leading into the darkness from whence she came, how can she be standing? Her nerves throb with pain but she doesn't feel weak. She wonders if she's in shock, and if perhaps she might have time to gather those bits and cover herself with them. Staunch the blood and maybe even give the skin a chance to reattach, find its place upon her once more, a rough and ready field grafting. She moves gingerly, the soles of her feet stinging, a wet slide to her flesh against the wood. Kneeling with a hiss, she reaches for the empty skin that used to cover her hand. It flops in her hold, the palm lined and cracked. Stroking it lightly with fleshless, bony fingers, she remembers. If only just a little.

She had loved with this hand. Held tiny fingers in her own, stroked soft cheeks and noses. Carried more weight than she could have imagined. The skin that used to lay on the back of her hand is dry, bunched in fine wrinkles. She remembers healing hurts with this hand, but it seems she cannot heal her own. Her attempt to slide the husk over raw meat fails, the skin splitting almost on contact. It no longer fits, and she gives up on the attempt. A deep, aching loss carves a pit in her chest as she lays the empty hand aside and looks for something else she can connect to. She scoots on her knees, blood pooling beneath them, further soaking the sticky pants she still wears, until she comes across another shred of herself. Large and floppy, a divot in the middle. She traces a bloody digit across two dark moles and knows that what she holds used to hug the curves of her belly. The faded pink c-section scar along the bottom of the flap of flesh confirms it, and she begins to feel the ground beneath her feet once more. *This* is who she was—who she still is. She used to hate this flesh, the stretch marks and sags and the rounded nature of it. She'd averted her eyes from pictures and reflections, but now she feels comfort and a warm love for this skin. This moment, all she wants is to feel it cradling her again, and dread tightens her chest at the idea of losing it forever. Straightening, she holds the flap against herself, wraps it around her middle, trying to line up scars and markings, find a sure fit for this macabre puzzle piece. It aches where it touches her and hope rises—perhaps the skin will reconnect, regenerate, remold. But no matter how she turns it or how tight she presses it to her body, the skin remains inert and dead. Even knowing it's a lost cause, she stays holding that belly for a while, regretting every second of hatred and disgust. What she wouldn't give to feel the warm connection of that part of her once more.

She lays it aside finally, for it's growing cold in this place. The shadows are darker, too, creeping from the sides of the path to blur the edges. She can't see as far as she could only minutes ago, and those parts obscured from her sight are lost to her. Is the dark encroaching, or is it her vision, fading as she loses blood?

A sense of urgency creeps through her, tightening her shoulders and quickening her pace. She looks around for more, something else to try, even a small piece to reconnect and find some shred of who she's supposed to be. She settles on the strip of shin and looks down at her legs in the fading light. Her pants end below the knee, shredded and stiff with blood. She forces herself to look at the moving red muscles, the ivory of bone peeking through. She waits for a wave of nausea, a panic attack, something to mark an occurrence like this. All these things are there, waiting in the wings of her consciousness, but for now the gathering storm is held back, the only sign a growing sense of pressure.

Looking at her exposed insides, there's less horror than she expected, seeing herself without her old skin. Disconcerting to see the way her inner workings flex and bunch and jump in response to her movements, but there is something hypnotically beautiful about it as well. It's freeing, standing in her pain. No tight restrictions, no leash of expectations. Her body is a thing of wonder and has always been so. She's almost reluctant to cover it up, but she cannot go on like this, exposed and raw.

With little hope, she finds where edges of desiccated shin line up with the bone and holds it in place, willing it to remember. Willing her body to come back together, even if only in this one place. But of course it does not. This skin, no matter how much she wants it, no longer fits her. Piece by piece she collects what remains, tries to fit it in place, and as she fails, lays it by her side. When there is no more of her scattered across the path, at least none she can see in the gathering dark, she puts her hands gently on her knees, against the stiff fabric of what she now recognizes as her favorite sweatpants. There were times in her life she'd spent months wearing them. Exhausted times of squalling infants, of working two jobs, of never being enough. Other times of deep and intense depression that made it impossible to take on the monumental task of dressing. Yet even then, in those hazy periods, she'd continued on. There was always something to be done, someone who needed her.

Someone. A flash of memory then, of two faces, blurred by time but precious nonetheless. She'd been needed, not long ago. There is a rush of love followed quickly by melancholy. Is she no longer needed? Is that how she ended up in this place in the silence of broken song? She doesn't know, and no further insights occur, so she pushes to her feet to steel herself for one last task.

Sliding bloody digits beneath the waistband of her pants, she feels the sharp pain of separation. It's as she feared. The only skin left is that protected by the cloth, but that's done little more than delay the inevitable. She pulls the fingers free and looks at them again, noticing for the first time the hunks of ragged skin and dried blood beneath each nail.

She did this. Not some freak accident or animal attack, no serial killer lurking, no strange chemical reaction. She must have pried beneath her own tissue and pulled it free, over every part of her body. Even as much as she wants to know why, she's glad she can't remember that part. What could have driven her to pull herself apart that way? Was that why she'd woken? Had the pain dragged her from slumber? What could be so important she would mutilate herself to wake up?

Hissing, she tucks her fingers once more under the elastic of the sweatpants and pulls down. Only an inch or so, and the separation of cloth from skin is excruciating, a wet ripping sound as the layers part. But it's not the sound of skin separating from cloth. Instead it is skin pulling free of muscle and fat.

She stops and stands with her hands still at her waist, holding as still as she can while agony washes over her. Why is she doing this? Why not leave on the last vestiges of her outer shell, hope for a chance to heal? It doesn't make sense, but she's compelled to keep going. The sticky press of the cloth against her legs is the unbearable itch of a job left undone. She can no more stop herself than she can force her body to reunite.

She steels herself against the pain, closes her eyes and yanks down hard. The cotton fights her, pulling taut in the stiffness of blood and connective tissue. Holding her breath, she digs in with bloody nails, scratching and thrusting beneath to gain purchase. She feels everything. Every cell letting go of the one beside it, every muscle fiber holding tight. Her fingernails are gummed with gore, losing their grip, and she wonders if she'll have the temerity to try again. Then the cloth gives and the last part of her old skin slides to the ground at her feet.

There is an intense moment of regret, awash in anguish both physical and spiritual, blackness crowding the edges of her vision. It is more than her skin she has stripped away, but still she cannot see what else is there. Warm blood oozes from her thighs and knees and she remembers to breathe as the pain ebbs just enough for thought to return. She gasps, hands held out to her sides, unwilling to touch this fresh rawness.

Blinking back tears, she is able to lower her gaze and see the puddle of gore and cloth at her flayed feet. Already it has faded to a gray hue, separated from her by more than physical distance. She crouches low, pushing back fresh agony in the wake of the movement. She reaches out and touches the crumpled, stiffening skin with one finger. She has always been bad at goodbye.

Standing, the stinging cold of fleshlessness covering every inch of her body, she looks at the dark path once more. It's almost completely obscured from her vision now, and she wonders what will happen when it's gone.

She frowns, her gaze catching on something pale, half buried in the floorboards. She bends down again to peer at it and with a jolt recognizes her own face looking up at her. She covers her lipless mouth with one hand and studies it, this flap of skin she used to peer out from every day of her life.

It doesn't look like the other parts of her, slimy with blood and frilled with dried, ragged edges. Instead the face appears to be sleeping, eyes closed but not sunken, cheeks still rounded from something below. She spreads her fingers from where they rest on her mouth and feels around, encountering what she expected—bleeding layers no one is meant to see. It *is* her face; she has no trouble recognizing it now. It's a good face, a little lined in places but kind, and now at peace. There are grimy tracks down the cheeks and she touches them, encountering the warmth of tears.

Tears. She remembers that. So many tears. Some were hers but those are unimportant, as they've always been. She can best handle her own, used to a lifetime of crying silently and looking away. But there were others. Crying that hurt her heart and soul, that spurred her to action, to do *something*, whatever it took to ease that pain. The song—the one she still cannot remember. The melody has something to do with calming those tears, with soothing aching hearts full of fear. She's been singing it a long time, feels its weight far back down the path, perhaps all the way to the beginning. Why can't she remember it? If she could only find it, she could leave this stark place of dark unknowns. If she could pull the threads of the lullaby back around herself, she could sleep once more, and stop all that heartache. Why had she woken? Why had she done this to herself? Perhaps she wanted to all along, and the song stopped her before. But now that's it's gone, she can't go back to sleep. She wonders if she'd be able to slip beneath the surface of consciousness even if she could remember the words. She no longer fits in this skin, in her life.

Dark falls completely on the path, and her detached face is lost to sight. She gives a shuddering sigh and stands, turns her back on the way home. Home isn't a concept that clicks anymore. It should speak of warmth and comfort, of respite from the world outside, but she knows it has been a long time since it represented any of these things for her. Perhaps that's why the path has closed—there is no going back. Panic fills her at the thought, her mind and heart grasping for a hold, anything to hang on, not lose her way completely. What if she never finds another path, forced to live in this half world with only partial memories? Why can't she just sing the song again?

A breeze tickles the exposed muscles of her back and shoulders. Her belly dips, her breath catching in her chest. The breeze feels like change.

She expects to see the blank wall still before her, but it is gone. In its place is a copse of trees, the way in lit only by a faint, warm glow. She looks down to see the wooden floor has been replaced by packed dirt. There are footprints leading out and away, back the way she came. They are smaller than she remembers, and at times they seem to have broken into a run, or a skip. She smiles, nostalgia for that kind of bright energy, the confidence of youth.

Hesitating at the opening, she studies the trees that gather close. Each pair flanks another path, all of them dark beyond the first few steps. She studies each in turn, guessing at where they might lead, seeking clues from the trees. On the front of each, a nail has been driven, and some kind of cloak trails down. It is this covering that seems to be the primary difference in the paths, and she steps fully into the clearing. A rush of air behind her, a feeling of displaced matter, then silence. She knows if she turns, the path will be gone, as though it never was.

But it *was* there. Even if all she has are broken up memories, she knows it existed, and that she once tread there, for better or for worse. Her chest aches momentarily for her loss, strong enough it takes her breath away. If she stays here with these thoughts, the grief will overcome her, freeze her in place. One benefit of age and experience is the surety that she cannot hide from harm—there is no armor strong enough to protect her from heartache. But she doesn't have to dwell here, either. Unsteady at first, she turns in a slow circle, taking in the clearing. Curiosity pushes back the hardening cement of loss and she moves close to the nearest tree. At its base are certain implements. There is a wooden flute of some kind, and a leather saddle bag holding a flask for water. A knife, some flint and steel. A lantern, glowing gently.

Haley wraps her arms around herself, holding in the inner parts that are now outer. She tips her head back and looks for stars. Much of the night sky is blocked by tree canopy, but she can see Orion's Belt. The only constellation she's ever been able to identify, and there is comfort in its presence here. Wherever *here* is, whatever this place is she's been taken to, it shares the same sky she has looked at all her life.

She reaches out to touch the nearest hanging cloak, pulling the cloth out to the side to get a better view. It is heavier than she expected, thick and rough. Frowning, she pulls it further to the side and gasps when she sees the slack face peering down at her, the nail upon which it hangs thrust through an empty eyelid.

She drops it and backs away from the tree, heart thumping. It's another skin, though this one is intact. Her breath coming fast, she turns and looks at each hanging cloak, recognizing them for what they are. Empty skin suits, some with clothing, others naked. They are different sizes, shapes, and textures, and she wonders if she truly had woken herself up, or if she's stumbled into the lair of a serial killer who skins his victims and keeps them for decoration.

Yet as she studies these skins, she notices certain similarities. Each has those same two moles on their belly, the scar down the shin, the hands she knows are her own. She has a flash of intuition that if she were to climb into any of these skin suits, the imperfections would match up perfectly with those she'd only just left behind.

She is in hell. There's no other explanation—it's the ante room of some endless torture, holding her while she comes to terms with being dead. Only she does not feel dead, nor is she afraid. The flicker of the lantern light prevents it, the scene before her reminiscent of adventure, of a beginning. The end is already behind her—loved and mourned for, but well and truly over. Is she meant to choose a new skin? Is that why she's here? Yet each one she studies seems wrong, somehow. She cannot put her finger on it, and knows if she were to step into any one of them, she would find comfort and learn to ignore the little things that made her uneasy.

She doesn't want to ignore those things anymore. She wants to listen when her inner voice whispers a warning, as it is now. She doesn't belong in any of these skins, and to her eyes, none are as beautiful as the gory, starshine blank canvas of her current body.

She may not accept the offering of flesh, but excitement tickles her belly at the idea of setting foot on one of the paths. It makes her think of epic stories of quests and adventures she'd read as a child. The breathless anticipation of the first step, leading to the second and finally far from home. That is what the flickering lantern light tells her; that a journey awaits.

But which path to choose? Even lifting the lantern, light does not penetrate beyond a few feet down each opening into the woods beyond. They are largely the same from that perspective, only minor differences in elevation, root structure, proximity of pressing trees. Down some of them she hears voices, ones she recognizes and that warm her heart. She settles on one of those paths, knowing that wherever she travels next, she wants to know these precious voices walk beside her. Gathering the materials left for her in the center of the copse, Haley breathes deep. Centering herself, focusing on the feeling of this moment. There is fear—a flutter of anxiety in her belly. Worries that the path she's chosen will fall off into a void of endless nothing, or that danger awaits her just out of sight. She cannot know, and the not knowing has always bothered her.

Yet staying here with the ground beneath her feet is no longer an option. The path of her prior life is closed, and this limbo won't last forever. Already the light is fading. She feels one last, tiny pang at the forgotten song that is her first memory now, but she doesn't need it anymore. She has slept long enough—her waking was brutal and bloody, full of pain and gore. It was well earned, and she has no intention of going back to sleep.

A smile splitting the exposed muscles of her face, her body raw and limitless, she sets her foot upon the dark path she has chosen.

The Magic Wood

Jonathan L. Howard

IN HIS QUIETER moments (others might have fancied them darker moments, but—as that was the timbre of most of his moments—a different adjective needs must be applied), he felt his claim to be a scientist rang false. A scientist strikes out into new country, after all, whereas well-nigh all his researches consisted of rediscovering that which had been found and lost. These researches, therefore, were more redolent of those of an archaeologist or historian than a true scientist stepping forth as an explorer. The pioneering in his discipline had all usually been done a long time ago, and then subsequently lost, forgotten, or suppressed, and it fell to him to rediscover them by dint of book reading, frequently preceded by book stealing, or questioning other previous researchers, often under duress, often while—technically speaking—they were dead.

Thus, when the happy chance fell to him to do something he felt assured was entirely novel, a melding of the old sciences that ignorant men call "magic" with the new sciences of the volt and the atom, it thrilled him in a way that few things did. Here he was, planting a flag upon an entirely virgin peak, and it delighted him.

He had poured this ingenuity into the more material form of blueprints and, cogent that their realisation lay beyond his own practical skills, he had taken himself into the heart of London to hire the necessary expertise.

Now, he stood at the counter in *Gideon's Scientific Apparatuses and Appurtenances*, a business that might reasonably be described as "interesting," not least for an idiosyncratic usage of the word "appurtenances." Gideon's bore the happy reputation amongst scientific persons of esoteric persuasions for the quick and sure construction of very much anything the busy scientific person of esoteric persuasion might need building, whether it was, say, an electrifiable deck for a submersible vessel or a reliable subjective chronometer for a transtemporal vehicle of some sort. All they asked was a workable set of blueprints and an eye-watering sum of money.

He unrolled the design for the device he required there upon the counter—a design for a machine of great novelty and sublime ingenuity—and awaited an appreciative gasp from the clerk who now examined it.

"Oh," said the clerk. "One of these."

"I beg your pardon?" said Johannes Cabal, a necromancer of some little infamy.

"An electric pentacle, sir," said the clerk, unabashed. "Yes, we have a gentleman we built some such for. He's been a good client for years."

"Some?" said Cabal. "Plural?"

"Three to date. A matter of improvements and, in one case, replacement. But I should be more discreet, of course." He smiled a bloodless sort of smile at Cabal. "We have a reputation to preserve, after all."

"And his designs were just like this?" Cabal was trying not to think of the painstaking evenings spent over a drawing board, cursing pencil and protractor.

"Oh, no, sir," said the clerk. "Even his first design was notably superior to this. If the gentleman would be so kind as to observe this detail, for example, the gentleman will notice that—despite an intention for his pentacle to be powered by portable batteries—there is no inverter in the circuit. The gentleman's tubes, therefore, will only glow at one end, and one feels sure that this is not the effect for which the gentleman is striving."

The gentleman was considering shooting the clerk, but controlled himself. "Very well," said Cabal, rolling up his diagrams and returning them to their tube, breathing heavily through his nostrils all the while. "Then I should like to order a copy of this savant's most recent design."

"Plainly impossible, sir," said the clerk with a quiet air of triumph. "The gentleman in question has not sanctioned the use of his design for general manufacture."

"Would it be possible to secure such a sanction?"

"I cannot say."

"Then might I have the gentleman's name and address?"

"Oh, but sir!" The clerk's outrage at the suggestion was as false as a clown's red nose and every bit as obvious. "We have our reputation to consider!"

Cabal was already reaching for his wallet. "How much?"

The address was an interesting one, and spoke to even Cabal's limited knowledge of London as suggestive of independent wealth and mild eccentricity. It was not a short walk from Gideon's in St. Giles down the Chelsea by the river, and so Cabal took a hansom to the embankment there. He squandered a minute watching the traffic upon the Thames, and then walked the short way to Cheyne Walk.

Outside No. 427, he discovered a brace of workmen gently manoeuvring boxes onto the back of a cart, and there swaddling them in yards of sacking under the anxious eye of a short, balding man, intriguingly clad in tweed and plus fours. As he approached, Cabal noted with interest that the last box to be loaded was an arm span in length and marked FRAGILE: *Scientific Equipment*. The man in tweed shooed them off on their way with admonishments to drive carefully and assurances that he would meet them at the station shortly. He then made to return to the house before whose open door he stood when he espied the approaching Cabal, intent apparent, and so paused.

"You have come to see me?" said the man, plainly flustered at this development.

"If you are Mr. Carnacki, then yes, I have."

"I am he," said Carnacki, "but I am sorry to say that you have called at a most inopportune moment. I am just in the process of leaving. I have a train to catch."

"To the countryside," said Cabal, nodding at the tweed. "Our business will be brief, I assure you. I require only a note of permission from you."

"A note?" Carnacki plucked his watch from his waistcoat and tutted. "Come with me, sir, while I gather my travelling bag, and explain what this note entails."

Cabal followed him to the hallway, where he gathered up a small case and plucked his hat from the rack. "My name is Cabal," said Cabal, "and I have recently devised a form of electrical barrier intended for the exclusion of certain... undesirable etheric elements." This brought Carnacki to a sudden halt and he gazed up at Cabal with frank astonishment. "I am given to understand, however, that my design has already been anticipated and, indeed, exceeded by one of your own. Gideon's would surely build a copy for me, but not without your permission."

"And what do...?" Here Carnacki was interrupted by the arrival of a hansom. "I'm afraid we must take this up at some other time, Mr. Cabal. My cab has arrived, and I do not have a minute to spare." He hustled Cabal out onto the doorstep, locked the door, and went to the kerb.

"Sir, my researches are constrained by the lack of this device," insisted Cabal. "A note permitting Gideon's to start work would take you a moment."

"It is not the writing of the note that is the concern," said Carnacki, climbing up into the hansom. "I would rather be sure of the timbre of these researches of yours before even contemplating the writing of such a note."

"Sir..." said Cabal, feeling his temper rise.

"Please write me a detailed letter explaining exactly why you require an electrical barrier of the type you describe. I shall read it upon my return and give you my decision then. Now, I must bid you a good day. Time is wasting." And so saying, Carnacki closed the door of the cab, and the cabbie drove on.

Cabal watched the vehicle diminish, and his teeth were gritted and his fists clenched as he did so. But he was not a man given to indecision. A moment later he had flagged down another hansom and, as he climbed in, he snarled, to the driver's inestimable delight, "Follow that cab."

～

Carnacki was surprised, not pleasantly, by a sudden appearance aboard the train as the service rolled out of Euston. He watched in wide-eyed astonishment as his compartment's door was wrenched open even as the train was pulling away from the platform, Cabal leapt aboard, slamming the door and throwing himself into the seat opposite him with greater vigour than is usually considered decorous.

"This is a private compartment," said Carnacki in a small voice.

"Good," said Cabal. "Then we may conduct our business in confidence."

"I have no business to conduct with you, sir."

Cabal drew a deep breath to slow his heart and spoke on the exhalation. "You recognised my name. I thought you might."

"I hoped you might go away, and I would never see you again. You should have used an alias. I shall have nothing to do with you, Mr. Cabal."

"I dislike dissimulation. It rarely ends well. Nor did I wish to start our acquaintanceship by lying to you."

"Acquaintanceship?" Carnacki regarded him owlishly. "I wish no acquaintance with a necromancer."

"I am a scientist."

"You are a criminal."

"Any criminality is a by-blow of my research. Is it so very long ago that surgeons had to deal with grave robbers? Great advances may blossom from such crimes."

"Surgeons deal with the preservation of life."

"I deal with the reignition of life."

"To what end?" Carnacki leaned back and crossed his arms. "Power and chaos, like the terrible business in that coastal town some years ago? Is that your noble aim?"

Here Cabal did something that confused and worried Carnacki greatly. He smiled.

"That 'terrible business' was the thinnest shadow of how terrible it could have been. Happily, there was an expert in the field of necromancy present who was able to nip the disaster in the bud."

"Oh?" said Carnacki. He pursed his lips. "Oh. I see. And it was purely a coincidence that you were there?"

"Not at all, but the circumstances were complex. Suffice to say it was not I who triggered those events, but it was surely I who brought them to a propitious end." The two men regarded one other stonily as the train entered the suburbs of London. "You're welcome, I'm sure," said Cabal into the silence.

"Is it thanks that you desire, Mr. Cabal? Or power?"

Cabal blew out his breath dismissively. "Power. What use have I for power? Do I look like the sort of man who hungers to place himself at the head of an army of the undead?" He thought for a moment. "I've got two in the woodshed, and they're more than enough trouble for anyone."

Carnacki decided not to pursue that particular line, and instead said, "Well, what then?"

Cabal did not answer that. He took a breath as if he might speak, but then let it sigh from his nose instead. Carnacki received the strong impression that he had cornered the man in a corner he did not relish occupying at all, and in that reluctance, he understood.

"Oh, my dear sir, I am so sorry," he said.

Cabal emitted a small growl of sublimating anger from the back of his throat. "Thank you, but I would rather have the plans for your electric pentacle."

What the statement lacked in diplomacy it gained in plain verisimilitude, and Carnacki found himself—if not warming to Cabal exactly—at least sensing common ground. At the very least, Cabal was an experiment in himself that might be worth the testing. Carnacki allowed himself a small, genial smile. "Perhaps you might prefer to see it in operation first?"

Now it was Cabal's turn to frown. "You would take me along?"

"Why not? You have already forced your presence upon me and, while I usually prefer to work alone, that is at least as much a product of necessity as mien. What the vulgar call 'ghost finding' bears few practitioners and most are, with the best will in the world, either rank amateurs or frauds. I do not describe them so to anoint myself, you understand—"

"Heavens forbid..."

"—but purely an observation based upon methods and results."

Cabal nodded. "And what of conclusions?"

"I have made none. I suspect it is beyond the ken of man or, at least, the ken of Carnacki to arrive at any. I am no philosopher."

"We all live within limitations, Mr. Carnacki. It is a wise man who perceives his own."

Carnacki laughed. Cabal felt an unfamiliar yet oddly pleasurable warmth grow in his breast. He carefully audited his emotional ledgers and found that there was a possibility that he might like Carnacki. This would bear monitoring in case he had to murder the man at any point.

"Let us find a ghost together, Mr. Cabal," said Carnacki. "Let us see what we may see."

It transpired that their destination lay in the Derbyshire Peaks; happily, not on a peak, but nestled more sedately betwixt. Pikewell House was a neoclassical building that—despite its columns and ionic capitals—wasn't even forty years old. It sat a little resentfully, conscious of its own pretension, in 200 acres in the hollow between three hills. As the dogcart they had hired at the station made its way up the avenue, both Cabal and Carnacki looked around them, while Carnacki gently plied the driver with intelligent questions as to the local perception of the hall and its grounds.

Cabal half listened while he took in the landscape, noting that the sun was almost setting for them, an hour ahead of the time stated in the almanac, the result of one of the hills lying to the west and occluding the horizon. He also saw that the grass of the lawns they passed was—but for some scrubby, yellowish areas of recent scything near the gate—hip high and untended.

The driver, however, was that particular flavour of taciturn that indicated that he had things to say, but liked, or at least respected, the tenants of the hall too much to air them, and Carnacki did not press him. For this mercy, the driver was eager enough to help with unloading

Carnacki's gear at the hall and was the soul of gentleness when transporting the equipment within.

Daniel Hogarth was the master of the house, and Cabal thought him too broad-shouldered and rustic a creature of around thirty years of age to be discovered wan and lurking at the threshold to the house. He also saw that Hogarth's attention kept darting past them as if anticipating another, unwanted visitor.

"I was only expecting you, Mr. Carnacki," said Hogarth as he shook their hands.

"I was a late addition to the expedition," said Cabal, playacting regret. "Please forgive the imposition, Mr. Hogarth. I have similar interests to Mr. Carnacki and I foisted myself upon him. The fault is mine."

"Mr. Cabal is here as an observer," added Carnacki, "and to assist if need be."

They were conducted into the study for tea, and as Hogarth absented himself to see about having another room made up, Carnacki said in a low voice, "You have taken note of the windows, no doubt?"

"The ground floor is shuttered on the outside, and curtained within, yet there is still light outside," replied Cabal. "They are no real defence against anything but sight."

Hogarth returned with a maid bearing the tea things. After she had served tea, she asked if she might be dismissed, and both visitors heard the urgency in her voice.

Hogarth looked wearily at the clock and nodded. "Of course, Lizzie. I shall see you tomorrow. Good evening."

When she had gone, Carnacki said, "Your staff do not live here?"

Hogarth laughed a humourless cough of a laugh. "They do not. I am usually alone during darkness. If I had not made the concession of allowing them home before nightfall, I would have no staff at all."

"I am very poor at social niceties, sir," said Cabal, "but this seems to be an instance where we may sensibly skip over them altogether. What is happening here? What is it that makes you so fearful?"

Hogarth glanced once more at the clock. "When the sun sets, it will come. Sooner or later, it will get in."

"Carnacki," said Cabal with some urgency, "we should not dither. In my experience, it is better to beard a lion than to hide from it."

The Magic Wood

Carnacki looked him with astonishment coloured with dismay. "What? But preparation is everything!"

"There are the three of us, I have my pistol, you have your pentacle. I am keen to see its operation; I suggest you set it up while we hear Hogarth's account. Then, at dusk, we shall throw wide the French windows and see what we shall see."

⁓

"My family's fortune," began Hogarth as Cabal badgered a befuddled Carnacki around until operations could begin in earnest, "was established by my grandfather, who built this hall quite late in life. He did not have long to enjoy it before his death, and it passed to my father, his only issue. My father was happy here, and raised us happily, my sister Amelia and me. He married young and was absolutely smitten with my mother every day of his life. This was a happy house, gentleman, a place of halcyon summers and joyful winters. When I became a man, however, I determined to find my own way as much as I might, and I travelled abroad, finally settling in Canada. My sister married and moved to Gloucester, but she visited here whenever she might, and her letters to me said that our parents remained content in our absence, my father maintaining the family business, and my mother integral to the social life of the district.

"Then... things changed."

Cabal paused in helping Carnacki mount one of the gas-filled fluorescing tubes upon its stands and said in a low voice and not unsympathetically, "They always do."

"I heard via my sister that our mother had died and that our father was in a state of emotional collapse. That he had failed to tell me himself seemed extraordinary, but as I later understood from my sister and the family solicitor, he was not in his right mind. Of course, I telegraphed him to say I would return home, but received a stern reply to the effect that I was to do no such thing, that the funeral would be long over before I could reach England, and that I could accomplish nothing there. It was at this point that I communicated with my sister and the solicitor, and they told me of his parlous state of mind, and that I should obey his wishes for fear of worsening matters. I did so, though it caused me great pain.

"I did not return to England for years, and was reliant upon my sister for news of him as he was slow to reply; brief and, I thought, evasive in our own correspondence. Her letters could tell me little more, as she had been all but forbidden to visit the house and was reduced to ridiculous meetings in local tearooms, as though they were enemies meeting on neutral ground. She did discover, however, that all the old staff had been let go and replaced by agency people, none of whom seemed contracted to stay more than a few months. Amelia told me our father seemed distracted during these meetings. He had left the running of the business to agents, and rarely left Pikewell. She also said his health seemed to be on the wane, and in this her sad observation was borne out when, seven months ago, I received word of his death. I was heir. I returned at once, of course, but what I found on my return....

"Pikewell was in an awful state. I had been away some eight years, and memory might lie, but I was shocked at the overgrown lawns, the weed-clogged ponds, the ubiquitous neglect. My first thought was that the business had failed, and the estate was impoverished, but when I conferred with the agents and saw the books, it was all in rude health. I could only conclude that my mother's death had pushed him somewhere further than mere eccentricity. Amelia arrived on the same day as me with her husband was equally shocked by the state of the hall and its grounds.

"Our favourite corner of the estate had always been an artfully wooded place in a sunny corner where the hill rises. Grandfather built a summerhouse in its heart, and as children we called it the 'Magic Wood.' Inexplicably, my father had had the wood fenced off with railings and protected by a locked iron gate. What lies beyond now looks more like a witch's lair, unkempt and horrible. It is a poor counterpart to our happy memories. None of the keys seemed to fit, so I said then I would have the lock broken and the fence brought down."

"But you haven't?" said Carnacki, removing five shallow silver bowls from a case and arranging them at the vertices of the rapidly forming pentacle. "Why is that?"

"To be frank, I'd forgotten about it until this minute," confessed Hogarth. "You see, something happened that first night we both stayed here that quite drove 'The Magic Wood' from my mind. My room—my father's old room—overlooks the aspect that lies beyond these windows. We had retired, but I couldn't sleep. I went to my window and looked out on the sad state of the grounds, illuminated as it was beneath a gibbous moon, a hair from fullness. I noticed that upon the unkempt lawn there were trails, which showed as dark curving lines against the pale heads of the tall grass. Of course, I assumed that they were made by animals, although certainly something quite large like a badger. For reasons I couldn't guess, they disturbed me, and I went back to bed thereafter and lapsed into a troubled sleep.

"I was woken at three by my sister's scream. I rushed down, accompanied by the household, and found her here, in this room, looking at the French windows with an awful expression of soul-deep horror as I had never seen before, and I would remind you gentlemen that I have lived in Canada. She was distraught and required time and a little milk and brandy to calm, at least to a state that she might recount what had happened.

"She told me that she had not slept well, despite her tiredness from travel, and had entered a sort of half-dream wherein she imagined that a cat or other harmless creature was at that window and desiring entrance. In this somnambulant state, she came downstairs and entered this study, coming to the window and drawing back the curtain.

"But there was no cat there. Only a deathly pale and bone-thin hand against the pane."

He paused, shuddered a little, and continued, "I assured her that she had been dreaming, but she swore she had been awake enough and knew what she had seen. Her husband took her away the next morning by the first train; would that I had shown similar good sense and left with them. For, after they had gone, I examined the window and found upon the glass of one of the low panes, perhaps two feet above the terrace, a handprint, perfectly defined and terrible in its thinness. And opposite the window, a new trail emerged from the tall grass that I swear was not there when I had looked out previously."

He sat on the edge of his chair and shook his head miserably. "It comes every night, gentlemen, and I am in despair. I dare not look upon it. I, who have faced grizzly bear and mountain lion without turning a hair, am afraid of that which crawls at night in the pleasant hills of Derbyshire."

"Night has fallen, Hogarth," said Cabal, "and the electric pentacle is ready. Step within it." He reached into the Gladstone bag he habitually carried and extracted a pistol that made up for in calibre what it lacked in elegance. "You, too, Carnacki."

Carnacki blinked at him. "You too, surely, Cabal?"

"No." Cabal worked a crick in his neck and checked the pistol's load. "I feel I have a better understanding of what is in train here than you. It transpires that it shall be you who is the observer on this occasion. If I am right, this all ends here and now. If I am wrong, you may regret not wearing sou'westers and oilskins as I may be very messily disassembled before your very eyes." He went to the window, drew back the curtains (this eliciting a low moan of horror from Hogarth), and then opened the French windows and their outer shutters wide.

"That is an ugly joke to make, sir," said Carnacki as he hastened to close the small bayonet switch that controlled the flow of current. The tubes delineating the pentagram about the pentacle began to glow an unhealthy sort of salty magenta uniformly—Cabal noted—along their lengths.

That is what an inverter does, then, he told himself.

"No joke. The entities with which I deal tend to be possessed of a very muscular malevolence. I am making an informed guess that my actions are the right ones. If I am wrong, you will truly regret lacking an umbrella." He checked the clock on the mantle. "I gauge ten minutes."

"Ten minutes for what?" asked Carnacki.

"For it to crawl here from the so-called 'Magic Wood.'"

He lit four tungsten lamps from Carnacki's gear, arranged them on the floor facing the open window, put out the electric lights, and then they waited.

At eight minutes, Carnacki nodded towards the gun in Cabal's hand. "You cannot shoot a ghost."

"I'm not expecting a ghost," replied Cabal.

At twelve minutes they heard the swishing of the tall grass, slow and rhythmic, though the night was still. Then the grass ceased its susurration.

"It is on the terrace!" whispered Hogarth, and so it was. By inches, hard fought and grudgingly won, it grew closer, drawn to the subdued lights of the study. A pale, clumsy thing it was, barely visible in the gloom outside, and every man there wished that it might remain so ill-defined.

But, by those inches, it grew closer and closer and then, after a moment's pause, it dragged itself over the threshold. It hesitated as if marshalling its strength and then, with evident difficulty, raised its head—a head crowned with tangles of filthy hair, dense with mud and brambles—and they saw its face.

It was dreadful to look upon, but more dreadful still was the cry Hogarth gave, a wail of animal horror that is usually the domain of the terribly wounded.

"Oh, God!" he cried. For a moment it was as if the air had coagulated in his lungs, curdled by shock, but then he spoke again. "Oh, God! My mother! It is my mother!"

"No," said Cabal, and Carnacki heard a tone of sympathetic regret there that seemed very alien to the man. "It is not your mother. Not now. Carnacki, turn him away. He should not see this."

Carnacki needed no second bidding, but took Hogarth by the shoulders and turned his face from the awful scene.

"Do it, Cabal," he said, and the shot rang out instantly.

Carnacki gave Hogarth a strong sleeping draft and stayed with him until it took effect. Then he and Cabal were up the whole night: Carnacki putting away the pentacle; Cabal seeking out a wheelbarrow in which to remove the remains from the house. Then they talked at length while they waited for dawn.

"It was Hogarth's father, of course, who did this terrible thing," said Carnacki.

"Of course," replied Cabal, "but do not think too ill of him for that. Grief is a powerful emotion." He said nothing for a moment, and Carnacki could see his mind was in some other time and some other place. "He grasped at straws, and he made a mistake. Once it was made, I imagine he believed its shortcomings could be rectified."

"And could they?"

"No. Never. What occupied the mortal clay of Hogarth's mother was not her soul. It wasn't human. It didn't even know how to walk upright. It had the intelligence of a slightly stupid dog." He sighed. "And the loyalty of one, literally undying."

Carnacki went to the open window and looked to the east and the growing light limning the ridges of the hills. "You were right, Cabal. This is not my area of expertise. What shall we do next?"

"When there is sun enough, we shall go to the 'Magic Wood' of his youth and break the lock. Inside the summerhouse are items I am confident it is better no coroner's court ever considers. Some things I shall take away, some we shall burn."

"The fence Hogarth senior erected around that wood," said Carnacki suddenly, "it was never meant to keep people *out*, was it?"

"Not primarily. But when he stopped going to the wood subsequent to his own death, what he kept there grew restive and came to look for him. We shall doubtless find the earth clawed away beneath the fence somewhere."

Carnacki shook his head. "This is a very tragic affair."

"Death shall ever cast its pall." Cabal rose to stretch and yawn. "We should find the kitchen. The morning's business will go easier preceded by tea."

"You should know, I shall never view your profession with anything less than opprobrium, Mr. Cabal," said Carnacki. "It is inherently abhorrent."

"That," said Cabal without hesitation, "is fair."

"But perhaps there is still hope for at least some of its practitioners." And Carnacki held out his hand to Johannes Cabal.

An Earth So Strange

The Dreambug Infestation of Half Moon Oaks

KC Grifant

THE CREATURE—ONCE someone's house but now a medley of wood, metal and debris—towered in the pale blue sky. Lance fired his six-shooter up at the monster while dozens of children and adults of Half Moon Oaks ran past him.

"Get as far as you can!" Lance hollered, sweat beading under his wide-brimmed hat. The creature screeched like buckling railroad but continued to rise, a two-storied building brought to life by the thousands of dreambugs wriggling in the wood. The beetle-like insects flashed emerald hues amidst the broken furnishings. Below the sound of their chittering rose something else: almost a whispering, like a dozen people hissing in unison. The noise made his skin crawl.

A handful of residents remained several feet away, firing at the creature. Next to the monster, the school building had emptied out and the rest of the townsfolk were safely evacuated.

Thank goodness.

"Sheriff'll be over in a jiff." Melinda's tall form appeared next to him. She dropped their bag of dwindling ammo and other supplies on the ground. She impatiently pushed her long dark hair back under her hat and grimaced at the monster. "Bullets?"

"Pass right through." Lance chewed on his lip and rubbed at the ever-present scruff on his chin. "Too bad we used all our dynamite. Other ideas, love?"

"We need to get it smoking," Melinda said, and he nodded. They had encountered plenty of strange critters on their monster-exterminating jobs and one thing almost always worked above all else: fire. "I told the lawman to bring over any firepower he's got."

The creature, which had been still, lurched toward the firing group of Half Moon Oaks residents. The semblance of an arm, bigger than an oak trunk and which looked to be made up of mostly kitchen components, nearly knocked one shooter to the ground.

"Watch out!" Lance shouted. The man ducked just in time, his bowler hat flying along with a scattering of the green bugs.

"Don't let them touch you! Psychic biters like these are bad news," Lance called to the three residents who lingered, firing uselessly at the creature. He wracked his brain to pull up the various monster facts he'd memorized before he and Melinda started their exterminating business. Not his favorite—he was more a doer than reader—but their mentor Abel had insisted. In fact, it was one of the conditions before Abel would loan them his custom weapons.

The half-page entry on dreambugs in one of Abel's journals floated back to Lance now and he repeated it to the crowd. "A few bites'll give you nightmares for weeks. More will put you in a stupor—if you're lucky. Let us handle this."

That was all the residents needed to hear to hightail it.

He and Melinda crouched on the side of a broken wagon while the creature grabbed the schoolhouse roof. Sharp cracks boomed as the monster tore off half the empty school building. Bugs poured from its makeshift arm and engulfed the wood, fusing it to its torso and legs, helping it grow into a giant-like human shape.

"Never heard of dreambugs doing this before," Melinda said. "Combining like that."

"Maybe their psychic tendencies are animating the inanimate somehow. And I'll be damned," Lance said. "Taking on a human form. What on earth for?"

"Don't matter much." Melinda started rummaging in their supply bag.

Lance peeked over and swore. "Slim pickings. Should've filled up after the Sunset Cliffs job."

"No time." Melinda extracted the custom electric-shocking gun from their supply bag. The shocker took a breath and a half to load and rarely worked.

"Don't know why we drag that one around, Mellie," Lance groaned. "We'd have better luck chucking torches."

"Got to do something while we wait for the dang lawman."

The vague outline of a giant face in the monster—near as wide as a barn door now—came together, with broken glass forming sightless eyes. Beams of wood crisscrossed to make eyebrows and a frowning mouth. The sound of the scuttling insects and whispering intensified.

"Here." Lance dug in his pocket and extracted two rifle bullets. "Last ones."

Melinda loaded and aimed. Meanwhile the monster turned its face upwards and stretched wooden fingers toward the sun.

"Looks like it's craving the sunlight," Lance mused.

He saw something flash in Melinda's eyes—almost like she felt sorry for it—before the look disappeared.

She squared her jaw and fired.

In the debris that made up the creature's body, the bugs' clicking hit a high, uniformed pitch as the bullet passed through. The creature turned at the second shot and screeched, a sound like splintering wood and clattering pipes. Debris made up of pots and knives and boards—along with a few bugs—rained down as the creature whacked the end of the wagon.

Melinda and Lance rolled out of the way and darted behind a single towering oak next to the dirt road.

"Close one!" Melinda brushed a few of the dreambugs from her duster and crunched them with her boot. Their smooshed wings changed from emerald green to a dark, pukish color, then black.

"Brave-making weapon for you," a voice rang out behind them. The lawman, judging by the flash of silver at his chest and the scar that ran from his nose to ear beneath black curls. He was a skinny fella who shifted more than a jittery colt, but his hands were steady. And in his hands, he held a monstrosity of a gun—what looked like a makeshift rifle with a long nozzle. The piece attached to a metal cylinder the size of a breadbox.

85

Melinda groaned out load. "Thought you were bringing us dynamite or something useful. Not an antique."

"Fire-maker," the lawman said proudly. "My daddy used it against a herd of ice wolves terrorizing the town back, oh, nearly a decade ago. Sulfur and proprietary concoction. Takes two people to operate it, though. Best one of you aim and I'll get the tinderbox going."

Lance glanced at Melinda. "Better than nothing, ain't it?"

Melinda crossed her arms. "I'll stick with the shocker."

Lance stifled a sigh and instead accepted the fire-maker. The creature took another step toward them, making the ground rumble. They staggered and tried to stay behind the lone tree for cover.

The lawman stared up at the monster. "You ever run into this before?"

"Not like this. But don't you worry, we've never run into a monster we can't handle," Lance said and knelt on the ground next to the tree trunk, hoisting the gun. The nozzle threw off his weight and he took a moment to adjust. "Heavy piece."

"The Fire-maker is a high card, even if it don't look it," the lawman said, crouching next to him to fiddle with the cylinder. "Think of this as a giant fire piston. When it's time, I'll ignite it. You'll get a pretty burst of flames out of that nozzle there."

"Tell me when." Lance took aim.

The creature was a stone's throw now, its wooden face shifting into what might pass as a glare. Bugs flicked down from it like sweat.

"One more step and it'll be within range," the lawman said.

"Shocker's loaded if we need," Melinda said next to them. "Lance!"

Lance glanced up. Melinda's tone told him something was wrong. His heart sank when he spotted what she was pointing at: a kid—couldn't be more than 12 years old—wedged between a stove pipe and floorboards in the upper right thigh of the creature. An impressive fluff of curls floated around her closed eyes.

"Aaya!" the lawman shouted. The girl's eyelids fluttered.

"Must've been in the school when it got enveloped." Lance paled.

"She's a special gal," the lawman said, looking panicked. "Orphan. Got a touch of the psychic in her."

"Psychic? Could be that made the dreambugs drawn to her. But for what?" Lance's mind ticked through the few facts he knew about dreambugs, but nothing he had read gave him an inkling.

"We got to get her," Melinda said, dropping the shocker next to Lance. "Fire at the other leg when I'm on it." She quickly climbed up the sprawling oak branches.

"Don't—" Lance started, and gave up as the lawman looked open-mouthed at her, then back at Lance.

"She's never going to make that jump," the lawman said. "Stop her!"

Lance ignored him. Once Melinda had her mind set to something he had about as much power to stop her as one of those squashed beetles.

Melinda crouched on one of the wider branches some fifteen feet up. She waved, drawing the monster's attention. It took one final step toward them, making the ground buckle.

Melinda jumped.

Lance held his breath for an endless minute as she soared through the air, duster lifting behind her like a cape. She slammed into the side of the creature's right leg and began to slide down before gripping a piece of stove piping. She found her footing next to Aaya and started prying off one of the boards imprisoning her. Beetles hurried over her duster.

"Don't fire, you'll kill 'em both!" the lawman said, pushing sweaty curls off his forehead. "All that wood will go up in flames quicker than a scared hare."

"Just get that fire piston going!" Lance took aim at the left leg.

The lawman drew in his breath sharply but began fiddling with the cannister.

On the monster, the beetles swarmed toward Melinda and Aaya. Melinda had the kid halfway out, but the large mass of bugs would be on them in a second.

The cannister clicked. "Ready," the lawman said.

"Now!" Lance shouted and pulled the trigger.

The blast of heat made Lance nearly drop the gun, but he held steady, squinting as best he could through the flames. It worked: most of the bugs scattered up the wood, running to the monster's makeshift face. Billows of black smoke poured out of its arms and legs as the fire swept up its body. The creature collapsed to its knees. Its chittering and whispers ascended to howls, like the wind itself was shrieking.

Through the smoke, Lance saw the kid's figure finally dislodge from the wood. Melinda gripped her and jumped; together they landed roughly in the grassy patch a few feet away and he breathed a sigh of relief. Through a breeze that snatched smoke plumes away, Lance could see they were covered in something dark. *Soot*, he thought at first, but the soot was moving.

They were covered in dreambugs.

Lance threw down the gun and ran, the lawman close behind.

"Kill the bugs!" Lance coughed, the smoke searing his throat and nose.

The lawman knelt next to the girl, Aaya, who was sitting up, rapidly brushing away the insects. Melinda, on the other hand, lay still as stone, except for her flicking eyelids. Dozens of the dreambugs scuttled over her, and he could see four fresh bites on her arms. Lance batted them away as fast as he could. They'd had plenty of close calls in their monster fighting days, but seeing her like this clenched up his throat and bowels all at once. "Mellie, stay with me!"

Lance used his handkerchief to swat bunches of the insects away. One of the dreambugs flapped its green wings and landed on the back of his hand. Before he could flick it, it reared up and stuck him in the hand with a stinger like a nail.

"Damn! Watch out for—" Lance started to tell the lawman when a gray cloud rolled in front of his eyes. "What the…?" The words snatched out of his mouth into the cold silence.

Lance blinked and blinked again, trying to clear his eyesight. Melinda and the town were gone. He looked to be standing in a white field. A dark grayness rolled overhead, reminding him of a murky, slow-moving river. Gray shadows shuffled at the sides of his vision, murmuring. When he turned to look at them, the figures dissolved like clouds. Their murmurs grew into the same whispers he had heard from the giant creature.

"What is this?" Lance tried to say, but whatever this place was, it didn't seem partial to allowing words.

He lunged toward the closest shadow, a willowy white figure. It turned to him, its face a smudge. In that blurriness, the figure opened a chasm of a mouth wider than humanly possible. What resembled a scream emitted: a warped wail that struck a chord deep in his ears.

Lance stumbled back and kept stumbling, as if the ground was disappearing as soon as he stepped on it. With the sudden movement he could feel—but not see—the dreambug on the back of his hand. He ripped it off.

The vision faded, and the smell of charred wood hit him as he hurled the dreambug that had bit him. The lawman and Aaya came into focus. They were trying—and failing—to sweep the dreambugs off Melinda. Her shoulders jerked and she went still.

Too still.

"You back with us, partner?" the lawman asked. "Your girl don't look too good and we can't get these blasted biters off!" In front of them, the creature had devolved into a mass of fire and smoldering wood, hundreds of dying dreambugs squirming around it.

Lance's gaze fell on the shocker Melinda had left beneath the oak tree.

"Work, dammit," he muttered as he scooped it up and dialed to the lowest setting. He took aim toward Melinda's chest.

"Don't hurt them!" Aaya cried.

"You crazy?" the lawman shouted. "You'll kill her!"

"Sorry love," Lance said to Melinda, grimaced, and pulled the trigger. For a split second nothing happened, and he figured they really were out of aces this time. Then the gun sizzled and snapped in a puff of bluish smoke and a kickback nearly knocked him over.

When he looked up, Melinda, her normally straight hair sticking out more than normal, was sitting upright. A ring of singed dreambugs twitched around her.

"You shot me," Melinda said, dazed. She brushed the insect carcasses from her shirt and pants, and Lance helped her to her feet.

"Sorry, love," he said and squeezed her hand. She was hot, maybe feverish. Her eyes struggling to focus. Might take a while for the bugs' toxin to wear off, but at least she was awake. Alive. He handed her his flask, and she promptly began to down it. "Perils of the job."

"Poor bugs!" The girl, Aaya, was looking at the electrocuted insects and blinking back tears.

"What are you talking about, girl? They nearly killed you!" The lawman exchanged a look with Lance.

"They didn't," Aaya insisted, smoothing down her curls.

"You seem dandy, despite being in the middle of what most would reckon was a deadly circumstance." Lance knelt next to her. "You want to tell us what happened, exactly?"

Aaya looked at him with sharp brown eyes. Her gaze was full of a calm intelligence that seemed to belie her age.

"They wanted to know what it was like," Aaya said.

"What *what* was like?" the lawman interjected.

"The ghosts," she said matter-of-factly. "Wanted to know what it was like to feel alive again."

The lawman cleared his throat and glanced at Lance. "She's had a knack for sensing things. She's done seances for some of the townsfolk to help with healing. But I never thought…" He trailed off, looking at the pile of smoldering wood.

Lance thought of the faceless screamer in his dreambug vision and shuddered. The pieces clicked into place. "Ghosts…communicated through the dreambugs?" he asked.

Aaya nodded. "I didn't mean for it to get out of hand. I found a nest of the bugs. They helped me talk with the ghosts. The bugs made a kind of, um, bridge and we connected." Her gaze brightened. "They were friends. I wasn't alone. Then more bugs came and the ghosts were so excited. They were able to communicate through the bugs and um, came through." Her lip twisted unhappily. "I didn't mean for anyone to get hurt. Or for the bugs to die."

"That's a potent power you got. You'll need to be more careful," Lance said.

"People will try to use it," Melinda agreed bluntly. "And use you." She looked to the lawman, her eyes getting clearer by the second. "You make sure that doesn't happen. And that she has the means she needs to take care of herself."

He nodded, turning as more residents gathered to stare at the fallen monster, now just a heap of smoking wood. "Take Aaya here to Ms. Bridges," the lawman instructed one of them. "And get a crew to start cleaning up this mess."

Lance leaned down to carefully pinch one of the last dreambugs still moving. He blew out the tiny fire on its back. "What'd you see when they bit you?"

"Dunno." Melinda handed back his flask. "Just darkness, I guess. Felt like a nightmare, but one I can't remember. Why?"

"Reckon we ought to take a sample home to Abel." Lance downed the last few drops from the flask before pushing the bug inside.

The lawman shuddered. "What for?"

"Folks at home study the monsters, see if we can get useful things from them. Medicines."

"Weapons," Melinda added, examining a dreambug bite mark on her arm and wincing.

The lawman shrugged and handed Lance a bound envelope from his pocket. "To each their own, I suppose. Payment for you. We thank you for your services. Where're you off to next?"

"Oh, we got a few more towns that wrote in need of exterminating. But first…" Lance glanced at Melinda. "Let's rest up, grab a bite."

"I'm game for anything." She shot a soured look at the bug carcasses, sprinkled like dark green and black confetti.

"Well, anything but barbeque."

Cruel Machinations

Pedro Iniguez

Prologue: Tunnel Rat

MARICELA OSEGUEDA RELEASED the duffel bag and let it drop into the abyss. When the bag landed with a muffled thud, she clambered down a set of rusty rungs until her tiptoes touched solid ground. Above, the manhole cover groaned as it slid shut, cloaking the world in darkness.

With a trembling hand, she flicked on the cheap plastic flashlight, the loose batteries clacking inside like broken eggshells. She swung the cone of dim yellow light every which way, illuminating the walls of a narrow tunnel. She could tell it was old because the wooden support beams propping up the roof looked decayed and discolored like some abandoned mineshaft. It was no secret the cartels had several of them intersecting the border.

The ceiling, damp and muddy, wasn't much higher than her head and barely wider than her flared elbows. As she padded forward, she felt a sudden tingle in the back of her brain warning her the tunnel would collapse on her, the weight of the world falling upon her slender frame, crushing her, never to be found. It was just her nerves, she thought, wiping a sweaty palm on her pantleg. She exhaled and continued along the snaking path. Maricela wondered why it hadn't just been a straight shot north. The path, she supposed, circumvented certain U.S. Customs outposts or ranches straddling the border.

They had given her instructions to follow the tunnel a few miles toward its end, where she would meet a man in jeans and a black jacket that read DEA. A man named *Deacon*. Maricela was to hand him the bag and come right back. It sounded easy enough. There'd be plenty of opportunities to make some more cash, they'd assured her, if she didn't fuck this up.

As she made her way deeper into the tunnel, the path seemed to slope slightly downward. Here, the air became frigid, needling her skin like a thousand thumbtacks. Her arms swelled with goosebumps, and she started to shiver. *Breathe in. Relax.*

Maricela needed the money in the worst way; to be independent, to afford her freedom from a life of restraints in a town that had kept her down, and would continue to do so unless she quickly changed trajectory.

A few of her friends at school had let her in on a secret. About those gigs the cartels had offered high school students. That was before they dropped out and ghosted her. Perhaps they'd moved on to bigger and better things with their new incomes. At least, that's what she'd hoped. Maricela wanted to attend a trade school. Perhaps even become a veterinarian. To treat the throngs of stray dogs this city neglected. To care for the sick animals the poor couldn't afford to do on their modest incomes. It would be worth it, she reassured herself. If this is what it took, she'd gladly do it. Besides, it wasn't like she was killing anyone.

Maricela tucked her elbows in and ducked her head as the tunnel shrank. Something seemed to change. The walls and ceiling appeared less the product of drilling machines, and more like they had been hollowed out by rudimentary digging tools, such as spades or pickaxes. Or hands. No more wooden beams or pillars or joists, either. Just dirt and mud. It was here that the stench of rot and decay became unbearable, like spoiled meat. She heard something and stopped. The distant patter of droplets smacking on mud. Or perhaps the sound of bare feet slapping against the soggy earth.

"Deacon?" she called out.

Only her echo replied.

The pitter-patter persisted, grew louder. Closer.

The masked men had reassured her she would be alone in the tunnel. Now, she wasn't so sure. Was she in danger? What was so important about what she'd been lugging around, anyway? Curious, she brought the duffel bag to her chest and opened it. Wads of newspaper spilled out. No drugs, no money, no severed heads. Just crumpled balls of faded sports columns and editorials. Oddly enough, the revelation did little to reassure her. In a way, she'd hoped to find something a little more nefarious.

Was this all some twisted joke? A loyalty test? Screw this. This didn't feel right. Just before she pivoted back toward the manhole, the shadows on the ground and walls came alive and slithered toward her. Before she could scream, the darkness enveloped her until she became a part of it.

Chapter 1: The Cab Driver

The phone rumbled, startling him awake. He peered out the windshield and waited for his eyes to adjust, for the world to take shape again. The neon lights stretched into long, fine-pointed stars against the black of night. He remembered now. He was parked in the Red-Light District.

Pepe Rodriguez slid his glasses onto his face and looked down at the cupholder. When he saw the number flashing on the screen, he immediately felt his heart contract as beads of moisture accumulated on his forehead. He thought about letting the call go to voicemail, but he knew there'd be no point.

He cleared his throat and flipped the phone open.

"Ismael?"

"Do you have it, old man?"

He swallowed a dry lump. "Listen, compadre, I'm still short some cash. Could you give me another two months?"

"I'm very disappointed in you." Ismael's words were cold, uncaring.

"You already know I'm doing everything I can. I drive the bus in the mornings and the cab at night. I have to care for my grandchildren all by myself. You know I'm going to get it for you, but these gigs don't pay enough."

"You should have thought about that when you placed those bets. One week. Then I come see your family."

The line died.

Pepe wiped the sweat on his brow with the back of his hand. He didn't understand. He attended church, he helped his grandchildren with their homework, he worked himself to the bone. And yet, the cockfights had put him in a hole. His thoughts drifted to Sara and Carlitos. Their sweet, plump faces. The world was ready to devour them and spit them out into a hollow grave somewhere in the desert.

Often he felt as if God, cruel and bored, had been toying with him like a marionette, pulling his strings for his own entertainment.

The rear door swung open.

A woman crouched and peered inside, her face bathed in red light from the neon sign above.

"Are you available?" she said.

"Yes, where to?"

"The Colonia Vieja."

Pepe arched an eyebrow. "Are you sure?"

"I'm sure," she said, scooching into the seat.

The woman gave Pepe an address. He pulled out and the old Toyota lurched forward.

"What brings you to the Colonia?"

"It's…personal."

"I see. It's just that nobody ever *asks* to go there."

Pepe glanced at the rearview mirror. The woman leaned her head against the headrest and sighed. She looked to be in her mid-forties, but the look of pain and regret had aged her about ten years.

"My daughter went missing a month ago. I've been digging around, getting nowhere. I'm visiting the only person that may be able to help me. He lives in the Colonia."

Pepe pursed his lips and nodded in solidarity. "I'm so sorry. Lots of girls go missing in this state. It must be hard."

The woman didn't reply.

"For what it's worth, I'm so sorry. I hope you find her."

The road became bumpy as Pepe pulled into the Colonia Vieja, where the paved streets gave way to dirt roads encrusted with rocks, rusted bottle caps, and shards of glimmering glass. It was an old neighborhood rife with mangy dogs, liquor stores, taquerias, and houses made of cinderblocks and corrugated sheet metal roofs.

There was a loud bang and a thump as the car jolted, as if a firework had gone off under the chassis.

"Shit," Pepe said, pulling off to the curb and popping the brakes. "Can you believe this?" He ran a hand along his hair, cursing under his breath.

"What's wrong?" the woman said.

"Flat tire. I just got a new set too. This is going to ruin me."

The woman reached in her bag and handed him some cash. "Thank you for the ride. I know you're a good man and things will work out for you."

"Wait, where are you going?"

She stepped out. "I'll walk from here."

"This is the bad part of town," he said.

The woman smiled. "I know."

Pepe watched as the woman ambled past the flickering street lights until she vanished down the street. He reached for his phone and dialed for a tow truck when something sparkled in his peripheral. He squinted as he scanned his rearview mirror. There in the dark of the backseat was the woman's purse. He hung up and lifted the bag. Inside, he retrieved a wallet loaded with cash. It was enough to give him a head start on his debts. He leaned back and sighed. Pepe thought about his cruel God again and wondered if he was being tested.

Chapter 2: The Mother

She found the address. The house was nestled in the middle of long street with cracked curbs springing thorny weeds. An old car sat on cinderblocks in the middle of an unkempt lawn. A single light shone through the kitchen window.

Lupe Osegueda knocked on the door. She reached for her bag, hoping to pull out a business card.

"Damnit!" She must have forgotten it in the cab. How was she going to get home?

The door creaked opened, leaving enough room for a single eye to peer through the crack.

"What is it?" a gruff voice asked.

"Josefino Cuevas?"

"Who's asking?"

"My name is Lupe Osegueda and I'd like to speak to you. It's urgent."

"I don't see visitors."

"My daughter's gone missing, and I need your help."

"Hundreds of daughters go missing here every year."

"I think she's being used as a drug mule in the tunnels. Please. Before it's too late."

The door opened and an old man waved her in. A discolored scar ran across his wrinkled neck.

"Make it quick," he croaked.

Lupe padded into the living room. The place was sparse: a couch, a dining table, a small desk with a typewriter, a waste basket full of crumpled paper, and a large planter hosting a drooping, wilted plant.

"My daughter ran away from home a little over four weeks ago. I don't know for sure, but I think she may have gotten in with the local cartel."

"What makes you believe that?" the man said, latching the door shut.

"Some of her friends from school told me as much."

"And what makes you think I can help you?"

Lupe nodded toward the couch. "May I sit?"

"Of course. Forgive me." Josefino rubbed his throat. "I'm a bit wary of strangers."

Lupe sat and crossed her hands over her knees. She looked down and shook her head. "I was too tough on her. She ran away. Wanted to be independent. Some of her friends told me the cartel likes to hire high school kids for menial tasks. Drug running, slanging on the corners. I think she may have run off with them."

Josefino stood there, watching her, not saying a word.

She tilted her head toward the desk. "What are you working on?"

He followed her gaze toward the typewriter. "A novel about a writer who learns his creations have become real. He ultimately abuses his power and becomes a cruel god."

"I see you've given up on the real world and created one of your own. You used to be a respected journalist. I know about your story on the K'oox Baal Cave System in Tulum and its sudden closure by the government. How the army began sealing off many of the country's cave systems. I know that they silenced you and terminated your position at the paper. How long has it been now?"

"Quite some time. That's behind me now. Besides, people aren't too kind to reporters around these parts." He lifted a pack of cigarettes from his shirt pocket, slid one free, and lit up. He closed his eyes, tilted his head back, and blew out a billow of smoke. "Seems the truth has a way of dying out here, if you catch my drift."

"I know about your son. How he was kidnapped. You're not the only one suffering."

Josefino's limbs went stiff. He opened his eyes, and they became glazed, burning orbs, fixing on the wall as if he'd been plumbing the depths of his mind for some misplaced memories. After a moment, he nodded.

"This world has stacked the odds against us little people. We're all we have in an uncaring universe." He sighed, regarded the typewriter. "We all have unfinished work. I'll help you."

Chapter 3: The Journalist

The F-150 rumbled slowly up the street, the masked municipal police officer manning the machine gun on the flatbed eyeing Josefino like a common thug. Before it turned the corner, the truck shuddered to a stop. He felt his heart jerk as the pickup idled there, the engine angry, grumbling. In his peripheral, Josefino could see the officer looking him over from head to toe. He knew the men in the cab were doing the same.

There was no way to know if they were crooked, so he kept his head down and hoped they hadn't recognized him. Josefino stuffed his hands in his coat pockets and continued to walk at a brisk pace. Satisfied with his inspection, the officer slapped the hood of the cab and the truck rolled on.

Journalists, reporters; if they didn't end up hanging naked from freeway overpasses or riddled with bullets, they vanished without a trace. No secret about that. The smart ones would leave town and find new jobs. He hadn't been in the game in years, but one could never be too sure around here. The scar would always be there to remind him.

He came to the northeastern edge of the city. An unfinished housing development in a little pocket of town that straddled the Sonoran Desert. Construction had stalled when the mayor abruptly cancelled the project.

Now, a slew of homes sat empty in varying stages of construction. Exposed beams, fluttering tarps, shattered drywall. Like carcasses picked clean. He pulled out the city planning map he'd acquired from the office of public records and followed it to the end of a cul-de-sac. He stopped when he found the only manhole not listed on the plans.

"Found you," he said.

Josefino retrieved a crowbar from inside his coat and hooked the manhole cover open. A pit of never-ending darkness peered back. He wasn't fond of confined spaces, much less ones built by killers. He sighed and descended a janky ladder until his shoes touched muddy ground. He flicked on his flashlight and swung the blue light around, piercing the veil of darkness. There was no doubt it was a cartel tunnel. It was bored hastily; shoddy workmanship, no regard for safety. Something to get someone from point A to point B.

He crinkled his nose. The air was stagnant and rank. Probably mildew or mold on account of last week's rains and flash floods. Josefino hunched slightly and followed the constricted tunnel as it wound this way and that, incrementally sloping downward ever so slightly into the earth.

His light caught on a pair of tiny sparkling orbs, halfway buried in the mud. He crouched and scooped them up, examining them in his palm. Earrings. Caked with blood. He stuffed them in his coat. As the tunnel rolled on, the darkness appeared to shift every time he turned a corner, but it was a trick of the eye, a dance of light and shadow, and nothing more.

After about a kilometer, the tunnel opened into a spacious, rocky cavern where the air stank less of mold and more of rot and decay. Here, his narrow blue beam did little to mitigate the well of darkness.

He aimed the light at the ground. It was littered with heaps of rags, much of it women's clothing. Shards of what appeared to be bone fragments had been assembled into evenly spaced mounds. A chunk of cavern wall looked like it had been chipped away so that it formed a cavity like an altar. Inside hung what appeared to be a pressure suit, similar to those worn by astronauts. Josefino shook his head. "What the hell is all this?"

Upon closer inspection of the suit, he made out a shoulder patch that read *Captain Archibold Johnson*. On the opposite shoulder, another patch, this one decorated with the symbol of an hourglass intersected by a stylized star with the words *Temporalnautics Agency* stitched across.

Josefino stifled a gasp with his hand. Further along the craggy wall hung a tapestry of splayed skins tattooed with rudimentary illustrations of simplistic figures and crude representations. A slew of shooting stars plunging into the Earth. Men emerging from pods. A tunnel leading downward. People sheltering beneath the earth, away from a monstrous sun. Or a plunging meteor, perhaps. Some figures appeared to have ventured into underwater caverns. Like the ones in K'oox Baal in Tulum. *K'oox Baal*. The word swirled in his mind. It meant *Wild Things* in Mayan.

Josefino suddenly felt dizzy, as if he'd stumbled upon a secret not meant for his eyes.

Following the figures further down the timeline, the illustrations became sloppier, cruder. Here, the men appeared transformed: webbed hands and feet, or clawed fingers and…tails.

A series of clicks and screeches pierced the silence, filling the cavern with jarring echoes. Josefino aimed his light at the darkness. Several shadows skittered from the dark and into the cone of his light. Naked, pale-skinned abominations grasped for Josefino, clawing at the air around his legs. As they slithered toward him, two limp appendages dragged behind their spines, like what may once have been functioning human legs. Their simian faces had two hollow orbital cavities where eyes should have sat, and their protruding lower jaws bared two rows of pointed teeth.

Josefino shrieked as he fled back the way he had come. His legs ached and his lungs burned, but he didn't care. The shrill, hungry cries at his back were enough to drive him past the pain. Upon climbing the ladder and tumbling over the manhole, he gasped for air and fell to his side, hacking and tasting copper. When he caught his breath, he peered over the manhole and aimed his light at the abyss. Nothing but motes of dust hanging on his beam of dissipated light.

It all clicked. The government; the army; sealing off the caverns all those years ago. How long had they known? The rags, the bones down there. Were all those people just sacrificial offerings? He shook his head, not sure he cared to know.

Josefino sealed the opening and fled the development as quickly as his legs would carry him. He'd tell Lupe that he'd found nothing, of course. That he offered his condolences. The shame that tugged at his heart would be pushed deep down where he'd never find it again. He would live with what he'd seen and carry it to the grave, and he would make himself believe the lies people told themselves at night. That those scores of missing women, in pursuit of a better life, simply fled north across the border. Or died crossing the river. Or met a gruesome end at the hands of jealous crime bosses.

The reality was worse. This country appeased its monsters. Offered sacrifices to keep them at bay in the shadows. Besides, who would believe that his country was besieged by bloodthirsty subterranean monsters?

Josefino knew he was a coward. He did, however, take some comfort in the fact that he wasn't alone in burying the truth. Everyone was complicit in that.

Chapter 4: The Police Officer

Mauro Lopez stood on the back of a pickup truck as he gazed at the night sky. The stars shone like the gleaming eyes of a drunkard. Or diamonds.

The truck rumbled to a stop on the fringes of the development northeast of town. The old man was sprinting toward them, winded, pale, screaming.

Mauro didn't blame him. He'd heard the rumors, too, of Los Subterráneos.

His superiors in the cab got on the radio and called it in. The Chief of Police squawked back his orders. Acquire target. His sergeant gave the nod and Mauro hopped off the flatbed and apprehended the old man, threw a sack over his head, and tossed him in the back.

"You can't do this to me," the old man said. "People will come looking for me."

"People go missing all the time," Mauro said, lifting his balaclava and popping a piece of bubble gum in his mouth.

They drove a few kilometers north to the ranch. The folks there had some questions for the old man: what he'd known, who he'd spoken to, things of that nature. Things above Mauro's paygrade. When they arrived, Mauro escorted the old man inside and brought him downstairs to a room with a white tiled floor, speckled with sparkling beads of moisture. It looked like a large shower. At the center of the room, the floor dipped slightly toward a drain. A water hose was spooled in a neat coil on the wall. Beside it hung an assortment of rusty tools like saws, knives, and bolt cutters. A few large trash bags lay scattered on the floor.

Mauro brought the journalist to a chair in the center of the room and made him sit. When Mauro removed the old man's mask, he gave the room a look-over and began to shiver in his seat, a stream of piss trickling down his legs, onto the tiled floor, and down the drain.

Mauro's phone rumbled in his pocket. A text from his wife asking him to call her immediately. Their daughter, Carla, had run away from home. He balled his hands into fists and felt his intestines tie themselves into knots.

Goddamn it to hell. Too many bad things had been happening to good people lately. Why him? There was no way, it seemed, around the cruel machinations of the universe. The hand of destiny was intentionally tipping down the scales on people like him. As if unseen forces were playing devious games with their lives. He wondered if anything could even be done against such malignant forces.

A pair of tall men clad in black tactical vests stepped inside the room. They nodded and Mauro returned to the truck.

He slapped the hood of the pickup, and they returned to patrolling the streets.

Pedro Iniguez was a horror and science-fiction writer from Los Angeles, California. He was a Rhysling Award finalist and a Best of the Net and Pushcart Prize nominee.

His work appeared in Nightmare Magazine, Never Wake: An Anthology of Dream Horror, Shadows Over Main Street Volume 3, and Qualia Nous Vol. 2, among others.

While conducting research for his unfinished novel, Cruel Machinations, he vanished in the K'oox Baal Cave Systems in Mexico. The government has no knowledge of his whereabouts. His work continues to be published widely.

The Fire Tower

D.K. Stone

THEY SAY BURNING *is a painless death. Once your skin blackens and peels off, the nerve endings are gone. You can walk right through fire, indifferent to your immolation. I don't know about that. (And frankly, I don't want to find out.)*

That's what they say, though.

You're not supposed to think things like this when you're alone. (They warned me about that when I came to the tower.) The human mind is wired for contact and—in the extreme lack of it—fills the silence with the worst of your fears. A branch tapping on the glass can conjure unimaginable terrors. Every creak in the floor a danger. Tonight, I heard something moving around outside. It's probably nothing. But then again, maybe it's not. Because there ARE things to fear here.

I haven't got it all figured out yet, but whatever came to the tower in April scared the last ranger enough the poor guy—

The trembling of Kira's fingers overtook her and she paused, unable to type the rest.

She stared at the screen. The words she wanted to write were alive in her mind: *Threw himself to his death. Killed on impact. Found the next day.* (The official report said he'd fallen.) Kira's index finger dropped down and typed an 'F,' but she couldn't go any further. *Fallen,* her mind whispered.

Unless that wasn't it at all.

On the floor above her third level bedroom, a narrow deck circled the observation room. A hastily added plywood square on the broken railing blocked the missing balusters where her predecessor had run out the door of the tower months earlier, breaking through the wooden slats and tumbling headlong to his death. She *wanted* to write about that, but something held her back.

"Fuck!"

Kira held down the backspace, deleted the 'F,' then moved backwards over the previous words until only the flashing cursor remained. It was one thing to have these disturbing thoughts rattling through her brain, another thing entirely to put them down onto the page.

She ran a hand over her face. "Should've brought melatonin to help me sleep. Should've been ready for this."

Outside, the wind howled in agreement.

The fire tower where Kira Tanwen lived and worked sat atop Starvation Peak, one of the jagged mountains jutting like canine teeth from the jaw of the East Kootenays. Visible for miles, the narrow building had been constructed like a Jenga tower from four pre-fabricated metal and wood boxes. The first floor housed the lounge and storage, the second floor the kitchen, the third floor a bedroom and bath, and the fourth floor the observation tower/office. The four boxes had been positioned by military helicopter, the base of the lowest bolted to the bare stone. They'd withstood thirty-seven years of rain and snow and wildfires.

They'd outlived their previous occupant, too.

This tower was Kira's home for the next four months. It gave her a view of the untouched land that few others had. Only a handful of mountaineers had ever summited Starvation Peak. The overgrown logging road, a hint of distant civilization, stopped halfway up the mountain. She'd made it to the end of that lonely road exactly once in all her time here, returning to the tower exhausted.

Kira's supplies arrived by helicopter once a month. She herself had been dropped off seven weeks before, when a two-foot layer of May snow still covered the now-barren peak. As snow receded and summer began, Kira began to explore the rocky mountaintop, with its fringe of pines. She'd found a decaying grave marker with an inscription that ominously read: "Frank Go," before crumbling into illegibility. Otherwise, the mountain was desperately, horribly empty.

Taking the job seemed a good idea when she and Mike broke up, but now…

The Fire Tower

The helicopter team found the ranger's body when Curtis didn't call in his morning report. His legs were mangled underneath him, but it was his expression that people in the rescue team still talked about. His terrified eyes were fixed upward, his mouth a silent scream of terror.

Kira swore and shoved the laptop off her knees onto the narrow bed. Sleep wasn't happening and trying to write about *why* was making things worse. She swung her feet to the floor, folding the laptop closed out of habit. Darkness absorbed her as the only light source abruptly disappeared. Her breathing kicked into double time. The feeling was back. The one that had awakened her after the sound.

I'm not alone out here. Not really. They found his body after he told the station he was being watched. There'd been an attempt on the satellite phone at 2:37 a.m., but the call had ended before anyone at the station answered. The broken railings suggested Curtis had run right through it. All the lights were on inside. Something had scared him enough that—

"Stop it!" she hissed. Her hand instinctively reached toward the light on the side table, but she stopped midway, fingers outstretched.

Turn it on and they'll see you.

"They?" The words had popped into her head unexpectedly, in a voice she didn't recognize. *A man's.* She laughed nervously at the thought of ghosts.

The whole thing was ridiculous! There was no one in the mountains to see, and no curtains or blinds in most rooms. A fire tower only worked if you *always* could see the horizon. That meant night too.

Kira took several slow breaths, waiting for her panic to recede. For a few seconds, she saw nothing. Then the faint light of the stars appeared beyond the uncurtained windows. The tightness in her chest eased. A few seconds more, and her eyes adjusted enough to make out the constellations and the jagged saw blade of mountains crossing the horizon. It was never *entirely* dark here in the Rockies. Not in summer, at least. Astronomical twilight gave the sky a faint haze even at midnight. When she could finally breathe again, she stood.

What *had* awakened her? A sound, yes, but what? Something big, moving nearby, she assumed. But by the time she'd fully awakened, whatever had happened outside the tower was gone.

Kira crept toward the line of windows that filled three out of four sides of the bedroom, staring out over the horizon. Far to the northwest lay Fernie. She'd awakened at 2:30, but it had to be close to 3 a.m. now. Mike was probably getting home from work. If she'd been home—*Not home,* her mind corrected. *You're the one who moved out*—she'd have talked to him about her fears, gotten his chill perspective. But there wasn't cell service here. So even Mike, who'd repeatedly attempted reconciliation over the last few weeks, wasn't an option. The radio was fire tower only. The satellite phone was for emergencies and, as she'd been warned, the line was monitored. Being flagged as "potentially at risk for mental health issues" wasn't a great look when you were on a probationary contract.

Kira had internet access, of course. She could use the radio to contact the command center and write a formal report about the sound. Or send an email—to Mike or her friends Mieka and Angie, or even her parents—but that seemed pointless. She might as well write out the circling thoughts of Curtis, whose sudden death had given Kira the job that provided her escape from a tangled relationship. She loved Mike, but couldn't—

A motion inside the line of distant trees jerked Kira from her thoughts. Her gaze shifted to a spot on the eastern horizon. There *should've* been an open patch in the lines of trunks. Tonight, it was blocked by a large, humped shape.

"What the hell?" Kira squinted and leaned closer.

There was something there. Unless it was just the angle she was viewing it from? Frowning, she struggled to recall exactly what fell inside the line of trees. Were there rocks? Perhaps the hump of another mountain in the distance? She remembered locating the logging road at twilight. She'd climbed a hill. Was this it? Here now, standing in the darkness of the bedroom, she couldn't remember.

Keep the lights off. Hide. Don't let them see you.

The hair rose on the back of her neck. There'd been no suicide note, but Curtis's logbook, which Kira still filled in each day, had grown increasingly frantic in its last few entries. One came to her mind now: *"Something in the tree line, blocking my view,"* Curtis had written. *"Will check in the A.M."*

She never knew if he did.

Kira crept back to the bed and opened the drawer of the table by feel. "Need to find out what this is."

Her gaze flicked back to the window. The humped shape—the size of a crouching man, if it was close to the tower, or as big as a bear, if it stood within the trees, possibly *much* larger if farther away—waited.

And then, inexplicably, it moved slightly left.

Kira gasped as her fingers searched blindly through the drawer. "It moved!" She had a pair of binoculars somewhere. But everything felt the same in the dark.

Hurry!

The shape moved again. Its rolling gait reminded her of a large animal, or a man creeping along on all fours. The undulating motion felt alive. Kira's breath caught. She'd seen bear scat on her foray down the mountain. By the shape of it—if this was a bear—it was massive. A fully grown grizzly could tear open the side of a car. The windows and thin metal sheeting of the fire tower were no match for brute strength. She redoubled her search for the field glasses as a new thought appeared: she needed bear spray too! But everything in the drawer felt exactly the same.

Her gaze skittered back to the window. The shape was closer!

With a swear, Kira fumbled with the light next to the bed. Sudden brightness filled the room and she saw, in frustration, that the binoculars lay on top of the bedside table, not in the drawer at all. She grabbed them and rushed to the window, scanning the trees. Her heartbeat drummed in her ears. With the lights on, all she could see was a reflection of the room's interior and her own terrified face.

"Motherfucker!" She spun back, flicked off the lights, and lifted the binoculars back to her eyes.

The shape was gone.

～

The next morning passed in slow motion.

"Kira Tanwen, Starvation Fire Lookout, reporting," she said, stifling a yawn. "All clear."

"Thanks, Kira. Fernie Fire Dispatch confirms all clear. Over and out."

There was a firm structure to Kira's thirteen-hour workday. Her shift started at 7:00 a.m. Every fifteen minutes, she patroled the perimeter of the tower's catwalk, avoiding the plywood section of railing as she surveyed the horizon for smoke. On the hour, she called in an official report using the tower's two-way radio. In between these intervals, she checked air humidity and weather conditions, prepped meals that could be interrupted at a moment's notice, or measured the rain barrel levels. She hadn't resorted to sponge baths—yet—but she'd been warned that in late summer, when drought loomed, it was a necessity. Electricity came from a gas generator—another thing to check—and like the food supplies, Kira needed to ensure she had enough to survive.

Today, her exhaustion was tangible. There *had* been something in the trees last night. She was sure of it. But when she'd checked this morning, she couldn't find prints, or even crushed grass in the tree line. That suggested that whatever she'd seen had either been in front of the forest—where the rocky slope didn't preserve prints like softer ground did—or behind the trees, and if that was the case, it was much, *much* larger.

What the hell could that be?

In daylight, it was clear there were no hills blocking the tree line. Just a sheer drop straight down to Starvation Valley. Nothing there.

But what if there was?

With a groan of frustration, Kira slumped down at the desk and buried her face in her hands. She wanted today over. Last night's events had left her nauseated from exhaustion. There was no way to call in sick if you worked in a fire tower. She just needed to finish her shift, then catch up on sleep.

Behind closed lids, the shape reappeared. Realistically, it made no sense for it to be a large object behind the trees. That left her only two options: In front meant the figure was smaller, but in many ways more dangerous… almost certainly a man. The second, equally likely possibility, was that it had been a bear—even if she couldn't locate its prints. She'd need to be careful about cooking anything with a strong odor the next few days. Either way, something *had* been outside. It had moved. And when she'd turned on the light, it had fled.

What if it comes back?

"—Fernie Fire Dispatch. Come in, Starvation Lookout. I repeat, this is Fernie Fire Dispatch."

Kira jerked awake. She'd missed her call in! With a squeal of wood against lino, she shoved the chair back from the desk and stumbled to the radio. The tangled cord caught halfway as she brought it to her ears, and she fought to release it.

"Sorry! Yes, I'm here. This is Kira—I mean this is Starvation Fire Lookout." Her gaze darted around the four glass-paneled walls of the top-level tower, praying for clear skies and no smoke.

"All clear here."

"Thanks, Kira." There was a pause rather than a sign-off. "Everything okay?" Geoff asked. "You're usually on time."

"Yeah, sorry. I was outside," she lied. "There was a bear circling the tower last night. I was looking for tracks."

"A bear?" Geoff's voice shifted into sudden concern. "Cause you any trouble?"

"No. Nothing like that. Maybe just passing by."

"Black bear or grizzly?"

"I, er… I couldn't tell. It was dark and I couldn't find the tracks when I looked."

"None?"

"Not that I saw. Mind you, it could have been out on the rocks."

"Any other signs? Droppings? Scratch marks?"

"Uh… no."

"You sure you didn't imagine—"

Kira interrupted him—breaking the first rule of radio transmissions. She didn't want anyone thinking it was in her head! "No. I was wide awake when I saw it. Definitely a bear."

"Well, keep your bear spray handy," he said. "File a report. And try not to be late next call in. Okay?"

Kira winced. "You got it, Geoff. Sorry."

"No worries. It happens to everyone." He cleared his throat, abruptly businesslike. "Fernie Fire Dispatch confirms all clear at Starvation Lookout. Over and out."

The radio clicked once, the connection broken. Kira stared out to the horizon, frowning. Tonight she'd be alone again. What if the thing in the trees came back? What then?

Kira's day ended at eight o'clock, an hour before sunset, though all fire rangers knew they needed to watch the horizon at all times. It wasn't a choice, just part of the job. Tonight, she couldn't have avoided it if she'd wanted to.

She ate cereal and canned milk rather than cook—one eye scanning the tree line—then showered quickly. She checked all the doors and windows on the main floor were locked. She wished there was more she could do to secure the tower—glass wouldn't stop a bear if it wanted inside—but the winter shutters had been stowed away long before she'd arrived and were so big they needed two people to install them.

Exhausted, she switched out of her day uniform and into her nighttime garb of track pants and tee, then crawled into bed. Around her, the sky bled from purple to navy and finally to black. Still, sleep wouldn't come. A woman's spry face appeared in Kira's mind. Grey-haired, she grinned at the camera, her orange shirt glowing against a bright green canopy of leaves. In bed, Kira shifted uneasily, fighting the memory. Mike had sent her a digital copy of the Edmonton Journal article when she'd announced she was taking the job.

"You'll be out there all by yourself," he said quietly. *"I get moving out, but why... there?"*

"Why not there? It's a job. I need one. Then I've got a place to stay too."

He frowned. "You could stay here. We could work things out."

"Mike, stop. I need space to think."

He opened his mouth, then closed it again. Kira waited for his logic. This was always the issue. Everything he said made sense, but her life felt like a cage and she needed to escape it.

"What?" Kira said. *"You obviously want to say more."*

His expression tightened. "I saw something the other day. It was about a fire lookout in Athabasca."

"What about it?"

"There was a woman there—older lady—she'd worked at the station for years. Pretty much an expert at living alone in the field, and..."

Kira swallowed hard. *"And what?"*

"*She disappeared and they never found her. Didn't call in one morning, so they came to check. No animal attack. No sign of forced entry.*"

Kira felt the floor waver beneath her feet, but Mike wasn't done.

"*There was a smudge of blood on the stairs and a boiling pot of water on the stove. Nothing else. Her body was never found.*"

With a groan, Kira shoved the memory of the grinning ranger away and rolled onto her side, staring out the black panel of glass. It was always a risk being alone in the wilderness, but it was higher if you were a woman. Back in Fernie with Mike, she'd considered that risk a fair trade for freedom. Tonight, though…

Her breath caught as a group of stars in one section of glass abruptly disappeared—blocked out by a dark shape outside the window. Shock surged like wildfire through Kira's limbs. Something had passed in front of the glass! Before she could react, the shadowy form moved around the other side of the tower, disappearing behind the wall against which Kira lay. On this side of the building, her bedroom abutted the bathroom and had no windows, but the walls were paper thin. Bottles rattled inside the bathroom cabinet as the black shape brushed against the outside wall. *The third floor wall,* her mind screamed.

Terrified, she rolled off the bed to the floor, crouching. There was something outside circling the fire tower. *The radio and satellite phone are up in the observation room!* On hands and knees, she scrambled across the floor to the stairs, her gaze darting furtively to the windows. Vibrations echoed from the other side of the tower as whatever or whoever it was moved slowly along the perimeter. She needed to be up before it reached the other side and could see her again!

Forcing her watery limbs to move, she bolted up the stairs to the fourth floor. The radio hung on the wall. She lifted the handset, clicking the automatic relay.

"Fernie, this is Starvation Lookout. Come in, Fernie!"

No reply.

"I repeat: Fernie, this is Kira Tanwen, Starvation Lookout. Come in, Fernie! Emergency! Emergency!"

Nothing.

The vibration grew. With a swear, Kira switched to the satellite phone, clicking the button and waiting. Buzzing filled the earpiece, the device searching for connection.

"C'mon... c'mon, just—"

The room where Kira stood abruptly burst from darkness to dazzling light. She dropped the handset, fell to her knees, and crawled toward the desk. The coil pulled the phone back with a snap, disconnecting her call. The light moved along the wall across from her, searching. Heart pounding against the cage of her ribs, she shielded her eyes. The light moved around the outside of the building like a car's headlight, or perhaps a search light, circling the observation room and illuminating it like a stage. None of it made sense. She was on the fourth floor!

As it neared her hiding place, Kira scrambled into the corner under the table, pulling herself into a tiny ball as far away from the piercing light as she could. Details sprang into focus as her eyes grew accustomed to its brilliance: there were flecks of red and orange in the green linoleum; the desk had been repainted more than once, a line of varying colors marking its underside.

All the while, the light crept closer.

Outside, a sound interrupted. *A helicopter? A military aircraft?* The rumble was of something large and loud. The light inside the observation tower grew brighter still, then abruptly winked out.

Terrified, she closed her eyes.

❦

Kira massaged her temple, the handset pressed to her ear. She'd been talking to Fernie Fire Dispatch for almost half an hour, but things weren't getting any better. Today was Geoff's day off. Sierra, his superior and the main supervisor for the entire Kootenay region, was taking the calls.

It wasn't going well.

"What did you do then?" Sierra repeated. "After the light, I mean."

Kira frowned, struggling to recall. "I-I went to sleep."

There was a long pause. "To sleep. Like, right there, in the observation tower?"

Kira shook her head. She'd made the official report. She'd filled in the paperwork, but in the stark light of day, nothing made sense. "Yes and no," she said lamely. "I slept, but only after I went downstairs to bed. I was really tired." Her frown deepened. She didn't *remember* going down the stairs, but her alarm woke her in her bed at 6:00 a.m. sharp. "I slept through to morning."

"Why didn't you call it in? It was late, yes. But stuff like this is supposed to be reported ASAP." Sierra's voice sharpened. "That's standard protocol."

"I know, I—" A headache began to pulse behind Kira's eyes. "I was tired."

Another pause. "Were you using any substances that we should be aware of?"

"What? No! Of course not!"

"It's a standard question," Sierra said. "And you've got to admit, the whole story seems a little strange."

"I'm telling you what happened." Kira's voice broke. "I made the report. I did everything I was supposed to do!"

"I don't think getting emotional is going to—"

"Just listen," she snapped. "It happened. Alright? There was something out there in the dark. A helicopter or maybe someone with a flare or a drone, or, or…" Her shoulders slumped. "I wasn't dreaming it. I wasn't stoned. I reported it exactly how I remembered it."

"Got it."

Kira wiped away tears of frustration. "Look. I should get going." She scanned the horizon and cleared her throat. "All clear at Starvation Fire Lookout."

The reply pause was just slightly too long.

"Fernie Fire Dispatch confirms all clear. Over and out."

With a click, the line disconnected.

~

The afternoon dragged by. Kira wasn't tired, but everything felt off. How *had* she gotten back to her bedroom? And who'd hung up the handset after she'd dropped it? That was back on the wall too. It wasn't a dream. Of that she was sure! She keenly remembered the terror she'd felt. The light at the window, then the sound of an engine, somewhere distant and unseen. But after the light flicked off, there was… nothing. It felt like the time she'd had her tonsils out. There'd been the strangest absence between when she breathed in the anesthesia, and then—without explanation—woken up somewhere, some *time* else.

This was still on her mind the first time Fernie Fire Dispatch didn't reply to her call-in. She frowned and checked the time: 6:01 p.m. She retried the radio.

Again, nothing.

Uneasy, Kira circled the observation deck. Her gaze skittering nervously from the top of the deck, then down to the ground, four stories below. If it had been a person with a flare circling the observation deck last night, they would have needed to climb up the exterior to reach the deck. That seemed unlikely. But a drone could reach this height. And a drone could arrive in silence.

Kira paused at the plywood cover where the last person to work at Starvation Fire Lookout had fallen. Curtis had been a ski instructor in Banff in the winters; a fire lookout all summer. Everyone swore he was an easygoing, happy guy, yet he'd thrown himself off the tower. Kira stared at the place he'd broken through. The splintered railing was hidden, but the chipboard square was starting to fade under the sun's relentless gaze.

He saw something that night... But what?

A nagging thought fought its way to the surface of her mind. Kira didn't want to let it in. If she did, she'd have to deal with it, and she wasn't quite ready. *Unidentified—*

"No!" She closed her eyes, taking a slow breath, just as the crackle of the radio came through. With a start, she bolted back inside, pulling the handset free.

"Kira Tanwen, Starvation Fire Lookout, reporting," she said.

"Kira, hi." It was Geoff this time—which made no sense at all, since this was his usual day off—but she didn't have time to ask why. "Sorry I missed the call in. You all right?"

"All clear at Starvation Fire Lookout," she said.

"Good." His voice was tight. "Things are crazy here."

"A new fire?"

"No, but a couple lookouts have gone silent." Somewhere in the background, she heard people arguing, though their words were indistinct. "I'm not even supposed to be on today. Got called in to cover for Sierra. There's—" His voice faded amid the sound of muffled shouting. "Sorry. Just... sorry, Kira. Everything's a shitshow. You sure you're okay?"

"Yeah… I mean, sort of, after the last couple nights. Have you heard anything about"—she flinched— "other fire towers seeing lights?"

"Honestly? I've been hearing a lot of crazy shit the last few hours."

Kira's palms grew sweaty around the handset. "Like what?"

"Like *everything*. Lights. Animals. Aircraft that doesn't show up on radar." His voice dropped. "Sierra's been on a private call for hours. Something's wrong! I'm supposed to hear from each tower every hour. Every single one. But they've been going down, and—" There was a piercing alarm, followed by someone barking commands in the background, and then Geoff's voice again. "Fuck. Gotta go."

"Geoff? What's going on?"

"No fucking idea. But whatever it is, it's bad."

"What does that mean?!"

"Stay safe. Fernie out."

The headset clicked off.

An hour passed. Kira did rounds and forced herself to eat. She called in at exactly 7:00 o'clock, hopeful to hear more from Geoff, but dispatch didn't answer. Kira fretted and spent another uneasy hour, then two, and then three, watching the sun set and the sky turn gold and then pink. There was a perfect stillness to the world. Even the birds quieted. If it wasn't for the darkness that crawled across the sky, Kira would have admired the beauty, but by the time night fell, her fear had grown into full-blown panic. She radioed Fernie dispatch one more time, already knowing there'd be no reply. Worried it might be the radio itself, Kira used the satellite phone. No one answered.

Outside the windows, the stars began to appear.

Hands shaking, she hung up the handset, then paused. She lifted it back to her ear again. Dialed from memory. There was the requisite clicking and buzzing as the relay moved from the distant mountaintop to the satellite somewhere far above earth, then back down again to Mike's cell phone. He'd be working. This would be the busiest part of his shift. Past the elderly diners and families with kids, and into the young couples and groups of friends.

Mike picked up on the second ring.

"H'llo?"

His voice was a low whisper.

"Mike?" Kira said. "Is that—"

"Oh my god, Kira. Are you okay?"

"Yeah, I'm fine. What's—?"

"They're in the building," he said quietly. "I can hear them upstairs."

"They? Who are—"

The connection crackled. "If you're safe, stay where you are," Mike said. "Do *not* come back to Fernie. No matter what. Stay away." She heard his voice crack. Mike was crying, sobbing almost. "I love you," he said. "Just know that."

"I love you too, but what's happening? You've got to tell me what—"

"No matter how things ended, I love you. I always loved—"

His voice disappeared. There wasn't a crackle of lost connection, just there and then gone, as if the satellite itself had disappeared. Kira clicked the handset again and again, but there was no buzz of connection. No clicking. Nothing at all.

She looked up to the windows. It was full dark. On the horizon, on the ridges beyond Starvation Peak, the shape was back. But not just one of them. Hundreds… all in motion.

Kira's legs wobbled and she sat down. "My God."

The things—whatever they were—were much larger than a bear, larger than the fire tower itself, and they writhed across the rocky landscape like insects. Her gaze lifted to the West where Fernie lay. The mountains glowed orange and red. A second later, she saw why. The shapes in the trees were setting everything alight.

"Got to call in the fire."

Moving like a sleepwalker, Kira tried the radio and the satellite phone once more. Nothing. She hit the emergency beacon next. Nothing. Outside the windows, great swathes of trees exploded into flame, burning up the mountainside towards her. Lit by the glow, the shapes in the trees finally grew details: spiderlike, metallic, and massive, flames spraying from their heads to the tinder-dry ground.

A strange calm overtook her. "They say burning is painless."

And as the flames finally reached the base of the tower, she wondered, for the very last time, if that was true.

To the Moon and Stars

Last Gasp

Stark Holborn

This story should be read with a coin in hand.
Flip every time you reach a **?**
[H] for Heads.
[T] for Tails.
Good luck…

"NAME?"

The border guard doesn't even look up. One of her eyes is glued to the lens that obscures half her face, the ghosts of some holodrama barely visible through the scratched plastic.

?

[H]
You push up your sleeve and set your wrist to the greasy looking scanner on the side of the kiosk. The flickering green data of your redacted existence fills the screen.

> *NAME:* xxxxxxxxxxx
> Somewhere in those crosses, the name your mother once gave you.
> *HOME PLANET:* xxxxxxxxxxx
> A place as good as lost.

EMPLOYER: EoM
Can a saviour be called such a thing?
CALL SIGN: Dust
Four letters. All you carry, these days.
The guard frowns. "The hell is this—"

[T]

You keep your sleeves firmly over your wrists.
"Dust," you say.
The guard snorts. "Warden name?"
"Journey name."
She frowns at that. "You wanna be careful. Holy Jo don't like other…"

Her voice trails off as she meets your eyes. Or tries to. There is the usual flicker of confusion as she attempts to focus on your face, only to be defeated by the grey shapes that morph and bleed constantly beneath the surface of the skin, flooding it with shadow. You are a living ink-blot test.

?

[H]

You pull your hat a little lower.

"Dust is the only name you need," you reply.

The guard scowls. You have her there, and she knows it. A security loophole of border stations like this: all that is technically required for entry is a valid call sign. And "Dust" is yours. Of course, you have another name. Have a title, even. Have a symbol upon your back, hidden beneath the worn coat. But this isn't the place to show it. Preacher's Gasp has a reputation, and in your experience, faith and fervour make for a poor cocktail.

[T]

You remember the feel of the micro-needles. "Dazzle," the underground tattoo artist promised as he worked his sub-dermal magic, pushing tubes filled with living ink beneath the flesh of your cheeks, your eyes, your chin. "Face full of dazzle, no camera's gonna be able to track you."

You only realised later what it meant: that no one would ever truly see your face again. You lived that way for years. An anonymous body, a collection of limbs, until *she* saw through your flesh and into the quick of you. Until she scoured you clean with her terrible kindness and sent you out to walk the world in Her name.

"Fine," the guard snaps, releasing the secondary airlock. "Freak."

You step into Preacher's Gasp.

To most, the Gasp is unremarkable; a ramshackle rest-stop, a clutter of junk and artificial habitats, wharves reaching like gnarled fingers. Except, in the centre is an atrium: a huge dome made from unbreakable plastic, like a bubble of air, a gasp in space. Legend had it a wandering preacher built the thing to hold sermons under the stars. Now, centuries later, it is scratched milky as a cataract. Sermons of other kinds take place there now. Prayers of bullets and blood. You pause beside a porthole and…

?

[H]

… look left, into a riot of lights; rusted droger's ships and vast water-haulers from Prosper, heavy-bellied conveyances from Jericho's warehouse cities, junkers, merchants, star-battered Accord Air Fleet fighters, private vessels of all kinds. A tidal pool of the system, threatening to spill from the clean waters of Regulated Space over the Dead Line and into no-man's-sky beyond, where Factus, outlaw moon, rolls like the yellow eye of a mad god.

[T]

… look right to see an airlock hatch marked with a neon cross fly open. A figure is ejected out into space. No suit. No helmet. Just a thin tether around their waist, linking them to the station. After a few seconds—not more than five—they are reeled back in, flailing weakly. You grimace. A form of baptism. Total immersion. Tells you everything you need to know about this place.

The sooner you're done here, the better.

But first you have business to attend to. The Gasp's market is a warren. Metalshops and doggeries, live contraband scurrying in cages, even a doxological stop, crammed with lockers dedicated to various faiths. Wire announcements blare, warning of quarantine laws and rotfruit bans and U-Zone permits. Outside an arepa seller, a radio plays the old familiar warble of Lester Sixofus—system's best beloved DJ—spinning songs on his endless wanderings between the stars.

?

[H]

You step up to the Doxological Stop. Veneration automats crowd the booth from floor to ceiling, dozens of gods and symbols and icons behind their scratched plastic doors, labelled and re-labelled with dozens of different prayers. You see slots marked with the all-seeing eye of the Munificence, wooden beads for the Congregationalists and their Old God, flaking gold paint for Quaesta, Jerichan goddess of profit. Some prayer slots are more specific. "For health," "for credits," even "for a new drive-shaft crank." You feel in your pocket. One pink all-purpose payment chip, one Delos piece and one Brovos marrowpence. All you have left.

You drop the marrowpence into the slot and press a button to send your supplication to the Munificence.

The machine whirrs, registering your prayer as you head towards the bar.

[T]

You make for the Credit Exchange. It is as you remember; an armoured kiosk with a service slot and two tubes, like a creature trying to show as little of its soft flesh as possible. You feel in your pocket. One pink all-purpose payment chip, one Delos piece and one Brovos marrowpence. All you have left. Glancing over your shoulder, you drop the pink chip into the left-hand tube. A scanner hums and a second later, the slot shoots open. Eyes stare out. Both augmented, sparking blue with technology.

"Source of credit?" a voice barks.

"Munificence."

The slot snaps closed. After a breath, tokens tumble from the right-hand chute. You bend to catch them. Five Delos pieces. Less than you'd hoped. You should have waited and found an official broker, but too late now. And anyway, you need a drink.

You shove the tokens into the pocket of your coat and make for the bar.

Blue light floods your eyes as you step back into the atrium. An image flickers, projected onto the unbreakable plastic of the Gasp: a portrait of a woman with grey hair cut into a severe bob, her skin mottled sand-brown and raw pink by radiation damage, her eyes rolled skyward in divine supplication, a pistol raised in each hand. Holy Jo, de-facto ruler of this place. She's Accord, but barely. A former Colonel, founder of the Pius XIX movement and by all accounts the only one insane enough to take the job as Steward. You try to think kind thoughts about her, but they do not come easy. Eventually, you turn your back on her image and push your way into the bar.

The oxygen in the Gasp isn't exactly fresh, but the air in the Barebones is something else. A Brovian place, cow-crazed, where boiling milk and old fat clings to every surface, until it is like trying to breathe marrow.

?

[H]

You glance cautiously from beneath the brim of your hat.

To the left, a noisy table of drogers are playing a drinking game. To the right, you clock a pair of bounty hunters. Sirenko and Prynne, aka The Twins. Your paths have crossed before. They smile at you with serrated teeth. In the far corner you think you see a figure, dull pitted silver-filled sockets where eyes should be, but when you look again, it is only a shadow.

Shrugging off a shiver, you walk towards the bar.

[T]

You stride to the bar. Your boots clang on the metal gratings. Better to be bold; that's what you had learned during your years of chasing marks across the stars. Hesitation breeds indecision and indecision breeds fear and fear leads to violence… especially here, so close to the Factus and its stories of ravening spirits that feed on the weak and the wavering and turn a falter in a firefight. Besides, don't you now have a calling to guide you?

"Yeah?" the bartender asks. His blond hair is slicked flat with neatsfoot oil. He looks tough as a tooth, one hand resting on the bolt gun at his hip, but still his blue eyes widen at the patterns that swim across your skin.

?

[H]
"Whiskey."

[T]

"Water."

He shrugs and pours, sliding the drink before you. You take a slow sip of the warm, slightly oily liquid. Your metal fingertips clink against the glass. No prints, anymore. Another part of you erased. Perhaps that's what makes the bartender ask:

"Here for the Intercession?"

You are not familiar with the term. "Intercession?"

"Same as happens every week. Sinners facing off to save their souls." He nods towards the pistol you wear beneath your coat. "You here to pray for your sins?"

?

[H]
You smile a rueful smile. "My sins have long been forgiven."

You reach beneath your coat and produce the pendant that hangs around your neck. At its end is your Vision: a human eye, blue and hazel iris preserved forever seeing, thread veins ending in the nub of flesh. The bartend blanches even paler when he sees it. You understand why. You too were disgusted at first, until you understood the gift of it. The kindness. It took the feel of that eye—the eye of Sestre Lamentation Prosguetel, Detectoress of The Munificence, Empath V, torn from her own head and placed in your palm, warm and unthinkable—to save you. To set you on the path.

[T]
"Her Reverence, the Eye of the Munificence, does not deal in prayer. She sees. She comprehends. And we enact her Kindnesses." You regard the bartender. "Perhaps there is a kindness to be done, here."

He stares, gloss-slicked lips hanging open. "You're a *nun?*"

You smile. "A Detectoress. Empath I. Still a tyro. But yes, I serve the Munificence."

The bartend swallows. Faith-fearing folk, Brovians. Most from the Western Sector are, in their own way.

He glances around. "You shouldn't be here, Sestre. Holy Jo don't like other creeds on her turf."

"The Eye of the Munificence must be cast into every heart," you murmur, and sip your drink. You have bestowed Her Kindnesses in more hostile places than this. With force, when you have to. But perhaps the bartend is right.

You reach for the pendant and hold your Vision, asking the sealant-hardened eye for guidance. Then, you take one of the Delos pieces from your pocket and place it on the bar. The bartend looks sick.

"What are you doing?"

"Letting Her Reverence guide me. Heads I stay. Tails I go."

?

[H]

It comes to rest on its head, a snake eating its own tail.

You gather it up. "I trust in the Munificence and will take my leave."

                                              [T]

It comes to rest on its tail, an infinity loop that reflects the blue light of the atrium beyond.

You gather it up.

"I believe there is work for me, here. I trust the Munificence to guide my way."

"What if it isn't the Munificence guiding you?" the bartend asks, a sheen of sweat above his lip. "What if it's something else?"

"Like?"

"Like..." His eyes dart to the window, to the Dead Line, to Factus. "Like *them*. The Ifs."

He should not have said it. Should not have named *them*. Too late, you see the oily grey shimmer to his eyes, the dusting of mica collected on his lashes. A 'cid addict. Which means he feels *their* presence, and must numb it, or invite *them* in. He looks at you desperately. "Can the Munificence see *them*?"

Before you can reply, the place goes silent. Slowly, you turn towards the door. Figures fill the frame, two hulking guards with blue crosses embedded in their brows. Between them is the queen of Preacher's Gasp, Holy Jo herself. Her eyes are lit from within by implants: her electrum-filigreed coat sweeps the floor, cut to emphasize the inlaid charge pistols that sit at her waist.

"Hear there's an Eye in my Gasp," she says.

You stand straighter, pushing back your jacket to reveal the Vision, and your weapon. "You are perceived," you reply.

Her thin lips twist. "What profit is there in my blood, when I go down to the pit?" she says, drawing one of her pistols. "Shall the *dust* praise thee? Shall it declare thy truth?" She levels the weapon at your head. "Do you trust your faith to intercede for you in my church, Sestre?"

?

Last Gasp

[H]

You stare her down.

In the mirror-backed bar, your face is a mass of shadow. She doesn't fear you, nor the Munificence. But she does fear *them*.

From your pocket, you draw the two-faced Delos piece.

"Let's find out. Heads and I will face you in the Gasp. Tails and you will let me leave in peace."

Holy Jo's eyes are fixed on the coin, jaw locked. She knows what danger it could bring, but the attention of the bar is upon her and she can show no fear.

"Very well," she says. "Throw."

[T]

You turn and begin to walk away.

Holy Jo's pistols ring out. Two shots, one for each shoulder blade, each an agonising rebuke that sends you sprawling to the greasy floor.

You twist and curse, reaching hopelessly for your weapon, flesh screaming as if someone has ripped wings from your back.

A shadow falls across you, Holy Jo, her pistols armed and levelled.

From your jacket, you fumble the bloodied two-faced Delos piece. "Let *them* decide," you choke. "Heads I die, tails you let me live."

Through a blur of pain, you see Holy Jo's eyes fixed on the coin. She knows what danger it could bring, but the attention of the bar is upon her and she can show no fear.

"Very well," she says. "Throw."

With a prayer to the Munificence, you send the coin spinning into the air.

?

Unremarkable

Alice James

1.

"WHERE THE BLOODY hell is my body?" I sit up on the gurney too fast; the world spins. "This isn't my body. What did you do with my body?"

I try to push myself up and jump down, but my arms are too short and my legs even shorter, so I miss the floor by a country mile and drop to my knees. When I attempt to get my hands out, they respond at all the wrong and I don't quite manage it. I end up performing an inelegant faceplant on the tiled floor, all four limbs flung out as if in ardent supplication, which isn't far from the truth.

"For the love of God, Luxi, whose body is this and what have you done?"

I hear footsteps and roll onto my back. Luxi comes into view. She looks down at me and shakes her head.

"You make such a fuss," she says. "Honestly, it wasn't anything special and you'd been using it for years."

I push myself up onto the heels of my hands. They feel plump and soft; they are going to be absolute rubbish at hotwiring engine carapaces. I grit my teeth but then stop in frustration because they fit together all wrong too.

"Luxi, for the last time, what happened to my damned body?"

She shrugs, already bored of my complaints.

"Look, it got broken, OK? And I got you a new one. Brand new; just out of the box." She sniffs. "Christ on a bicycle, there's no pleasing you, is there?"

All the fight drains out of me. I lie back down on the floor and stare at the ceiling. The eyeballs in my sockets feel wrong too, so does the tongue in my damn mouth. I raise my arms up to the ceiling and then lower them to rub my face vigorously. I feel something. Hair. No, not hair; stubble. I reach tentatively down towards my groin.

"Oh crap. Luxi…"

"No. Don't start."

I drop my hands to my sides and raise my head very slightly, just high enough that I can bang it against the floor. When I work out how to stand up, the very first thing I'm going to do is kill her.

"Oh, bollocks. I'm a man."

2.

I drag it out. I force myself to eat a healthy breakfast and let her check all my vitals before I haul myself to the washrooms. I try to stare at myself in the mirror, but all I can see is the top of my head; Luxi might claim my previous incarnation had been getting a bit long in the tooth, but I had got agreeably used to being just shy of two meters in my stockinged, feminine feet.

"Ship, lower the mirrors," I bark, and watch grumpily as my features hove into view. "Seriously? All the bodies in the world and she picked me this one?"

The face staring back at me is that of a young man—part Caucasian, part Asian would be my guess. My thick wavy hair isn't quite true black, but I'm not sure it's even brown either. I'm shortish but not enough to comment on, stocky maybe but not really fat. I'm…I'm a bunch of not quites; not quite handsome, not quite plain, not quite anything at all. I am the most unremarkable person that I have ever seen.

Ah well, in my line of work it could be worse. No one wants to be a memorable bandit, do they?

I stomp around the ship until I find Luxi. She's in the bay examining our haul, her back to me as she delves into shipment chests.

"Have you stopped moaning?" she says. "You nearly died, you know."

She turns around but then starts, jerking backwards.

"Who the devil…" She breaks off. "Oh, sorry, it's you of course. For some reason I didn't recognize you."

"Yeah, it's me." I kneel next to her. "I don't remember a lot. What happened and what did we get out of it?"

"Hmm," she said. "I think we learned a lesson. You remember leaving this ship? Boarding the *Ever Chance of Mars*?"

"Yeah, but not much after that."

We stole our ship off Manny the Rat; we nicked the engines from a shipment Cherry Jones was ferrying between satellite hubs. Then we screwed the parts together and used our supercharged ride to rip off enough bounty from the interplanetary trade route to pay the pair of them both back and agree that bygones would be bygones. They say there's no honor between rogues, and they might be right, but there's a balance and you can pay it down. Manny and Cherry wouldn't trust us now as far as they could throw us, but what of it? They never did before, and I think we notched up in terms of respect.

Anyway, the ship's a military prototype that Manny swiped off Chupta the Fence, and neither of them knew what to do with it because they couldn't sell it. And the engines came from a research ring up by Lunar Nine; they didn't pass their safety tests, but no one told Cherry that, so honestly, we did everyone a favor. The boys and girls got some money, and we ended up with a tiny mosquito of a craft that could jump latch onto one of those massive transports, purloin a few chests and be off into the stars before anyone was any the wiser. In a few years, the powers that be will have all have installed something that can see us coming but for now… for now we're like kids in a sweet shop. We just got our knuckles rapped this time.

"Well." Luxi is prizing open a chest. "You went in, magged out four or five blocks and a couple of containers, and we were about going to split when some alarms went off. The airlock you'd jammed started to close and you had to jump for it." The graphene casing cracks under her pry bar, and she levers off the lid and throws it to one side. "Seriously, Mal, you were cut in half. I got you in a medic unit in time, but it was close. Anyway, one of the containers you'd brought on was marked as holding body blanks, so I took the one with the highest spec and dumped you in it."

I grunt.

"You could have just left me in the medic unit to regrow."

"Yeah, sure. I could have manned this baby on my own for four or five months so that you didn't have to get used to new teeth. Fuck that, Mal, and grow a pair. Oh, hang on; you just did."

I roll my eyes and help her tear insulating foam aside.

"Fair enough; thank you for saving my ungrateful hide. What the actual? These are guns."

We rifle through the contents, and I purse my lips. I might be a bandit, a burglar, a pirate—pick your idiom—but I'm not into violence. I'm a smash-and-grab girl and, if someone catches me in the act, I'll scarper rather than fight for the spoils. And if you're going to judge me, let me say for the record that I only rob rich people. Or other robbers; I mean if you can't rob a fellow robber, what's the universe coming to?

But guns… They're for people with different family values to me. And these are nasty little next-generation weapons, the type that blows a small hole and then tests your DNA before deciding whether to terminate you with vengeance. Dealing death with a side order of bigotry… Not for me.

I can tell Luxi's read my expression, even in my brand-new face, because she just pats my arm.

"We'll let Manny have them," she says. "He'll just peddle them round the Saturn rings. That whole bunch of sister fuckers is so inbred that the bullets won't know whether to self-destruct or ask for a new family tree. Look, if you don't like that body, there were two; you could see if you prefer the other one."

I shake my head.

"I'll keep this one," I say. "It's fate. But let's have a look at the other. A quality blank's worth a fortune, and we could do with some good fortune right now."

Fuel is expensive. Engine parts are more expensive. Docking fees are worse, and that's before you even think about oxygen. And ever since our Prime Minister ramped up tensions between the systems, prices have just headed higher until it feels like breathing is a luxury you should consider saving for saints' days and Christmas. I can hardly blame the Martian rebels for kidnapping her son. Honestly, some days I feel like throwing it all in and just retiring to a hut by the sea, and then I remember that I don't have citizenship anywhere that has huts, let alone a sea, and that I've been on the run for a hundred and seventeen years for a crime I probably didn't commit but can't remember. So I just get out of bed and rob another supply ship and drink a beer.

Anyway. I feel we're due a run of luck. It's about time we throw something that isn't snake eyes.

3.

I look down at the body blank. She's tall. She's athletic. She has jet black hair down to her waist. Her eyelashes, curled and even, arc above cheekbones so plump and delicious my mouth waters. She has skin so dark it eats up the light. She is absolutely literally fucking perfect.

"Seriously," I say to Luxi. "I said I'd stop moaning, but you picked *this…*" I wave my plump hands in front of her face. "You picked this over *that*?"

Luxi has the decency to look embarrassed.

"I didn't even open this container," she confesses. "Yours had a higher spec on the lid and I was in a hurry. What can I say? Mea culpa. I meant well. If you're that unhappy, let's ditch your charming persona and you can have this one. You'll be up and running by tomorrow."

"No way."

The words are out before I can stop them. I'm a fool, I know. It's paranoia, and things have moved on, but I lost a friend to a bad transfer, and I'm left with this phobia. There's always this unholy terror that I'll leave a perfectly adequate form and never wake up in the next one. We all fear death, but I fear bringing about my own through shallow ambition. It's hardly sensible, but people get hung over worse things. I could have therapy, but that would mean accepting that my fears aren't actually deep-down just sensible instincts for self-preservation, and I'm not there yet. Luxi knows, but she still thinks I'm an arse.

"Fine," she says. "We'll sell it. Oh, bollocks to that."

"What?"

"This body; it's not empty."

Oh crap. So now we're not bandits; we're kidnappers. This isn't good.

4.

"You're sure we wake her up?" Luxi asks.

"Yup."

I've moved our stowaway into the medic unit to bring her round safely. She lies there like sleeping beauty waiting for a prince. I would kiss her—goodness knows she's pretty enough—but she's also unconscious and I'm into consent.

"Or we could just, you know, not?"

I press a few buttons and hear the unit start to hum. A few hours to heat her up gently to thirty-seven degrees and rekindle the electronic and metabolic pathways and she should be fine. Just like me.

"She was locked up in an unmarked body blank case on board a renegade Martian supply vessel carrying questionable weaponry," I say. "I can't imagine she got there voluntarily. We wake her up and help on her way. Like decent space pirates do."

"Hmm."

Luxi's unconvinced, and I get it, but it's like the guns. There are some things I won't do. I don't kill people and I don't rob the poor, and keeping people on ice just feels wrong. I close the lid.

"Let it go," I say. "We're better than this. Now, let's get drunk."

We don't get too drunk; just a bit. We loll around and watch some immersives and a few news reels. They're a blast. The Martian collective is still running riot, the Prime Minister's son is still missing, fuel isn't getting cheaper, and some actor somewhere has released a new mascara. Luxi says she despairs sometimes and when is he going to update his eyeshadow range, and we laugh and then sleep it all off.

I wake before she does and wander through to the washroom. A total stranger stares at me from the mirror and for a moment I'm confused. It's the new me, exactly the same as yesterday, but somehow, I don't recognize my face. Weird. I push the strangeness to one side and take the time to shave—haven't missed that—and take a piss; OK, that's more fun than I remember. I head down to the stores, naked, and ask the ship to adjust some clothes for my shorter, wider stature. I find I've chosen things to fit the new anodyne me, in-between colors, nothing to hold the attention, and super casual tailoring that doesn't catch the eye or stick in the mind. I'm dressing for the unremarkable man I've suddenly become.

I get two mugs of hot coffee and bring them up to where Luxi's unconscious form is still slumbering restlessly. I turn the lights up, but not too aggressively.

"Rise and shine," I say. "Wonderful adventures lie ahead of us, stretching out in our new lives as—hang on, let me check this—two broke crooks in an illegal jumper ship without any prospects or plans. Let's seize the day."

"Bugger off." She stretches and sits up. "When do…" She breaks off with a shriek. "Who the fuck are you? Get away from me!"

I back off, hands raised.

"Whoa, sister. It's me, Mel, remember. New body, short bloke, good hair. Hell, girl, I brought you coffee."

She blinks and relaxes.

"Sorry, don't know what happened there. I didn't recognize you. Just sleepy." She takes the mug from my hands with an apologetic shake of the head. "Seriously, just not awake yet."

I pat her shoulder, but my mind is whirling; I didn't recognize me either. That's forgivable—I haven't changed my body in twenty-two years—but Luxi changes hers with the weather and so do her friends back on Luna. Perturbed, I change the subject.

"Whatever," I say. "Ready to wake up our stowaway?"

She rolls her eyes; she said her piece, but I think she broadly agrees with me.

"Sure," she says. "Let me get dressed and we can draw straws to give Snow White a kiss, eh."

Snow White is bang on thirty-seven degrees. She does indeed look like a princess, lying there in her utter perfection as though a hundred years behind a wall of thorns couldn't taint her beauty. I press a few more buttons and the lid of the chamber draws back with a pneumatic sigh. After a few moments, her dark eyelashes flutter.

"Wakey wakey," Luxi says cheerfully. "Rise and shine, sister. Stairs to climb, worlds to conquer."

The girl opens dark eyes that are just as lovely as you would expect them to be, nestling in that face. Their expression is fearful, wary, cowed.

"Please don't hurt me again," she says. Her voice breaks a little. "I promise not to run away this time."

I back away, raising my hands in a pacifying gesture. Next to me, I feel Luxi doing the same.

"No way," I say. "I mean, no one here is hurting you, lady. We accidentally stole your body. I mean, we stole you, but we didn't mean to. You're not a prisoner. We don't even know who you are."

She blinks, her hypnotic eyes welling up.

"I'm Vikri Sakovos," she whispers. "I'm the Prime Minister's son."

5.

"Well, this is crap," I say, scrolling through the news feeds. "There's a lovely four million terran dollar reward out for your safe return, but if either of us tries to claim it we'll probably be interred for slightly longer than it takes for the universe to decay into entropy and seed over again, so probably not worth it."

Vikri giggles. She's younger than her body in lived-out years and hasn't got used to breasts or peeing sitting down. She and Luxi spent a hilarious half hour in the washroom together while I called unhelpful advice through the door. We're kind of friends when it's done; I think she knows we mean her no harm. She's all out for trying to find a way we get the reward.

"For sure you should have it," she says. "You're returning me safely, right?"

I shrug. I'd like the money—don't get me wrong, I've always wanted to be part of the undeserving rich—but I also value my freedom. I was banged up once before. It was more than a century ago, but I've never forgotten. And I'm still on several most-wanted lists as a result of using a get-out-of-jail-free card that firstly wasn't mine and secondly wasn't free. Water under the bridge, my friend, but the long arm of the law—so I hear—isn't exactly a floating limb. It's attached to a sturdy shoulder of justice that's set just below a head of legal precedents containing a brain with a long, unforgiving memory of sentences passed and yet mysteriously unserved. The money, I fear, will go unclaimed.

"I hope we are," I say, prevaricating. "You look safe to me."

She turns and gives a little jump.

"Sorry," she says. "I didn't recognize you for a minute. You just…" She tails off. "Maybe being on ice did something to my memory."

I growl.

"It's not you," I say grumpily. "It's me. I'm literally the least memorable man in the solar system. I swear, no one is every going to remember my face."

There's a silence. I think about what I've said and mentally smack myself in the head with both hands. I don't do it for real because I haven't got used to these hands yet and I might accidentally gouge out an eyeball with a wayward thumb or something.

"Holy shit, I just worked it out," I say. "I mean, it's for real, isn't it? No one is ever, ever going to remember this face. That's what it's for."

Luxi give me a look.

"What are you driveling on about?" she asks. "You're still complaining about that body, aren't you? I'm going to break your damn nose and then let's see how unmemorable you look. What?"

But I'm laughing because I've worked it all out. With a little forethought, I probably can net us four million dollars.

"Watch and learn, ladies," I say. "Watch and learn."

6.

One change of clothes should do it. Anything more sophisticated and I'll trip over my own ambition. I just ask for the money in bearer bonds, in an envelope left leaning against the bin just outside the toilets in the main terminal at Lunar Seven. I take the package, knowing every eye is on me, and walk nonchalantly into the washrooms. Then, during the brief thirty seconds when they're all cooing and distracted by Vikri emerging at the far end of the concourse, I strip off my clothes and stuff them in a cistern. Underneath I'm dressed as a terminal janitor. They're waiting outside, of course, but they're not waiting for me. They're waiting for the smartly dressed, short guy who took the money. But they let me past because… because no one remembers what the hell I look like. No one's ever going to remember this face.

It's utterly forgettable.

That's why the spec on this body was so high. That's why it was nestling next to some speculative military hardware destined for the revolutionaries. That's why Luxi gives a little jump whenever I come into the room, and I look in the mirror and every time wonder who the hell the dark-haired guy with the round face is. Seriously, I wonder what they planned to infiltrate with this wonderful, forgettable face in its slightly-below-average-height unmemorable frame. How they did it, I don't know, but they did. It's going to be one hell of a ride. Luxi and I are going to have a lot of fun with this body—let's hope four million dollars is only the start.

I'm just an unremarkable man.

Who's Afraid of Little Old Me?

Sarah L. Miles

Now:

LUCIAN WAS SITTING behind his large wooden desk, an anachronism from a different world, but one he felt lent him gravitas, a sense of leadership he was determined to maintain despite his inner fears. He rested his head in his hands, elongated fingers massaging his temples, at the sight of the younger man in front of him.

"Steve. Steve. *Stephen.*"

Steve's ears cocked at the use of his full name. His shoulders slumped as he attempted to sink further down in the metal of the chair in which he was uncomfortably slouched. The response did nothing to improve Lucian's mood.

"You understand why you're here, yes? Here *again*, I should say."

Steve mumbled something under his breath, in the way of teenagers across the ages. His sullen expression was not aided by his long jaw, which caused his mouth to seem permanently downturned.

"Stephen, you will address Lucian with respect," came a voice from behind him. "Sit up straight and stop being such an embarrassment."

Steve winced at the sound of his mother's voice. It was like claws down a metal panel. If it wasn't for the fact that his neck was already scruffy and unkempt, he'd have expected the hairs there to rise of their own accord.

Lucian dropped his hands and glanced over at Janice, nodding to her in acknowledgment of her interruption.

"Stephen, it has been brought to our attention, once again, that your foolish—dare I even say childish—obsession with humanity has once again risked our safety here. We simply cannot allow this to continue, do you understand?"

A few days earlier…

Steve stood as quietly as he could to the side of the single metal door, listening intently, his head cocked slightly to one side and his large ears standing up straight. When there was no movement from inside, he slowly slid the access card over the door panel, wincing at the loud beep it gave off as the door swooshed open. He entered the lab as quietly as he could, feet making slight taps on the metallic flooring, holding in his breath in case there was someone working late. Glancing about as the door slid closed behind him, he let his breath out slowly. The lab was empty, and the equipment still running. He sat down in the spinning metal chair at the main console, and deftly began maneuvering the cameras in front of him. Attached to satellites around the globe, they were the property of television networks, oligarchs, and governments, but the colony had adapted the technology used to their own needs. Thanks to the work of the previous generation, they could now look at virtually any area of Earth using its own kit, without anyone on the planet noticing.

Steve enjoyed using them clandestinely, knowing that he would never be allowed the opportunity if he hadn't stolen the access card from his mother, one of the leading lights of the science program. Luckily for him, she was the embodiment of the ditzy scientist cliché, constantly losing tablets and equipment. She never noticed that they occasionally turned up in Steve's room. Although, that was more a reflection of how little attention she paid to her son than anything else. He had long become used to coming second to her work, and none of the males had wanted to claim him as their son, despite the fact that he was born long after the colony was established. Janice wasn't exactly the most desirable female— he shuddered at even thinking that of his own mother—and given that there were other, better options available, he didn't blame them for leaving him fatherless. This of course did nothing to improve his own standing, a fact that had hurt him for a number of years before he simply adapted to the situation and learnt to like his own company. He sighed and turned his attention back to the console in front of him, its large number of keys, toggles and joysticks combined into one large system, much of it cobbled together from old Earth tech and scraps unused elsewhere.

Steve angled the satellite currently in operation to point at his favorite spot, Kings Park, Long Island. The others didn't understand his strange obsession with this one spot in particular, but then they were all mature adults, not a juvenile like Steve. As the youngest member of the pack, and given his long-established loner status, he often felt lonely, and seeing these other juveniles hanging around gave him a sense of belonging, even from 250,000-odd miles away. The one time he had been caught looking, he had managed to shift the location of the cameras to a few hundred miles away. Of course, that had just led to more scorn from the older males, as despite being so far away from the planet they all still felt the need to mock New Jersey.

Now...

Lucian called up a series of alerts on the screen behind him, each seemingly random, but as Steve assessed the data, he felt a deepening sense of dread. Lucian clocked the expression on his face, and almost felt sorry for him, for a flicker of a second. He sighed deeply.

"Why do we live here, Steve? No, it's a rhetorical question, you don't actually have to answer."

He held up one long-fingered hand as the youngster started to open his mouth.

"We are safer here, we do not have to deal with prejudice here, and most importantly *no one knows we are here.*"

Lucian once again massaged his temples.

"That was the agreement we reached before we came here. We stay away from them, we send them occasional updates on progress as and when required, and in return, *they leave us the fuck alone.*"

Steve's ears flicked back at the cussing. Lucian never lost his composure normally, and it was a bad sign that he was doing so now.

Steve cowered back into himself slightly, his shoulders caving over his hollow chest as he attempted to make himself look smaller. Which is easier said than done when you're pushing seven feet tall whilst still growing. The mass of alerts behind Lucian continued to appear, as his gaze flicked between Steve and the increasingly busy screen.

"We've held a conclave." The gasp from behind Steve did not make him feel any better about what Lucan would say next. "The decision has been made on behalf of the colony. It is for the best; contact has been made with the planet. They are due to send up an unmanned shuttle shortly to appease the curious, and it's an election year so those in charge need a visible win. A new discovery about the Moon should win the incumbent some votes. We've agreed to provide them with some of our data in return for their ship bringing back a passenger. It'll still be unmanned, of course, just with you on board."

The howl from Janice chilled Steve's bones almost as much as Lucian's words. It was a noise of grief, and anger, and pain, and yet did nothing to quell the bubbling sense of excitement that sparked in the pit of his belly. He kept his composure even as he sloped away from Lucian's office, avoiding eye contact with those he passed—news clearly traveled fast, based on the range of looks he got, from sympathetic to smug—and leaving his mother to hopelessly plead his case with Lucian. Steve tried his hardest to look downcast, even as he realized the enormity of Lucian's decision. Finally, the chance to make contact, to find out what made those on earth tick, why they were just so… different.

∽

The shuttle landed several kilometers away from Statio Tranquillitatis, settling easily onto the pad that had been hastily assembled for that specific purpose. The pack didn't keep a permanent shuttle pad near the site, as they had very little face-to-face contact with the earth-based scientific teams, and very few shuttles actually touched down. The majority of their work was done through emails and shared spreadsheets, in no small part due to the way the Earth-based teams looked at those who lived on the moon. It was… less than complimentary. They clearly preferred to stay on the International Space Station and simply beam data to and fro, rather than actually setting foot on the surface.

Steve waited impatiently, bouncing from side to side on the balls of his feet. He had a messenger bag slung over from shoulder to hip, his few meager possessions stuffed inside, his long limbs virtually vibrating as he watched the landing pod go through its final, automated checks. As soon as the outer door hissed open, he loped quickly towards it, throwing himself inside in a fit of excitement.

He settled into the single chair inside, adjusting the belts to settle over his long torso as much as he could. He shuffled the bag to a comfortable position between his feet, pulled out a tablet loaded with American comics, and removed his external breathing apparatus. Lucian had been very clear on the point that the shuttle would contain the right mix of oxygen for his comfort, which he thought was strangely generous of the scientists. As he heard the machinery within the shuttle starting to come to life, there was also a strange hissing sound, followed by an unusual smell. He assumed it was an oxygen input, even as he passed out from the gas slowly filling the chamber.

In the light of the moon, the four men grunted as they shifted the bag. Whatever was inside it was oddly shaped, and heavy—heavier than they'd expected. Regardless, they'd been paid to do a job, and it was a matter of pride for them to do it well. They shuffled sideways to their van, and threw it into the back, choosing to ignore the slight huff of sound that came out. They were being paid to do a job, not to ask questions.

Setting up the gas canister as instructed, two of the men jumped in the front of the van, leaving the others to tidy up behind them as they hit the road and headed north. The drive was due to take them about twenty hours, and they had oddly specific instructions for where and when they could stop. They were in no mood to waste time, though, and the driver chose to take a few shortcuts on back roads that he knew, ones where he could get away with driving well over the limit and not have to worry about the local cops pulling him over.

Thanks to his creative use of the itinerary, they made it to their location, a deserted building well outside of New York City, a few hours ahead of schedule. Picking up the bag, the two men were surprised at how light it felt compared to several hours before. Their instructions clearly stated they were to deposit the bag, unzipped but unopened, and leave. But where would be the fun in that, after such a long drive? Dropping the bag at the dictated spot, they unzipped it and were surprised to find a teenage boy inside, wearing ill-fitting clothing that had gone out of style several years earlier, and no shoes. He looked and smelt like he'd not washed in weeks, and his tousled hair was verging on matted. Exchanging a look, the two men pulled the edges of the zip back together and quickly headed back to their van. Whatever a group of science nerds back in Florida were doing with some kid, it wasn't worth their time finding out.

꩜

The sheer size of the building was intimidating even to Steve. He leaned his gangly frame back as he took it in. Floors upon floors of brick and glass, nothing like the enclosed metal pods he was used to. The grass under his feet felt almost obscene in how organic it was. There was a breeze—a word he only knew from reading it—and the feel of it in his fur was transcendental. He luxuriated in it, flexing the muscles in his back to extend the sensation across his skin. He allowed himself to extend to his full height, stretching his double-jointed arms far over his head and reaching up to the wall above him. His claws scratched through layers of grime and graffiti, leaving deep gashes.

Even as he enjoyed his newfound freedom, he was curious as to how he'd gotten here so quickly, and why he couldn't remember the journey. But he understood he'd not grown up on Earth, and so hadn't got a good idea of how things really worked down here. There wasn't much reason on the moon to leave the base, and he could easily lope from the labs at one end of the base, to his room at the other, in under an hour. He wasn't even sure where he was supposed to be staying, or how he went about getting a place to stay or find people to hang out with. However, he'd seen Kings Park plenty of times, and it shouldn't be that hard to find the teens he'd been watching for so many months.

Who's Afraid of Little Old Me?

Loping off to the side of the building, he took a quick glance round to gain his bearings, his gaze sliding over the graffiti and broken windows, the moon glinting in the fractured glass. The grass between buildings was surprisingly well kept, given the state of the buildings that were rising around him. Halting at the rise of a small slope, he dropped down to his haunches and paused for a second. The sound of cars came from his right, the low rumbling bass of their music causing him to nod along. He paused for a second, licking his palm and slicking his hair back to try and make himself look at least a little presentable, before setting off towards the sound.

The response was less than ideal. As he moved round the corner of the building the clouds pulled back from the moon, highlighting his frame in all its gangly glory. As the assembled cars and teenagers saw him appear, they froze. Freezing Steve could deal with; it was the screaming that he found disconcerting. And the running. The running provoked a feeling in him that he hadn't felt before. It was primal, animalistic, disconcerting to his very core, as he considered himself a scientist at heart. He retreated behind the building, shaking as he fought the urge to run after them, feeling his teeth in a way he wasn't used to, his ears picking up the gravel rattling under the car tires, the screech of brakes as the cars hit the main road, and the terrified voices in the cars.

He leant back against the wall, looking up at the moon and wondering if he had made a terrible mistake, and slowly slumped down the wall, head falling into his hands and a mournful howl releasing from his lips. He failed to see that one of the teens hadn't fled, instead remaining sitting in a beat-up old car, engine off, staring intently through the windshield. The kid was so still, he could have been holding his breath. But Steve was too caught up in his confusion to notice, pacing round the buildings and adding more scratches to the graffiti-covered walls, howling his grief to the ever-present moon.

∽

Janice felt her heart constrict in her chest, the camera in front of her angled to Steve's usual spot. She knew he was only a pup, but she had thought he was at least a little street smart. He knew they didn't go to the planet's surface for a reason, surely? He couldn't have been so innocent as to think the American teens would simply accept him as he was. Maybe he would learn to adapt; to make the best of the time he could have with the people his own age. But she wasn't convinced, and that was on her. She had failed him as a parent, working under the assumption he would stay on the moon and not have to deal with the humans directly.

Maybe she could appeal to Lucian? Show him the footage of Stephen being rejected, appeal to his kinder side. If he had a kinder side...

Maybe he could take the car that had been left behind and drive back to Florida, persuade the scientists to bring him back? It's not like there was any reason for him to stay on Earth now.

～

Steve woke with a start, panic setting in before he remembered where he was. Things felt different, though. He could see the sun rising behind the abandoned buildings, which looked a lot less impressive in the daylight. He felt the sun on his skin, though, and it felt warm and glorious. The realization very slowly dawned on him that he could feel the sun on his skin. Not his fur. *Skin*.

He looked down at his hands, marveling at their appearance. His fingers looked short, almost stubby. The claws were gone, replaced with short fingernails, his fur replaced with light brown skin, tiny hairs standing up on the skin of his arms as the breeze blew over them. He shivered, feeling naked, and went to stand. This in itself was an unusual feeling, as his legs didn't unfold in their usual way, his feet weren't able to flex and bend as he expected them to. Looking down, he saw that it wasn't just his hands and arms that were changed. His legs were shorter, paws truncated and flat. He was still wearing the same shorts and t-shirt as the night before, but now they were baggy on his form, loose fitting and making him look scruffy. He felt small, uncertain. It was an unpleasant sensation, even for someone who had been the runt of the litter for his entire life.

He turned and looked at the wall behind him, baffled at the difference between his current height and the claw marks above his head. As he studied them, he became aware of a presence behind him. For the first time in his entire life, he jumped in surprise, confused as to why his hearing hadn't alerted him to the young man now standing next to him. They both look startled, and after staring at each other for a moment looked back up at the gouges in the wall.

Steve glanced across at his new companion surreptitiously, only to find him doing the same. He looked back at the wall straight away, self-consciously tugging on one of his ears. The young man broke the uncomfortable silence first, coughing into his hand before grinning lightly.

"Dave."

Steve looked confused, and turned to him.

"Sorry, no, my name is Steve?"

The man chuckled, and put out his hands,

"Yeah, I'm Dave, you're Steve, nice to meet you."

He faltered slightly and Steve looked at his hand, and then looked back up at Dave, utterly baffled by the entire interaction. Dave sighed and dropped his hand

"You're not local, are you? Most people don't hang around the asylum during the day. The cops tend to come and yell at trespassers, and they'll ticket you if you give them attitude." He faltered as he saw the expression on Steve's face. "Are you okay, dude, you look like you've seen a ghost. Or a werewolf? That's why I'm here, bunch of my friends were down here last night and there was some weird shit going on, so I hung around to check it out."

For the first time ever, Steve started to sweat. He wasn't sure what was going on, but he had a strange sensation in his belly, which itself was much lower than normal and therefore feeling weird anyway. He looked at Dave, perplexed, both at what he was saying and what he was feeling.

Dave trailed off and closed his mouth. He glanced at the marks on the wall once more, then back at Steve in his ill-fitting clothes; cargo pants that hung low on his hips, a worn t-shirt advertising a festival from a decade ago, and bare feet. He set his mouth in a lopsided smile, and put his hand on the back of Steve's arm.

"Do you want to go get some breakfast, man? If we stay here much longer, a patrol will turn up, and then we'll have to bail. So, we may as well head off now. Whaddaya say?"

Steve didn't know how he'd ended up in this situation, but he was seated in a booth across from Dave, wearing a pair of borrowed sliders, a plate of waffles in front of him dripping in butter and maple syrup, a pile of bacon to the side. His mug of black coffee steamed by his hand. Dave was chatting away merrily about the history of the buildings they had just left, and Steve was just letting it wash over him. He'd never really shared a meal like this, being more used to eating on his own in the canteen and trying to keep his head down so that no one would notice he was there.

It was actually really nice to have company, other than his mom. He smiled lightly and picked up his cutlery, trying to mimic Dave's movements, unused to the size of his hands. The food was delicious, like nothing he'd ever had before. The flavors were sweet and salty on his tongue, the fluffy pancakes mixing with the crispy bacon in ways that he had never experienced, his eyes rolling slightly back in his head at the sensation. Dave watched him eating, clearly enjoying his reaction. Steve felt heat in his cheeks, unused to the expression on his companion's face.

The conversation flowed easily once Steve loosened up, filled with coffee and breakfast and feeling less concerned about his situation. He tensed slightly when Dave started talking about werewolves again, but did his best to hide the response. He wasn't sure where the time went, but soon enough they were walking out of the diner and back to Dave's car. Settling into the passenger seat, he happily chatted about comics and movies, pleased that Dave had the same taste as him, and getting into friendly arguments about who would win in fights, and whose runs were better.

As the sun slowly came down, Dave pulled the car back into the road that led up to Kings Park. He had gotten quiet as they drove back, and Steve was worried. They both got out of the car and walked back towards the main building, surreptitiously shooting looks at each other as they kept an eye out for cops. Dave broke the silence first.

"Listen, Steve." He paused, collecting his thoughts. "We've chatted all day and you've not once said anything about where you live, or what you do. I don't want to make any judgments or anything but, are you okay? Like, if I leave you here tonight will you be alright?" He looked concerned, and reached his hand out.

As soon as his hand connected with Steve's arm he flinched back, looking down at what he had touched. The sun was sinking below the horizon and the moon had appeared in the sky, full and close. Steve's arm had thickened while they walked, fur sprouting from all sides. As Dave watched, Steve doubled over, holding his arms over his belly as his back extended and he dropped into a crouch. Dave backed away, slowly, and so as not to startle Steve. Not in a fearful way; he seemed almost respectful.

After his experience last night, Steve had expected screaming. His conversation with Dave had been enlightening as to what had happened that morning, the lack of moon and how legends said that werewolves needed to be bathed in moonlight to transform. He'd never realized until that day that humans and werewolves could look the same; growing up on the moon, his mother had never told him, and it wasn't covered in their lessons. It was all "humans are dangerous, humans hate us, humans want us dead." Dave had been different. He'd been kind, and gentle, and interested in what Steve had to say. Most importantly, he wasn't running away as Steve felt his bones extending, stretching out the limits of the clothes he was wearing, and tearing through the ends of his fingers and toes as his claws flexed back out. The pain was indescribable, but he did his best to muffle his own screams. He didn't want to scare Dave, or hurt him, and he was worried about the feelings he'd had the night before when he saw the people in the car park.

Dave crouched down into a squat, slowly reaching one hand out to place it gently on Steve's shoulder. Steve's head whipped up, his long nose and sharp teeth closer to Dave's face than he was comfortable with, but Dave didn't even flinch. Instead, he smiled slowly, and nodded.

"It's okay. I guessed when I found you this morning, after last night. I'm not scared of you, Steve. I think you're a decent guy. Just… a little different. And that's okay, I'm a little different too. Not like you are, obviously, but still…"

He trailed off as Steve stood to his full height, towering over Dave but trying to make himself look smaller. He reached his paw out in the way Dave had that morning, which felt like a lifetime ago now. Dave, still smiling, took his hand, not in a handshake, but linking their fingers together.

"Please, don't try and make yourself small for me. I'm not afraid of you."

A Hundred Thousand Eyes Gaze Upon the Core of You

Khan Wong

THE CREATURE LAY belly down as the first scans were run. Before the dissection, Saba and her colleagues wanted to document the strange geometries of its skin. Hues of blue, green and violet morphed into each other in a fractal-like pattern, some hidden code of the deep, maybe. Crystalline growths sprouted from the smooth surface, opaline and translucent. Its tail—twice the length of the body—flared out, edges draped over the table, nearly to the floor. Stretched out, it would be, at its widest point, wider than its body was long. It must have been magnificent in the water. The body was sleek, like a missile. No legs or appendages. A hooded head bore glossy eyes, reflecting the lab in miniature a dozen times.

Saba made note of these details and more—the fine silver filament that connected the crystalline outgrowths, how the outgrowths were faceted in patterns of three, six, nine. How the same silver thread connected the eyes, making them, like the crystals, appear to be jeweled studs upon a net draped over the creature like the costume of a popstar from the old world. The thought of the song and dance girls brought up an old resentment—how could they be so shiny and happy as the world was burning up and falling apart?

A dorsal fin traversed nearly the full length of the body—scarlet at the base of the head, it faded into a golden orange, then a pale yellow by the time it reached the origin point of the tail. She knew these colors, these patterns, this tail. Somehow.

"This is by far the largest one." Saba's colleague Hutcherson waited for a response he probably knew wasn't forthcoming. At least not easily.

He continued, "A preliminary scan of the hemolymph indicates no known relationship to any genome on Earth."

"Mmm hmm." That was as much as Saba had to say about it at the moment.

"We think it may have come through the anomaly—"

"We have no reason to believe traversing the threshold is possible." She really didn't want to think about the implications of that, yet the possibility licked at her brain. So uncomfortable.

"And yet…" Hutcherson gestured at the creature before them.

"I don't see any gills," Saba said as she walked a slow circle around the table, observing the thing from multiple angles. When she reached the head and stared into the twelve-eyed face, she tapped a command into her tablet and a holographic projection of the creature's insides appeared in the air above the body. "There doesn't appear to be any sort of respiratory system."

"The skin is covered in very fine pores," Hutcherson explained. "We'll know more after dissection, but we suspect it's a tracheal system."

"But that wouldn't allow it to breathe under water…" Oh, she didn't like the implications of that.

"Yes. And?" There was a hint of a smile in Hutcherson's voice, as if he was waiting for a moment—

"So this thing drowned? But then it couldn't be a sea creature." Saba resented the panic in her voice, the incredulity. "It was found in canyon 1122A? It's at, what, two thousand feet?"

"Just about fifty meters from the anomaly."

She met her colleague's eyes, crinkled with suppressed laughter. Why did he so enjoy her discomfort?

"That doesn't prove anything."

"Why are you so resistant to the obvious?"

She shook her head. "It doesn't prove anything."

A Hundred Thousand Eyes Gaze Upon the Core of You

Waves surged against the glass of the observation sphere. The sea roiled, agitated but not quite stormy. When it got like this, the elders—most of them anyway—got sick. Seasickness, they called it. They had lived on land in their youth, and knew stillness and solid ground. But those Saba's age and younger, while they had known conditions from calm to turbulent, had never known stillness. Even when conditions were calmest, the ship shifted with a subtle bobble, ever present.

Saba was situated in her favorite alcove right at the midpoint—she loved this liminal space between containment and the wild sea, between the calm of the depths and the surface churn. It helped her think and make connections. An irony, then, that her mind insisted on disregarding all evidence that the strange creatures the team had been encountering over these past weeks did not originate from this sea, from this world. Maybe she was thinking herself away from the obvious to preserve the reality she knew, and her sanity. She could outthink herself. It had been known to happen.

A dozen eyes gazed at her, locked into the very core of her. She closed her own eyes, but that only made the vision stronger, more detailed, more finite. Opening her eyes again, she focused once more on the cresting, splashing horizon on the outside surface of the glass sphere in which she sat, one of four that hugged the central structure of the ark. The warmth of the mug she clutched tightly between her palms grounded her. Other pods with other occupants—mostly pairs and small groups—were distributed throughout the space, and Saba's gaze flitted across all of them. She usually sat alone here. Hutcherson had once asked why she didn't just stay in her quarters if she wanted to be alone, and she'd replied that she enjoyed being solitary in public.

"Doesn't that get lonesome?" he'd asked.

She had kept her answer to herself.

Sudden murmurs intruded on her thoughts, and everyone was looking at something outside. A shadow emerged from shadow: some large, wavering form heading for the sphere from deep water. The giant octopus situated itself right outside the base level observation deck, its chromatophores streaming colors in rapidly morphing horizontal lines across its body. It was clearly looking in at them. Many creatures came by the ships, swam close to the alien-to-them waterless environment contained by the glass bubbles. Schools of fish, pods of whales and dolphins, sharks, jellies, mantas. Cephalopods were rare, but not unheard of. It was thought the heat the engines gave off attracted them, or maybe the lights, or merely the enormous mass of the vessel. Not for the first time, she wondered at the intelligence of these animals, if the octopus was a scientist or explorer of its own kind, investigating this strange structure and the strange creatures inside. Now, why did that feel familiar, just like the skin of the creature in the lab?

What did this visitor know of the anomaly? Had it tasted the secrets held by that shimmer? It could be mimicking the shimmer with its shifting pigments.

It could be mimicking the shimmer with its pigments.

It could be—

Saba pulled her datatab out of her satchel and tapped to footage of the anomaly captured by one of the probes. There was no mistake—the colors and the mode of fluctuation were identical. She knew those colors and that wavering pattern were familiar! On the lower level of the sphere, where the octopus hovered, polished screens of recorders glinted in the low light. She slipped her shoes back on and, leaving her things behind, headed down.

A hush had descended among the observers, as everyone seemed to grok the octopus was actually attempting to communicate. It held its position, perfectly framed by two curved girders that hugged a segment of glass between them, like parentheses containing an aside. Saba walked the catwalk to the deck over which the octopus hovered like a stage. Was this a performance for their entertainment by this eight-armed showgirl of the deep? It was even bigger close up—its head as long as an average man is tall, its armspan quadruple that.

All its arms were arrayed outward from the nucleus of its body, ribbons of color forming the spokes of a wheel, the radiant beams of a halo, the arteries of a pulsing heart. Saba walked right up to the glass and met the alien eyes gazing at her from the other side of it. No doubt it was looking at her. The rippling hues settled into a vibrant yellow that pulsed in a steady rhythm before shifting into more ordinary mottled browns and reds. Its pupils were dark, elongated crescent shapes set in golden orange eyes. Then it brought all its arms together and, pointing itself like a missile, it dove down down down into the darkness that opened below them.

Murmurs arose all around once more, breaking the reverent hush that had descended.

"The anomaly was that same color in the last footage," somebody said. It was Chen, one of the other researchers. He held a tablet out toward her, playing footage of the anomaly from one of the remote cameras. It was indeed that same yellow. She knew it, the color, the patterns. But that made no sense, and yet.

It felt like a greeting. A call to return.

⁂

Later, Saba met her friend Ruby in the canteen for supper. Protein cake and greens, some seaweed salad.

"It really is the strangest creature," Ruby was saying. "Its bones are hollow, like a bird's. The shape of its body suggests it would swim, and yet it drowned. And there's the matter of its mode of breathing, of course. It can't be an aquatic lifeform."

"What do you suppose that means?" Saba pushed food around on her plate. She didn't have much appetite, as her mind was full of eyes looking at her: a dozen dead eyes on a table. The living eyes of the octopus with its crescent moon pupils.

"You know what Hutcherson thinks."

"That it came through the anomaly."

Ruby nodded. "There's strange radiation coming from it. Microwaves. Gamma rays."

"So what do you think?"

A look Saba couldn't quite parse swept over her friend's face. She finished chewing, swallowed, sat quiet for a moment. "That there are things in this world we don't understand."

Saba set down her chopsticks. "And what does that mean?"

"Maybe it's a portal or a wormhole or something."

"Do you really believe that?"

A sigh. "The only thing about all this that I believe for sure is that maybe we are being called to believe the unbelievable."

Saba grunted. What the hell kind of answer was that?

Back in her quarters, Saba reviewed footage of the octopus that had been uploaded to the central server. The colors flickered even when she looked away, shapes blinking in and out of existence: luminous tails. Clouds. Stars streaking in their cosmic dance. She slowed the footage down to half speed and watched the mesmerizing waves of colors. The pattern of them unlocked some kind of code within her, she didn't know what. She was more aware than ever of the remove at which she held herself, her invisibility in the eyes of the community of the ship. She was more aware than ever that this was her preferred state, and of the feeling in her bones that she was among these people but not of them. These feelings frightened as much as they allured. Then the golden yellow of its final emanations before it took off. The same yellow as the anomaly down in the deep. Was Ruby right, that it was a portal? To where?

The moment of eye contact with the octopus came to mind and those eyes with the alien arcs of their pupils replicated until there were dozens, hundreds of them all looking at her, seeing her.

Seeing her.

When Saba finally put her tablet away and lay down to sleep, the dark behind her eyes wasn't dark. Shadowy figures glinted from the recesses of her mind—were they her unconscious fears and thoughts taking on nebulous shapes? Octopus arms reached out to her with radiant glimmer, enfolding her in streaming colors. Constellations emerged and the stars were little gems, gems like—

She opened her eyes and sat up in her bunk, knowing that sleep was futile tonight. She pulled on coveralls and shoes and made her way to the lab. She exchanged perfunctory smiles and nods with those she passed—familiar faces, but nobody she knew all that well.

"Late night?" a man about her age asked as they passed each other.

"Thoughts," she blurted out. "Racing thoughts."

"Okay," he said as if trying to calm her down. She couldn't tell if she liked that or not.

Hutcherson was at the lab when she arrived and didn't seem all that surprised to see her. The creature still lay on the slab; the dissection was to begin in the morning. It looked different. What had changed?

"It was in the icebox," Hutcherson explained. That's what they called the freezers where they kept specimens. "I was getting ready to leave for the night when I heard this clattering sound." He held up a plastic tub full of diamonds. No—not diamonds.

She stepped up to the carcass and spotted the difference—the body had less shine to it, less shimmer. The crystalline growths were gone. "Are those—?"

Hutcherson gave the tub a little shake and the little crystals or whatever they were tinkled. "They all fell off," he explained. "Whether that's a typical postmortem phenomenon with these guys or a reaction to the cold, I don't know." He set the tub down. "But my head hurts thinking about it. I need to get some shut-eye. You up for a while?"

She nodded. "A bit."

"Well, I wish you deep and pleasant contemplations. See you in the a.m."

When she was alone, she walked to the creature's head and, resting her hands on the table, bowed down and looked into its eyes. Was it the light playing tricks, or did the eyes seem no longer clouded over with the fog of death? They twinkled. They beckoned. *Look into us, look into you*, they seemed to say. *Come home*.

She gazed into the dozen eyes, clear, blue, like marbles. Each eye a moon, a world unto itself. From the orbs of those worlds, a dozen inquisitive minds like hers gazed back and wondered what the devil sort of thing she was.

The fallen crystals lay gathered in the little tub Hutcherson left on the table. They sang to her, a keening. She plucked one up—it was cool in her palm.

こ

When it came time to perform the dissection, she could swear the crystal in her pocket vibrated, she could swear it sang a song of farewell. A clear, mournful tune rang in her ears. The others didn't seem to hear anything—but she had claimed the crystal in her pocket, so maybe it only sang to her? Still, she was a little afraid the others would hear it, but nobody seemed to.

The team ran through the standard protocols: tissue samples, the weighing of organs. The creature was even more confounding once they looked at its innards. The hemolymph was the only fluid—there seemed to be no waste matter, no digestion. A sort of heart, a dense brain that bloomed to quadruple the size when it was removed from the skull. How the hell did this thing survive? Did it eat, drink, breathe? The breathing they had a hypothesis for—the pores of its skin, the tracheal system. But the rest of it made no sense. Its musculature resembled that of a snake's.

It was when they got to the eyes that things got really strange. From the scans, they determined each of the eyes contained a lens in the form of a solid sphere—similar to fish eyes. But they were not prepared for what they found when they removed one. Its surface was opalescent, and when it was magnified by their microscope, it looked like it contained a field of stars, a whole cosmos, alien constellations.

"Wow," Ruby muttered as she gazed at the display.

"Do you suppose all twelve eyes are like that?" asked Hutcherson.

"My guess is yes," Saba said, transfixed by the patterns in the eye. What were those spots, those glints? Did they effect the creature's vision? And through twelve eyes? What did the world look like to this thing? There was something cogent in the patterns—a language she could almost understand. Not understand. Remember.

"We need to send a probe through the anomaly," Hutcherson said. "See what kind of environment it came from."

Saba had wanted to object that there was no evidence it came from anywhere else, that the anomaly was a portal to some mysterious other place, but something echoed in her at the sight of the patterns the microscope revealed, the singing of the crystal in her pocket, the streaming colors of the octopus. A recognition she did not get from the people around her, that she never got, her whole life.

"I have to see it for myself. The anomaly. Can I get down there?"

Hutcherson and Ruby gave her looks like they were trying to figure her out, which she was used to, from everyone, all the time.

"Only the physics teams are authorized for direct observation," Ruby said. "You know that."

"Why do you want to see it anyhow?" Hutcherson asked.

How could she explain that it was calling to her through streaming colors and pinging tones? "There might be something to your idea that our friend," she gestured at their cut apart subject on the table, "came out of it. I'd like to investigate."

"We have all the telemetry," Hutcherson said. "Plus video capture."

"What are you thinking?" Ruby asked. Saba appreciated her friend's inquisitiveness, as opposed to Hutcherson's naysaying.

"Oh—I don't know—" She fumbled for something reasonable to say. "Maybe compare ionic charges from the creature and what's coming out of the anomaly. Maybe if we use a lens from the creature's eyes and filter the camera capture through it, something will show up. Maybe these things—" She picked up the tub of crystals that Hutcherson had gathered, sitting on a side tray, "do something. Have some kind of reaction. Isn't it worth checking out?"

"Wow, when your skepticism breaks, it really breaks, huh?" Hutcherson teased with a faint smile.

"I do tend to go all or nothing," Saba said.

"Well, you can ask," Hutcherson said. "But I think if you want more than the telemetry and footage we already have, it's going to be nothing."

꩜

She licked the crystal, unsure what compelled her to do it. But she did. She licked it and the tingle, and a strange sweetness lingered on her tongue for days. In the privacy of her quarters, she gazed upon it intently, turning it over and over. Its glint entranced. Once, she thought she'd spent only a few minutes looking at it, but it turned out to have been a couple of hours. She should have been concerned. She wasn't. In public, she worried it in her fingers, hand in pocket. Sometimes, she'd pat the outside of the pocket, to feel it through the fabric, to make sure it was still there. She didn't want anybody to see she had it—especially Hutcherson and Ruby. They'd know what it was right away. And how could she explain that she had an inexplicable urge to swipe a specimen? How could she say it called to her?

One night, Ruby pinged her tag—her friend's face looked bewildered, excited, scared when it appeared on the screen. *"Get down to observation sphere 1 right now!"*

Sphere 1 was the only one of the four spheres that lay fully below the surface. Saba's skin prickled with an anticipatory tingle and a light sweat as she dashed down to it.

"Headed to 1?" asked a woman in engineering colors.

"Yeah, I got a call."

"Any idea what's happening?"

Saba shook her head.

As the lift reached the sublevel where the sphere's main entrance was, the hush was palpable. There were whispers and murmurs, but it was largely quiet—the sort of quiet that only a large crowd gives. The quiet of presence, not emptiness.

It was crowded—more crowded than the spheres typically were. On the decks of every level stood groups of people with mouths agape and saucer-wide eyes. When Saba caught sight of what was outside the sphere, out in the water, she understood why. Dozens of octopuses encircled the outside of the dome, each as large as the visitor from before, each with all eight arms extended, making starbursts of their bodies. The tips of their arms touched the tips of their brethren above, below, and to each side of them, forming a sort of net. It reminded her of the pattern on the creature's skin, with each octopus head serving as one of the jeweled connection points.

They were all streaming colors in unison, the colors of the gateway: blue, green, yellow, violet, pink, red. It was as if they were filled with LEDs running a programmed sequence. Then, one at a time, at random intervals, they changed to yellow—that bright golden yellow color. The color of a flower her grandmother told her about once. Buttercups.

Ruby caught her eye from across the crowd and waved her over. She joined her friend on the deck, right up against the glass. "This is so wild," Ruby whispered.

Gasps rose all around as the pattern shifted again. Saba turned her attention from her friend back out to their visitors—a golden yellow S glowed in the octopi network.

"Are they really making an S as we understand—" Ruby began to ask but then the letter A cut off the flow of her words.

Then a B.

Then another A.

"Holy shit," Ruby whispered.

Those among the gathered who knew Saba turned to look at her, their faces fearful.

Saba herself was not fearful. A strange elation bubbled inside her.

∽

"No. Absolutely not," the Commandant said again.

"This is an unprecedented opportunity for interspecies communication," Saba said. She had never felt more lucid and direct.

"We're not expending resources to send you down there. And what the hell are you going to do once you get there anyway?"

"See what they want?"

"Don't be glib."

She could see there was no arguing with the man. She could see the fear in his eyes. And was that a tinge of jealousy? She had been called to a higher purpose and he sure as hell was not going to let some peon in the system of his ship get any sort of higher purpose glory, was that it? No. No, she was projecting and getting grandiose. It was this realization that prompted her to drop the matter. For now.

She left the Commandant's office and meandered her way back to her quarters. Everyone on board knew who she was now, and curious glances and stares met her walk to privacy. People gave her as wide a berth as the narrow corridors allowed, sometimes pressing up against the bulkheads so they wouldn't even brush shoulders. What did they think would happen?

Her tag pinged with communications from Ruby and Hutcherson, but she ignored them and silenced notifications. Once in her quarters, she pulled the crystal from her pocket, lay down on her bunk and turned it over and over in her fingers as she gazed into it. *SABA*, the octopuses said. They said her name. They glowed with the colors and the pattern of the gateway. There was no doubt an invitation had been issued. Could she hijack the deep-dive shuttle? She didn't know how to pilot the thing; she'd probably crash it or get lost in the dark waters. But how else could she get down there?

The crystal glinted at her. Colors streaked in it, like stars smearing with faster than lightspeed. Or at least how that impossibility of physics was depicted in old movies. Stars of another cosmos. Her inner cosmos. Her inner—

The tingle that had haunted her tongue for days returned, the glimpse of all those eyes. Before she could stop the mad impulse that overcame her, she did it—she swallowed the crystal. Then she waited.

～

It came upon her in the middle of the night, a cold sweat, a sharp pain in the belly, rushes of electric tingles through her body, down her arms and legs, searing behind her eyes, to the very top of her head, every hair a livewire. Her vision was distorted—rainbows around everything, even in the dark, and she saw two, three, four of everything. After switching on the light blinded her, she quickly dimmed it to its lowest setting. She ran to the mirror. Her eyes had a shimmery glaze over them, and bulbs were pressing outward from beneath her skin. A scarlet red ridge emerged from the crown of her head. Her skin was starting to look blue with hints of violet—

The gateway—Hutcherson was right. The anomaly was a gateway, and she had to get there now. She had to get off the ship. Already her breaths were growing shallow, and she didn't know how she knew, exactly, but some instinct told her that her lungs would stop working soon, and atrophy.

Her cabin door slid open to Ruby's astonished face.

"You didn't show up for shift and—" Her face betrayed her terror and alarm. "Oh my god Saba, what—what's happening?"

"Water," Saba croaked. "Out." She pushed her way past Ruby and headed for the nearest diving deck.

"We should get you to medical," Ruby said, grabbing her shoulder.

"No!" Saba bellowed, shoving Ruby so hard she stumbled backwards and fell to the floor. She began running. Vaguely, she heard Ruby calling somebody for assistance, but there was nothing anybody on this ship could do. Her course was set.

When she reached the deck, nobody was there—there wouldn't be unless a dive was scheduled. Ruby and Hutcherson arrived moments later and pounded on the door she had locked behind her, pressing their faces to the glass porthole. They cried her name, begged her to stop, but their voices were distant, unintelligible. She shucked herself out of her coveralls quickly—she could feel her arms beginning to lose mobility and fuse to her torso, she could feel her legs turning into not legs.

The door swung open, and Hutcherson called out, "Saba, stop!"

She faced her colleague for the last time, felt nothing, and dove.

The water was not as cold as she expected, but it also was not the environment she needed. Here, in this in between state of becoming something else, she could manage it, but soon she'd not be able to hold her breath any longer. She recalled, dimly, that the creature like what she was becoming had drowned. She pointed herself at the gateway, driven by some primal need to get to that light she had never even laid her own eyes on.

She wasn't alone in the water, and felt undulating arms wrap around her. It was an octopus—it was *the* octopus—the first one that had come. It enveloped her in a multi-armed embrace and dove. She wasn't breathing, but she didn't need to. She felt the increasing pressure of the water, but it didn't bother her. It was as if the octopus emitted some sort of field that cocooned her, but deep down she knew it wasn't going to last.

Down and down they dove, into a depth of darkness she had never known, yet she could see. A pod of sleeping whales. Sharks on the prowl. Down and down and down towards a golden light in the distance, on the side of a cliff wall. She had more eyes than two when they arrived at the golden glow that wavered with warmth and vibration. Some kind of energy. Familiar.

The octopus held her out with a few of its arms, as if she were a human baby it had been coddling. She looked into its crescent eyes. *Go home*, they said. It pushed her towards the light, and by her now many-faceted sight, she guided herself to it, propelling her body by instinct, as if she had been this way and moved like this her entire existence. She had to get through, get through the shimmery heat, get through the sucking sensation pulling her through a tunnel of light or a tunnel of light pulling itself through her—it was all the same—

She emerged into a field of stars, and she wasn't alone. There were hundreds, thousands, like her. They felt her coming. They felt her arrival. The flock of thousands of her kind floated in the void. Their tails fanned gently, glimmering in the light of a distant sun. A gas planet loomed below them, pink and orange and purple. They could swim out here, but they lived down there, in the clouds. That was home. The human she had been was gone, and she was this new thing now, but she was still called Saba.

And for the first time in her existence, she basked in the gaze of those who saw her. And it was what she wanted.

Donhagore

T.L. Huchu

IT HAD BEEN nearly three years since I'd been home when I received a letter from my grandfather telling me that a person I didn't know wanted to see me before they died. It arrived on a sunburnt yellow page with jagged edges, ripped out of a school exercise book. Grandfather wrote using tiny cursive, neat, but hard to decipher. Because the Shona language is non-gender specific when referring to people, and the name Donhagore is unusual, I couldn't tell whether the person was male or female as I wracked my brain trying to remember who they were. Maybe it was one of a hundred distant relatives whom I had great difficulty keeping track of, but they were surely old, for no one in my generation had a name like that.

The letter was urgent, though it had been sent last month and it had taken four weeks to arrive, Zimpost being what it was. A small miracle it got there at all, but our village Mamombe didn't have mobile reception despite neighboring Sanagwe and Porovi being connected. There were Econet and NetOne masts nearby, but because of some electromagnetic anomaly, you couldn't get a signal at ours. It didn't help that when the letter arrived, it was exam season at the National University of Science and Technology in Bulawayo where I was doing my undergrad in Applied Biology and Biochemistry. I was unsure why I took this particular course, which was only going to lead to unemployment after I was done. Zimbabwe isn't a beacon of biotech, and I'd tried to swap out to Actuarial

Science or Medicine after my first year, only to be rejected by the university administrators.

"You had the grades to do Medicine if you'd wanted to, but you chose this biology course with a lower entry requirement. It was an odd thing to do, Tamuka. You've made your bed and now you must lie in it. It would be unfair to the other applicants if you took a place on a course they could have gotten into, only for you to swap out later. In any case, the bursary you're on doesn't allow you to change course," the dean had said, after calling me in for a meeting when I'd appealed to move again after my second year.

I was stuck in a dead-end program, which I was acing, and in my final year the dread nothing was waiting for me after I was done was killing me. The university brochure had promised career opportunities that didn't exist in Zimbabwe. Instead of working in a lab in the city as I'd imagined, I'd have to go back home to raise cattle and grow maize, the same subsistence shit my ancestors did for hundreds of years. You don't need a degree for that. I'd screwed myself.

The one chicken bus that went to our district was an AVM from the Rhodesian days, a rust bucket whose metal flooring had holes through which I could see the chassis and dust road rolling underneath. It was packed, and the stench of sweat and boiled eggs was so thick, it overpowered the fumes that poured in from the broken exhaust. I had to stand for three hours before we broke down two kilometers from Porovi. This wasn't too bad; the bus looped from that village and went out towards Masvingo City anyway.

I grabbed my satchel and disembarked out into the burning sun, joining a group of women dressed in black as though coming from a funeral. They carried sacks of nyimo and nzungu on their heads with babies on their backs. Two of them had crates of Chibuku beer, and another had bottled beer. In my left hand I held my small leather-bound journal, and I had a ballpoint pen tucked behind my right ear.

"Are you not the graduate—Sekuru Jengaenga's grandson?" the older woman asked.

"I am," I replied, embarrassed I didn't recognize her.

"Greet me properly, child. Have you become so arrogant you think you are an Englishman now, with your dress pants and Edgar's shirt?" she said with a mocking laugh.

She was a sturdy woman, her face was cracked like elephant hide polished with Vaseline, and she had one overlong incisor that poked out even when her mouth was closed. I clapped my hands and gave her the "Makadini henyu" greeting the elders demanded when you hadn't seen them for a long time. The other women eyed me suspiciously, like I was something obscene that had washed up mysteriously. I had changed since I went to university, not just in the sense of turning twenty-one, but I tried to dress more like the city boys now.

"I hope you can at least still walk the fifteen kilometers home, or have you become too posh for that?" the old woman said.

"They fill their heads with English in the city and make them forget their own people, Mai Marange," her companion wearing a torn doek replied.

"I'm coming back to see Donhagore," I said.

"Who's that?" Mai Marange asked with a frown.

I kept quiet, feeling silly, and followed a few steps behind the women. Despite the load on their heads, they kept up a relentless pace and sweat rolled down my face and poured out from under my armpits. The strip road towards our village wasn't well maintained; grass spilled in from the verges. The tar was potholed. Miombo woodland stretched out into the horizon, and I dreaded the long walk ahead.

There was something very wrong with me, and I hadn't been able to tell anyone. The journal I was holding, in which I carried Sekuru Jengaenga's letter too, was one I'd been keeping since I was in high school. I didn't write in it daily, but every so often when something of note happened, the numerous times I'd fallen in and out of love with women I never told, wisdom gleaned from conversations with my lecturers, details of parties, that kind of thing. But when I read the bits from home in Mamombe it felt like I was reading someone else's work in my own handwriting. The passages sometimes made no sense or referred to things I simply couldn't recall. There were illustrations of pods with compartments which I couldn't recall ever drawing. This scared me.

At NUST, a good few students flamed out or freaked out. My friend Varaidzo, who was in the second year of an Applied Mathematics degree, was currently detained in Ingutsheni Central Hospital after she stripped naked and chased people on campus with a butter knife, unprovoked. She'd been screaming obscenities in Latin and her folks said she'd been bewitched by relatives jealous that Varaidzo was the first in her extended family to go to university. Others' grades dropped, and they flunked out, nervous wrecks, where they'd once been confident and smart. Was this how it started, losing your mind? I had to keep my shit together, but I was scared that my relatives were using juju on me. They were trying to steal my destiny since I was an orphan; my parents died when I was still a child.

Flies hovered around my head, and I swatted at them with my journal, but they wouldn't leave me be. The chemicals I was using to soften my afro must have attracted them. The women sang songs from the Zion Christian Church as we walked. These were sad songs, and I remember feeling like we were doomed. Fire and brimstone, that kind of thing.

The temperature dropped suddenly, like I'd been plunged into an ice bath though the brilliant sun was overhead. I shivered and didn't say anything as the women sang on like nothing had happened. I blinked hard. There was something not quite right. Maybe we'd changed direction without me noticing, but the sun had been over my right shoulder and now it was to my left. My shadow was short like noon though it was surely past four. I checked my phone. The time was correct, but the signal had gone.

"Why are you still following us like a lost calf?" Mai Marange asked. "The path to your homestead is that way, and we will join you tonight."

"Oh, of course. I, I, yes, I remember," I said, hiding my uncertainty. There was a path branching left from the strip road, leading towards a small conical hill bare on top with trees and shrubs growing on the sides. There was a homestead at the foot of the hill and some fields. The roofs of the huts reflected silver sunlight like large mirrors instead of the grass thatch used by the other villagers. This was home? It was. There was an entry in my journal about climbing the hill to gather the Resurrection Bush, which Sekuru Jengaenga liked to boil for his evening tea before bed.

Those were my memories. I was sure of it even as I stumbled and nearly twisted my ankle stepping into a mole hole in the unfamiliar path. I steadied myself and checked that my foot was okay before limping back.

Two sandy colored mongrels barked aggressively as I approached the gate to Sekuru's homestead. They were skinny, ribs poking out, and they stopped, growing excited, and wagged their tails to welcome me. The gate had long fallen off its hinges, and there was no fence around the property.

It's as if Grandfather had decided we needed a gate along the path because that's what people in the city had. He was out sitting in the shade of the musawu tree drinking beer with Chief Chauke, who ruled over our district. My grandfather was the Sabhuku who governed our village on the chief's behalf.

"You are too late, Tamuka," Grandfather said. "Your best friend is dead, and they've left us in quite a pickle."

"It's bad luck for a foreigner to die in one's village. You cannot mix their ancestors with yours," Chief Chauke said.

"My great grandfather gave Donhagore land to settle on with the understanding they would soon return to their kind, but they never did. It was the same mistake we made with the white man when he came to our corner of the earth. We've been stuck with them since."

I gasped involuntarily. If Donhagore had been settled by my great-great-grandfather, that would mean they were here before 1890, when Zimbabwe was colonized by the British. I'm sure it was the beer speaking or I had misheard. One must never say their elders misspoke. Instead, you blame yourself, even when they've said the wrong thing. And how could Donhagore be my best friend, yet I couldn't remember?

"Your grandson looks confused. It seems he has forgotten about our guest," Chief Chauke said.

"Before Tamuka was circumcised and became a man, he spent all this time in the cave on the other side of this hill with Donhagore," Sekuru Jengaenga said.

"Don't be too hard on the young man, even I had to be reminded," the chief replied.

The two men laughed. I placed my bags on the ground and crouched in the traditional style, waiting to greet the elders by their clan totems. A red hen walked across the ground with five chicks following it. I was exhausted and felt strange. My throat was dry.

"No need for such greetings. This is a funeral. Grab a seat on the ground near me and let me see you. How you have grown!" Sekuru said.

"If we bury them here, we are allowing an unknown spirit to lodge within our lands. In the towns, people are grappling with the ghosts of dead white people who have no relatives left to pour libation for them," said Chief Chauke.

"Their njuzu spirits are also grabbing people and turning them into mediums who do rituals with brandy. It's improper."

"This one will cause us problems. How do we calm their spirit, Jengaenga? It was your people that settled them on your lands."

"You could have overturned that. We have no land apart from what you have given us. Every tree, every creek, even the ants crawling on the soil know this country we are in belongs to the Mlilo Clan."

The chief smiled; Grandfather had spoken well. He'd exaggerated the Mlilo's importance, but even they were under the supreme overlords, the Hungwes. By marriage, our clan were the Hungwe's in-laws, and Grandfather once revealed to me the Chaukes were ever wary that the Chieftainship should be wrenched from them and given over to our clan, since the Chaukes were Shanganis, migrants to this land who'd come north, fleeing South Africa when the Zulu Empire fell. They'd won their place here, but knew what was given could be taken away.

"We must consult the ancestors," I timidly suggested.

The elders ignored me. I'd tried to plant a seed. It was simple, even if I didn't fully understand what was happening; whenever there was a problem we turned to the ancestors, though every Sunday we pretended to worship the Christian God. The old ways were strong, rooted into the soil that gave us sustenance.

"I know you're tired from your traveling, but come, it's getting dark. Let us go and see your friend, Tamuka," Sekuru Jengaenga said, rising from his seat. "We already consulted the spirit medium, and she said you were the only one who knew what must be done."

"The boy looks even more lost than before," Chief Chauke said.

"They forget our ways so quickly when they go to the city and start eating with forks and knives, these young ones."

"Even his accent—"

I followed the old man to the circular path that went round the hill. It was possible to go over the hill, but Grandfather was more stooped than I recalled him ever being. His cane was silver and shiny, fragile looking like a fishbone. It had a sulcus in it, a groove running along the shaft. What manner of beast had that come from? Both he and the chief were dressed in black, and once again I felt out of place. I no longer quite fitted in the village I grew up in. My feet ached and so did my heart.

It was getting dark, but the shadows were still short, mine stubbornly under my feet. There was still a bit of sunshine, the horizon tingeing orange, yet the stars were already brilliantly visible in the sky. The msasa and mopane and munhondo trees were mixed in with shrubbery lining the path, but once we got past the muuyu, as we rounded the hill, the plants changed. I passed what resembled a purple cactus, thick and fleshy, with three branches pointed up like a garden pitchfork. The ground near the path was filled with fleshy round balls of the same color. It looked like someone had grown a large cabbage patch stretching out at least twenty hectares.

"I don't remember these plants," I said.

"Yet, you used to tend their garden," Grandfather replied.

"Have you tried eating these?" the chief asked.

"If I had a dollar for every time you came here and asked me that question, I'd be a rich man," Grandfather said.

"I wonder what else we've spoken about during my visits."

"Maybe this time you'll remember to collect our taxes."

Sekuru Jengaenga laughed loudly, and I remembered that he'd told me that the people of Mamombe had not paid their dues for two hundred years. I retrieved my phone and took a photo of the strange purple plants. I noticed how they pulsed as if they had a heartbeat. They smelt like rubber and sugar. No, it was more cookie dough. The scent was thick and cloying, sticking onto the hairs in my nostrils.

There was a large skeleton, much like a whale in the middle of the field ahead. The bones of this thing were silver like Grandfather's cane. There was a clear spine running from curved front to the back, but instead of ribs there were lattices, interlocking bone arcing towards the ground. It looked familiar, something out of a dream artificially sculpted onto the purple cabbage patch.

There was a cave on the northern aspect of the hill. It had a narrow entrance one could easily mistake for a crack given the size of the granite dwala.

"Tisvikewo," Grandfather said, clapping his hands and entering the cave.

I briefly hesitated by the mouth of the cave and then followed. The walls near the mouth of the cave had Khoisan rock art of animals, the eland and the giraffe, rendered in an oxblood tone. They showed men and women hunting with bows and spears. It felt much colder within the cave, and the rock art gave way to purple symbols, which I'd have called hieroglyphs, but they seemed too wavy and were all connected, such that there was art from wall to ceiling in the cave. These glowed in the dark as we reached a large, yawning cavern.

"Did they ever tell you what these symbols meant?"

"They are beautiful," I replied. "That's someone human like us, pointing to a star. Which constellation is that?"

"What is the boy talking about?"

"Tamuka used to say he could read all this when he was five years old. I think that's when Donhagore took an interest in him."

The floor of the cave had more symbols, and in the middle of the floor was a body under a blanket. It was small, barely four feet tall, and I found myself fighting back tears. An overwhelming sadness overtook me, and I fell onto my knees. You can't hold back the ocean, and I began to sob. The grief was sharp and turned me inside out. Donhagore was dead and I'd not remembered them. It was as though the loss of my own parents had come back to me, magnified.

Grandfather put his hand on my shoulder.

My best friend had died away from their people. I'd not been there for them.

"They were as mortal as we are," Chief Chauke said. "Death is truly the master of this universe."

"Their soul will be left to wander the wilds if you do not tell us the necessary rites," Sekuru Jengaenga said, anxiously.

"The worst fate of all."

Our people went to the halls of our ancestors, kin meeting kin, in a land where the grass grew tall and the cattle were fat, beer was plentiful, and the rains always fell on time. But Donhagore didn't eat meat. They liked sorghum and rapoko, though—the only food of the Earth they would partake. I looked at the star charts on the walls of the cave and recalled nights standing atop the hill, or at the mouth of the cave with them pointing out different stars with their two slender, nailless fingers. I didn't know if those were worlds they'd visited, for they had no language. They wore no shoes and walked on stumps like stilts that didn't bend at the knee like we do, but there was something resembling an ankle at the bottom of the stump.

On the drawings on the cave walls was a star they returned to again and again. It was clear this was important to them, and I thought that was their home world. These hieroglyphs were bringing back to me what my own writing had failed to. Then, I recalled Chief Chauke saying that he too had to be reminded every time he came back.

"Donhagore makes us forget," I said.

"Only when you're in this village can you know of them. Once you leave, they slip your mind like a brief acquaintance," Grandfather replied. "That's why I doubted when you said you were going away to study so you could help them. Their knowledge far exceeds ours. How can you aid that which you cannot understand?"

"But I promised to get them back. I failed," I said. I'd not even started in truth.

Since I was a child, I'd taken to playing within the bones of the whale outside. I was a nerd and didn't have too many friends. Most of the village stayed away from this side of the hill with its strange plants. It was too quiet, but I liked it. Donhagore would come out at twilight and watch me play. They were never out during the day; the sun was too bright for their fragile golden flesh. I thought they looked like dripping honey glistening even in the lowest light. There were no eyes on their face, though they had a narrow opening like a mouth large enough for a straw. They weren't blind; their skin could see whichever side of them you stood at.

I'd hide behind the strange cactus plants and watch them going over the whale. It changed depending on the season. When it rained, a bulbous tarp grew, covering them. Donhagore was most active with them, pottering around the whale, checking different bones, standing high up on the spine, feeding it the cabbage-like bulbs, trying to coax it to grow. They'd arrived in its belly. Grandfather heard a story from his own father about how it fell from a cloud with a thud and Donhagore had emerged, a seed falling out of rotten fruit. Others claimed the whale had grown out of the ground like a seed, leading to claims they were a demon from Hell below the Earth.

I watched how Donhagore stroked certain parts of the bones with their fingers, and the work they tried weaving dangling bits of flesh together as the women in the village made reed baskets. Young and brave, maybe foolish, I tried to help with the weaving. It tingled my fingers. Donhagore would watch me and occasionally fix something I'd messed up. They pulsed sometimes, and I took that to mean they were happy. We'd be under the wet, fleshy whale and they'd point up to the stars.

Donhagore liked the sound of drums. They came nearest the homestead whenever we had a bira or jiti, celebrations for death or harvests, when people would come from all over the village to drink beer and dance. Then Donhagore would sway; maybe that's how they danced, swaying in, approaching the bonfire where young men and women danced mbakumba around the fire. In those moments, they would be one of us, a small golden alien dancing to the beat of the drums. One day, I heard their voice in my head during the drumming. A reedy voice. It spoke a language that sounded like a sad song without pause and made my skull feel like it was being sawn in two. This only happened once. . . or twice. Visions of kaleidoscopic mountains like jelly with beings like Donhagore going up and down them on all fours. This in a dark place, a dull brown dwarf shining overhead.

I believed that song was a call for home.

If we could fix the whale, Donhagore could go back to their kind. This is why I'd chosen my course, because I believed I could help them if only I understood more about this craft that grew itself, but always wore out. Maybe our soil made it sick, its exterior thick with a mucous-like membrane first thing in the morning. I worked when Donhagore wasn't there, and they inspected my work in the evening. They tried to show me things, but I only imitated them. I never understood what they were trying to say. No one could. Their thoughts, feelings, intentions were lost to us.

"How did you know they wanted to see me before they died?" I asked.

"They said your name," he replied.

"You mean to tell me they spoke?"

He shook his head and placed a finger on his right temple.

"What shall we do with the body?" Chief Chauke asked.

"Bury it beneath the bones of the whale," I replied.

"But we can't have their spirit lurking here."

"I'll be its medium and finish their work and send them home. This rainy season, I'll do the weaving until the whale is ready," I said.

"That means you will have to forget your studies. No more Bulawayo, lest you forget again," Sekuru Jengaenga said, gravely.

Donhagore had lived far longer than us and they were patient. Their work was one of decades like the building of a cathedral. If I left uni, I'd do the things I'd seen them do. I'd tend to their ship for them. When our people died, they became ancestors and came back to guide the living using mediums who embodied their souls. I would play the drums and call Donhagore's spirit back to our village and be their vessel back to the stars.

Grey

Ren Hutchings

ON ALL MY official documents, my place of birth is listed as *Bell,* which happens to be patently untrue.

Now, if you're going to be pedantic about it, nobody has ever been born on Bell itself. Barely anyone has even set foot on the planet's surface yet, and most of the people who live up here in the orbital industrial cities probably never will. It's just the way Central Admin records things; surface, orbit, station, whatever, it's all *Bell* to them.

But listing Bell as *my* birthplace is a little more untrue than it is for most. Because the ship I was born on was still in transit when I made my appearance. I arrived earlier than expected, and I took my first breath on the thirteenth of the month of Augg, while my mother's ship was passing through the warp channel on the way to the Bell solar system.

Which means—not that I can really wrap my head around the wormhole physics involved here, but as far as I understand it—I wasn't even technically in our current plane of existence when I was born.

Quite understandably, that was way too much of a hassle for the record clerks to bother dealing with. When my mother's ship docked up with a day-old passenger that wasn't on the manifest, some overworked administrator took the quiet and remarkably reasonable decision to just bump my birthday one day forward on my registration.

And so, as far as the official record is concerned, Edurin Grey Winstoane was born on the *fourteenth* of Augg, about two hours after that ship arrived at the orbital. A very normal birth, and very much within the nebulous administrative borders of Bell.

In some of my more superstitious moments, I wonder if some spell was cast upon me with that decision—if it was something in that lie that tied me to Bell permanently, and prevented me from ever finding the will to leave. Because I have never again entered the warp channel. I've never even set foot on another spaceship. I'm still here, living in the same orbital city I was supposedly born in, a lifelong part of what they call the Builder Generations.

Preparing this planet to be settled is actually going to take more than three centuries, and the effort is barely at the halfway mark. I've spent my whole life looking at billboards and simulations showing Bell's beautifully terraformed vistas and thriving mega-cities… but we're not at the phase where even a single piece of building material has been shuttled to the planet yet. The asteroid-mining rigs to extract the metals to even *make* those materials were only activated last year. We are a generation making the building blocks of a dream we will never see realized.

Most of the time, though, I'm not exactly sure how anything I'm doing is helping build anyone's future… least of all mine. Today is my thirtieth birthday, and I'm working as a Customer Experience Specialist in the Hyperreal Theater. And so far, this shift has been a total disaster.

It started when the ticketing system bugged out right after I got to work. As I stood there rebooting the core terminal with my fingers crossed and a prayer on my lips, I already knew in my gut that it was going to be One of Those Days.

And sure enough, before the 'start' prompt had even reappeared, Andee stuck her head into my pod with an apologetic grimace and said, "Hey, Grey. The cleaning bots are down for maintenance right now, but there's an incident in DSA. Could you please grab the mop?"

I had to hold back an eye roll. DSA stands for Deep Sea Adventure, one of our two dozen virtual experience chambers—the one that simulates a dive into some of Bell's underwater caverns. Of course, we'll all be long dead before anyone *actually* plunges into the planet's oceans, besides the automated exploratory dive-craft. But here in the Hyperreal Theater, you can experience swimming with deep-water fishes and bizarre sea-mosses. Right after a descent that happens to make a small percentage of guests intensely nauseated.

Andee is our shift leader, and she's one of my best friends at work—but she will not hesitate to pull out her seniority over me as soon as mop duty is mentioned. So I didn't even bother protesting; I left the core terminal still humming through its reboot sequence, locked up my pod, and headed for the janitorial supply closet.

I wish I could say it got better from there. But it's now four hours into my shift, and it most decidedly did not improve after the mop situation.

The customer currently standing in front of my pod is sticking his handheld device into my face, showing me an entertainment pass that isn't even valid for our compound. His group is looking for an opera performance that's happening in another arm of the orbital. I *think* he's yelling at me about how they're supposed to get way over to the Opera House in time—like it's my damn fault they went to the wrong place—except I can't actually hear him over the two small children who are having a screaming contest next to my pod.

Finally, he snatches up his device and storms off, and a parent appears to collect the two shrieking toddlers. I take a long, steadying breath as I go to process the next customer's ticket.

"Welcome to the Hyperreal Theater," I say, pasting on my chirpy customer service smile. "How are you today?"

"One for First Footfall," the woman says without a word of greeting. Of *course*, because the rudest guests pretty much always book that one. First Footfall is the Hyperreal Theater's most expensive premium package, our longest and most detailed experience. A full-day simulation of the whole process of settling on Bell's surface. It follows the journey all the way from orbit to the balcony of your new-built, solar-powered house in the shiny new settlement. *Belltoll*—that's what the city will be called a hundred years from now, when it's actually built.

I scan the guest's code for her, and immediately, I can see that we're going to have a problem.

ERROR 138—RESERVATION CODE ALREADY REDEEMED

I try not to sigh out loud. "Hmm. I don't suppose you already scanned your ticket at Entrance B, did you?"

"What?" The customer shoves her loaner experi-goggles up to the top of her head, as if to ensure I can fully see her glaring at me. "No, I obviously just got here! What's the problem?"

"Not to worry." I tap my way around the touchscreen, seeing already that there's nothing I can do to dismiss the error. "It's juuuust... ugh, hang on a second—"

I cast my eyes around the visitors' hall, looking for Andee, who's out there covering for one of the Floor Greeters. She walks cheerily along the guest lineups, making sure everyone's got the right lanyards on, telling them all about refreshments and ticket collection and the location of the gift shop. I mutter under my breath—I sincerely hope nobody in line for DSA is getting refreshments.

Andee weaves her way over to me through the crowd, a satellite dipping out of its orbit. As always, she wears something from her vast collection of space-themed button-downs. Today's is a high-necked ruffled blouse with huge sleeves. The whole thing is covered with images of craters and rocks, like the surface of a small moon. Like the asteroid I wish would obliterate us.

"What's up, Grey?" her mouth says. Her eyes say: *Never-ending shit today, huh?*

"System's saying this ticket's been used already. Five minutes ago, Entrance B." I point at the red letters on the screen. "But the guest says this is the first scan."

"Ah, yep. Error 138," says Andee. "There's probably been a duplicate reservation."

The customer glares spectacularly. "Which means...?"

"Just a little glitch in the system." Andee swats at the terminal with a smile, beaming at the irate customer like she just won a prize. "Means two reservations accidentally got generated with the same code. It happens sometimes if a booking is made just as the ticketing system reboots—"

"Look, I don't care," the customer snaps. The experi-goggles on her head almost go flying. "Can I get in or not? Just give me another ticket, right?"

"I'm so sorry. It looks like First Footfall is completely booked up for today," says Andee. "I'd be glad to give you a voucher for a future session. In the meantime, I can get you a complimentary pass for our Deep Sea Adventure, or the Mining Rig Close Look—"

"A *mining rig* tour?" the customer says, as aghast as if Andee had just suggested a tour of the nearest airlock. "Absolutely not! Why can't you make the *other* person take a voucher? This is *my* ticket!"

And that's about when I decide to leave Andee to it, and I slip away for my break. She totally owes me for the mop incident. Besides, it's my birthday.

I head out through the staff entrance and hide in the darkened catwalk that runs between two viewing chambers, and I finally catch my breath in blessed silence. Maybe in some alternate universe, whoever had the other copy of that duplicate ticket came to Entrance B five minutes later than they did. I wonder if that customer would've been as much of a pain in the ass when we refused entry... or if they'd have been even worse. Some days, the universe seems to deal out the shittiest possible version of everything.

I stand in the catwalk with my eyes closed for a long time—probably much longer than my break should've been—until Andee comes back there to find me.

"One of those days, huh?" she drawls, leaning on the guardrail. "Well...the good news is there's just three hours left on this shift. The bad news is there's three whole hours left."

"Yeah," I sigh, more dramatically than I meant to. "Happy birthday to me, huh?"

"What? It's your *birthday*?" Andee whips around to look at me with an incredulous laugh. "Grey! Why didn't you say anything! Damn, I would've at least let you off mop duty."

"It's just another day, what does it matter?" I shrug. "My official birthday's not till tomorrow anyway, if that isn't enough proof it's just a number."

"Wait, what?"

"They fudged my registration and changed the date on all my docs, 'cause I was born outside this plane of reality."

"Right." Andee laughs, but she gives me a look that's half pity and half consternation, like maybe this hell shift has finally broken me. "Tell you what... how about you fudge your hours today, then? Give me your staff pass and I'll clock you out when your shift's done. Scoot out early."

"I haven't made any plans—"

"Chhht!" She presses a finger to her lips with a hiss that brokers no argument, and holds her hand out for my staff pass. "Gimme. Go. Grab a coffee, take a walk, take a nap, whatever. But you're not gonna spend your birthday moping in the ticket pod on my watch!"

I should've known better than to mention my birthday to her. But when Andee makes her mind up about something, there's no budging her.

So I grudgingly relinquish my pass. I go grab my backpack from my locker and slip out one of the back doors. And—for reasons I can't fathom—I hop on the mag-train, and I ride it for an entire hour until it terminates at the Bell spaceport, at the far end of our orbital segment.

I don't make a habit of hanging around near the spaceport; one might even say I actively avoid it. Something about it has always felt *off* to me. I just get a strange vibe from it, ever since I was a kid. Like I have this deep-seated aversion to even the *possibility* of leaving Bell.

Some people would tell you it's the so-called "uncanny things" that make the spaceport feel so weird. There's this whole myth about supernatural energy emanating from the mouths of open warp channels... like some of that *thinness* that lets ships slide between solar systems is leaking out. 'Course, that's not solid science—you can't even tell where a warp mouth is located without special equipment. Nothing actually comes out of it, besides the ships that went in. But you can't argue with folk wisdom.

The old hands who've been in the orbital cities longer than I've been alive say you should never eat or drink anything while the warp channel is open, just in case some unspecified creepy thing should happen. Some people even put an offering of sweet water near their doorways the night before a ship is meant to come in, to ward off the "uncanny things."

When I was a kid, I had this book of old Earth folktales about the fae. I learned about how you shouldn't ever accept food or drink from them, lest you get trapped in faerieland. I wonder if that's related to the stories about uncanny things in the warp channel.

In any case, I think it's probably for the best that the truth of my birth wasn't properly recorded. Because I can only imagine what some people would think about *me*. Between that and the two little star-shaped birthmarks on my wrist—which our elderly neighbor used to call *fae marks*—I'd probably have been taken for some kind of witch-child or changeling. I laugh to myself, because if I had anything like supernatural powers, I certainly wouldn't be working in Customer Experience at the Hyperreal Theater.

When I hop out of the mag-train at the spaceport, the whole place is practically deserted. There's no ship due to leave today, so there's nobody in any of the waiting lounges. No one is here except a few maintenance staffers, and a round silver bot that's meticulously polishing the lobby floor.

The information signs high above the lobby show that the next inbound ship is expected later tonight. That means it's currently what those superstitious folks call the *witching hours*. The warp mouth is open—the incoming ship having entered the channel on the other side—and it'll stay that way until the ship pops out at our end.

I head up toward the observation lounge, that long, oval-shaped viewport where you can watch the orbital's docking bay. I wonder if anybody was up in this lounge thirty years ago, when the warp mouth opened ahead of my mother's ship. They had no idea that Bell's new Climate Regulation Technician was about to board the orbital the next day with a five-and-a-half-pound administrative nightmare.

When I get upstairs to the viewport, I go straight to the self-serve refreshments counter. I consider the single screen of beverage options for far too long before I settle on a cup of plain black coffee. It's only when I turn around again with the quick-printed cup in my hand that I realize someone else is already up here.

There's one guy sitting alone at a table right by the observation window, holding on to his own cup of coffee with the kind of two-handed grip that suggests he's barely keeping himself together. But when our gazes cross, he gives me a little tilt of his head, and motions with his hand like he's asking me to come sit down with him.

Being as we're the only two people here—two weirdos who've come to an observation lounge to look at nothing—it seems kind of rude to refuse. So I take my coffee and I head on over there.

As soon as I see him up close, there's a strange familiarity about this guy that tugs at me. He's a complete stranger, but I feel like I've seen him thousands of times before. I tell myself that maybe I've spotted him in the queue for the Hyperreal… but surely I would remember where I've seen someone as fancy looking as him.

It's immediately obvious that he's not from the orbital cities. He's probably a visiting investor, because he's dressed in a sharp-cut patterned jacket and bow tie, like one of those rich people that graduate from Starling. He looks the part, right down to the thick, jewel-encrusted eyeglasses that are definitely a fashion accessory. He's got heavy facial mods, too—pointed ears and little swirls of embedded pearls and shells and gold leaves that grow out of his cheeks like barnacles. It's the kind of over-the-top modding that looks real silly to me, if I'm honest... but if you can afford that stuff, you're far beyond rich enough not to give a damn what anyone else thinks of it.

As I approach, he's pouring sugar into his coffee—one entire packet, then two, then another. I grimace inwardly; I've never been one for sweet coffee. Andee jokes that I take it like I take all things in life: bitter.

"Mind if I join you?" I ask him. Despite his clear wave of invitation, I'm the kind of person who still needs reassurance that I'm not misreading things. I hate the idea of barging in on anyone.

"Not at all," he says. "Please." He's got a lilting, mellifluous accent, like aristocrats in the holos have. Definitely a Starling guy. Probably raised on a planet with normal gravity and everything.

I slide awkwardly into the chair across from him, feeling incredibly underdressed in my wrinkled work t-shirt. My own coffee is too hot, and it burns at my lip when I take a sip. I wince as I spill some of it right down my shirt.

"You, uh... you look sort of familiar to me," I say by way of conversation. "You ever been this way before?"

"A long time ago," he says. "But I was way too young to remember it." He makes a little discontented sound before he picks up his coffee again, and he takes a long, beleaguered sip, the way someone would take a fortifying drink of spirits. "I think I probably *should* have grown up here. Maybe I did, in another life."

"What?"

"Sorry," he says, blinking after a beat. "Spaceports... they turn me upside down."

I look at my coffee, and then at him again, puzzling out his odd phrasing. I don't understand exactly what he means. But just about all the super-rich folk I've encountered seem a little bit strange to me. Especially the ones who came after the resource harvesting started. I bet he's here to look at one of the mining rigs.

"So... what brought you back here?" I ask him after a while.

It's the kind of question that makes me cringe even as it leaves my mouth, one of those terribly vague platitudes you ask a stranger. I expect him to give me an equally vague answer, like *work* or *business* or *my investment portfolio*. He might give me a friendly, conspiratorial aside about why this or that asteroid-mining company is the hottest rising stock… if I looked like the type of person who has ever bought a stock in my life.

What he actually says is: "It's my birthday. Existential crisis."

"Oh!" I startle in surprise. "Well, damn! Me, too!"

I guess it's not *that* unlikely to share a birthday with someone. There's only four hundred days in a standard year. Still, I imagine it's substantially less likely to meet one of them *on* your birthday, while having an existential crisis in an empty observation lounge at the spaceport where you supposedly came into this world. I doubt very much that he was born in the warp channel, though. I laugh to myself at the thought.

"Well… in that case, we should toast to a good year," he says. He gives me a half-smile that looks almost sad. But maybe I'm projecting. It's kind of hard to read subtle facial expressions on someone with that many mods.

I wonder how old this guy is. From what I can see of his actual face, he looks about my age, but anyone with the currency for those luxury mods could probably afford life-extension treatments too. For all I know, he could be old enough to be my grandfather.

"Happy birthday!" we say at the exact same time, raising our cups to one another.

And then we drink.

I tip my cup all the way back, draining it like a shot. The sugar that's settled in the bottom rushes into my mouth, and I crunch it up between my teeth. Maybe three *was* too many packets.

As I set down the empty cup, my companion is fishing a napkin out of his backpack, dabbing at the coffee he's spilled on the front of his t-shirt. It's got a company logo on it that looks like a happy cartoon mouse—a grinning critter wearing big blue goggles. *Experience The Hyperreal*, it says. An ad for some kind of theater, probably one of those experiential places.

He crumples the napkin and puts it down, and for a second, I think he looks a little sad. But maybe that's just what people look like with natural facial expressions. I really don't know many un-modded folks.

In this light, it's easy to imagine that maybe he looks a little bit like me… what I would've looked like without my mods. If I'd been allowed to stay with my mother, and grown up in one of the orbital cities here above Bell.

If I hadn't been the first person ever to be born in a warp channel.

I don't remember my mother at all, but I've met a few terraformers from the old Climate Regulation department who knew her. Somebody told me once that she fought hard to keep me on the orbitals with her. They probably said that to make me feel better, but honestly, it only made me angry. Apparently the med-staff wanted to register my birthday as the *fourteenth,* and write down that I was born after the ship docked. They asked the administration to just fudge the numbers and avoid the whole logistical fiasco.

But I guess the clerk on duty refused, and said it would be against protocol or something. Of course, because when has a local administrator *ever* bent the rules?

After that, someone called the space labs at Starling, and that kicked everything off. I was taken to the university to be put under observation when I was eight weeks old. Edurin Grey Winstoane, living science experiment. One of my old nannies used to call me a changeling because of those little star marks on my wrist. She said one of the fae must've had their hands on me, that some uncanny thing grabbed my arm at the moment I was born.

I stayed under the Science Dean's guardianship until I was seventeen. But as it turns out, there was nothing special about me at all. No discernible physiological or neurological differences from a child born in regular space. And certainly no supernatural powers. I was completely ordinary, it's just my life that wasn't.

Eventually, some new scientific ethics board reviewed my case, and they determined that my guardianship was seized illegally by the university. That caused all kinds of PR mess and legal precedent, and pretty much everyone agrees now that it should never have happened. I never should have been taken from Bell.

Of course, I did get a free education out of it. I went to the top preparatory schools in the sector, and I graduated from Starling. I also got a huge financial settlement that was put into a trust for me. With a few smart stock buys in asteroid-mining, I've made enough money in the last ten years to put a serious investment into that new city they're planning to build on Bell.

I can easily afford life-extension tech, and if the current advances in bio-nano keep up, I might even live long enough to see the first landers come down to Belltoll.

But sometimes I feel like somebody *else* got my life. My real life, my ordinary life, the one I'll never get back. The one I was *supposed* to have.

I imagine it sometimes, what it would be like to meet him. What it would be like to *be* him, that uncanny changeling that came out of the warp channel and took my place.

For some reason, I've always thought he goes by my middle name, because it sounds like fog.

I always call him Grey.

By the Saber and the Spell

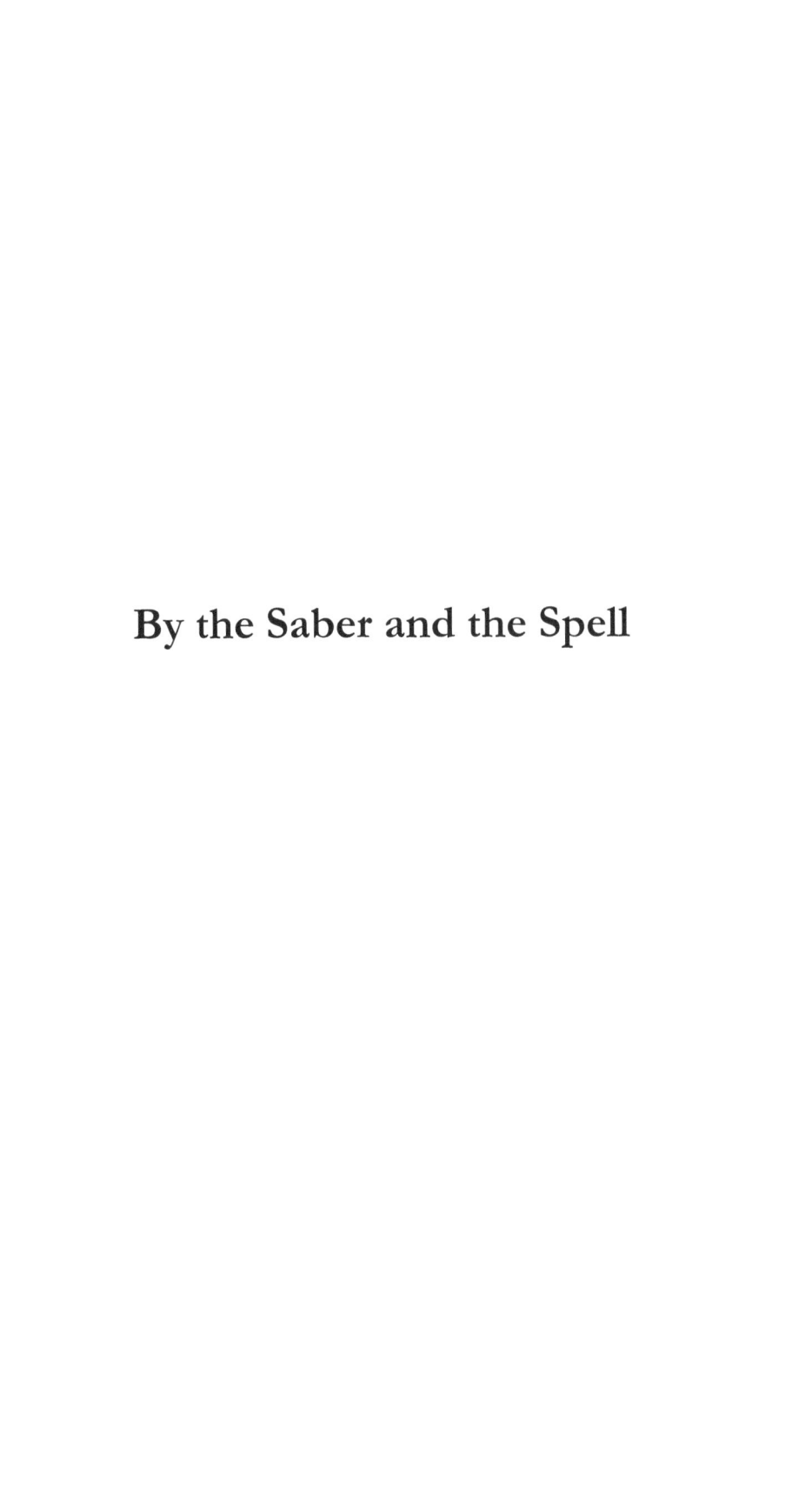

Holy Fools

Adrian Tchaikovsky

WHEN NENIVAR HAD been a child, there had been Ustorath, in the Golden Sanctum. The building that doubled as a grain storehouse, because Ustorath was a god of growing things. Nenivar's mother had been one of the priests, doing Ustorath's will "up and down" as she said, which meant she made sure the mighty of Jarokir received their proper tithes, and the impoverished their handouts. At the age of six or seven, Nenivar had assumed he would—being a boy, ergo ineligible for the priesthood—become a sweeper or a counter or a guard at the Sanctum, some lay role that kept him close to home. That was his future.

When the Palleseen had come, and defeated the Jarokiri muster, and raised their flags over the palaces and city halls, they had brought their laws, which were many. But chief among all those laws was just this: *No gods.* The Palleseen brought perfection, the best of all ways of doing everything. An ideal that divinity could not be allowed to meddle with. And so the Pals had broken the temple doors and drained the relics for their magic power, and taken away the priests, Nenivar's mother amongst them. Taken them away for "re-education" and, whatever they had learned there, they had not come back to share it. And the Pals had told everyone that they were liberated now, from those old chains of superstition, and here was the long list of new restrictions and forbiddances, to help people live more perfectly.

A lot of people had fled. Jarokir was no longer home, and the Pals made sure that anyone associated with Ustorath or any of the temples would never be permitted any decent work or station or peace. Nenivar's father, the lay sweeper, had fled, by spectacular mischance, to a farm on the outskirts of the city of Ilmar, across the sea. Because why would the Pals come *there*?

Nenivar remembered the flight, and the arrival. Somehow his father had maintained an iron purpose, taking them so far across the sea. They were going to start a new life. Raise a shrine to Ustorath on foreign shores. Sing the old songs and tell the old stories. Preserve what they were, in the name of Nenivar's mother and the Golden Sanctum.

Then they had reached Ilmar, the foreign city, with its lilting gabble of a language and its melting pot of immigrants, its new factories, its feuding factions, all of it. They, who had been Ustorath's chosen, carrying the god's faith away from those who would destroy it, had found themselves just two more foreigners in a strange place that didn't care about them or their songs and stories. And Nenivar, the child, standing in the crowded bustle of an utterly unfamiliar street, had understood that they had not, after all, brought Ustorath's grandeur to a new home. Because the Pals had murdered Ustorath back in Jarokir. Killed his priests and drained his relics and repurposed his holy places, so that the temple became just a grain store, and the priests' quarters a counting house.

Nenivar's father didn't live much longer than that, as though he had left some part of himself, some vital organ, back in Jarokir. But Nenivar—sixteen by then—was young, strong, and knew farm chores. Ilmar had a whole patchwork hinterland of agricultural plots, and there was always work.

Then, years later, after a string of other conquests that the Ilmari had watched philosophically, telling themselves, *They won't come* here *though*, the Palleseen army had marched in and brought their perfection to Ilmar.

          ~

The farm was owned by an Ilmari couple named Shem and Almhaiv. Of their three children, the dull one was still hanging around the farm with intent to inherit, the gifted one had won a scholarship to the Gownhall, and the brave one had been killed fighting the Pals in the early battles.

Before the Pals came, the family had gone every holy day to the Mahanic Temple in the city. They'd had icons on the mantle and quoted Mahanist maxims over dinner. There had been a lot of pressure on their foreign farmhand, Nenivar, to come along. He had sat, head bowed miserably, beneath the gilded ceiling and the resplendent candlesticks, as the priests had droned on about civic duty and acceptance. Dressed in opulence as they preached that everyone had their place and should stick to it. Nenivar, the immigrant, felt that he had no place. No place in the Mahanic Temple, certainly, and no place in the grace of fallen Ustorath. Through no decision of his own, he was as devoid of gods as the Palleseen.

After the Pals took Ilmar, it turned out that civic duty and acceptance suddenly lay in submitting to their rule. The Mahanic priests had decided that their creed allowed them to bend the knee even to the god-devouring Pals, if it let them keep their nice ceiling and candlesticks and costumery. And the Pals, cynical, pragmatic, placed grey-uniformed observers in the temple and vetted the sermons, and let the charade limp on because it was doing their job for them. And because they could afford to be patient, after all.

Shem and Almhaiv, new in mourning for their brave child, stopped going to Temple. Stopped mouthing holy writ at dinner times and trying to convert their farmhand. Nenivar recognised the looks on their faces from his own in the mirror. The way the Pal knife came in and severed you from your beliefs.

Life got hard, and then it got harder. The Pal grip closed about the city, and then there was an uprising that went very badly and became just an excuse for that grip to clench more tightly still. The tax gatherers who came calling had Ilmari faces and accents but wore Pal uniforms, and each year they took more.

Then came the infestation.

"I think we've got rats," Shem said, one dinner. It was the one meal Nenivar joined them for, as per Ilmari rules of hospitality. Conversation—previously mostly pious in nature—had become a matter of practicalities. The farm had never been easy, and new Pal taxes were just one more burden squeezing the life out of it and putting new lines on all their faces. Dinnertime talk had become a grim roster of everything going wrong, and of the latest bad word from the city, about who had been arrested and which businesses had closed down.

"You *think?*" Almhaiv asked him. "Either we've got rats or we haven't."

"There's something in the barn," Shem said. "Things getting moved about. The dog knows it, but he hasn't caught anything. The cows won't go in there."

Rats that spooked cows and couldn't be caught by dogs. But then rats had a dire place in Ilmari superstition, and also, there were worse things in the world than rats.

"Goslav's got a good terrier and some vermin charms," Almhaiv said. "And he owes us for milk. Nenivar, go to his place tomorrow. Tell him."

Goslav's good terrier didn't like the barn. When Goslav finally goaded the dog inside, it stood growling and snarling at nothing at all, and tried to bite its master's leg when he wanted to shoo it further in. He was a big man weighed down with his own bigness, all his flesh sloping and sagging, as though wanting to be done with his bones so it could take up a separate life somewhere else. His habitual mournful expression wasn't improved by the dog's recalcitrance.

He sat beside Nenivar to eat a lunchtime pasty, which from his expression tasted of bitter tears. He'd set his charms inside the barn, little papers with magic words on them, tacked up about the place. It would take time, he said. They might as well eat.

"Ain't rats," he confided, which Nenivar had already guessed. When they went in, all the charms had been defaced, as though some small creature had clawed at the sigils.

"Going to level with you," Goslav said. "Place is haunted."

"Ghosts?" Back in Jarokir they'd known how to propitiate ghosts. Jarokiri ghosts, anyway.

"You know Parnalli?" Goslav said.

"They arrested her," Nenivar recalled.

"She's freed. Misunderstanding. They thought she was a priest. Some places, that's who does the exorcisms."

Nenivar nodded. Jarokir had been one of those places.

"Anyway, they took most of her stuff and melted it down for magic, but she still knows the tricks. She owes me a favour. You quit me with Almhaiv, I'll get her to do this for you." Because nobody had spare coin, now the Pals had brought in their laws and taxes, but everyone owed favours.

※

Parnalli was younger than Nenivar had thought, an exorcist's apprentice thrust into her trade because the Pals had got through a few of them before accepting that Ilmari exorcism was not a priestly thing. Her box of occult paraphernalia rattled in a mostly empty way and her protective stole had been heavily darned. The Pals had not outright outlawed her trade, but made it plain it was frowned upon, tantamount to imperfection. Business had not been good.

She set up her circle and chalked her marks, going through the whole supernatural business with as much numinous reverence as Goslav had when he kicked his dog. She sat and listened, and then she tried some different marks, and then a whole other set she said she'd learned from an Allorwen conjuror, in case it was some sort of demon and not a ghost.

Then she sat and had lunch with Nenivar, just like Goslav had, because that was the way of hirelings together in Ilmar.

"Well, you've got something," she said, unhelpfully. "Definitely a presence. Not a ghost, though." Meaning no cast-off echo of some dead person that had latched onto the barn to prevent its eventual dissipation into the world. "Not reacting to any of the ghost stuff."

Nenivar pictured Shem and Almhaiv's reaction on being told they had some nonspecific supernatural infestation that nobody could shift. "What else have you got?"

She shrugged. "I'm out of ideas and you're out of luck." Then, after a sidelong look, "There's a man in the city."

Nenivar returned that look. "Hmm?"

"He's mad," Parnalli explained. "Or weird."

Nenivar, the Jarokiri whose childhood ways would have seemed very weird to the Ilmari, grunted.

"I heard of something similar, though. Where he turned up. Took it away."

"It?"

She waved at the barn, shrugged. And this man wasn't even someone who owed her a favour, just someone she'd heard about. Some penniless beggar on the streets of Ilmar, about whom a weird mystique had gathered. The holy man. The man with the box.

~

Nenivar didn't like going into the city. Still too crowded, polyglot, too noisy, unwelcoming, just as it had been when he'd first got off the riverboat there with his father. Now noisier, because the demon-fuelled factories ran day and night. Now even more unwelcoming, because there were Pal uniforms on the streets, keeping peace and enforcing ordinances.

The Pals had no time for beggars, and they flat-out arrested holy men, but Nenivar found Parnalli's man eventually, begging. Followed a chain of rumors and sightings. *The madman, the idiot preacher, the man with the box.* And maybe the man was or wasn't holy, or a preacher, or an idiot, but the box was a big giveaway. Not many people on the streets of Ilmar with a big wooden box on their back, holes knocked into it as though he was a mendicant pigeon fancier. He had a bowl in front of him, but in deference to the occupiers' preferences he was tucked in a side-alley where official eyes might not remark him. Nenivar and his father had begged on these streets, in those first weeks before the farm had taken them in and given them work. You got nothing, stowing yourself out of sight. And yet Nenivar watched the man from one chime of the city clocks to the next, and his bowl was never quite empty. There would always be someone stopping by with a coin and a word. Sitting with the man, sometimes. And it seemed to Nenivar that more passed between the holy man and his momentary companions than just money or talk. An invisible commerce. Unspoken penitence and wordless benediction. Exactly the sort of thing the Pals took you up for.

A dangerous man to be seen talking to, perhaps, but they needed a barn that the cows would actually enter.

The man glanced up brightly when Nenivar picked his moment to approach. Not the timeworn hermit the rumors had suggested. Under the grime and the multiple layers of cast-off clothes was someone of about Nenivar's own score and a half of years. Not some foreign mystic, either. Just some Ilmari down on his luck, and with nothing but that weird box to his name. Nenivar sat down beside him, trying for just enough distance that he could deny everything if some Pal informant were watching.

"You look like a man who's lost something," said the holy man. A voice devoid of awful grandeur, just that faintly musical Ilmari accent, which Nenivar hadn't quite grown used to, even now.

He frowned. "Not lost, no. Gained, maybe. I…" Abruptly he reconsidered. This was, of course, ridiculous. Here was a mad beggar with a box less holy than holed, and here was Nenivar, allegedly sane, about to ask him to come clear the barn of… what? He didn't even know.

He wanted to get up and leave. This was just one more Ilmari displaced by the uprising, living on the streets with some weird gimmick that somehow induced people to donate. Except Nenivar gave the instruction to his legs, and his legs seemed to say *Don't you feel something about him, though?* and didn't pole him to his feet and carry him away after all. Just kept him sat there until, eventually, he asked the question you never did, in this city, under this regime. "Are you a priest?"

The holy man smiled, almost embarrassed. "Me? God, no." And then, as though someone had prodded the correction out of him. "Used to be."

"A good business to be out of, these days," Nenivar allowed.

"Me and God, we parted company," the apparently-not-so-holy man said. "I broke His rules. He disowned me." Again that weird moment of unheard interruption. "Or it was me disowned Him. Disowning was involved." As though there was someone at his shoulder, sticking their nose into the conversation, save that the only thing at his shoulder was the punctuated top of the box.

Nenivar, who hadn't had any contact with the numinous since the fall of the Golden Sanctum, felt his skin creep, ever so slightly, and the hairs on his arms prickle.

"I suppose," said the holy man, "you want me to come and look at it. This thing you've gained." He peered at the handful of coins in his bowl. "Far, is it?"

Nenivar had given him a coin, but it was a very small coin, and also not legal tender under Pal regulations. He had promised the man milk and eggs and bread, though, and a roof and a blanket for the night, even a little of last year's salt beef, on the basis that Shem and Almhaiv wanted rid of whatever was in the barn. And the man had agreed, and they'd walked the long stretch out of Ilmar, along the good roads and then the poor roads, until they got to the farm. Then it had been dinner time, and the holy man had sat with them at table, which had been spectacularly awkward. A weird, pregnant silence that Shem's usual complaints had fallen into and been swallowed by. Until they were all glancing at the man, waiting before each bite. As though he might suddenly begin officiating at prayer, and they'd have to be solemn and on their best behavior.

And at last, the confession. Shem just blurting out, "We don't go to Temple anymore. We're sorry."

The holy man blinked at him.

"It's the Pals," Almhaiv added. And then, because that might just mean they didn't want the Pals to see them bowing the knee to the Mahanic altar, "After the priests started saying we should obey the Pals. Just so they could keep what was theirs. I couldn't." She spat, then looked embarrassed. "I'm sorry, Father."

"I'm not—" The look on the holy man's face suggested he'd had this conversation more than once. "I was never anything to do with the Temple," he said quietly. "But there were other gods, before the Temple took up all the space. Great gods once, and then later they were little gods. There were so many gods." He shooed away the unmoored apology. "I should be sorry. I don't do blessings. I don't bring good fortune or painless birthing or a decent harvest or any of that. I never did. None of it was every any use, really. A lot of nonsense. I don't blame the Pals for wanting rid of it." He smiled wanly. "But maybe I can help with the barn. Who knows? Stranger things have happened."

The next morning, Nenivar took him to the barn, and the holy man sat there, with his box on the ground, as the farmhand described the symptoms of the infestation that Goslav's dog wouldn't touch, and the haunting that Parnalli couldn't remove.

"I see." And the man did see. Nenivar's skin, which had just about recovered from sitting next to the man in Ilmar, started crawling all over again. There was nothing there, and the holy man's gaze was fixed on that nothing, following it as it moved restlessly around the barn.

Nenivar swallowed, and wanted to leave, then. Go, and hope the man did what he did, solved the problem, and then left. But he felt his duty, to the farm and to their visitor, and forced his feet to stay where they were.

"I was the last priest of a god," said the holy man. Then, at that unseen prod, "*Not* a great god. A very mean and insignificant god. The last priest and last worshipper. And we fell out, and so I stopped being His priest." He glanced up at Nenivar. "All my life I'd lived with God, you know? Seen Him. Not actually a blessing, honestly. He wasn't easy to live with. But He was there. And then I stopped being His priest. And there was a gap, in me. A God-shaped gap. And through it I saw all the rest."

Nenivar wished he'd gone when his instincts had prompted him, because this wasn't talk that could possibly profit him.

"This city, this land, used to have a lot of gods, before the Temple," the holy man said. "And then a lot of people came here from other lands—for work, for trade, for sanctuary. And they had gods too, and sometimes their gods were left here, like things stranded on the beach after high tide, you know?"

"Are you saying," Nenivar said levelly, "that we've got gods. In the barn. Like rats? Is that even a thing that happens?"

"All the time. Every place you ever went, that had a *feel* about it, you know? Maybe there was a god. Maybe the sense of welcome, of unease, of calm, of sadness. Maybe that was some little leftover god, still trying to be what it was supposed to be. Unseen, unheard."

"Except by you."

"Unfortunately, yes," the holy man agreed. "I don't really want to be the person who sees all the unwanted gods, mostly because they get very demanding once they know they're being noticed. But that seems to be how it's fallen out. This one is some sort of beast god. A hunter god, I think."

Nenivar started, trying to see the invisible nothing that the holy man's eyes were tracking. "Here, now?"

"Explains why your cattle weren't happy here, anyway," the man said.

"What beast god?" Nenivar asked, feeling... an absence, inside himself, where reverence should be. The absence that had grown after Ustorath had gone from his life.

The holy man's face looked infinitely sad. "I don't know," he said. "It can't tell me. Maybe some god whose groves or temples fell a thousand years ago. We forget our gods, you see, but that doesn't mean they go away."

He left after sharing lunch with Nenivar, and when he set back off towards the city, it was as though there was an extra burden in his box. After that, the cattle had no qualms about going near the barn, and the dog went in and caught rats there, and all was as it should be.

On the infrequent occasions Nenivar went into the city, after that, he sought out the holy man. In some alley or other, following a chain of rumor. Amazing how many of the occupied seemed to know where he might be found, and yet the occupiers never came for him. A curious odour of sanctity around the man who denied that he was still a priest. If there was a spare coin, Nenivar ensured it went into the bowl. If there was a heel of bread or a rind of cheese left over, likewise. And the man nodded politely, and gave no indication he even remembered who this random Jarokiri was. But he did, as later events showed. Ilmar was a city that had never hesitated to punish charity, before or after the coming of the Pals.

The next year, things got worse. Of course they did. That was life under the Palleseen Sway, a gradual and inexorable tightening of the noose. The excuse this time was some war they were fighting, somewhere else. A costly war, meaning the taxes went up. A bloody war, meaning Nenivar had to dodge the conscription squads seeking to make quota. And then the new man came. The chief Pal of an occupied city, they called the Perfector. The old one had been lethargic, corrupt, bloated by the curses of a city ungrateful for the perfection he had brought to it. He had been reassigned, or died, or gone mad, something like that. The new man arrived with a mandate from the Palleseen treasury to squeeze for all Ilmar was worth. Not money, or not just money, but magic. The Pals' dominion ran on magic, decanted from every artifact and relic and trinket they could get their hands on. From magicians, too, when they got hold of them. The new man came with a host of prying inquisitors, witch hunters and priest-finders. He came with special lenses that let him see the least possible glimmer of power that he could siphon away. The Mahanic Temple, preach obedience as it might, lost its candlesticks and its gilded ceiling, and any priest who dared to object. The Allorwen quarter lost half its indigent summoners and hedge wizards, and the stock of its arcane pawn shops and antique dealers. Trite, perhaps, to say that the Pals were draining the magic out of everyone's lives, but also literally true. When Nenivar walked the streets of Ilmar they seemed more grey and drab each time.

Around this time, the holy man started to call. Leaner and more harried now, because both begging and being a weird little holy man were trades that the Pals were even less tolerant of, under the new man's aegis. The farm wasn't his only port of call. He walked a wide beat, around the hamlets and houses in Ilmar's hinterland. But he remembered where he'd been made welcome, and he remembered where he was owed.

Shem and Almhaiv didn't want anything to do with him, but Nenivar met him, took him into the barn the man had reclaimed, and brought him a little lunch. Sat with him to eat, like you did, one worker with another, of whatever trade.

"I hope you don't mind," said the holy man, "if I leave something here."

Nenivar eyed him.

"Something precious. Something at risk. It won't be any trouble. I hope." The box was at the man's feet, as he sat on a haybale. Nenivar's gaze was drawn to the holes. Imagining things creeping in, or creeping out.

"You took something from us once, that we needed rid of," he noted. So many stories in so many cultures, about accepting the help of uncanny people, and the cost of that.

"I won't bring that back. I found a better home for a hunter than a barn." A little smile, a man incredulous at the words coming out of his mouth. "But other things. More fitting these surroundings, perhaps. Only…" And he trembled, just a little, just briefly. Shook, and then looked embarrassed at the fuss. "There are so many."

"These lost gods, that only you can see." Nenivar did his best to sound disbelieving, despite the services the man had performed in this very barn, a few years before.

"Well," said the holy man, "that's not really the case anymore, I'm afraid. The new man." Everyone referred to the current Perfector that way. "He can see them. He has people. Ratcatchers, they call them." A crooked little laugh. "All the little gods. And it's not as though there's much power in any of them, but if you get enough of them together…"

Nenivar eyed the man's box. When the holy man had arrived, he'd been bent under it as though smuggling lead ingots. When he stood to leave, he shouldered it without effort, and Nenivar looked about the shadows of the barn that his imagination was peopling with… what…?

"Nothing that will do harm," the holy man said. "Nothing that will spook the cattle. I promise. But there are so many, and I have to save them. Or what am I for?" A real question, Nenivar understood, because this wasn't some divinely ordained task, but just a man doing some tiny good in the world, under the shadow of the boots of the Pals.

The last time he saw the holy man was past midnight. A tap at the window of the little side-room Nenivar lived in, that had three outside walls and was never properly warm. And there, in the sliver of a dying moon, that slight, embarrassed-seeming figure with the box.

Nenivar brought him in, quietly so as not to wake Shem and Almhaiv. Stoked the fire and got some tea on. Eyed the box the man put on the kitchen table.

"I won't be long," the holy man said, when Nenivar offered him a place in the barn overnight. "In fact, I'll be very quick. You don't want them to catch me here." His face was haunted. "I just wanted…"

"To leave something else here," Nenivar finished for him. *You don't want them to catch you here.* Meaning certain activities had been noted by the occupiers, by the new man. Meaning even the tiny sparks of divinity the man had been sneaking out of the city were more than the Pals could permit.

None of the man's previous deliveries had so much as spooked a calf, so Nenivar shrugged. He'd thought the man would let his invisible burden loose in the barn, as usual, but that eerie gaze was watching a shred of nothing emerge out onto the table, right here in the kitchen.

Nenivar opened his mouth to say *No*. To absolutely forbid the release of any stray mote of divinity here in the house, where it might get him into trouble with the family. And stopped. Felt, in that empty place, a curious cascade of associations. His mother. The words of prayers he should have long forgotten. The hollow resonance of the Golden Sanctum. The hiss of grains against one another, poured out in offering.

"I…" he said.

"I think you lost something, when you came to the city," the holy man said. "It can be very distracting. A lot going on, and one's own beliefs seem very small. Hardly worth keeping hold of. Believe me, I know."

"Stay in the barn," Nenivar said. "Hide there. If they come, I'll lie to them."

He met the holy man's hollow, melancholy gaze at last.

"I really must be getting back to the city," the man said, shouldering an empty box.

"But the Pals—"

"There are so many more to save, you know?" That weak little smile, this weak little man. An inconsequential weight on the scales of the world, against the might of the Palleseen.

The next day, Nenivar went to a corner of the barn, and with a few loose grains of corn and some stones, made a little shrine to Ustorath, the grain god. It was not the Golden Sanctum, and his mother would have despaired, but it was all he had, and it would have to do. He looked about the barn, and wondered just how many other forlorn godlings the deity of his childhood was sharing it with.

Later, after he heard how the holy man had been taken up for begging, for religion, for *god-smuggling*, if that was even a thing, Nenivar went to a cabinet-maker who owed him for some eggs and a jug of milk.

"Make me a box," he said. "A box with a few holes." And the cabinet maker looked at him oddly and said, "Funny, you're the fourth person this week to ask for just that."

Hunger and the Lady

Peter McLean

THEY WERE EATING corpses in Messia by the end.

Nine months of brutal siege and the city was on its knees; even Billy could see that, young as he was. He only had eleven years to him, as he reckoned it anyway, but that was almost a man grown and he'd had to grow up fast after Da was killed on the wall. Faster still, when Ma took sick.

He caught rats for them to eat, him and Ma and little Joan who was just six. He was good with his sling, and he could drop a nice plump rat at twenty yards or more. There wasn't much meat on them, perhaps, but they were a lot better than nothing. He could bag two or three of them in a good day's hunting. Three was a good day indeed; that meant they got a rat each. He'd seen little Ellian from the houses down by the river eating a tallow candle the other day, trying to fill the gnawing hole in his belly. Both his folks were dead, Billy knew, and he didn't think Ellian would be far behind them on his journey to the gardens of the gods.

Not that the gods of Messia were still watching what went on in their holy city.

Not anymore they weren't.

"I saw the Great Temple on fire today," Billy said to his ma, when he came back that night. "There was soldiers everywhere, and all the priests was hanged by the neck from lamp poles."

"Enemy soldiers," Ma said, huddled on her pallet bed of louse-ridden straw.

Billy could hear the sickness thick in her voice, like there was too much snot built up in her throat.

Joan just looked at him from the bundle of grey rags by the cold hearth where she slept. She was grey too, the dirt on her face so ground in it was hard to tell where rags ended and sister began.

"Did you get anything, Billy?" she whispered.

"I did," Billy said, and he couldn't keep the pride from his voice as he held three rats up by their tails. "I got three."

Today had been a good day, as such things were measured now, but he had to admit the rats were nothing like as plump as they had been a few weeks ago. Even they went hungry now.

"You're a good lad," Ma said, but Billy could see how she kept worrying at her front tooth with her tongue when she spoke, and how it moved every time she did it.

It made him feel ill to see that. He turned away and took down their precious flint and steel from the cracked mantle over the hearth, and set about making a fire from the meagre store of kindling and sticks they kept carefully dry at the back of the room. Joan took out her little knife and started to skin the rats while he did it. Da had always done those things before, but now Da was gone and done on the wall and Ma didn't move much these days.

Billy met Joan's wide eyes over the first blush of the fire.

I know, that look said, but neither of them wanted to say it.

Neither of them could give voice to what they knew. Joan was too young to find the words for it, and Billy was too weary and too scared, but they both knew.

Ma was dying.

Ma was dying, and then it would just be the two of them.

There were so many dead in Messia that Billy couldn't have guessed how to count them. Nine months of siege and starvation and disease. The walls had finally fallen a week ago and now there were soldiers in the streets, looting what little was left and burning what would burn, working their way south through the city. Soon they would reach the street where Billy and Joan and Ma lived, and what then?

He had his sling, and he was good with it, but against grown men in mail and helmets?

No.

No, Billy knew he wasn't going to be able to protect his family when the soldiers finally came. He was only eleven, for the love of the gods.

He sniffed back a tear and put a skewer through the first of the rats Joan had skinned and gutted, and propped it up over the fire to cook. He supposed you didn't ought to eat just one thing all the time, and that might be why Ma's teeth were coming loose and Joan looked close to starving, but when there was only one thing to eat that was what you had and you made the best of it, so far as he could see. It was better than candles, and no mistake.

"Did you see the soldiers?" Joan whispered.

Billy nodded slowly. She meant the enemy soldiers, he knew that, and that it didn't need saying any more. They both knew there weren't any of their own left.

"Yes," he whispered back.

"Are they really demons, like the priests said?"

Billy shrugged. He didn't think so, but then he didn't know what demons looked like. They had just looked like men to him, and a few hard-faced women among them. All of them had looked fierce and hungry and dirty and angry like soldiers always did, whichever side they were on.

"Don't know," he said after a moment. "I think they're just folk, like ours. Made to fight by their priests, maybe, same as Da was by ours."

"Do they even have priests, where they come from? I heard they was godless."

Billy bit back a sharp reply that he knew his little sister didn't deserve. How the fuck was he supposed to know? He didn't even know where they had come from. Da had said they came from somewhere up north, but that was only because someone in the army had told him that. Da had been a potter not a soldier, before he was conscripted and forced up onto the wall with a spear in his hands to die alongside all the other men, so how would he have known?

"I expect they have their own priests," Billy said, after a moment. "Different gods, maybe. Maybe that's why we're fighting them. Don't know."

I don't care, Joan, he thought. What did it matter why the men were fighting? They were, and that was that, and that was why Da was dead and Ma was dying and everything was burned and dead and gone and there was nothing left for them to eat but fucking rats.

He started to cry then, hot and hard and angry. He didn't want to and he even less wanted Joan to see him doing it, but he just couldn't help it. Everything was gone and ruined and Da was dead and he was only eleven years old and it wasn't fair.

"It's going to be all right, isn't it, Billy?" Joan whispered.

Away in the corner on her straw pallet Ma choked on her own phlegm, spat a great reeking gob of it onto the floor, and sagged back into her blanket with a wet gurgle.

No, Billy thought. No Joan, it fucking well isn't.

Joan was the first to die, a couple of days later. The night had been freezing, and Billy woke in the pre-dawn light, cold and hungry as he was every morning. He lay there on the floor for a moment, huddled in his pile of rags and listening to Ma's gurgling breath coming from her pallet in the corner. It took him a minute or two to realise that he couldn't hear Joan's usual snuffles coming from her own bundle.

He sat up and poked the shape of her body with his toe. She didn't move, or make a sound. Moving quietly, not wanting to wake Ma, he wriggled over and pulled a grey cloth that might once have been a wall hanging away from Joan's face. She was quite still, almost peaceful but for the blue around her lips.

Billy knew at once that she was dead. He might only have had eleven years to him but he had seen enough dead bodies in the last year to know what he was seeing now. His little sister was gone.

Billy pulled her into his arms and held her close, sobbing quietly into her filthy hair as their bundles of rags entwined, his warm from his sleeping body and hers as cold as the holy sepulchre she would never have.

"I'm sorry," Billy whispered, his lips almost touching her cold, dead ear and the tears hot on his cheeks. "Oh Joan, I'm so sorry. I tried my best, I really did."

He held her like that for what seemed like a long time, rocking her tiny, stiffening body back and forth in his arms until he had cried himself out. At last he pushed her corpse away and wriggled out of his bundle, pinching his eyes between his finger and thumb to clear away the tears.

There was no time for tears; he had to be a man. It was just him and Ma now, and Ma hadn't got out of her bed since Da was killed on the wall. Billy was all she had left in the world.

He stood up and pushed his feet into the ruin of his boots, pulled the blanket that served him as a cloak around his shoulders, and picked up his sling and Joan's knife. He looped the sling though his rope belt as he did every day, patted his pouch for stones, and tucked Joan's knife through the other side. Armed, he felt more like a man grown.

I've only eleven years to me, Billy thought, but he pushed that thought away with a scowl. Childhood was past and done, ripped away from him, a luxury he couldn't afford any more. Be a man or starve, that was the choice before him, and Billy had Ma to think of.

He looked over at her, lying on her side on her pallet and drooling green snot onto her pillow of stinking sacking, and he sighed. He was young, yes, but he wasn't a fool. He knew Ma didn't have long left.

Joan's death was what finished Ma off in the end, Billy reckoned. She couldn't forgive herself, the way he saw it, not that it had been her fault. He remembered burying his sister's pitiful little body in the yard behind their house, and he had wept doing it but even rats were getting scarce by then and a small, wicked part of him was glad to have one less mouth to feed.

Two days later Ma was gone too, choked on her own slime in the night, and then Billy was on his own. He looked at Ma's body, and remembered how much work burying Joan had been, and shook his head in silent remorse. Burying Ma would take more strength than he had, and he knew she wouldn't be there to thank him for it. Her spirit was already walking in the gardens of the gods, so what difference did it make?

He left her where she lay, and he took what little they had left and he headed out alone into the ruins.

He didn't think he'd ever be coming back.

It was hard, that first day alone in the rubble of Messia. There were soldiers everywhere, sacking the city, but most of them were drunk and noisy and they were easy enough to avoid. Billy had spent a long time stalking rats through the alleys and middens of Messia, and he knew how to be quiet when he needed to be. No, it wasn't the soldiers who were the problem.

It was the other survivors.

The sun was just starting to go down when they grabbed him.

It was a lad, with maybe seventeen or eighteen years to him, and his woman had maybe sixteen to her. Her belly was already swollen with child but there was no motherly love in her face as she pressed a rusty blade to Billy's neck while the lad searched him.

"Knife and a sling," the boy said, disarming Billy with ease like he was a child.

Gods curse it, he *was* a child. He might be almost a man grown, perhaps, but this lad was a foot taller and twenty pounds heavier and there was no almost about it with him. Billy never stood a chance.

"Give me that back!" Billy shouted, and the girl pricked his neck with her blade until blood blossomed against his filthy skin.

"You shut up now," she hissed. "If the demons hear us we'll all burn."

"They ain't demons, they're just men," Billy said.

"Horseshit," the lad said, and he punched Billy in the guts hard enough to make him puke up what little watery filth was left in his empty belly. "They're fucking demons, you little cocksucker. The priests said so. We wouldn't have lost otherwise, would we?"

Billy drew in a shuddering breath and spat bile onto the boy's boots, earning himself a cuff to the side of the head for his trouble.

"Check his pouch, Lissa."

The girl thrust a thin, rough hand into Billy's pouch, her stinking armpit in his face as she rummaged.

"Stones for the sling," she said. "Hang on… flint and steel!"

"Give them to me," the boy demanded.

Lissa passed them over, but Billy couldn't help but see the flicker of reluctance that crossed her face as she did so. A flint and steel was a treasure indeed in Messia in these times, and now his had been taken from him. He had nothing else of worth.

"Now what do we do with him?" Lissa asked, looking at the hard-faced boy with wide eyes. "Don't hurt him, Jared."

The boy, Jared, just shrugged.

"You ain't keeping him," he said. "Got a brat of our own on the way, ain'ts we? I ain't feeding another one."

"But…"

Jared half-raised his hand, and Lissa cowered.

"No, Jared," she whispered.

"Right, well he can fuck off then, can't he?" Jared said.

Lissa looked down at Billy, and there was something on her face then that was almost an apology. Billy shrugged and backed away, hands held up to say it was done. He backed away a few more steps, then turned and fled into the darkness.

That was life in Messia, during the sack.

Billy was alone in the alleys, and the rain came down like the wrath of the gods. He huddled in his blanket-cloak, grateful that they had left him that at least. The doorway offered him scant protection, but it was better than nothing.

He was hungry, he knew that much. Oh gods, but he was hungry.

He would have eaten anything, had the world let him, but there was nothing moving and now he had no way to hunt anyway. Cold rain ran down his face and he considered going back to the house, but Ma was there lying dead and he didn't want to face that.

He huddled in the doorway, and he wept, and waited to die.

Come the dawn the rain had stopped and Billy hadn't frozen to death in the night after all. He rose shuddering with cold and made his way out into the thin grey light. He could hear voices in the distance, men who spoke with a strange accent.

Soldiers.

Instinct told him to run and hide, but what was the point? He had survived the previous night, but he knew his chances of doing so again were vanishingly small if he didn't find food and shelter soon. Soldiers would have food, at least.

Billy hugged a wall and crept toward the noise, his grey rags blending in with the damp stone and helping him to hide. He reached a junction where the alley met a rubble-choked road, and he made himself as small as he could as he peered cautiously around the corner. He could see smoke rising from behind a broken wall, hear raucous voices and smell... oh gods in their gardens, he could smell pork cooking!

Billy's mouth flooded with saliva, and he stifled a groan. He hadn't tasted pork in the better part of a year, and now his empty stomach tore at him with longing. He was shaking with fear as he crept closer, but need drove him and he forced himself to keep going.

Down on his belly in the rubble, Billy wormed his way up against the broken wall and held his breath as he risked a look around the edge. There were six soldiers, five of them rough men and one a scarred woman, all in mail and tattered cloaks. One of the men wore open robes over his mail and had a black hood pulled up over his head, but they were all intent on their food and no one saw him.

"Oi, Cookpot, there any more?" one of the men asked in his strange, thick accent.

"You've had today's ration, I ain't cooking no more now," another replied, a round-faced man who sat closest to the fire.

More, Billy thought. They've got more.

He stared at the soldiers' makeshift camp, trying to work out where the food might be. They didn't have a lot, just some bedrolls and a rough length of canvas that they had rigged up as a shelter, flapping in the wind. Behind that... behind the canvas was a pack. It was perhaps twenty feet away, on the wrong side of the wall. Billy swallowed.

He crept slowly forward, pulling his filthy grey rags over his head to help him blend in with the stone and rubble all around him. Ten feet. Six.

"Whassat?"

Billy froze, his heart hammering so loud he swore they must be able to hear it.

"What's what?"

"I heard something, down there."

One of the men was on his feet now, pointing away down an alley in the other direction. The scarred woman was on her feet then, swinging a loaded crossbow up to her shoulder almost faster than Billy could follow.

"I don't see anything," she growled, her voice rasping over the wind.

Billy took his chance to clamber over the wall and scuttle toward the pack. He plunged his hands into it and pulled free two packages of meat wrapped in oiled cloth. He stuffed them inside his shirt and managed to get back behind the wall just as the hooded man turned to look his way.

"We're all jumping at shadows," the man said. "It's probably just rats. Lady's sake, Bloody Anne, sit down and eat. There'll be killing enough later."

"Aye," the woman said, but Billy barely heard her.

He was already wriggling back the way he had come as fast as he could, with the precious meat clutched to his chest. Today was a good day.

Billy put his head in his hands and wept, the neatly wrapped packages of pork lying on a broken flagstone by his side and the dry sticks it had taken him all morning to scavenge piled in front of him. He had no flint or steel. Jared had taken those, so now he had no way to make a fire. He couldn't eat it raw. Raw pig was poison, Billy knew that, but the tearing hunger in his belly screamed at him to eat it anyway. Tears ran down his cheeks, tears of frustration and rage, grief and loss and sheer starving misery.

Something broke inside Billy then, and something woke and spoke to him.

"You can do it, my love."

It was a woman's voice, and for a moment she sounded just like his ma. It wasn't, though. Ma was dead, and the dead spoke to no one.

"You can do it," she said again, this lady who wasn't there. "Just push."

"Push what?" Billy whispered, choking back snot and tears. He got no answer, but somewhere in his head where the thing had broken he could feel something else, something that hadn't been there before. It felt hot, like a flame.

Billy reached for that hot place and he pushed at it, pushed with his mind in a way he'd never done before. It hurt, bright and sharp in his head, and he clenched his teeth.

"You can do it," the lady said again. "If you want to live, you'll do it. Push!"

Billy pushed and his head screamed fit to burst with the pain of it. The fire caught, sudden and hot in the pile of sticks, although he had no flint or steel and he hadn't even moved. It caught hot, and it burned bright. He quickly fed more sticks to the blaze, his hands trembling as he worked. The lady be praised, he wasn't going to starve after all.

They found him an hour later.

It had been foolish to leave the fire burning, he supposed, but he was almost warm for the first time in days and he had no idea if he could do the trick again. He'd tried, once he had eaten the first piece of pork and sucked the grease off his fingers, pushing this way and that with his mind, but nothing had happened.

So of course they saw the smoke, and they crept up on him and the first he knew of it he was surrounded.

"I think we've found our pork thief," the round-faced man said, the one called Cookpot, but he didn't look angry about it. "You must be starved, you poor little bugger."

Billy scrambled back on his haunches and made to run, but the scarred woman was there with her crossbow in her hands and he knew he wouldn't get ten yards without a bolt in his back if he did.

"It's all right, boy," the hooded man said, his accent strange to Billy's ears. "We won't hurt you. My name is Tomas Piety, and I'm a priest of Our Lady."

Billy's eyes went wide as he stared at the man.

"It's all right, my love," the woman who wasn't there said to him. "You can trust this one. He's one of mine."

"The lady," Billy said softly. "I know the lady. The lady speaks to me."

"Does she now?" the man asked, and frowned. "I think you'd better come with us, my lad."

And that was how Billy first spoke with Our Lady of Eternal Sorrows, and how he used the cunning for the first time. That was how he first met a man called Tomas Piety, too, and that was more important than either of them knew at the time.

FIRST PUBLISHED IN GdM ISSUE 18

Reprinted by kind permission of Adrian Collins, Editor in Chief.

His Lord Recalcitrant

J.L. Worrad

One

THE PORCELAIN HULK stung my eyes. The great vessel shone pale as a glacier beneath the fat red sun. I watched it from a distance, sat upon the sandalwood boards that jutted from the howdah of our pond skater, my legs dangling above the supernaturally flat sea some twenty feet below. I had travelled more than half a year to reach this place. I would trade for the dead.

"I am here," I whispered to the distant vessel. I touched the silver locket that hung from my neck. "My love, my love. I am here."

The porcelain hulk was a ceramic island-city half a mile long, a gloss-white colossus dappled with swirls and stripes of royal purple. The hulk had the vague outline of a ship's hull, its vast prow rising to a fever-dream acropolis that constituted the aft. This aft, of sorts, was festooned with countless buildings and sculptures, though at this distance it was difficult to tell one from another, their shapes being so very indistinct. Either way, they were all a part of the greater whole, as if the porcelain hulk had been cast of a single titanic mold. And all of it deserted. So it seemed.

"Like staring of gods, yes?" my host, the pond skater's pilot, called to me. His words I took for gibberish, some concept of his people warped by his poor grasp of Imperial speech. Now, setting down these words, I am far less certain.

I turned to face him. He was prowling toward me along the footboards, one hand to the guide rope that was nailed along the thorax of the giant pond skater we travelled upon, his body snake-thin and inhumanly white.

"Indeed, sir," I replied. "You are certain this is the right hulk, yes?"

"Dead fingers lie never." He knelt beside me and grinned, his teeth like two ranks of battered shields. He held up his ornate compass with its mummified finger. Its blackened nail pointed toward the porcelain hulk. "See?"

"The compass, yes." I would be glad to be free of this man's constant presence, along with his hissing voice and his loud, hourly urinations. There had been no way to escape him on the back of this giant insect. "The hulk's captain, this king of the dead—"

"His Lord Recalcitrant," the pilot hissed. His smile vanished.

"This Lord Recalcitrant. What manner of man is he?"

"No man." The pilot's smile returned. "No longer."

"I know," I replied. "But I mean how does he behave? What is he like?"

"Miserable," the pilot said. "Saddest thing he."

"Why?"

The pilot held silent awhile, his milky blue eyes studying me. The sun baked my neck through my high collar.

"They say miserable, he," the pilot said at last, "for the thing he needs... he has."

With that he stood up and headed back toward his skater's reins. Baffled, I returned my gaze toward the porcelain hulk. We were closer now, our pond skater having drifted closer to it. What I had thought buildings or sculptures were neither and yet both. The hulk's levels were covered with abstract contours and bulges that only hinted at monuments and edifices. The structural equivalent of embryos, one might say, only half-formed. An architecture locked in gestation.

The pilot and I had not arrived alone. We were part of a small flotilla of giant skaters, water-borne insects of elephantine proportions sporting six legs that one might be tempted to call "spindly" if they were not the width of lamp posts. They were native to the Pond-Oceanic and had evolved a way to float on this eternally flat sea despite their weight. The skaters had a strange musk, like green tea and sulphur, and my nostrils looked forward to being clear of it.

One of our skaters was already approaching the hulk. Tied to its howdah was something the size and shape of an oak's trunk shorn of root and branch. The trunk-thing was entirely wrapped in a tarpaulin mottled with black stains. The skater's crew banged a deathly gong.

The pond skater reached the hulk's colossal hull. Things stirred upon the porcelain decks. Lion-sized quadrupeds loped out from hidden nooks and high ledges, slinked their way toward a sort of jetty near the approaching skater. The gong rang faster across the flat sea.

I stood upright and, holding on to the rope handrail, made my way over to the pilot. He clambered back into the pilot's seat above his skater's neck. The beast's house-length antennae twitched, testing the air.

"Sir?" I said. "There are creatures upon the hulk."

"The Lord's hounds," he answered, never looking up from his task of gathering the reins. "To them, gift must be made." With a growl, he handed me a small telescope made from a human femur and bound with copper wire.

I gazed through its glass. The other skater's crew had unwrapped the tarpaulin from their log-shaped cargo and were in the process of lifting one end up to the white jetty and the hounds.

The hounds, nine in all, had heads like eyeless hummingbirds, each tipped with a black beak the length of an elephant's tusk. The hounds were bereft of fur or feather, their hides all sunburned flesh.

It was no log that the pond skater's crew held up to them. The thing was another skater, a youth shorn of its six long legs. I could see it still lived, its antennae shivering with a pathetic docility.

His Lord's hounds sniffed at it, held still a moment, then lunged as one at the great insect's face.

I could not watch. I turned my gaze to the hulk's upper ramparts and spied movement up on a high veranda: a door, apparently of dark wood, flew open. A naked man burst out and tumbled forward, out of my line of sight. I waited for him to reappear, to get to his feet, but it was not to be. After some minutes I realized the incident had to be some trick of the light, of distance and moving shadow, for even the door I thought I'd seen the man emerge from had vanished. Light and shadow played oddly upon the white porcelain with its purple mottling, cheating the eye and provoking the subconscious.

I returned my gaze to the hounds. They had disabused the skater of its hundred milk-white eyes, leaving its head a pulpy mess. Apparently satisfied with the eyes alone, the hounds already loped back into the angular shadows they had crawled from.

The crew pitched the dying skater into the flat waters. Its fall cast ripples which the Pond-Oceanic soon absorbed.

I handed the telescope back to my pilot. He shoved it back in his belt and jerked the reins of his mount. The beast lurched forward.

I lifted the locket on its chain around my neck and studied it. Behind its crystal window lay a lock of her black hair. Ermaline, lost Ermaline: her amber-dark skin, her sapphire eyes, her smile and the aftermath of that smile. Her touch. The way that she had felt for me and I her. Our love, to put it glibly. Intangible and real.

I counted myself a man of reason. Surely madness such as mine was reasonable enough? I would trade for the dead.

Two

"Greetings," a man said as I stepped on to the porcelain jetty. He stood some distance away, his face shadowed beneath a half-formed arch, and it seemed entirely possible he'd been stood there all along. His white dinner jacket and trousers were practically a camouflage on this island.

"Greetings," I replied, gripping the shoulder strap of my satchel. The skater crews ignored the man, busy tethering their beasts. "My name is Pilchro," I said. "Sebastian Pilchro. Am I right in thinking you His Lord Recalcitrant?"

The man strode toward me. I had thought his face shadowed by the arch, but in truth his countenance was as a chopping block's: a mass of old scar tissue, the scars purple. His lips were purple too, like those of a fresh cadaver.

"I am counted among his servants," the man said. "I am Señor MisterMonsieur. I welcome you here… Sebastian Pilchro." Something about my name amused him. The old scars on his face stretched as he smiled.

"Thank you, Señor," I said. "I seek an audience with your lord... should it please him. I wish to trade for the dead."

"Why else would you be here?" Señor MisterMonsieur replied.

I felt a singular rush, a giddy brew of hope and terror. I remembered the object in my satchel, the trinket I would use for my barter.

"Then it is true," I said. "The dead reside here?"

"In the bowels of every hulk upon this pond," the scarred man said, "are spirits of those dead and those yet to be born."

"To be *born*?" I asked.

"Time is a patchwork here, not a thread." He eyed me up and down. "You will come to learn this. Follow me."

I did so. I took one last look at my fellow travelers the skater nomads, unloading veiled cargo from the backs of their beasts. I'd never enquired what they had come here to trade for, or what with. It was not a thing to ask.

Three

His Lord Recalcitrant's chamber smelt like old incense in a seldom visited chapel. The chamber was scant larger than a chapel too; paneled from floor to ceiling in the glossy white porcelain with its purple markings.

Most of the chamber's floor had been taken up with a statue, also fashioned from the hulk's milky ceramic. Indeed, there was no divide between the statue, the floor or the rest of the hulk itself. The statue was of an obese male giant, naked and lying on its back. Its legs--slightly raised at the knees--were thick as sewer pipes, its fists white boulders. The head, supported by a giant pillow cast of dark gold, had the face of an eyeless hummingbird. Exactly like those of his lord's monstrous hounds.

Señor MisterMonsieur and I stood before it.

"His Lord Recalcitrant will meet us here?" I said.

"He is present," Señor MisterMonsieur replied.

I frowned at the statue with its folds of disquieting, stone-hard flesh. A beautiful and troubling masterpiece. "His Lord is in there?"

"He is in the statue. He is the statue. He is this hulk entire."

"How..." I found myself stuck for words. "How shall he speak?"

"He conveys his meaning to his servants always," the Señor replied. "Presently, I shall speak for him."

I was being made a butt of some outlandish joke. This Señor MisterMonsieur had a smile about him, certainly. A knowing smile. Could it be that he was this Lord Recalcitrant? Anger tickled me. Yet my mission remained. I thought of Ermaline and the love we had known. I could not fail.

"I seek a spirit from the belly of the hulk," I announced to the slumbering statue.

"Its name?" said Señor MisterMonsieur beside me.

"I once loved a young woman called Ermaline Solipsee, who—"

"There is no spirit here of that name," he interrupted.

"I know." I paused here, hungry to see confusion in the man's ruined face. Señor MisterMonsieur showed no hint of such. I continued regardless. "Ermaline still lives, and lives comfortably enough for all I know. She is married to a respected man in my home city's hierocracy. They have a boy-child and a holiday cottage on the west coast." Louder, I said: "I could not care less for Mrs. Ermaline LeCanthus."

Señor MisterMonsieur smiled in his maddening way. "Then His Lord Recalcitrant wishes to know why you allude to her."

"I seek not the spirit of Ermaline," I said, "but that of our love. The love we knew existed between us. Foolish. Profound. Lost to the haunts of the dead."

I shut my eyes. I pictured Ermaline and me, caught in the summer showers of home. Her laugh, the rainwater pouring down her cheek. Her kiss.

"You ask for much," MisterMonsieur said. "The spirit of a feeling, not a person, is hard to seize once expired."

I opened my eyes and faced him.

"Can it be done?" I said.

"Who would pay for such a service?" he asked. "The price, Sebastian Pilchro, would be far too high."

"And I can pay it, sir." I opened my satchel and searched for the object. "Believe me, I can…"

I pulled out my bartering chip: a quartz prism wrapped in copper wire.

"This is a sinusoidal discharger," I announced to the statue. "In my homeland we have perfected the science of trapping—and releasing—many and varied forms of energy. In here," I nodded at the prism, "is something I am certain no other porcelain hulk in these flat waters possesses. The very essence of a wave! One merely dips it in the Pond-Oceanic and—"

"His Lord has no use for such," Señor MisterMonsieur interrupted me again.

"But think of the advantages," I pled to the statue. "This device can generate a great wave. It will grant you predominance of the pond, I assure you. And you can use it again and—"

"What else can you offer?" Señor MisterMonsieur asked, his scarred face implacable.

I had not considered bringing another gift. Surely the sinusoidal discharger was enough? After all, the urge for power and domination is universal in all intelligent beings.

A second possibility gnawed at me. I undid the clasp of the silver chain about my neck. Only when I held the locket out did I notice that my hand shook.

"Inside this," I said, "I keep a lock of Ermaline's hair. His lord can work some enchantment with that, can he not? If his lord can keep souls, I imagine he can take them too. Well, take hers."

"His Lord Recalcitrant has no desire for this woman's spirit," Señor MisterMonsieur replied, his smile a lilac slit. "In that regard, Sebastian Pilchro, you and he are identical."

I wanted to lash out at this man, murder him before his lord and statue. I threw the locket across the floor.

"Damn you, I'll pay! I have travelled too long, travelled through wretched lands a wretched man. I am broken and I am hollow, and I will pay *whatever* is required. Name it. I must have that love I once knew!" I glared at the obese statue with its hummingbird head. "You hear me? I must have it!"

My shouts echoed through the chamber.

"You should have said so from the beginning," Señor MisterMonsieur said. "But it is vital that you rest now. I will take you to your room."

Four

Indeed, it *was* my room: an exact replica of my bedroom back home. I should have been astonished, but all I could muster was a bitter amusement.

Oddly, "my" room was dark, lit only by a flickering candle that rested upon my bedside table. I stepped into the center of my bedroom and looked up at the modest glass dome above. It was a moonless and cloudy night.

Bemused, I returned to the dark wooden door I had entered moments before and opened it. Sunlight poured through. Beyond lay one of the hulk's many higher levels; a balcony-like expanse I recognized, for Señor MisterMonsieur had only just led me across it to get here. The noontime sun beat down upon the porcelain level. Exactly as I had left it.

I gazed a little longer until I noticed one of his Lord's hounds in the mid-distance, basking upon a tower-like outcrop. Its eyeless hummingbird face was fixed upon me. I closed the door.

Back in the bedroom's nocturnal gloom I sighed with incomprehension. No other windows existed save the dome above, so I could not ascertain if my home city at night lay beyond my room (the insanity of the door notwithstanding). I'd no way of clambering up to the dome to see the truth of it but, even if I could, what then? I might well see my home city, with its spires and transmitters, its hierocratic palaces and vertical gardens, but would it be the same city? Or some doppelgänger landscape, a fiction presented by the porcelain hulk?

Ah, it mattered not. I was simply exhausted. I removed my clothes and climbed into my impossibly familiar four-poster bed. I snuffed out the candle, lay my head upon the pillow and fell into dreamless slumber.

I awoke in darkness. I felt a presence nearby, as if someone were stood next to my bed.

This is no man, I thought, for the thing above me drew no breath.

This presence was that which I had long sought. Not Ermaline, but her love for me and mine for her, combined in a single form. Resurrected. I knew it to my bones. His Lord Recalcitrant had made good on my request. I had traded for the dead.

I closed my eyes and smiled. "Come."

The lost love fell upon me, cold as an ocean's floor.

No longer tethered to its makers, the love Ermaline and I had known was a stale and twisted thing, its touch withering cold. A beast of the gloom, from the unseen belly of the hulk, the belly of death.

I screamed. I leapt from my bed and bolted across the floor. The love clung to me, leech-like, hungry for what few drops of joy remained in my soul. I groped for the door handle and, despite blind madness, found it.

Daylight scorched my eyes. I ran through the doorway and stumbled face forward onto the deck of the porcelain hulk.

Five

I do not recall how long I lay there, the sun above cooking my naked back, but at some juncture a pair of white leather shoes came into view.

"You have rested," Señor MisterMonsieur said.

I did not reply. I could feel the shadow-thing, that lost love, bedding down in my nerves, smearing my soul with coldest filth. I staggered to my feet.

"Señor," I muttered, "I..."

Señor MisterMonsieur's face was smooth and pale. It was entirely free of the old scars that had once obscured it.

"Your face," I whispered. "Where are the scars?"

"I have never possessed scars, Sebastian Pilchro."

"But—"

"Time is a patchwork here," he said, "not a thread. No doubt you—"

"—will come to learn that," I replied, finishing his sentence.

"Quite so," he said. "His Lord Recalcitrant is an entity of singular aesthetics. If his whim should be I mutilate my face..." He shrugged. "...then it is so."

I couldn't take in what he had said. Too much ice within me; that thing that had once been love. Like an insect's sting left to fester in flesh.

"I'm broken," I mumbled. "Miserable."

"Naturally," he replied. "For you have the one thing you ever needed. Now sir, regarding the payment..."

He stepped away and I saw a new landscape before me. The Pond-Oceanic was half-full and rising. Fed, I suppose, by countless unseen springs below.

We were stood upon the aft of the porcelain hulk, yet the thing was only half built. Its skeletal framework, now bare to the world, was a complex lattice of dark gold. Countless hummingbird-faced hounds climbed over it, vomiting a milk-white liquid from their beaks wherever the insane design of the hulk required it. They had been busy: half the hull was built already and had hardened to porcelain in the sun. Other hounds helped themselves to pond skater eyeballs that hung in bunches here and there upon the framework of golden struts and transoms.

Somewhere below me lay a small ledge of the white ceramic, fully dried and as hard as stone. Upon it rested a huge and empty pillow of dark gold. Four hounds worked the edges of the ledge, vomiting the wall foundations of a chamber that would be little bigger than a chapel. It would be a chamber I had once stood in and made bargain.

Of course. Payment for services rendered. Time to place my head on that golden pillow. My loyal hounds would do the rest.

Shadow Wraith

Dennis K. Crosby

KASSIDY ALWAYS BELIEVED she was a good fighter. Not great, but good. Just a few short days ago, she'd bested Azra-El, the Angel of Death and, technically, her boss. Perhaps, on some level, that had made her cocky. Perhaps she was fatigued from the physical and emotional toll of that battle. Whatever the reason, she was quickly learning that *perhaps* she wasn't as good as she thought.

Her current fight wasn't expected, but the same was true of the last two she'd had in as many days. Word about what she'd done was out, and every Reaper in existence was hell-bent on avenging their Primus. Where Kassidy had been able to get away and hide in previous fights, the speed of her present skirmish kept that opportunity just out of reach. Coincidentally, out of reach was where she'd hoped to be to avoid the punch coming toward her. All she could do was brace herself and hope for the best.

Unfortunately, the *best* had a painful end as the speed of the blow was surpassed only by the velocity at which she flew through the air.

"Ungh!" she let out as she violently slammed into the concrete wall of the abandoned warehouse on Chicago's south side. She crashed to the floor, losing her breath, some blood, and her orientation. Being grabbed by her hair seconds later did not help her catch her bearings.

"Motherf—"

Her face met the knee of her opponent.

Suddenly upright, on unsteady feet, a kick to her abdomen propelled her backward to the wall with which she was now well acquainted. Her eyes misted. She felt the throb of her body's attempt to heal itself.

All this because of Azra-El.

"Now, young Reaper, you will answer for your crime," said her attacker.

Kassidy knew her. Not well, but she'd seen her before. Elizabeth was her name. Like Kassidy, Elizabeth was a Reaper—a supernatural being tasked with escorting souls to the afterlife. Elizabeth was from a time when rules were followed, not side-stepped or blatantly ignored. A time where everyone had their station until otherwise redirected by their leader. Thanks to Kassidy, there no longer *was* a leader.

And there were consequences for that.

Consequences which Elizabeth and others apparently felt duty bound to carry out.

"No. Wait. I can explain," said Kassidy.

Her words were ignored. Kassidy watched as the silver-eyed reaper stalked forward, her hands dematerializing only to reappear as sickles. That was not the signal for a secret Reaper handshake. There was to be a reckoning.

Instinctively, Kassidy transitioned to the Nexus, the way station for souls on their way to the Beyond or the dreaded Void. In the Nexus, Reapers had no power beyond their ability to enter and leave. They could not manifest weapons and it was understood that in this place, violence was not allowed. The Nexus was a place of peace out of respect for the passing soul—even the dark ones.

"You can't hide here forever," said Elizabeth.

Kassidy looked up and found Elizabeth standing over her. Her sickles had transitioned back to hands. Her eyes were still silver, but the intensity had eased. All this because Kassidy dared to challenge Azra-El, battle him, and defeat him. Despite his death, Kassidy felt no massive shift in the balance of things. Not having a Primus didn't turn the universe on its ass. She wondered if Elizabeth knew his true goal. She wondered if *any* Reaper knew. Would it matter? Kassidy knew that the only way to end this was to end Elizabeth. She didn't want to, but she needed this to be over. As resolve filled her and some strength returned, Kassidy stood. She felt her eyes transition to silver.

"You cannot fight here, Reaper," said Elizabeth.

Kassidy closed her eyes and kept them shut as she transitioned back to the real world. She knew Elizabeth would immediately follow. Letting her senses take control, Kassidy steadied herself. She felt a shift in the air around her, sensed a presence before her, and immediately thrust her hand forward and squeezed. When she opened her eyes, she saw a shocked Elizabeth. Kassidy also saw the dark orbs that were her own eyes reflected in the silver of her adversary's. Startled, but choosing to ignore it, she set her gaze downward to find her hand had successfully phased through Elizabeth's chest.

"What…are…you?" asked Elizabeth.

Kassidy retracted her fist from Elizabeth's chest and opened it. There was no blood. Only an audible gasp from her adversary. The orb that pulsated in Kassidy's now open hand was the life force of a Reaper. Everything that made Elizabeth supernatural lived within it.

And Kassidy promptly swallowed it.

"No!" screamed Elizabeth.

Kassidy stepped back, willed her right hand to transform into a sickle, spun, and slashed through her attacker's throat. Again, there was no blood. No pain. And this time, not even an audible gasp. Just the slow transformation of flesh to ash.

And ash to nothing.

Sore, confused, and exhausted, Kassidy fell to her knees.

"This has to stop. Please make it stop," she whispered—to anyone.

Since her battle with Azra-El, Kassidy had been constantly looking over her shoulder. Like a fugitive on the run, she had ducked and dodged every Reaper that had come after her. Tonight was not her first fight. But it was the first to almost end her. She was still just a kid. Old enough to vote, too young to drink, and wanted by the supernatural world.

Are all the Reapers against me now?

CRASH!

Kassidy looked up to see a large swirling dark cloud slam through a warehouse window. With it came shards of glass, dread, malevolence, and the promise of true death. The wind died down and the cloud coalesced into a human form. Nothing more than a silhouette. Tall. Dark. Terrifying. Atop its head was the outline of something that seemed out of place. More shadow than man, its face was featureless.

But its eyes...?

In the Reaper ranks, eye color denoted station and power level. When using their powers, Reapers had silver eyes. Azra-El, their Primus, had red eyes. Black eyes were something Kassidy had only encountered once, though somehow, she'd seen her own turn that color—twice now after tonight. The being before her had neither silver, nor black, nor red.

Its eyes were living flames.

It raised its arms, and an unholy sound escaped it. Part scream, part cry, it echoed through the abandoned structure. More glass shattered. Holding her hands to her ears, Kassidy fought hard to dematerialize. After what seemed like an eternity, she finally transformed into vapor and fled to the skies.

The flame-eyed shadow followed.

༒

Unable to maintain concentration, Kassidy materialized mid-air as she descended from the skies above St. John, New York. She crashed through the window of the local bookstore and rolled unceremoniously several feet until she found resistance in the form of a wall. Her head throbbed, and the discomfort was exacerbated by the roar and wailing of the dark cloud making its decent. Again, she transitioned to the Nexus. She wasn't certain what this creature was, but she hoped that if it followed her into the Nexus, the same rules would apply.

The Nexus was just like the regular world, everything looked the same, only it existed on a plane just beyond our own. Kassidy was still in the bookstore, but in that transition, the real world gave way to a greenish gray existence. Along the ground was something she had once described as living fog. Seemingly sentient tendrils of smoke and vapor covered and moved about the surface. When the creature that followed her landed and took form, Kassidy watched for any signs of awareness.

There were none.

She dared to stand within inches of the entity...and nothing. No reaction. Just a constant search for its prey.

"It doesn't know I'm here," she whispered to herself. "Good. Now to get what I came for."

She'd been to this place before. Three times, in fact. The first time, she'd simply stumbled in during an assignment given to her by Azra-El. An assignment that resulted in her saving a group of girls and killing a strange being with black eyes. The second time, she'd come to steal. The third time, she'd come to return what she'd stolen. The items she'd taken were daggers. Special weapons made from something called celestial onyx, a metal that was believed to be the only thing that could injure, or possibly kill, an immortal. She'd stolen them to use against the Primus and found that the legends were true. It stood to reason that if they could destroy Azra-El, they should destroy the thing currently stalking her.

Kassidy moved deeper into the bookstore toward the hidden room shown to her by its owner, a rather unremarkable man. Keiron was the name she'd remembered. In addition to the books he sold, the guy seemed to live in a world of wonder and legend. He'd told her about the daggers and their alleged power. If only she could tell him just how true the legends were. But he was only human. There was no chance he'd fully comprehend the depth of the power at his fingertips.

Reaching the entrance to the secret room, Kassidy quickly transitioned to the real world, immediately dematerialized into vapor, and infiltrated the room through a small crack. She knew her time was limited. That creature would descend upon her and unleash unknown power. She quickly moved to the wall where the daggers were displayed to secure them and prepare for battle.

"What the hell?!" she whispered.

The hooks that had once held them were there, but the weapons were gone. Everything else seemed unmoved from what she could recall of her last visit to the place. She continued to search, and then, out of nowhere, she found one.

At her throat.

In the hand of someone behind her.

"I remember you," said the man. "You know, some property of mine went missing. From this very room. Almost a day later, though, the missing items reappeared. Like magic."

"That's—"

"Weird. Right?" said the man. "That's what I was thinking. Because not only is this room always locked, but there's only two ways in or out. And I would have seen the thief at either location."

"I mean...glad you got your stuff back," said Kassidy.

"Me too," he said, releasing his grip on Kassidy and backing away.

Kassidy instinctively rubbed her throat, then turned and looked at the bookseller. Given the aggression with which he'd grabbed her from behind, she was surprised to find how relatively calm he seemed.

Peculiar.

When she'd first met him, she chalked it up to him being some nerdy, albeit handsome, bookstore owner in a nondescript small town in upstate New York. Now, she wasn't so sure. How the hell had he snuck up on her so easily? Was she that distracted by the thing upstairs?

The thing upstairs!

"Look, I don't have time to explain. But...I kinda need to borrow that," said Kassidy, pointing to the dagger in his hand. "Two, in fact."

The bookseller looked from her to the dagger and back. She took measure of him. Confusion and indecision were present on his face...but only on his face. One of Kassidy's other gifts, one that existed long before she'd become a Reaper, was her empathic power. She could sense the emotions of those around her. She'd spent her entire life learning how to control the ability because as amazing as it was, it was also debilitating at times. In places of extreme emotion, like weddings or funerals, she'd be overwhelmed. But there was no extreme here. The man before her—the otherwise unremarkable, nerdy albeit handsome bookseller, was feigning surprise and confusion.

Shit!

Kassidy dematerialized into vapor, reformed behind the bookseller, grabbed his left arm, and held it behind his back, then grabbed his dagger hand, twisted it, and brought it upward to place the blade against his neck.

"Two weeks ago, I killed the Angel of Death," began Kassidy, "and somehow that's the least interesting thing that's happened to me."

She pressed the dagger closer to the bookseller's throat.

"At least now I know where my weapons vanished to," said the bookkeeper.

"Look, Keiron, right? Don't bullshit me, man. These daggers? They did exactly what you said they would. You knew they would, didn't you?"

He said nothing.

"I need them to take care of something unbelievably bad roaming around in your shop. Something trying to kill me for what I did."

"Right," he began, "because you killed the Angel of Death."

Kassidy heard the skepticism in his tone, but she didn't *feel* it. He held no sense of doubt in her claims *and* there was no fear in him. She was holding a dagger to his throat, she'd shifted from human to vapor and back again…and he was as calm as the waters of the nearby lake.

She removed her hold and shoved him forward. Her eyes never left his. He didn't look away. His hand didn't go to his throat to check for blood. He simply straightened his shirt and took a deep breath.

"Who are you?" asked Kassidy. "None of this seems to phase you."

He responded with a raised eyebrow.

And a grin.

"I'm a friend. At least, I could be," he said. "Tell you what, talk to me about the thing following you. Then afterward, I'll share more. About everything. What do you say, Kassidy?"

The sound of her name felt foreign. But there was something more. Not just the sound of her name, but the fact that this unremarkable, nerdy albeit handsome bookseller had remembered it. After all this time, he'd remembered. She felt…seen.

And somehow, safe.

"I…don't know what it is," she said. "It's unlike any Reaper I've ever seen. A shadow. You can make out that it's a man. In fact, weirdly, it looks like a cowboy from the old west. It's got like…a hat or something on its head. Otherwise, it's featureless. It shrieks this god-awful sound, and its eyes are—"

"Made of fire?"

For the first time, Kassidy felt concern from Keiron.

"Yeah. Fire," she said. "You know what it is, don't you?"

"Yes," began Keiron, "it's a Shadow Wraith."

"A what now?"

"A Shadow Wraith. Nothing like a regular Wraith, though."

"What the hell is a regular Wraith?" asked Kassidy.

"You don't know?" asked Keiron with surprise in his tone.

Kassidy raised her eyebrows and shrugged.

"A Wraith is much like a Reaper, only with augmented power and black eyes instead of silver."

Kassidy's heart sank. That's what she'd fought when she'd saved those girls. But…that didn't explain why her eyes had—

"The Primus created them to act on his behalf. A color guard, if you will, to help police the Reaper world."

"And a Shadow Wraith?" asked Kassidy.

"Neither Reaper nor Wraith, it is a being created solely for one purpose. To track, hunt, and reckon whomever or whatever its master deems an enemy."

"What you're describing as a Wraith, I've beaten before," she began, "but it was nothing like this."

"If that's true, consider the fact that you also beat the Primus," he said. "So you can do this."

"How?"

"Shadow Wraiths are created with different power. Power that is *attached* to a soul instead of *infused* into it. They wear that power, much like a shadow wears the form of a person. All you need to do…is strip the shadow away. It will take additional power, but it can be done."

"Oh," began Kassidy, "is that all?"

"I understand your apprehension, but you're capable. And you won't need these," said Keiron, holding out the onyx daggers.

"If we're going to do this, we'll need to go someplace people won't see or get hurt."

"I know just the place," said Keiron.

"Then tell me what I need to do," said Kassidy.

"I'll tell you on the way."

⁓

Kassidy surveyed the area. There was a playground and other amenities, but in truth, the grove was nothing more than an open field. Probably perfect for football and soccer. Seemed large enough even for a festival or fair.

Or a battle to the death.

"What is this place?" asked Kassidy.

"Jacobs Grove," said Keiron. "It's our local park."

Whoosh!

Kassidy watched the dark swirling wind above touch down and coalesce.

"The Shadow Wraith," whispered Kassidy. Now that she knew what it was, it felt slightly less menacing. But only slightly. "Are you sure this will work?"

"I mean...yes?" said Keiron with a shrug.

"Oh great!"

"Look, we don't have much choice. Just remember what we talked about," said Keiron.

The Shadow Wraith began to stalk toward them.

Kassidy shot one last look at Keiron before turning and charging ahead. With quick strides, Kassidy replayed the plan in her head. Every part of it sounded insane.

"You'll need the power of the Nexus. The Shadow Wraith can't enter. It's too dark an entity. Even if it could, you wouldn't be able to battle it there because you'd have no weapons at your disposal. But you can, with enough momentum, bring the Nexus with you. At least a portion of it. For a brief moment."

Not just improbable, but flat out impossible. Yet somehow, the bookseller felt she'd be able to do it. Closing in on the Shadow Wraith, who'd also picked up speed, she allowed her power to build within. There was no other sound except for the voice in her head.

Three.

Two.

One.

Kassidy shifted to the Nexus. Still running, she counted to five. She continued running and tried to manifest her sickles.

"Try to create your weapons in the Nexus. The attempt alone should propel you right out. And with that, you'll bring some of the Nexus with you. That'll be the added power you need."

It did just that.

Kassidy was thrown from the Nexus back to the real world just as she was about to make contact with the Shadow Wraith. Lowering her shoulder, she struck it, center mass. The violent collision resulted in a spark of light and energy that threw them both backward.

"Umph!"

Kassidy landed on her back and rolled several times. When she stopped, she shook off the pain and sprang to a crouch. Eyes watering, she looked ahead and saw two distinct forms.

The shadow with its fiery eyes, and a man lying face down, a cowboy hat off to the side.

"Holy—"

"Now!" yelled Keiron. "Do it now!"

Kassidy sprang up, opened her arms wide, transitioned to vapor, and began to spin. Faster. Faster. Faster still. Until her speed began to pull the shadow toward her. It shrieked. Kassidy felt pain manifest from it. It resisted, so she tapped into every bit of energy she could. The shadow roared and wailed. Its grief echoed in her mind. It pulled against her, but finally Kassidy was able to consume it.

When she slowed, her form became visible. Her feet touched the ground before her winds dissipated, and she immediately fell to the ground. Her insides ached. Her skull throbbed. Pressure was building as something unholy desperately tried to escape.

"Ahhhhh!" she screamed.

Hot pins poked at her from the inside. The taste of bile set up residence in the back of her throat. She wrapped her arms around herself and felt the winds that had just died down begin to swirl again.

Only now, it was in her head.

"Here!" yelled Keiron.

She could barely hear him. The bookseller threw something toward her. Unable to make it out at first, Kassidy was hesitant. It was a purple jewel. Octagonal in shape.

"Infuse it with the power! Release it *from* you, *into* the jewel!"

She caught it, closed her eyes and concentrated. She felt power leave her body. Again, there was resistance. The shadow was trying hard to take control of her. Every nerve in her body lit up. White hot pain consumed her. Her head was ready to burst. Kassidy felt her very breath leave her body. With one final desperate push, she thrust the erratic Shadow Power forward and into the jewel.

Another burst of light and energy filled the area. Kassidy felt the weight of the heavens leave her. Her breathing hurried. Intense. She tried to transition to the Nexus to see if she could find relief.

"My…my…powers," she gasped.

"You'll be okay," said a voice next to her. "Take your time."

She felt an arm around her. There was comfort there. When she finally looked up, she saw Keiron walking quickly toward her.

Shadow Wraith

Who the hell is touching me?!

"Let me help you," said the man next to her.

With a great deal of assistance, she stood. The man next to her was gentle. At full height, he was taller than she, even without the cowboy hat. A Black man with a heavy mustache, he wore a wool suit, weathered, complete with a vest and dress shirt. He wore no tie. On his left lapel, a five-point metal star that read:

U.S. MARSHAL. DEPUTY. OKLAHOMA TERRITORY.

"Who…are you?" asked Kassidy.

"Deputy United States Marshal Reeves, ma'am. Bass Reeves," he said, tipping his hat.

Kassidy felt like that should mean something to her.

"Are you all right?" asked Keiron, running up to Kassidy and the Marshal.

"I will be. I think," said Kassidy.

"Marshal," said Keiron, acknowledging the man next her.

The Marshal inclined his head to Keiron. She caught some glimmer of awareness, at least from Keiron. From the Marshal, she felt nothing. That was not normal.

"You two know each other?" she asked.

"I know him by reputation. By legend. But…we've never met," said Keiron.

Despite the sensation in her gut, Kassidy let it go. There was already too much weird happening. Even for her.

"You have, uh, rescued me from a most untenable existence, ma'am," said the Marshal. "I am much obliged."

"You're welcome. I don't quite understand everything that's happened. But you're welcome."

"Marshal Reeves was one of the most revered lawmen of the late nineteenth century," said Keiron. "I'm guessing the Primus used his power to transform the Marshal into that Shadow Wraith. A combination of magic with the Marshal's natural tracking ability would make a formidable sentinel of sorts for extra special assignments."

"That's so…" Kassidy just trailed off, lost in thought.

"There's a problem, though," said Keiron. "The Primus attached that shadow power to a body that can no longer sustain life. The soul inside is his…but it's weak and needs to transition."

At those words, the Marshal dropped. Kassidy shifted her vision to view the Marshal's aura. His life force was on a swift decline.

"'Fraid that's pretty accurate," said Reeves. "I'm...meant to be dead."

Kassidy and Keiron worked together to ease the Marshal to the ground.

"So you tracked people and brought them to justice?" asked Kassidy.

"Yes, ma'am. All manner of man...and other things."

"Were you good at it?" she asked, trying to ease his thoughts.

"They say...I was one of the best, ma'am," said the Marshal.

Kassidy sat with that for a moment.

"Trackin' is an art," he continued. "Findin' people that don't wanna be found, or even people that's just lost and need help back...s'all an art. Requires patience, understanding, and heart. In some ways, it was a way for me to help find myself. Might could help you. If you're feelin' a certain way."

How does he know?

"He needs to transition, Kassidy. If his soul doesn't move on—"

"Yeah, I know. Bad things," said Kassidy with a nod. "Thank you, Marshal. And...I'm sorry. For what happened," she said.

"Not your fault, ma'am. B'sides...you're makin' things right," said Bass, placing his hand on hers.

With renewed strength, Kassidy transitioned to the Nexus. Reaching into the body of the Marshal on the ground before her, she searched for the spark that was his soul. It was faint. Weary. But she found it. Gently, she helped it exit the body. Standing at full height, the Marshal looked down at his body, then turned to Kassidy. He inclined his head, tipped his hat, and moved toward a swirling blue light.

Back in the real world, Kassidy helped Keiron bury the Marshal's body. Once complete, the bookseller handed Kassidy the purple jewel.

"What's this for?" she asked.

"A witch created this," said Keiron. "It's a powerful talisman on its own. But now, with that shadow power you transferred into it, it can help hide you from other Reapers and Wraiths."

"No way!"

"True story," said Keiron.

Kassidy felt overwhelmed, and strangely…free.

"We have some things to talk about, sir," said Kassidy, some sass returning.

"Indeed we do," said Keiron. "Let's get back to my shop."

"I think I need a drink."

"Are you even old enough?" asked Keiron.

"Not technically," said Kassidy. "But what are they gonna do?"

Keiron shrugged.

"Tell you what," he began, "I'll let you try something. I doubt you'll like it, though. It's for grown folks."

"Tequila?" she asked with disdain.

"Bourbon."

"Ew!" said Kassidy. "You mean for *old* folks, not grown folks."

"Don't knock it till you try it."

"Fine," she acquiesced. "On the way, though, tell me more about the Marshal."

"Happy to. He was one of a kind. Honest. Dedicated. Relentless. A man of honor," said Keiron.

"And he traveled around finding people?"

"Mm hmm."

"Can you do that job without being a fed? Finding people and such?" asked Kassidy, thoughts of a probable future on her mind.

"Absolutely. More money in the private sector, too. Certainly more freedom."

That word again.

"Good. Cuz I'm not really into working on a team. The last group I worked with…well…you know…"

Keiron chuckled.

"Bass Reeves didn't work on a team," he said.

"No?"

"No ma'am. I guess you could say he was more of a lone ranger."

The Bike

Mya Duong

"WELL, THAT'S EVERYTHING." Collette closed the last box for the movers to take. "Try not to pack too much, just what you need for three days."

"Okay, Mom." Lydia ran back into the house.

"What am I forgetting?" Collette mumbled as she searched the garage.

Boxes lined the walls. She thought she had closed everything but hesitated at an open box. She knew what lurked inside. Sitting on top of the pile were the papers that had caused so much grievance this past year. That had instigated the nightmare that turned into a fiery storm.

Divorce papers.

Collette picked up the document. She looked at it one last time and tore the papers in half. Walking through the side door, she tossed the remains in the trash. She knew she had an electronic copy in her computer.

Collette took a deep breath as the memories surfaced. She had been devastated when her husband said he didn't want to be married any longer. They had tried to go to counseling, only to have him show up a few times and not participate. The marriage had been over for him. Something had been lost, and he couldn't get it back.

Then, a year and a half ago, he had begun divorce proceedings.

Collette had tried to fix things, tormenting herself, trying to think what she might have done wrong. How could she have let her marriage get to this point? It became pointless, a failure she would have to shelf under life's experiences. He didn't fight her on custody. He didn't blame her for the dissolution. He just didn't seem to care any longer.

She brushed yesterday's memories away. She could only move forward now with a heavy heart.

Collette scanned the property. There wasn't much left in the yard since Lydia no longer needed a jungle gym. Only Collette's high-quality bike remained. She used to ride it often, but even that had gone to the wayside.

Time to sell the thing, she thought to herself.

Collette dusted off the bike and went inside. She put an ad in one of those apps where one buys and sells used goods. Fast and simple, that's what she wanted. Some kind of closure. Even though the mountain bike was her own purchase, it was her former husband's idea to buy it, something for her to ride around and get away on her own.

It was a happy memory. Lydia was younger and grandparents were around to help, spend time with the family. They were both doing well in their careers, so money didn't feel as tight as when they first got married. Everything fell into place. Everything felt good. Until it wasn't.

Collette's phone pinged. A potential buyer wanted to come over today to look at the bike. As she walked into the house, light flashed in her face, followed by a gust of wind. Then it died as quickly as it came. The same thing had happened this morning, a brief change in weather. Collette didn't think much of it. Where she lived, this seemed normal, as the weather could change drastically.

Please don't rain and ruin this sale. Collette had enough to do. The movers were coming in a few days. They would be out by the end of the week.

"I like it. It rides well. How much?" the buyer asked.

"Two hundred. I'll even throw in the spare tire."

"Deal." The buyer gave her cash, then loaded up the bike. "Thanks, again! Can't wait to take it on the trails."

"Have fun!"

The buyer drove away with the last remnant of her former life.

Collette went back inside the house to resume the move. Even though she had sold items they wouldn't need, she lacked a sense of accomplishment, as her to-do list continued to grow. The movers would pick up all the bigger items. She and Lydia would just keep their essentials—a few kitchen items, some clothes, and personal items. They planned to move into a two-bedroom apartment, since the current house wasn't practical or affordable on one income. Collette didn't need a house this size, and the memories would be too hard. She needed time to figure out their next plan.

Collette put her hand on her head. "Lydia, I'm going to lie down for a bit. Just heat up the leftover food."

"Okay, Mom," Lydia said, her head never turning away from the television.

In a few short moments, Collette felt herself begin to drift off. Soon, she'd fall into a deep sleep...

Her phone pinged again, startling her awake. She didn't know how long she had slept, but it felt like only a few minutes. She looked at the time. Over an hour had passed. Collette read her message.

I'm sorry to contact you, but I can't keep the bike. There's something wrong with it. It's hard to explain. Could I please return it?

Confusion filled Collette's mind. *Something wrong with it?*

She hesitated for a moment, then replied to the buyer. *OK, I'll refund your money. Please bring the bike back when you're free.*

I'm on my way. I'll be there in 30 minutes.

Collette wondered if she'd had a change of heart.

･

The buyer drove up to the house and unloaded the bike.

"I'm sorry, I just can't keep it." The woman quickly handed the bike back to Collette, and Collette returned her money.

"Can I ask why?"

The buyer hesitated, "It's not for me. It's not meant for me."

"What does that mean?"

"It doesn't seem to…like me or want me to use it."

"*What?*" Collette looked at the buyer strangely. "It's just a bike."

"I know. It sounds strange." The buyer appeared distraught. "It's not the same for me. It didn't feel right. I think it was meant for you." The buyer took a few steps back. She scanned the driveway on both sides. "I'm sorry. I wish you all the best." She walked quickly back to her car, got in, and drove away.

Collette stood there, dumbfounded. She examined the bike for any loose parts. Nothing. She climbed on the bike and rode it on the sidewalk. She pedaled slowly, then quickly, changing gears and checking the brakes. She rode the bike on the street. It moved smoothly and efficiently.

Collette parked the bike back inside the garage.

I don't know what she's talking about. The bike is fine. Everything works.

Collette received another ping on her phone.

Another buyer.

Hi, can I look at the bike? I've been searching for one like it.

Collette replied, *Sure, ok. Can you come today? We're moving in a few days.*

Yes! I'll be there in an hour.

Collette went back inside the house, still confused about the issue with the first buyer's claim that the bike wasn't right. There was nothing wrong with the bike.

"Honey, someone else is coming by to look at the bike. I guess the first buyer didn't like it."

"Okay, Mom." Lydia turned off the television, then faced her mom. "I think you should keep it. You liked it. Even Dad thought so."

A sharp twinge ran through Collette's body. "That was before. It's time to let it go."

Lydia shrugged her shoulders. "Whatever you say."

Collette tensed. "I'll be...upstairs."

She reached the top of the stairs and noticed the landing window open. A chill drifted inside. She closed the window, wondering when she had opened it. She didn't remember doing it. Shrugging her shoulders, she went into her room to sort out her belongings.

Her phone pinged again. Buyer number two was in the driveway. Collette sighed, hoping for a successful transaction. She dawdled down the stairs to greet the new buyer.

"Hi! I'm here about the bike."

"Great. Let me open the garage door."

Collette presented the pristine bike to the buyer.

"This looks amazing. It's one of a kind. You really kept it maintained."

"Yes, I took good care of it. Try it out. Think it'll fit you."

The buyer hopped on the bike and rode away. She rode down the street, made a U-turn, and headed past the house. Collette watched her maneuver back on the sidewalk. She pedaled smoothly and tested the brakes.

There's nothing wrong with the bike, Collette thought to herself.

The buyer rode up the driveway. "It rides so smoothly. I want it." She handed Collette the money. "Can't wait to take this out on some trails." The buyer loaded up the bike.

Collette watched the driver and her former bike speed away. Relief and wave of sadness rushed through her. She didn't know why; it was just a bike. But she knew this was the last remaining detail of her former life.

Collette collected her thoughts and walked into her house. She had work to do. She had numbers to crunch and data to send back to people waiting. Clients and an employer who paid the bills. She could push herself even harder to one day make partner. That would bring her the income her small family needed. That might give her the financial happiness she wanted.

Did she want that?

Something halted her instantly.

A chill ran through Collette like she has never felt before.

"What the hell!"

Collette nearly tumbled but reached the side of the house, her hand braced for balance. Her body shook from the abrupt change in temperature. Shock and confusion surfaced from her rabid thoughts: why was this happening to her? She knew she was healthy, in good shape. Collette scrambled to stop the downward drop before it became too late. She wrapped her arms around herself and rubbed rigorously. The coldness subsided, allowing her blood to return some warmth to her body. The last of the chills dissipated enough for her to feel her core return to near normal. Collette stood up straight, lost to what had transpired. Just when she felt stable, a sudden thrust to her lungs pushed her off balance. She braced against the wall again. She couldn't catch her breath; her breathing labored. Collette grasped the base of her throat.

Oh my god. This can't be happening. I'm going to die! She clamped down on the force pushing her in different directions. *Lydia! Who will take care of my daughter?*

Then everything came to a standstill.

Collette slowly stood straight up, testing her body movements. The tightness, chills, and aches disappeared. She looked around the front yard to organize her thoughts. Everything appeared the same.

What is going on?

Collette hurried inside the house and swiftly moved toward the couch. She sat down, hands shaking. She placed her palm on her forehead. No fever. She reached for her water tumbler on the end table and gulped down all the fluid.

Am I having a nervous breakdown? Collette closed her eyes.

After a few moments of contemplation, she went to the sink and poured herself more water. She drank all the fluid in the tumbler and added more. She wondered if she was dehydrated or had forgotten to eat. Maybe the stress of moving was throwing her body out of control. Collette grabbed a leftover cheeseburger and a can of cola from the fridge, devouring both. She unsealed a box of cookies. It'd been a long time since she had eaten this kind of junk food. She savored the unhealthy meal, not caring how many calories or how processed the food she was consuming.

After the meal, Collette went into her office and buried herself in work.

∽

Collette abruptly woke up. She scanned her room. She couldn't remember when she had stopped working yesterday or when she went to bed. She couldn't remember talking to Lydia that evening. Everything felt as if she had moved on autopilot. A wave of panic reached her as she looked at her phone. It was after seven in the morning. A string of missed calls and some text messages appeared.

Buyer number two had tried to reach her.

A twinge of fear rippled inside her body.

"Lydia."

Collette rushed out of her room and stood at Lydia's door. She quietly opened the door, fear raced through her mind. But Lydia lay sleeping in her bed. Her room appeared the same: boxes lined the wall and her suitcase lay flat on the ground. Collette closed the door and wondered if she was starting to lose her mind.

She opened the text messages from the buyer:

I need to see you. Can I come over this morning?

I can't keep the bike. Something happened.

There's something wrong with this bike.

Uneasiness drifted inside of Collette. She put her phone to her ear and listened to the message:

"Hi, I'm sorry to call you. I bought your bike yesterday. I'm not sure how to say this, but I can't keep the bike." A pause. "There's something wrong with it. I was riding it around yesterday, and I…fell. Actually, it felt like the bike pushed me off. I know this sounds strange. I can't explain it. I just can't keep this…thing. Please call me."

Collette felt lost for words. She stood there for a moment, contemplating what to do. Then went back inside her room. Collette looked at herself in the mirror. Dark circles had formed under her eyes.

Is this for real? What is going on?

A bike? Two riders who can't ride my bike? Afraid of it?

Collette texted the buyer back to ask her to come over in an hour.

༄

The buyer lifted the bike out of her SUV. They faced each other, both wary, uncertain who should speak first. Except that Collette couldn't hide her wide-eyed staring. The buyer had cuts and bruises on her face, arms, and legs.

The buyer trembled. "Here, you take it back."

"What happened?" Wild thoughts ran through Collette's mind as she imagined how this person, this stranger who had gleefully bought her bike, had obtained her injuries.

The buyer shook her head. She gathered her thoughts and took a deep breath. "I…was riding the bike. Everything was fine. I felt good, enjoying myself. Then, the bike stopped. It just stopped. I tried to pedal again, but it wouldn't budge." The buyer swallowed, her lips trembling. "I pushed harder on the pedal. It still wouldn't move. Then the bike jerked forward and threw me off, like a bucking horse. It threw me across off the trail."

Collette's head spun. "Wait—*what?* Are you telling me a bike threw you off, that you just didn't fall off a trail?"

The buyer appeared annoyed. "I'm telling you that bike of yours…that *thing* has a mind of its own. It literally moved by itself and threw me off. It did not want me on it." They both turned to the bike propped against the side of the house.

Collette didn't know if this person was crazy, or if she was having a series of bad luck that just wouldn't quit.

"I…don't know what to say, what to make of this." Collette reached into her purse and returned the money to the buyer. "I'm sorry this happened to you. I can assure you nothing strange has ever happened with this bike."

"*I've* never experienced anything like this. It just didn't want me." The buyer spun around, then turned back to Collette. "It has its own mind." She quickly got into her car and drove away as fast away as she could.

Collette sighed. The headache throbbed.

It's just a bike.

She looked at it, leaning against the house. "What is wrong with you?" Collette shook her head. "Now I'm talking to a bike."

She wondered how she'd sell the bike, especially after two people claimed the bike didn't want them, had a mind of its own. A bike. With its own mind. Resolved, Collette grabbed the apparatus of enjoyment and hopped on, forgoing her helmet against her better judgment.

In seconds, Collette had pedaled down her street. She maneuvered her ride, letting the wind flow through her hair and the afternoon breeze consume her. She inhaled the fresh air, air she didn't remember feeling this clean. Her lungs filled with the goodness she hadn't felt in a long time. She soaked in the afternoon warmth as the sun brightened her day. She pedaled further and further, taking her to the place unknown. Collette giggled. Collette laughed out loud for the world to hear.

She felt free.

She welcomed peace. Finally, welcoming the ease that once lived inside of her.

Collette pulled up to the house and parked the bike in the backyard. With newfound determination, she embraced hope, a confidence that she would be okay, and the new direction she and Lydia would take would be a steady path.

The Bike

"Lydia?" Collette walked through the kitchen from the garage. "I've made a decision."

No answer. "Lydia!"

Lydia turned her head, taking out her ear pods. "Yeah, Mom?"

"I'm keeping the bike."

Lydia tilted her head. "I knew you would."

"You did?"

"Yeah, Mom. It was meant for you. It's not meant for them."

"What? How…would you know?" Collette's eyes widened, and confusion and disbelief filled her thoughts. "Did you hear them talk to me?"

"No, Mom. The bike just knows." Lydia gave her mom a half smile.

Collette took a step back. Fear crawled up her spine. How could her daughter know those things or say those words to her as if she knew what the bike thought? As if she knew the bike had a mind of its own?

Collette scanned the room, which suddenly tilted, nearly causing her to lose her balance. She managed to plant her feet firmly on the ground to hold her in place.

Then the room shifted from what it currently looked like to another room design she remembered seeing some time ago. Perhaps many years ago.

"What is going on?" Collette stared at a calm Lydia; panic filled the core of her body.

"It's okay, Mom. You'll understand."

The room began to shake.

"Lydia!" Collette reached for her daughter, but couldn't seem to grasp any closer. Lydia remained still, sitting there without a care in the world. She turned away from her mom and put her ear pods back in her ears.

The room stopped shaking.

Collette ran to her daughter, embracing her. *"Lydia!* I think it was an earthquake. We need to get under a table…or just go."

"We don't need to go anywhere, Mom."

Collette let go of her daughter. Confusion, hesitation, and a sense of déjà vu overcame her. She took a step back. She looked at her surroundings and saw the layout had shifted from moments ago. It appeared the same as she had once remembered.

There were no boxes lined up against the wall. The kitchen wasn't packed up. In fact, the home design appeared quite familiar, as it had been once—and perhaps it had never changed. Yet.

Collette went out to the garage and opened the door. A few boxes still lined the walls. She gathered her thoughts of mixed emotions; a calmness now permeated through her from the frantic feelings she had moments ago. Collette walked outside. The tree in the front yard appeared a bit smaller than she had remembered, the shrubs not fully grown.

A car drove up her street. This car looked familiar. The driver pulled into the driveway, smiling at Collette. He parked the car and got out.

"What are you doing here?" Collette asked.

The man wrinkled his face. "Huh? I live here." He went into the trunk and removed two bags of groceries. He walked into the garage. "Why are there boxes against the wall?" He looked at Collette, confused. "What's going on?"

Collette appeared stunned. She knew something had happened, a series of life events leading her to this place in time of packing and moving. Yet, something now told her otherwise.

"Collette?"

"You have bags."

"Yeah, the groceries you asked me this morning to pick up after work." He looked weary. "Are you alright?"

She paused, taking in a deep breath. "I'm better now. Everything seemed...off today. But now it's better."

"Well, okay." He shook his head, then gave her a kiss on the cheek. "Lydia can help me put away the groceries while you...continue to do what you're doing." He walked into the house. Lydia greeted her dad as he came through the door.

Collette stood in the garage, unsure if she had sleepwalked all day. She turned her head, noticing something against the wall.

Her bike.

She remembered leaving it outside after her ride. Or had she?

Collette closed the garage door and walked inside the house.

An Asexual Succubus

John Wiswell

LILI CALLED THEM "triple puppies," but they didn't sell under that name. After a month she had to change the sign back to "Cerberus dogs." One three-headed hellhound had gotten famous, and now the buying public called the entire breed by his name. That was like calling all humans "George," or calling all succubi "Lili."

The Cerberus dogs sent wood chips flying everywhere, scampering up to the glass window of their pen, triads of tongues dangling out of their mouths. Lili hauled a bag of chow to the pen, and when the puppies clustered in, she scratched the tops of a few of their heads. The heads snapped at each other, greedy for the affection, and she had to jerk her hand away.

She groused, "And you wonder why nobody buys you?"

While they were distracted with in-fighting, she filled their dishes. You couldn't fill that many separate dishes with three heads apiece watching. She'd only sold one Cerberus dog in the last two months—the one she'd named "Saul" after her favorite TV lawyer. Hopefully, he was happy with the old man who'd bought him.

Today's mail came in. Golden Fleece Pets had sent her another mailer about buying out her store. They were such a big company that their envelopes were literally coated in gold. Lili was barely keeping the lights on, but she'd be damned if she'd sell out to that supernatural puppy mill.

She struggled to haul the bag of dog chow back to storage. She made it three steps before tripping, pinwheeling her arms, and falling face-first into bags of bird seed.

To her right, inside one of the cages with tinted windows, the mogwai all giggled at each other. They high-fived paws audibly.

Lili reached for her ankles. The mogwai had tripped her up with a stolen power cable. It was the second trap they'd sprung on her this week. She rubbed her face and glanced at the gilded shine of the Golden Fleece Pets letter.

"Why do I bother doing this...?"

Rising, she spotted a familiar face in the store. The chubby white boy had been in every day for the last week. He wore the same extremely bulky jacket, probably living in that phase of internalized fat-shaming where he thought large clothes made him look smaller. Lili knew that phase too well.

He was squeezed almost into a ball on the floor in front of the Cerberus dog display. His breath fogged the glass like he was daring the dogs to a smooshing contest. A few puppy heads sniffed at him before biting each other out of jealousy for his attention.

Lili sang to herself, "And they called it puppy love."

The boy was probably too young to know that song. He jolted, mumbling apologies, and looking like he thought he had to leave.

Lili gave him a casual wave to calm him down. She said, "Welcome back to my little store. Any creatures I can show you today?"

The boy's shoulders climbed up like his head wanted to hide inside his own torso. He had powerful body language. "Uhm. Hi."

She said, "You know, one of those is a lot of work for two hands."

His voice shot up like he was defending the puppies. "It'd be worth it, though."

That was a deep voice for such a young guy. Puberty was probably ruining his life.

Lili said, "I like your spirit. Have you had mythical pets before?"

"I read that whole thing." He gestured at the thick pamphlets for three-headed dog care. Most people ignored the reading materials she left out. "They have a bad reputation, but they're loyal. One guarded the gates of the underworld for, like, ever, right?"

Lili felt herself smiling for the first time all day. "So you like loyalty, huh?"

Maybe it was too much attention, because the boy started avoiding eye contact. He mumbled, "Yeah, I guess."

"You can browse all day if you want, okay? You just need an adult to come in if you want to buy one of those. It's the law."

The shop's bell dinged, and Lili turned her optimistic smile on her next customer. There stood a familiar old man in a tweed jacket whose frown seemed older than the rest of his face. He all but dragged a Cerberus dog by its leash. The dog had two heads drooping down, with the third up and sniffing as though confused. She'd recognize the white freckles on those three brown snouts anywhere, like snowflakes on red oak bark. The dog was Saul.

Lili spent the next hour handling the man's complaints that he couldn't feed Saul effectively. Lili's assistant had offered him lessons about this, which he'd clearly ignored. According to him, a decent dog would eat however he wanted it to.

Ultimately, Lili took Saul back, and the man left grumbling about her generation ruining the world.

She fought the urge to eat people again. She didn't even like sex, but some customers were just begging to be succubus snacks. They'd make better chow than pet owners.

The anger dissolved into something more toxic in minutes. As she led Saul into the pen, she wondered if Golden Fleece wouldn't do better with mogwai and Cerberus dogs. Maybe this whole store was vanity.

"Lili," she told herself. "Don't make decisions on an empty stomach."

She went into the backroom, to the box with the warming lamp where gryphon chicks spent their early months. Petting them meant carefully stroking one fingertip from their beak to the nape of their neck, making them squint with joy. They all chirped and cheeped for her hands, and the platonic affection gave her a refreshingly warm feeling inside. This was probably how her friends felt about peanut butter granola bars.

Not a minute after Lili started her lunch, her cell buzzed. No matter how she moved her lunch break around, her dad always managed to call during it. He insisted he wasn't psychic. But your parents didn't have to be psychic to mess with you.

She sat by the gryphon cages, grooming chicks with the fingernails of one hand. They nuzzled into her touch, feeding her stray nutritious affection. That emotional feedback was delicious. It was enough to keep a discerning succubus alive.

It was like eating with one hand. With the other, she held the phone to talk to Dad.

He started with, "How is your weight?"

"Better than yours."

"Did you get that offer from Reggie at Golden Fleece?"

She squinted at the cracked screen of her phone. "Are you why they sent that?"

"Reggie's a friend, and they've got good money. You can do better than a pet store."

"Dad. No."

"I don't see how that vegan stuff can be healthy."

She'd never enjoyed the flavors of succubus life. Petting these gryphons kept her full all day, and she left them healthier for it. It definitely beat the gross impulses of traditional succubi feasting.

She said, "It's not veganism, Dad."

"Your mother calls it veganism."

"I'm asexual."

She heard Dad scratching the stubble of his chin. "Whatever you call it."

"I don't need the family business."

"Do you know how many asexual succubi there are?"

The glass reflected how little she was enjoying this. She checked her teeth. "I've got at least one in the store right now."

"You would make a killing as a traditional succubus. Young people don't know what the business really used to be like. Do you ever ask yourself why you settled for a pet store?"

"I've got a customer. Talk to you next week."

"You should call your mother—"

However much people liked sex, it couldn't feel as good as hanging up on her father.

Lili checked the aisles and caught the boy withdrawing his hands from the glass wall of the dog pen. Saul was the closest dog to him, all three heads butting up against the glass, like the boy had been pretending to pet them through the glass. Without the glass, Saul would've utterly overwhelmed the poor kid with sheer size.

She threw the kid a bone. "Want to help me fill their dishes for dinner?"

With his fixation on the pups, she figured this would make his day.

A great shadow swept over the front of the shop, blotting out the front windows. It was like the sun had set at 1:15. An orange high heel bigger than a delivery truck came down and rested on the sidewalk outside. Next a few giant fingers came into view of the shop's windows, waving painted nails for intention. Lili thought she might be getting summoned outside.

The boy retreated to the other end of the Cerberus dog display, eyes on his sneakers.

Lili stepped out through her door and into the shadow of a hundred-handed titan. The lady was taller than the building across the street. She took up several curbside parking spaces to loiter, wearing a loud leopard-print pantsuit, and watching the puppy-loving boy through the shop window. Several dozen of her hands were texting people, presumably some of them about the boy.

The titan said, "I'm sorry if he's bothering you. I can get him out of your hair."

"He's not hurting anything. It's better he spend time here where it's safe rather than go to some seedy library and get hooked on reading." Lili offered a handshake to the titan lady. "I'm Lili. This is my store. How can I help you?"

The titan answered by daintily poking her palm with a fingertip. It easily could've crushed Lili. She appreciated gentle giants. They always took surprisingly great care of their animals.

The titan said, "I'm Chéri. That in there is my nephew, Leo. He and his mom just moved in with me. I live uptown. He's having trouble fitting in."

"That's never fun."

"I try to be the good aunt, but he keeps sneaking out. His parents are having an… ordeal of a divorce." Chéri winced mid-description, and her tone made Lili imagine the Trojan War if it was run by lawyers. They had to be in the middle of an ordeal, for his aunt to be the one who came looking for him. On the other hand, that made her one heck of an aunt.

Chéri went on, "Leo will feel better once his hands grow in. He's not developing as fast as some kids his age."

"I was a late bloomer, too."

"You're sure he's not causing trouble?"

"If Leo caused any less trouble, I'd have to pay him a salary."

"If he wants a pet, I'll pay for it. We have room for whatever he wants."

"And his parents aren't going to try to return it in a week after misadventures in paper training?"

Chéri waved the idea away with fifty dismissive hands. "I promise that's not going to happen. He and his mother are living in my house. I make the rules."

"You know what? I wish I'd had an aunt like you."

Lili stepped back into her store. Leo was over by the mogwai cages, pushing his toes together, trying to pretend he wasn't looking at his aunt's titanic ankles. He wouldn't be considered tall for a human. His teenage years were going to be a nightmare of growth spurts.

He studied packets of gryphon seed with an intensity that would've read as fake even if she didn't know the text on those packets was boring. Lili said, "You've got a great aunt. Literally, she's bigger than my whole family."

"Is she mad?"

"Nobody who is mad at you right now is worth listening to. Trust me. I have good taste in people."

"I don't know. My parents are mad a lot. Do I have to go?"

"You can stay. Focus on what you want right now. What would you like?"

"Of anything?" he asked, as though he wasn't obviously side-eyeing the Cerberus dogs. "I just don't want to be so lonely."

That crumpled up Lili's heart like an empty to-go cup. But she had to check him.

Crouching slightly to be at eye level with Leo, she said, "A pet is a living being with needs. You must take care of it, even if other people don't do what they should. Do you think you're up to taking care of something every single day?"

"I want to try."

"What would you like to see?"

"A triple puppy."

Lili checked the sign beside the pen. The boy corrected himself.

"A Cerberus dog. Although I don't like that name as much."

"You said the magic words. Pick one out, my man."

Leo pointed across the dog pen and over to Saul. The triple puppy's heads were too busy trying to smell in different directions to notice. One nipped at the other two.

Lili said a quick prayer that the critter this boy was begging for didn't wind up biting him. Part of her wanted to close the entire business to avoid that level of disappointment. Let Golden Fleece handle heartbreaks like that.

The store had an enclosed room in the way back, behind where the gryphon chicks slept, with foam mats on the floor where customers could have private hands-on time with the animals. Saul strained against three leashes as she guided him in. All three of his snouts went straight for Leo's lap.

"His name is Saul. Be careful with him," Lili warned. "Remember, those heads are a lot to handle."

She held onto the leash, straining against the excitement of three puppy brains all set to compete for affection. If Leo picked the wrong head, the others would get jealous immediately. Lili maintained hold on the leash, ready to dive in if she had to.

Leo knelt and whispered, "Hello, Saul. I'm Leo. I only have one head."

He shrugged off his jacket and petted the triple puppy under their chins. His fingers worked under all three of them, all at once, leaving them drooling and open-mouthed. He never missed touching any of the heads, not for a second. At first, Lili didn't see how.

The boy had at least three hands, and more than three shoulders. There were lumps where more arms were beginning to sprout, tucked inside his t-shirt beside his thick belly.

He was going to live up to his hundred-handed family after all.

Saul didn't know this boy was unusual. The triple puppy's foreheads kept bunting into Leo's palms, and the heads yipped with irrepressible excitement. After several moments of the affection assault, Leo giggled along with Saul's three-mouthed yips.

There was nutrition, and then there was this. No petting of gryphon chicks or frolicking with mogwai could compare to bringing joy and peace of mind to another person and pet. It filled Lili up to the brim—not simply spiritually, but in the entirety of her succubus being. She wouldn't need to eat a crumb for a month at the least. It was an overwhelming reminder of why she'd started her business in the first place.

Leaning on a box of paper towels, she said, "You're perfect for each other."

Leo tried to hug around all three necks, and the triple puppy tackled him down onto the foam mats. Leo petted between three sets of ears, and his giggles turned into husky, huffing sounds, like he'd had air in him he'd been holding down for weeks. He inhaled hard over and over, like he was setting up to cry without actually crying. The triple puppy's head licked his cheeks and nose before tears could even manifest.

Then Lili was trying not to cry. She dabbed a knuckle at the corners of her eyes.

Sniffling and using one hand to blot his eyes, Leo asked, "Are you sure I can keep him?"

Lili took one tissue for herself and handed him the box. "We'll get your aunt to talk to your mom about it. I'll give you a killer discount on monster chow."

"That's all? That's all I have to do?"

"Well, if you make any friends who might like a puppy with too many heads, send them my way?"

"Are you kidding? Everybody's going to want one. Look at him."

Saul's entire hindquarters wagged along with his tail. Leo alternated his three hands along the three heads, like his hands were jealous of each other and wanted to ruffle every pair of ears. All of Saul's heads licked each palm in turn. They couldn't get enough of his taste.

Leo stretched up, looking at her with a lopsided smile. "Can I get one of those hero chew toys? Or maybe three?"

Leaving a customer with a pet unobserved was frowned upon, but the toy bin was right next to the register. She dipped outside for a second, scooping up an armful of rubber Hercules, Achilles, and Teddy Roosevelt figures. Triple puppies loved chewing on presidents almost as much as heroes.

She took a detour just long enough to go by the stack of today's mail. She tossed the Golden Fleece's letter into the recycling bin, before returning to the young titan and his triple puppy.

To the Rescue

David Quantick

"MIND IF I join you?"

She looked up. Sitting across from her on the other side of the tiny pub table—she'd chosen it because it *was* tiny—was an enormous man. He stank of outdoors and rum and something else—salt? seaweed? she didn't know and didn't much care either—and he had a massive beard, the kind you could lose a hand in if you weren't careful.

"Yes," she said. Then, when the man—who also had, she noticed, a long white scar across his cheek, like a dragon had clawed him—said nothing, she added:

"I do mind if you join me."

He grinned, revealing a mouth filled with two kinds of teeth: gold, and none.

"Thought you'd say that," he answered, but made no move to go.

"I'm waiting for my friend," she said.

She could see her reflection as she spoke, strained in the tinsel-decorated pub mirror. To her annoyance, he shook his head.

"Heard that before."

She cast her eyes around for help, but nobody was looking her way. Everyone was laughing, chatting, drinking, lost in their own Christmas outing.

"Lonely time of year," said the man.

"I like it that way," she replied, thinking *don't engage, don't engage.*

"I'll go in a moment," the man said, seeing her expression.

She rolled her eyes. She didn't need this, not tonight. Tonight she had plans. That's what people do at Christmas, she thought, have plans.

"No, you won't," she said. "You'll say you're going to go, then you'll think of one more thing you had to say, then you'll tell me I look nice, and if I don't say 'thank you,' you'll get nasty. And it'll just get worse from there."

In answer, the man took something from his pocket. It was a coin, but unlike any coin she'd ever seen before. It was very flat, for a start, with uneven edges, the face on it (no face she recognised) half worn away by centuries of fingers, and it was made of gold.

"What's that?" she asked.

"For your time," said the man. "Nothing else," he added. "You pocket that, you listen to me, I leave."

"What if you don't?"

"I will," he said. "On my oath."

On my oath. That was what did it for her.

She picked up the coin, put it in her pocket. "You've got five minutes," she said.

The man nodded. He picked up his tankard—she thought, *that wasn't there a moment ago*—and took a swig. He wiped his beard with the back of his hand, and said:

"I have not always been the man you see."

She laughed, despite herself.

"It's true," he said. "Once I was a lad, and before that a boy. And before even that, I was a baby."

"That's what happens," she said.

"Not always," the man replied. "Some never get past babyhood. Some don't get to be babies. I was, at least, lucky in that. My mother bore me to term, she was allowed that by her people. Whether she loved me, I cannot say. But I know she could not keep me."

She fingered the coin in her pocket. Any minute he was going to ask for it back, or demand something, she knew it. She thought of her plans for the evening. All she wanted to do was slip away.

"I can't listen to—" she began.

"Five minutes," he said, and this time there was an edge to his voice. "We have a deal."

"All right. Get on with it," she heard herself say, and for some reason regretted it.

"Sorry," she said.

"I was lucky to be born, as I said," the man went on. "But as soon as I came into this world, my mother abandoned me. There's no other word for it. Not to be wanted is a terrible thing."

He stopped, drank a mouthful, and looked her in the eye.

"But then you know that."

Before she could answer, he went on.

"The moment I was born, I was given up," he said. "Handed in, like lost property. For that's what an orphanage is, is it not? A lost property office where all the property is human, and not so much lost as thrown away or wrested from its rightful owners. And there's more chance of an umbrella or a hat being claimed than an unwanted child.

"I spent the next few years in that orphanage, treated neither well nor badly, like all the others. And all I wanted was—"

She leaned in, despite herself.

"To be rescued," he said. "For my mother to come for me, or if not my mother, my father—whoever he was—and if not them, then... someone. Oh, I dreamed of it. I would be standing in the playground, or sitting in the classroom, or lying in my bed and then they would come in—whoever it was—and they would say, 'Edward'—for that is my name, 'Edward, I have come to take you away.' And I would be *saved*."

She said nothing. A voice at the back of her mind was whispering *it is time to slip away* but for now she wasn't listening.

"I would be saved," the man repeated. "And I would be free. I knew it was a dream, but it was my dream. To be rescued. I saw children arrive like a constant tide, and sometimes I even saw them go. They found new parents, but I remained. I was alone. Oh, I had friends, but not many. How can you have friends when nobody stays? I became myself, because there was nobody else to become."

He smiled, the corners of his black beard bristling like a thousand whiskers.

"I was solitary, I did not play games, but I read. There was television, sometimes there were films. And then one day I was rescued."

The voice in her head was louder now.

Slip away.

"I'm glad," she said. Then: "I have to go."

"There is a minute left," he replied.

"I don't care—"

He slammed his mug onto the tiny table. Ale went everywhere. "We have a deal," he said.

She sat down, one eye on the clock. There was still, she couldn't help noticing, a minute to go.

"When I say that I was rescued," the man went on, "I do not mean that my mother, or my father, or a kind family, arrived to take me away, because no-one ever did. I mean that one day I opened a book," he said. "Or I saw a film, or I turned on the television set. I forget. And they were there. Beckoning to me. They had swords, and flags. Muskets, and lasers. They were knights, and warriors. Aliens, and pirates. Creatures, and fair maids."

"Did you drink a great deal as a child?" she asked. "Or was it—"

Slip away

"—drugs?"

He ignored her.

"I was frightened," he said. "Books don't beckon to you. They just stand there, waiting to be opened, and when you do open them, they're only great clumps of words. Aren't they?"

"You tell me," she said.

"TV," he went on. "It's wallpaper, they say. It makes you stupid."

"Maybe it does."

"Films. They don't talk back."

"I would hope not."

The man wasn't listening to her. He was looking in his pint mug, as if seeing something. For a moment, she thought she could see it too: a puff of cannon smoke, a flash of red light.

"One day I was more alone than ever before. Completely and utterly alone. You know how it is. I was too old to be there. Everyone was young, or gone. I had nowhere to go."

"Talking of which—"

She looked at the clock. A minute still to go. *Really?* she thought.

"I started thinking of ways to get out, but there were no good ones. Find someone who liked boys, maybe. But as I say, too old. Oblivion was a possibility. I don't have to tell you where that leads."

She said nothing, scratched the back of her hand.

"I was isolated. There's a word. It means you're on an island. And I felt I was on an island. I was a castaway, and there was a tidal wave coming towards me. I mean, literally. I could see it. A huge tempest crashing towards me like a herd of elephants."

"Look," she began.

"And I saw them. They had a ship. Or a plane. Or a spacecraft. Or they were riding a leviathan, I don't know. But they were there, and they were real, and they rescued me. And here I am."

There was a loud *clunk* from the clock.

"Five minutes," she said.

"You seem like you need rescuing," the man said.

"Thanks."

He laid a cutlass on the table. Nobody else seemed to notice this. "Join us."

"Join—"

She looked up. Behind him stood a terrible crew. A squire in chainmail. A pirate lad. A thing with tentacles and a cheerful expression. A maiden fair with a bloody broadsword. Something that was both silver and vapour at the same time. A wise child.

Outside it was snowing. A choir was singing.

She examined her glass.

"Did you put something—"

"We are real," the captain said. "And we are here to rescue you. If," he added, "that's what you want."

She remembered a moment, one she had carried with her, as if in a bubble. A girl, reading. She thought of what she had planned to do, of slipping away.

"When do we leave?" she said.

Wish You Were Here

Renan Bernardo

I TAKE MY clothes off to collect a coin's wish in the greenhouse fountain.

My feet slosh in the water. I kneel to touch the coin.

The water ripples. The oscillation that flows through me lacks only your body to share wish and water.

I wish I could fly, the sorrowful voice of a young woman resounds in my ears.

A good wish. Sincere.

The fountain's water crawls up my body and sheathes me, twigs and leaves scratching my skin.

Today could be like one of those Friday nights when we fulfilled what others would give blood and life for. We'd use the maps in your app to track the fountains around São Paulo, use your methods of sifting the good coins from the dark ones. And then we would revel in the whims of other people's wishes.

I gasp, inhaling rust and staleness as water penetrates through the pores and holes of my body.

The moldy scent of the fountain's tiles becomes that of old carpet.

I appear in a small bedroom, illuminated only by a blue cone cast by a cell phone vibrating with notifications. Rock bands are plastered on the walls. Airplane models neatly set on a workbench cast their shadows on the carpet.

The young woman is crying on her bed. Crossed legs, hands rubbing her eyes. The reflection of my spectral body casts an apricot halo on her. Light pulses around me like threads of thin hair exuding from my skin. Some of them get free and die out in the air.

"Who are you?" The girl lifts her head and recoils, back against her pillows. She digs her nails into the bedsheets.

"I came to fulfill your wish," I say, extending a hand and offering a smile. "My name is Alice."

"You're not real. Go away."

I don't move. My hand remains with its palm up, inviting the girl to fly with me.

Your glowing, translucent arm had extended to me that same way when you invited me to dance that day, fulfilling the wishes of a man who had yearned for something as abstract as the peace of angels. We'd been transported into his shabby residence and did what we could. Mostly you carrying me along with the waltz. I chuckled and tucked my head against your neck, wishing our forms held the scent of something different than water and dead leaves.

"Why are you crying?" I ask the girl.

"I broke up with my boyfriend."

I step forward and touch the girl's arms so she knows I'm real. She startles. Some people flee us, not used to radiant spirits flustering through the air. But those who wish upon coins have a tendency to embrace the uncanny.

Quivering, the girl takes my hands. As our fingers interlace, I hover. She hovers too, above her bed, gaping down at legs that don't touch the mattress anymore.

We fly through the night and above São Paulo's never-ceasing lights. That's when I ask the question I'm here for, my heart pounding, bursts of electricity inside my spectral chest.

"Have you seen a curly-haired woman that ... glowed like me?"

"Another angel?" she says without taking her eyes off the world down there.

An angel. Yes, you're an angel, Joana. One that's probably stuck in a wishworld. You'd once told me wishes of death, pain, and ruin have a way of crimping one's mind and fastening our spectral selves to a wishworld, even though you believed dark wishes could be reined somehow.

"Yes," I mumble to the girl. "An angel."

She chuckles. "No, you're the first."

No surprise. I've been hearing negatives for a while. My heart slumps anyway.

We fly for another hour, and I take her to the airport to feel the planes vibrating in the air. Before the city's lights fade and the dark horizon gleams with orange, I bring her back home. By then, I've already held the tears for too long.

The last thing I see before coming back to the fountain is the girl's smile morphing into my taut jaw reflected on the stale water.

I'm wet, shivering, and all my body prickles with twigs and leaves as it regains its consistency in the fountain.

You weren't there, Joana, but I promise I'll find you even if I have to fulfill the wishes of everyone in the world.

The last bonsai in our apartment is shriveled and grey. I pick it up and set it aside for disposal. I dust out the moths that gambol on your books about sculpture, mythology, and folklore, shifting a few that I've placed wrongly in my last cleaning. Theme, then author. Always this way, always your way. I roll my finger over their spines to check whether they're correctly ordered. Those which don't have their titles clearly on the cover confuse me sometimes, but you'd know them from a kilometer away.

My finger arrives on our special shelf. I drop the dust brush and grab our box of coins. I clink them on my hand the same way you did when you put a new coin in there. *We'll run out of space in here before death do us part, Alice.* Since you vanished, I've been collecting wishes without bringing the coin back as a souvenir. It's a way of saving the space for when you get back, for when we can wishcollect together again. Besides, what's the point of a solitary collection? It's supposed to be our chest of shared memories. We can remember every bit of our fifteen years together just by sorting these coins.

I take the coin which is separated from the rest, protected by a plastic layer. Our marriage's Penny. It takes me back to that day. Gilded bamboos were sprinkling water inside stone ningyos' mouths. The Japanese mermaid creatures had their arms upward, as if inviting us to celebrate. After we kissed and made our own vows without anyone else's presence, we responded to the ningyos' call. We grabbed the Penny, brought a young woman to her mother's distant home, and spent our one-day honeymoon on a deserted island. It was on that day you'd explained to me that, eons ago, families and clans had experimented with magic, so their descendants were capable of dabbling with water's powerful properties. We're their genetic legacy, as you liked to say.

I put the coin back in the box and go to my bedroom before the living room seizes me.

The app we developed together is still open on my mobile when I unlock its screen. I scroll the map and filter the places that are most likely empty in São Paulo, all those you'd catalogued as having magic fountains. I tap the greenhouse's fountain and mark it as Done. No success finding you there. Another one pops up as a suggestion, just three subway stations from here. I fill my backpack with some towels, a bunch of clean clothes, and set a route.

Loosened mosaic tiles lie on the bottom of a tiered fountain with carvings of deceased authors. The water is uninviting, with a saffron quality to it, but the coins are there. At least a dozen.

You would recognize this library, even if it's desolate now. It was here you acquired *An Antique Treatise on Magic and Specters*, by Anonymous, with its sticky pages reeking of rotten wood. It's still there in the apartment, wrapped in a plastic bag for conservation, waiting for you to come back. I'd stayed awake on the day you arranged to buy it from the library, my head on your lap just to watch your widening eyes and pinching lips for every new fact you gleaned from the book. And sometimes you twisted your nose when a puff of dust rose from turning a page. In the morning, still in your lap, you'd told me wishworlds are places where we can flow as specters, unbound by the laws of nature, endless layers of our own world, each accessed by a person's sliver of thought. It had nothing to do with wishes at all, but you'd coined the term because you found it cute and appropriate.

"What really happens when we interact with coins," you'd told me, "is that we link ourselves with—stop it!"

I'd grappled with your arms and kissed your face all over, knocking you down on the sofa. You pushed my face, laughing, and only after we made love you continued.

"We connect our minds with the last thoughts of the coin's owner. And what does a coin in the water mean? Rarely anything else than a wish."

I drop my backpack near the library's main steps, undress, and enter the fountain. Slimy, warm. We used to avoid those which have disgusting waters, but I don't care as long as I find you.

Kneeling, I peer over the basin and check the coins. A one-Real coin, a couple of twenty-five cent coins, at least five ten-cent coins.

"There are people overrunning with boiling emotions. Hate, pain…" you'd told me over a feijoada in the restaurant near our apartment. "And they have wishes, powerful ones at times. I wish we could fulfill them and maybe free them from their dark thoughts. But it's greater than us. It's dangerous, evil…"

I touch the one-Real coin.

You differentiate a good coin from a dark one by the first touch. Good coins trill your body with pleasant sensations: surprise, excitement, orgasm. A dark coin draws your color and rattles your bones, sucking you in like quicksand.

The water flutters. The other coins sway and tinkle at the bottom. A tingling sensation runs through my body. Whiffs of musty, old-fashioned cologne elevate from the surface. I bite my lips, and for a moment, the pressure of your cheek on my shoulder is more real than anything else. I moan when the sensation fades fast.

I wish my son would visit me.

A good and fulfillable wish. I seize the coin.

The fountain's water spirals up and whirls me in its embrace. I close my eyes.

I'm in Ibirapuera Park. Pigeons skitter by and fly away. An old man sitting on a bench raises his head and interrupts his knitting. His eyes crinkle. Not surprised. Our spectral selves usually frighten people, so you taught me your triad of trust: smile, move slowly, extend a hand.

"You again?" he mutters, before I can put the triad into practice.

"What do you mean?" I say.

He tilts his head forward, then shakes it and resumes his knitting. "Oh, it's not the same. You glow alike, though."

My heart quickens. I cough and feel as if the fountain's water is chuffing out inside my specter. My arms and legs puff out in clouds of light that quickly flock back into their original forms.

"This…person you saw…" My voice falters. "What did she say? Where did she go?"

"I'm not sure, my dear. My memories fail me these days. She talked some nonsense about my son. I shooed her away, she obeyed. Shall I shoo you away, too? I'm not fond of spirits."

"Is she…in pain?" If you'd fallen to a dark coin, you might be suffering and trying to escape its grasp.

The man squints at me. "Can't remember, but I'd say she was as healthy as you. I mean, as long as being so shiny and translucent is healthy."

Perhaps you're confused, stuck, trying to find your way out—to find me.

"You—your son… Do you still want him to visit you?" I'm not eager to fulfill wishes right now. I'm trembling. My specter spurts out tiny beads of light-thistledowns. But one time you'd told me that since we're using these people's thoughts and their privacy to traverse wishworlds, then we owe them at least one wish, if it's not impossible.

"My son is dead, my dear. Please spare me from the memories right now. Those damned coins I spent and the prayers I've recited are way too late." He unfolds his needlework. It's an elongated shape crisscrossed with fuchsia threads on a blue background. I squint at it and recognize it from one of the big books you read on the weekends—second shelf from top-down. The boto, the folkloric weredolphin who seduces girls and makes them pregnant. "Your friend said she liked it, said it reminded her of where she lives. What do you think?"

"It's—"

The boto fountain in the Folklore Museum. We'd never been there, but I'd come across its thumbnail several times in our app. Why there?

My lips parch. The old man lifts his arm in front of his eyes. His body and the park behind him wither. I cough and spit out water from my lungs, losing the connection with the wish.

I'm back at the tiered fountain, hair plastered on my cheeks, heart throbbing, and shivering all along with dead authors judging me from above. But I smile. For the first time in about a year, I have a lead.

I place the tenth and last bonsai on the stand facing the window, its branches curling as if to embrace the sun. I'm not completely sure of the way you'd like it arranged, only that you never identified them with plaques. But I do know you better than anyone else. Collector, organized, shiny. That's how I describe you to my relatives and friends. Still do, after lying that you're temporarily working in Argentina. I'm so overwhelmed with hope right now that I even told the friend from whom I bought the new bonsai that you're going to come back soon. That I was going to get you in a few days.

How bare of you this place is and how much of you it needs. You'd raised it from a broken-tiled, empty apartment to something that pulsed with your personality.

Our coins are lined up in front of the bonsai. I've sorted them in chronological order, from our first wish bringing a lost letter to a grieving mother to the ones of the weeks before you vanished. You'd been tired then, reading until the first morning lights, hardly sleeping at all. You must've been exhausted to the point of being unable to escape a dark wish's grasp before it was too late.

I go to the door and inhale the crisp air lent to the room by the bonsai. It's how you'd like it. Tidy, good-smelling, curtains only partially open. I grab my mobile and scroll the app's map until I find the Folklore Museum location.

"Why?" My stomach curls. I slide my finger over the picture of the pink boto. Why would you wait for me in a dry fountain? I inspect the building date, the maintenance schedule, and the description text, but nothing hints that the boto fountain has anything special for wish collectors. Just bare stone.

I need to check for myself, though. It's the only place that fits the old man's description. I pack my things and leave.

Renan Bernardo

∽

The Folklore Museum's garden is public, so I have no problem getting there at 4 A.M. A boggy odor weighs on the place. The lampposts seem to stoop over the cobblestone road that leads to the museum's entrance. Shadows lengthen over the grass, drawing weird shapes and casting the building in complete shade. The fountain lies in the middle of a small garden. I pull out my mobile and turn its flashlight on.

The stone boto is sculpted leaping up from rocky waves. Its beak is broken, its eyes but small holes casting an accusatory glance as if I'm not supposed to be here. And am I? This place gives me the creeps, and your app indicates it has no use for us.

I turn the mobile's light to the basin. It's not completely dry as stated in the app. Various puddles pockmark the bottom. Puddles are water, and water is all that's needed for a coin to transport me to a wishworld. I sit on the fountain's edge and seek for glints. The Museum still opens during the days, but people usually don't make wishes on dry fountains. Brings bad luck.

But there's a coin dipped in one of the puddles. I jump inside and walk to it, my feet sticking and clacking on the bottom's loosening tiles.

It's a one-Real coin, almost completely burnt and with dented edges.

I place my mobile like a lantern propped on the fountain's wall and touch the water with the tip of my finger. It probably won't work. Who would wish upon a burnt coin, anyway?

My finger runs through the water until it finds the coin, and—

My neck stiffens. My teeth clench and rasp into each other as my body shudders with the water. It bubbles and wraps my finger, knuckles, hand, wrist…

I can't pull it off—

The brisk and wooden scent of bonsai suffuses right into my nostrils, but it comes like a sting. Instead of the cooling sensation of water dominating my skin, it scrapes as if it carries glass in it. I try to scream. My teeth won't let me. Only a sob comes out.

I wish to be free. The wish is simple and comes as a whisper. But it's definitely dark.

The water hoods my face.

My body relaxes.

I gurgle and scream.

My chest heaves. I can feel water wobbling inside of me, inside my—specter. My eyes take a while to adjust.

An apartment.

Bookshelves face each other on two opposing walls with books organized by color. On a circular table slightly out of the sunlight's path, five bonsai add their earthy scents to the living room with little plaques stuck on their pots. You never liked plaques. This place is you, but not the same you that has vanished on a Saturday evening while I was out. I close my hands in fists. My nostrils flare. I could percolate this place with the weightlessness of my specter and wreck it, make this fraud unrecognizable as it deserves.

Who made this? Who dared to mimic our living room?

But the answer is obvious.

You float from a bedroom at the end of a long hallway. You come as I love you: naked, shimmering in spectral gold, knees slightly bent as you hover forward, hair clouded around your head.

"Alice?" I ask. Your eyes widen, your lips pinch. "What are you—how? I came to…get you." My voice is feeble. It's not worth repeating it. "What is this place?"

"My apartment." You stop by the hallway's door, some safe inches from me. Hardly the reencounter I'd imagined. "Hi."

"Hi."

We stand like this for a while, two wordless specters facing each other. Both golden, your shade slightly darker. Particles of light escape us and die out.

"This wish is dark," I finally say. "Are you stuck?"

I know the answer already. And you know me well enough to realize my question is hollow. I just need to dawdle until I decide what's happening and what to do.

"Why?" I look around the apartment. Each of its bonsai and the color-organized books make me queasy. One day I'd asked you whether the wishworlds were just alternate realities of our own, if we were just fulfilling wishes from alternate people in other universes. You'd laughed and said that was silly, that we could find those people in flesh and bone and all of them would still remember their experience. But the way this apartment girdles me can't be anything else than an alternate reality.

"Have you never thought I could've just left you?" you say, shivering. For a split second, your specter becomes a shapeless mass. And I wish you'd stay this way, but your body rapidly re-clusters its loosened parts.

I shake my head.

"I wanted to talk, to tell you the truth, but—" You draw a deep breath. "We both know you wouldn't accept, we would fight, you would beg for me to stay, and—it wouldn't be nice for us. So I left you with everything we built together. I didn't want to take anything from you."

"You took everything and didn't even leave a note." My voice is brittle.

"I'm sorry, Alice." Your shoulders slump. "I was in need of a change. You know I wanted to pursue dark wishes for a long time, to know what they're really about. What I found out is that dark is just an intensity. There's nothing inherently evil in a human wish. Take mine, for instance, it—"

"I don't want to know." I raise a hand. "You—What do you mean *yours?*"

"I wish to be free."

The voice. The whisper, ringing through my ears while the fountain's filthy water ripped through my pores.

"Is that—No…" My hands sparkle in amorphous fingers and knuckles while I take it all in, all the implications of what being free means to you, the only person I loved my whole life.

"That wish was my turning point. It was when I couldn't bear anymore. I was in pain, keeping it all inside me, and I couldn't speak to you. I wasn't able to tell you the truth. So I just—gave up."

"Your collections, your books, the Antique Treatise…" The list stutters in my mouth. "The bonsai, the coins. All those coins you were so proud of. Why would you leave it all behind?"

My eyes burn. I'm crying, but specters don't have tears.

"I have started a new collection." Your gaze flits away from mine.

Books sorted by color, plaques for bonsai, a new collection. You don't live alone.

My specter prickles all along, sending shivers across my body. Lightning breaks around me in gold and silver and red.

You raise your hands and step forward. "Let me send you back. I've learned how to master these intense wishes. They're just wishworlds that affect the mind."

I extend an arm, my veins pulsing in glowing lines of purple like trails made of amethyst. My palm is open, but the fingers are rigid, pressing against each other as their tips crackle with lightning.

"I came to fulfill your wish."

You flash. "Alice, please, you just need to get back. I'm sorry for what I've done, for leaving you without a word. I was a coward."

"And I need to make you free," I say.

I dazzle forward and blaze through your body.

You morph into a cloud of light.

I zap and flicker around you, trying to rip your specter. You once read to me, my head on your lap, about the fragility of our specters. We flow like ghosts, but we're as weak as dispersing rain clouds. We're not made for frays.

"Stop it!" Your voice snaps, loosened, scattered through the apartment.

I zap like a bolt across the room, puncturing your books, ripping through them. One of the shelves falls. I defoliate and tear your bonsai, shriveling them as you have left yours back in our—true—apartment.

"What is that?" A bald, tall, spectral pink woman stands in the bedroom's doorway. "Is this... Is this Alice?"

I stare at her, mouth agape. It's her. She's mind-controlling you, keeping you amnesiac and enslaved in a dark wish.

I fizz toward her, spreading across the air, a gob of what I was. A mass of distorted light and frustration.

"No!" You scream and take shape in front of the pink monster. Total. Complete. You as you were to me. Collector, organized, shiny. For a moment I think I'm capable of sniffing your perfume, of squeezing your hands to bring you to the couch so we can relax together as you read chapters of the *Antique Treatise on Magic and Specters*.

You grapple with my lumpy and deformed specter. Your touch is enough to kindle and cluster me back into my shape.

"Please, come back to me, to our place," I say, my voice perfectly clear. "She's controlling you."

"She's not," you murmur, nearing your mouth to my ear. You grip my wrist.

We explode.

I flash back into the fountain, coughing out water from my lungs, my arms and legs regaining their opacity. Thin streaks of blood run down my body. You appear in front of me, the real you, flesh and bone, curly hair falling over your shoulders like servants of gravity.

You extend a hand and help me sit, back against the basin. If I had any doubt, it's gone now. The lines around your mouth are taut, dimpling how they did when you were about to say something serious. You're not being brainwashed or out of the dark wish's control.

"Don't come back, Alice," you tell me. "You were amazing, and I loved you… Maybe I…maybe I still do. Love is weird. Who am I to know anything? But right now, this is who I want to be."

You kneel in front of the puddle, not taking your eyes off me.

"You promise you won't follow me?"

I shake my head and whisper, "I can't promise… I…"

You lock your gaze on mine and we stay like this for a while. Then, you touch the burnt coin. The water swirls around your body and it's consumed, draining most of the puddle's remaining water.

You vanish. Again.

I turn and crawl to touch the coin. It's completely dry now. Burnt copper. I pick it up and stand, my legs heavier than before. The coin trembles in my hand, a flake of energy still sizzling through my fingers.

I can just throw it in another puddle and touch it again. I can get back to you…

I sit, curling my knees and folding them with my arms. I fidget with the coin. I can try to reason with you, negotiate, show you whatever kind of love that woman gives you, I can also give.

…and I can close doors.

"I wish for the peace of angels," I stutter, weeping, and flip the coin into a puddle. It splashes, clinks, and locks me out of your wishworld. Of you.

Long Last Alice

Cynthia Pelayo

I AM SITTING by the tall open windows. There's a gentle breeze blowing in. The smell of honeysuckle fills the room. The young man is seated beside me. To me he is young. To others not so much.

We have a beautiful spread of tea in front of us, pretty sandwiches and brightly colored cookies and savory and sweet scones, and of course tea. He's bitten into the raspberry scone I baked this morning, chewing with his mouth slightly open and his eyes wide. Crumbs are plinking down onto the porcelain plate set in front of him.

"What is it, young man?" I ask.

He reaches for the white napkin on his lap and brings it to his mouth and dabs the corner of his lips. He then sets the scone down onto the plate. "They're so blue. Your eyes. I've never seen eyes so blue. They remind me of your dress." His eyes flash to the black rectangular device beside the plate.

"You're recording our conversation on that?" I raise the teacup to my lips and savor the taste of Earl Grey tea.

"A cell phone. Have you seen one before?"

I smile and return the teacup to the table. My eyes turn back to the window, focusing on the slope of the great, green land. I knew of cell phones, and I knew of cars and I knew of other things, but I liked to keep things this way, the old way.

We both hear the purr of a cat and our eyes move down by his brown pantleg where she's rubbing against the fabric.

"Is this?" The young man reaches a hand down and starts petting the top of her head.

"Indeed that is my darling cat, Dinah."

The young man looks up at me. "She does not age either?"

"No, neither of us do. That is the way things went after that day. The door, the path, and well, we all know the story. Those of us who have read the story."

Dinah slinks away to the living room.

"What if the story is no longer read?"

I reach for a cucumber sandwich and place it on the plate in front of me. "Well," I say, my eyes training upwards to the ceiling in deep thought. "There is no sure way of knowing until the very last child, the very last person has read my story. I suppose, then and maybe only then, that's when the effects of age would take place and well, it's all a ticking time clock from there now, isn't it?"

"Is that why you live here?" the young man asks. Looking around the great house. "To escape the possibility of time?"

"Yes, to be frozen in the way things were so that I could have some familiarity. Everyone is gone. Mother and father, cousins and aunts. There are others. Great-great-great this, that, and the other, but after a while, people start raising eyebrows like 'Dear cousin Alice, why are you still a little girl?' That is very difficult to explain, and so I came out here in isolation so I no longer needed to explain. I moved to the ends of the Earth and in doing that I also escaped the newness of things. It's not that I shunned innovation. Of course there's something marvelous about advancement, shifts and change, sparks and plugs, but given my journey I thought it would be best I retire someplace that felt familiar. What feels familiar is land and green and trees and…"

In the distance I notice a small white mass appear and disappear. I feel my lips pull back in a smile, and a warm sense of peace fills my chest.

"Rabbits?" the young man asks.

I shake my head "No," but that is a lie. There is no need to tell this visitor about the things that I see, about my life past and my life present, and future, even though all of it has melded into one. I look down on my hands resting on my lap. *How much time has passed?* I wonder. People like the idea of eternity, immortality, to live forever, but rarely do they ponder the cost of a constant that knows no end. I live in this great house, and on this great swathe of land, but what else is there when my life is on repeat. My life will be repeated as long as they read my story and in ways, I like that I bring them joy. I like that my travel written on pages brings them wonder.

This young man who presented himself to me today, he has come to learn about me. He wants to know why I know no end and he wants to know how I found the door, but I think that he's not asking the most important question.

The young man starts telling me about the recording and how he plans to take it back to his paranormal psychology society. I am neither paranormal, nor do I think that I am fascinating enough to be psychologically studied. My days are simple. I wake. I wash. I walk. I prepare meals for myself and I think of my kitchen cabinets with white porcelain plates and cups and saucers. I think of my bedroom drawers full of socks and chests stuffed with delicately stitched quilts. But there are many other sorts of doors, car door, barn doors, cellar doors. A little door in a tree. A rabbit hole even could be considered a door of sorts.

A door can open in. A door can open out. One can enter. One can exit. There are many more considerations. Not many people think of these archways in their homes that lead from one room to another. A threshold. A doorknob. Knock. Turn. Push. Pull. It's all very ritualistic if you think about it, and every moment, every room entered generates a shift, a change, something more. Transformation. Metamorphosis.

I pick up my sandwich and take a small nibble. "I don't know how you found me. Still, I find it quite exciting that you have tried for so long."

"I've been trying all my life," he says and while yes, he does look like an old man to the average person, to me, he is still a very much a young man.

"How old are you?"

"Seventy-eight. And you are…"

"*Alice's Adventure in Wonderland* was published in 1865, so that makes me 158 years old."

"Did he know? Lewis Carroll, that you were going to pop right off the page?"

I wipe my hands on the napkin on my lap and reach for my teacup and take another sip. "I don't think anyone could anticipate the absurdity of any of it. Mad Hatter and the Queen of Hearts. A duck. A dodo. Caterpillars. A Cheshire cat. More. People like me, what's happened to us, it takes time to process, to truly understand the story that we've lived."

The young man raises a hand. "Us? Who is 'us'?"

"You can't believe that I'm the only one who has leapt off the page by my creator to live a life. There are things that no one really intends and understands, like how a story is written, how it progresses, how it changes and changes you. No one thinks of me, not at this age. They don't think, 'Well, Alice is 158 years old!' No. They like to speak of me as young, a little girl."

They will tell you I was looking for adventure, that while yes, parts of that may be true, there's so much more that I wish I could tell you. Like, I wish I could tell you that in the summer months when the June bugs shimmer across the blue-black sky that you should find cheer because you are surrounded by magic. And if you catch a June bug in a mason jar, or cup one into your hand, be sure to whisper to it your wishes and release it, for it will then race off to the nighttime clouds, beyond, to make sure your dream is set in motion.

A June bug is your own personal genie, your private Tinker Bell. There's wonder everywhere.

The problem is you can't see this wonder anymore because you have grown, and while yes, I have grown too in ways, I made sure along this life path to clutch onto it tight, that heart of fire, that passion and joy and intensity. You've come here to learn about the rabbit hole, but I think you want to know more about doors and how they can change you. That is the question I think you seek an answer to.

Maybe I will tell you more about the rabbit hole one day, about the clock and the potion and poison and the ocean of tears, but your journey is just starting. I have much time still too, don't believe that this age means that my travels are done. I just need to relay this message before the timekeeper disrupts our tea. He has a tendency to do that in his fits of madness.

"You want to know about the power of doors. First, you must recognize that each door is not just a rectangular passage, but a portal and how you step through it, what you believe as you step through it, what you say as you step through, that will become manifest. Please nod your head, please confirm that you're listening to me, because this is very important."

The young man nods, a look of astonishment on his face.

I hear the queen and her court marching up the lawn.

The young man stands slowly and looks out the window. "Is that?"

"Unfortunately, they're early today, yes. I did tell them to please reschedule as I would have company today, so I suppose I have to make this quick."

The door leading to the library creaks open and there is a cat perched atop it, smiling. The young man's lower lip twitches. "And that is…"

"The Cheshire cat enjoys a dramatic entrance, but please, pay attention. Doors. Portals. They're everywhere you see, inside and outside. You just have to choose. You just have to believe. You just have to *know*."

"And then what?"

"Then what?"

The young man reaches for a glass of water and takes a gulp. He seems nervous, but I understand. "Then I just disappear? When will I reappear?"

I scratch my chin. That is a very great question. "Who knows?"

"Who knows?"

"Yes, that's part of the adventure, don't you think?"

The Red Queen and her court begin chanting, a very ominous chant outside. Off in the distance the White Rabbit can be clearly seen, standing on its hindlegs looking at a gold pocket watch.

"That's…"

"The White Rabbit, yes."

We both sit silent for a moment and then I finally say: "Well, it's time for you to be off. Make your wish. Set your intention, pick a door and walk through it."

"And just like that?"

"And just like that it happened for me. Just like that it will happen for you. You have to speak the words, and you have to believe the belief and you have to feel what it is you want to be and then you stand at that threshold and then you push open that door and you become that thing you want to be, you live that life you want to live."

Eat me. Drink me. We are all changed at one time or another, by this, the way through doors.

The young man stands and walks over to the door where the Cheshire Cat is no longer lounging.

"What is it that you would like, young man?"

Standing at the threshold, with his back to me, the young man says, "I would just like more time. More time to enjoy the joys of life. More time for adventure. More time for wonder. I didn't appreciate what it was I did have and now it's gone, but now, another chance, to learn from you, the queen of time, in ways, and the queen of doors, and the queen of wonder."

"Believe it," I say, motioning for the young man to walk through.

He closes his eyes, holds his arms out just a little, just a bit, just enough to fit through the door frame and he steps and he steps and he steps right through and there, off he is gone.

I lean back in my seat, and I look at the cookies I baked and frosted and decorated. EAT ME, some say, DRINK ME, others have written.

I take the right cookie and I shrink myself down.

It is time for another adventure in my Wonderland.

Toward the Light

Outrider

Antony Johnston

SHE SHOULDN'T BE in here alone. But what choice does she have?

Savage walks cautiously, head-mounted flashlight forming a claustrophobic tunnel through which she moves. Travelling fire-blackened corridors, ascending charred stairwells, skirting pipes seeping oily drizzle, passing doors burned off their hinges. The building creaks and groans like an old man straightening his crooked back, a never-ending litany of structural despair embedded in its shifting walls.

This is far from her first trip inside the Block, but Savage isn't complacent. She knows the pitfalls. She turns in a watchful circle, only to find a new balcony now in front of her. She glances up at a sound from the ceiling, and almost falls down a shaft created a moment ago. She tries to retrace her steps, but the stairs she mounted are a solid wall.

Nobody else is here. She knows that, expected it would be this way unless a streamer is doing a run at the same time, but that's unlikely. Few come in here to begin with, and the bribed cops who look away when she passes the cordon normally drop hints if the Block is "occupied." Nobody wants their livestream spoiled by running into another person.

Savage isn't streaming. She can't, and there'd be no point anyway.

She's here to find Hideo. Which she knows, she *knows* is impossible. A waste of time. Does she really think he could have survived in here for however long it's been?

(Two months, four days, twenty-one hours.)

No. Hideo is dead, and like all the others lost before him, his body will have been swept away, sacrificed to the Block's perpetual renewal.

She didn't stop crying for three weeks when he failed to return. Savage warned him the streamer was sketchy; a superfluous act, because he knew damn well already. But the client was a big shot, offering big money if Hideo would be his Outrider and get them to the rooftops. Almost nobody gets up there, but Hideo had made it four times already.

Twenty minutes inside, everything was going great. Then a rotating support pillar caught Hideo off-guard, and he lost sight of his streamer just long enough for the shadows to lead the big shot through a doorway that became an elevator shaft. Livestreamed to millions of followers, plus Savage, who had tuned in nervously and now screamed in vain as the gunmetal floor rushed to meet him.

End of stream, because Outriders don't wear Shadowcams. Why bother, when they can't see shadows anyway? Besides, they're not the star. Their job is to keep the star safe. Hideo failed to do that, and never came back out.

So now here's Savage, blundering alone through the Block's hollow, reverberating paranoid darkness. Not for engagement, or follows, or sponsor deals. She knows she won't see anything; no shadows, no Hideo, nothing but her own grief and desperation reflected in a rank puddle of ebony tears.

Then she sees the girl.

~

Imagine a city block. Imagine, one day, it *changed*. No warning, no visible force, no explanation. Suddenly it looked like it had been gutted by fire (but there was no fire) and everyone who lived there was gone (but there were no bodies). The whole place was simply vacated. Empty.

The government ran a cordon around it and sent in drones, returning the pictures they expected of black, fire-damaged surfaces. Empty buildings and apartments. Clandestine pipes and guts, life's occult arteries, brought to light and bleeding through disemboweled walls.

What they didn't expect was the drones getting lost. Not just the GPS (which the Block scrambled somehow) but where they flew in through a door, they flew out into a wall. Where they had turned left, the corridor now turned right.

That wasn't even the weirdest part.

～

"What the hell are you doing in here?" Savage asks the girl. Seven, eight years old at the most, barefoot in an incongruous summer dress. "Are you streaming?"

The girl makes eye contact, defiant and silent.

"Talk to me, sweetheart. How did you get here? Who did you come with?"

The girl says nothing. Savage approaches slowly, not wanting to spook her. She knows she looks intimidating; has spent years cultivating it, with the mohawk and boots and tactical augments. But she hears the environment's tell-tale noises, the moan of shearing metal, and knows if she's not careful this corridor could become an atrium, stairwell, even a solid wall.

"It's OK," she whispers. "You're safe now. I'll get you out of here."

Something slams behind Savage. She turns in time to see the corner become a doorway, firmly shut. She doesn't bother trying the door; knows it won't yield.

When she turns back, the girl is gone.

～

The firefighters they sent in after the drones all killed themselves, or each other, and nobody could figure out why. Their bodycams showed the same building, eternal reconfiguration notwithstanding, but one by one they either walked into empty air or turned on their colleagues.

Next up: a mixed team of scientists and soldiers. Advisors objected, because what better way to go crazy and kill your companions than with a fully-loaded assault rifle? But the decision was made, and in they went.

What happened next changed the world.

One scientist wore an experimental implant of their own devising, a neuro-optic waveform compound visual processor. To you and me, that's a camera that looks through your eyes. Meaning it records not what really *is*, but what you *see*.

She saw shadows.

˷

Savage runs, calling out, angry that she took her eye off the girl. Nobody so vulnerable should be in here. But there have always been young streamers: barely teenagers, risking everything for engagement. She would rant to Hideo that the perimeter cops should set some kind of minimum age, making him laugh at the incongruity. She'd insist it wasn't safe for kids like that to enter, and he'd shrug, and say, 'It's not safe for anyone. That's why we go in with them. Those young streamers all have Outriders.'

He was right, which only made her more angry.

She pushes those thoughts and memories from her mind now. She knew looking for Hideo was futile, and coming in here alone is the most dangerous thing she's ever done. But, having exhausted her tears, she couldn't sit idle. Savage cancelled all her regulars and decided she wouldn't take another gig until she'd tried to find him. A coping strategy, something to aim for no matter how unattainable.

Now, she buries it alongside all her other abandoned hopes and dreams, ignoring the mourning cry of yesterday's Savage. This, today, is real. This is important. Her new mission, to find the girl and get her to safety.

She takes newly-created stairs two at a time to the upper floors.

˷

Shadowcams (based on that neuro-optic tech, now with added wireless livestream protocol) set the market ablaze with the heat of a thousand suns. The must-have surgery this holiday season. Even people on the other side of the world, nowhere near the Block, emptied their savings. Watching livestreams was one thing, but seeing shadows with your own eyes: that's the ticket.

The first to venture into the Block were a couple of young streamers with new implants. Sneaking inside, broadcasting to millions. Shadows, shadows everywhere. So many tuned in, the platform crashed.

When they finally resurrected the servers, the boy was dead at the bottom of a stairwell with the girl sitting next to him. She held his hand and whimpered while shadows swarmed around them. Seventeen minutes later her stream cut off.

Meanwhile, on the other side of the world: nothing. Turned out shadows only appeared inside the Block. Those early adopters, their life savings spent, now merely regretful cyborgs. Disappointment turned to anger, and suspicion of a hoax. Editing. VFX. Tricks of the light.

Hideo was one such skeptic. He travelled halfway across the globe and went in with a Shadowcam-enabled streamer. Sure enough, he didn't see a damn thing. But his partner's stream, side-by-side, showed different. Dozens of shadows, passing so close it was impossible Hideo couldn't see them. And yet.

When frustration subsided, confidence filled the gap. Unencumbered by flickering silhouettes that hid a shifting landscape, or malevolent whispers that obliterated reason, Hideo guided his partner onward in safety and saved him from a dozen fatal missteps.

The world realized not everyone saw shadows.

Hideo realized this was a business opportunity.

༄

Stalking down a corridor, checking each skeletal apartment as she passes, Savage wonders, is she mad? Or is the girl a shadow after all?

She doesn't *think* she's mad. But she *knows* she can't see shadows, not with her own eyes. It's the defining attribute of her role: the streamer sees, broadcasts, takes a bow while the Outrider remains off-camera, anonymous, seeing only the Block's shifting form. They keep the streamer safe, and both make it out alive.

Savage has seen shadows on livestreams, though, through the Shadowcams' technical magic. She knows what they look like. Blurred, hazy shapes lacking clear definition, defying detail.

The girl is none of those things, which means Savage must be mad. The grief and loss of Hideo has done something to her mind.

She presses on, up and up.

∽

The government extended the cordon street by street until the Block sat inside a dozen others, deserted and abandoned. A pale reflection.

Occupants had no choice, but it didn't take much to persuade them. Some feared it would spread; others, with perfectly rational irrationality, worried that if it happened again it would strike in the same vicinity. Whatever their reasons, everyone snatched the meagre compensation and ran.

∽

Savage crashes through a door and sees stars.

She's on the rooftops. Her first time.

It's nothing special. Burned and dilapidated, like everywhere else. Beyond the Block is the perimeter buffer of empty buildings, desolate and silent. But then the city stretches away in all directions, life and hope surrounding this event horizon of death and gloom.

Savage smiles, remembering how she and Hideo met. They were both trying to bribe the same cop at the same time. She was with one of her regulars, he was with a notorious risk-taker she wouldn't touch with a ten-foot pole. Savage knew who Hideo was, of course. By now everyone knew his dark eyes and cocky grin. To her surprise, he recognized her in return. Said he liked her mohawk.

They argued about priority, then they laughed when the cop worried they might fight, then Hideo backed down and let her go first in return for her number. Savage thought she'd come out on top, but then after her own run she watched him and his streamer climb onto the roof just in time for sunrise. It was a glorious, beautiful moment, now one of the most watched in Block history, and Savage was so angry she almost applauded at how expertly she'd been played. When Hideo got out, he immediately offered to buy her a drink to apologize. She called him a sly bastard, and he grinned, and they kissed.

They agreed early on not to run together. Streamers rarely needed, and certainly didn't want, more than one Outrider at a time. No simultaneous runs, no shared clients. A façade of independence, masking new-found inseparability. Hideo's fans came to despise her, but Savage didn't care. Anyone niche enough to follow an Outrider was already inclined towards the odd.

Now she remembers how they parted. Two months, four days, and twenty-two hours ago she rolled on top of Hideo and tried again to persuade him not to go. She didn't like it. Bad vibe. He laughed, lifted her off, and dressed. Left her lying on his pillow, infused with the scent of him.

Standing on the rooftop, as dawn's inevitable light burns away the exhausted dark, memory emulsifies sorrow and joy in the crucible of her heart.

A young girl cries from below, and Savage rushes back.

In the old stories, most people were blind to ghosts. Only a select few, blessed and cursed in equal measure, saw beyond the veil.

Are shadows ghosts? Nobody knows. Some say they are. Others call them devils, aliens, time travelers. What we know is that they exist, and cameras can't see them, but humans can. It's not a rare blessing (or curse) after all. It's… normal.

Well. Normal for ninety-nine-point-nine-something of the population.

Maybe half a million worldwide are "insensitive." That's the official estimate, though this extrapolated statistic rises from unsafe ground because less than two thousand people total have ever been inside the Block.

The new stories aren't like the old stories. Now, entire servers are dedicated to Block fanfic. Streamer/Shadow, Streamer/Outrider, Streamer/Outrider/Shadow, Shadow/Shadow, all humanity and otherwise is there. Some have even tried Outrider/Shadow, though most reviews dismiss them as too unrealistic.

❦

Savage takes the stairs three at a time. Four when there's a step missing, exposing space and air through abrupt rents in charred steel that rings under her boots, every step filling the suffocating air with a metallic din. The only other sound she hears is her own heartbeat.

She keeps the tunnel of light fixed in front of her to prevent transformation. Around her, the building wails and mewls like a thwarted infant. She knows if she only glanced to the side, she'd see walls expand, doors birthed, spaces collapse; is no less certain that when she looked back, she'd step into void.

The sound of the girl matches her descent, always a floor below, until Savage is certain she's taken more stairs than there are floors. Still they continue, and still the sobbing reaches her ears.

"Stay where you are!" she cries, not knowing if the child can hear or understand her but compelled, nevertheless.

It works so well that on the very next landing they almost collide.

Startled, the girl stops crying and looks up at Savage. Something about her eyes is familiar, but the Outrider doesn't have time to think about that.

"Can I come with you?" the girl asks, and Savage's heart melts.

"Of course you can, sweetheart. Of course you can."

She reaches out, hesitating just long enough to wonder if there's anything to touch. Or is she truly mad, and this is mere illusion given form by her damaged mind?

Savage touches the girl. Solid, pliable, palpable skin and bone. She wraps the child in her arms, unable to explain why she's crying. She wipes her eyes, releases the girl, and takes her hand to lead them back upstairs.

Except there is no upstairs anymore.

Idiot! She took her eye off the landscape and the Block seized its chance. The stairs are gone; now Savage and the girl huddle in a cramped windowless corridor. She swears in frustration, screams obscenities at the building. She can almost imagine it twitch and quiver in response.

It's not her imagination.

The ceiling cracks and splinters, cascading debris at their feet. The ground trembles. Black dust billows into the air.

Savage instinctively moves in front of the girl to protect her, is already moving to gather her up, when she realizes there is nothing to gather. The girl is gone.

"Come back!" she yells, spinning around, furious that she didn't even ask the girl's name. "Come back to me, we'll find a way out!"

"You won't find her, Sav."

A voice emerges from the darkness. A hand reaches out through the suspended dust. Hideo takes her hand.

"Maybe she'll find you, but first you have to live. Come on."

She has a thousand questions, so many they jam in her throat. Instead, she cries, "No, no, the girl… we have to find her, I promised to take her with me…"

A slab of blackened concrete smashes to the ground beside them. Hideo smiles sadly, the same way he looked at Savage when she begged him not to take the sketchy gig, and squeezes her hand. He doesn't need to speak.

Filled all at once with sadness and light, she holds on as they run through the thundering destruction which she somehow knows is the end.

The Block is dying. She will be one of the last to see it. Nobody will witness this but her, Hideo, and the girl.

Walls crumble in the darkness. Girders twist and snap, falling into newly-formed chasms inches in front of them. Doors disintegrate before their eyes. Grimy soot chokes the air.

Savage stumbles over an erupting beam. Hideo catches her, pulls her along. Has the girl made it out? She wants to go back, to find her, but knows it's hopeless. As hopeless as it was coming in here to find him.

Dawn light shines somewhere ahead. She coughs on noxious air but forces her eyes to remain open, fixed, keeping the exit in sight as firmly as she grips Hideo's hand. She never wants to let go. But then he drags her to the opening, neither door nor window but something indefinable, and she must let go to pass through.

Outside she keels over, and the Block collapses behind her, and firefighters run towards her, and despite dawn's light Savage's vision succumbs to the dark.

Later, lying on her bed, she projects the security cam footage from those last moments onto her ceiling. Everyone in the world has seen it, saved it, analyzed it. What happened in there? Why did the Block collapse? What did Savage do?

The firefighters insist she came out alone. No bodies have been found in the wreckage. No shadows have been seen.

She watches it again and again, looping the moment before she jumps clear. There, in the shivering dark, right behind Savage, obscured by pulsating walls. Is that a figure? A trick of the light? Her own shadow?

It's OK. She knows they'll never be apart again.

Inside her, the baby kicks.

Glitter Town

Kali Wallace

FOR A FEW moments, in the disorienting space between sleeping and waking, Daniel imagined himself as part of the movie. The crowd of travelers flowed around him. They had no faces. They jostled him, and he tried to mumble apologies, but he could not speak. The sound of the approaching train grew louder. There was no color, only flat shades of gray. The sky cracked open, and people began to scream.

A soft slap of sound, unexpected, and Daniel woke. He was slumped in Dimitriou's armchair. *Silver City*'s opening scene played on the screen in front of him. The mournful cello swelled over the sound of the train.

It was a wallet that had awoken him. The plain folding kind, now lying open on the tile floor. In his sleep-muddled mind, Daniel thought: *That's new.*

Tiff had put a layer of throw pillows down to catch whatever came through, but the wallet had missed by a couple of inches. It had fallen from an ember-ringed hole in the screen about two feet off the ground. The hole was closing now, the screen knitting back together, leaving no trace except a tendril of smoke.

The holes always looked as though something were burning through the screen, but there was never anything visible through them except an iridescent darkness, like oil spilt on asphalt. Some would grow to eight or ten inches across, but no matter their size, they were impossible to reach through. Daniel had tried, once. The scars on his right hand tugged every time he made a fist. The memory of the pain made him nauseous. Tiff still woke with nightmares sometimes; she didn't like the smell of grilled meat anymore.

Daniel pushed himself out of the armchair, stifling a groan as his back twinged. He watched the hole close up completely before he switched the projector off.

The film had been playing all night, which wasn't possible. It was a single reel, not quite the standard thousand feet long; there was damage at the end where the last several feet had been torn or burnt away. At twenty-four frames per second, with the soundtrack, it should play for about ten minutes. Those ten minutes encompassed *Silver City*'s long opening credits and the beginning of its first scene. That melancholy score, all cello. The black-and-white ground-level view of a train passing by a busy platform. There were voices, but they were indistinct. At around eight minutes the travelers stopped walking abruptly. In the distance a few people craned their heads and pointed upward. The music stopped and, at the same moment, there was a terrible crack, like thunder. The travelers screamed and cowered.

And the reel would—impossibly—start over.

A single reel was all that remained of Konstantin Dimitriou's final film. That same clip existed in digital form all over the internet, but everybody believed the original reel had been lost with the rest of the movie.

Daniel and Tiff hadn't known any of that before. They weren't really into movies. But after Tiff got the job as Dimitriou's nurse, they had found paperwork for a bungalow in Silver Lake. The house was outside the domes, in one of the parts of Los Angeles that had been evacuated and restricted nearly thirty years ago. Scavengers had been picking over that territory for almost as long, but Daniel had still gone to the bungalow, looking for souvenirs, artifacts, random junk from Hollywood before before the studios left L.A., from before the city outside the domes was cleared. All of that was in fashion among collectors and film buffs. He had thought he might find something worth selling.

Most of what he found was the normal detritus of a city that had become a ghost town. But he had also found the single damaged film reel and the old-fashioned projector. Dimitriou had cried the first time Daniel and Tiff played it for him, big fat tears leaking over the ropey burn scars on his face. They'd had to hold him back from lunging for the screen when the first hole opened.

It wasn't possible. Daniel and Tiff weren't scientists, they were just a guy who sold snacks and contraband from a cart and a home care nurse, but they weren't idiots either. The holes in the screen, the items dropping through, the single reel that played for hours, none of it was possible. It happened anyway.

Down the hallway, Tiff's alarm beeped briefly. Their bedroom door opened; the bathroom door closed. Tiff always woke up looking like she'd lost a fight with a wind tunnel during the night, but in an impossibly short time she would emerge from the bathroom tidy and pretty as a picture. Daniel loved looking at her either way.

He opened the back door to clear the faint scent of smoke from the room. In this quiet hour before dawn, the view across the city was soft, indistinct. The Torrance and Long Beach domes hunched over the landscape to the south, filling valleys and tipping over hills, just starting to glow with the day's first sunlight. The ruins in the middle ground were a dark sprawl, interrupted by the cluster of skyscrapers jutted upward like charred sticks, and specked with faint, scattered lights. There were a few bright spots that indicated bigger encampments, but most of the campfires were solitary: loners who had survived another night.

That had been Daniel, before the house in Silver Lake. He hadn't left the domes since. This was the most dangerous time of day for scavengers, just before dawn, when the mind was most easily muddled. It had always been nearly dawn when Daniel heard and saw the things only scavengers knew about. Shadows that moved when there was nobody there. Loping creatures on empty roads, moving too fast. Sounds that weren't quite voices echoing from sinkholes in crumbling pavement. There were old-timers who swore a person could walk through a doorway in one of the half-collapsed sound stages over in Burbank, or poke around the old Palace Theater downtown, or prowl through the ruins of a Malibu compound, and at the right time of day, in the right lost and lonely frame of mind, they would find themselves surrounded by echoes of how the city used to be, thriving and vibrant and alive—but if they lingered, they might never want to leave.

Daniel rubbed his face and yawned. He left the door open to shuffle over to the screen. He bent down to collect the lost items into a cardboard box. Tiff had written "Lost and Found" on the box in black marker, with a couple of smiley faces.

Today there was a gold watch, the brand name on its face an unreadable scramble, its second hand ticking backwards. A silver bracelet with a little dog-shaped charm; the dog had two heads, and one was snarling. A small crucifix on a delicate golden chain, but the figure on the cross was no Jesus Daniel's abuela would have revered, not with claws that long and a grin that wide. A small purple butterfly barrette that looked so normal Daniel spent a full minute searching for its oddity, but found nothing. A few careworn comic books from a series called *Dust City Detective*. Other issues had come through before, legible enough to piece together that it was the story of a private investigator in a Martian city. Daniel already had a collector in mind.

Standard stuff, the right degree of strange. Easy to pass it all off as scavenged goods, slightly warped, from outside the domes.

The wallet was new. It wasn't more personal than the watch or necklace or comics, it wasn't more *real*, but something about it made Daniel nervous. He was being ridiculous. He flipped it open. Inside there was some cash, words and images all messed up, a few faded slips of paper, and a single plastic card. The card was an ID, with jagged lines at the top that almost said *California*. In the photo a young white man smiled awkwardly. A cowlick stuck up from the part in his combed dark hair.

Daniel could just make out the man's name: Winslow Poole. Most of the address was jumbled, but Daniel decided that Winslow Poole probably lived in Pasadena.

Nothing had come through with the owner's name before. Daniel had only ever speculated about the people on the other side. About who they were, how they existed. If they were real. He wasn't sure he liked knowing a name and a face. His scarred right hand itched. He tucked the ID back into the wallet.

A door opened, soft footsteps padded, and Tiff pressed sleepily against his back. "Good haul?"

"Not bad."

She had been wanting to visit her mother for months; her sisters called every week to discuss another health concern. But the nursing service imposed a penalty when Tiff needed a replacement, so they couldn't afford both the time off and the trip down to San Diego. A few more sales and it might be doable.

The house's alarm beeped as the kitchen door opened. Pilar, Dimitriou's cook and housekeeper, punched in the code before bustling in.

"Visitors today," she said. Pilar rarely bothered with greetings. She wouldn't be out of place in one of Dimitriou's films

"They won't be here for hours," Tiff said.

Pilar sniffed. "Even so."

Tiff rolled her eyes, but only after Pilar turned away. "I'll get the old man up." She gave Daniel a kiss. "It's going to be hot today. Be careful."

"I'll stay inside the stations," Daniel promised.

The visitors were a film school professor and some students, eager for an interview with the great director Konstantin Dimitriou, right here in the Laurel Canyon home where he had lived as a recluse for decades. They would be disappointed; Dimitriou didn't speak anymore. His manager only set these things up to prove the old man was still alive. Tiff and Pilar would deal with it.

Daniel headed out to the garage to load up his cart. He went heavy on cold drinks for the morning, ice cream for the afternoon. He put the items from the Lost and Found box in a hidden compartment. It had been months since any cops had hassled him about selling scavenged goods—"looted," they called it—but it was better to be cautious, and collectors paid more if they thought there was risk involved.

He popped back inside to tell Tiff goodbye. She was in Dimitriou's room, helping the old man into his wheelchair; his legs were like scarred, knotty sticks jutting out from the sagging adult diaper he wore. Daniel left quickly and told himself it was for Dimitriou's sake. The tabloids used to say Dimitriou had been injured by experimental cosmetic surgery gone very wrong. It wasn't until after Daniel found the *Silver City* reel and tried reaching through the screen that had he and Tiff deduced the truth: sometime in the past, before the reel was lost, Dimitriou had tried to climb through to the other side.

Outside, the velvety dawn was fading into flat, mustard-yellow daylight, giving the streets and houses and trees a jaundiced look. The Laurel Canyon dome was one of the oldest in the city, built back when it had been a grotesque example of the wealthy wrapping themselves in protective walls while the world burned. Now, there were better places to live, and everybody who wanted out had already moved away. The downhill walk to the station was long, but it was peaceful.

The commuters were used to Daniel; they moved aside to make room for his cart on the train. He sent a few messages to collectors before tucking his phone away.

Dimitriou's face glared down from the ads all along the train car. A film festival: AUTEUR OF A DYING WORLD. A KONSTANTIN DIMITRIOU RETROSPECTIVE. TICKETS ON SALE NOW. That was why the professor and students wanted an interview this week. The ads cycled clips from Dimitriou's movies: the empty beach from *Roulette*, the broken wine glass in *Long Time Forever*, the woman's limp hand dripping blood at the end of *The Wastes*. That one was about the failed Martian colony, the kind of movie where everybody died by the end, and the hand belonged to Angelica Boucher, Dimitriou's favorite actor. It had been her last movie. She had died in one of the Malibu firestorms thirty-some years ago. Daniel remembered the news, remembered his aunts staring at their phones in shock, remembered the sky glowing red.

The ads for the film festival followed Daniel all morning. He headed to the Long Beach station, and the wine glass broke a dozen times on the screens above the platform. He passed cold drinks to office workers and snacks to day laborers, and Angelica Boucher's fingers dripped blood. He sold the watch, the bracelet, the crucifix, and the purple barrette to a twitchy collector who called himself Lincoln. Lincoln, who spent ten minutes telling Daniel that creatures from outside had learned how to change themselves into shadows and slip through cracks where the domes were failing.

"You can only fight them with light," Lincoln said. He leaned closer to Daniel and opened his jacket; he smelled stale and unwashed. There was a string of LEDs draped around his neck, sparkling against his sweat-stained t-shirt. He said, "They're afraid of light. That's how you keep them away."

"Thanks for the tip," Daniel said. He passed over an iced tea and a bag of chips. He didn't know if Lincoln had someone looking after him. "On the house. Stay safe out there."

After the lunchtime rush calmed, Daniel started to close up the cart to move to another station. He bent down to secure a panel, and when he stood again, there was a man watching him.

The man at the end of the platform stood out from the other passengers only because he was so very still. He didn't look at the train as it slid into the station. He looked only at Daniel. A knot of unease tightened in Daniel's gut. Even the cops didn't stare so openly when they came around to hassle him.

Daniel met the man's eyes briefly. White guy, young. Dirty jeans and a ratty hoodie. A little familiar, but Daniel saw a lot of people during the day.

The train left, and the platform was empty but for the two of them.

Daniel's right hand itched. He reached down—he didn't look away from the man—and opened the hidden compartment beneath the cart handles. Felt around—still didn't look—until he found the wallet. He fumbled it open.

The jumbled letters that probably said California. The distorted address that was probably Pasadena. The low-res photo. Daniel's stomach dropped, slick and sudden, a sensation not unlike falling. He looked up again.

Winslow Poole was thinner now, almost gaunt. The cowlick stuck up from his unruly hair.

Daniel hesitated, then held up the wallet. Gave it a little shake. He felt ridiculous; he wasn't trying to tempt a stray dog with a treat. But he wasn't about to shout across the platform: *Hey, did you drop your wallet?* He had watched the wallet fall through the screen just a few hours ago. Winslow Poole in his ratty hoodie and jeans had definitely not followed. He didn't have two heads, or claws. All of his features were in the right place. His clothes badly needed a wash.

Winslow Poole startled and took a step back, like he was surprised to be noticed. His mouth dropped open, and his jaw moved slightly. If he spoke, Daniel couldn't hear it.

A group of loud-talking construction workers spilled from the escalator onto the platform. Their hardhats and high-vis vests obscured Daniel's view. When they packed into the next train, Winslow Poole was nowhere to be seen.

Daniel looked for him, peeking around the columns on the platform, peering up the escalators and into the tunnels, but the man was gone. Hysterical laughter burbled up in Daniel's chest. People were starting to stare. He couldn't risk that. It didn't matter if he was losing his mind; it would be a hassle if somebody alerted the station security guards that the snack cart guy was acting weird.

So he finished packing up his cart. Locked the wallet away. Got on the northbound train, like he did every day. Beneath the film festival advertisements—breaking wine glass, bloody hand—he considered the possibilities.

The simplest: He was mistaken. That had just been some guy, a stranger wondering why the snack guy was gawking at him. The resemblance was coincidental.

Slightly more concerning: That man was the Winslow Poole from this world, the alternate version or doppelganger such as Tiff and Daniel had theorized must exist after reading some stuff about parallel universes. It was either unlikely chance or sinister design that he had been on the platform with Daniel.

Most concerning: That man was Winslow Poole of Pasadena, the same man who had lost his wallet, and he had come from wherever the wallet had come from, and somehow, for some reason, he had found Daniel.

He hadn't come through the screen in Dimitriou's house. They would have noticed. But there were other possibilities. Daniel had looked for more reels of *Silver City*. Dimitriou's personal records proved the rest of the film *had* existed at some point, although nobody but Dimitriou had ever seen the finished movie. First Daniel had searched in person, at the house in Silver Lake and places Dimitriou was known to have worked. Later, when Daniel stopped scavenging outside the domes, he trawled message boards and discussion forums, chasing down rumors. Tiff had even asked Dimitriou, but she had not expected, and did not receive, an answer. Daniel and Tiff never stopped wondering if the rest of the film would do the same as the opening scene, if every reel would play until it was stopped, if every screen would burn and heal, burn and heal, while detritus from another world tumbled through.

They never found any more of the film. But it might be out there, which meant somebody else might be watching the reels, catching what dropped through. Maybe even studying the film and the items—maybe they had more luck convincing scientists to listen. Maybe in different scenes, a whole person might fall through.

Maybe it wasn't *Silver City* that mattered at all. Lincoln was seeing shadows inside the domes. There were echoes in old soundstages, music in old theaters. Glints of light in the ruined skyscrapers. Some people wanted to look backward and invent a particular catastrophe to explain what the city had become: an industrial accident, a nuclear explosion. Chemicals, drugs, viruses. But Daniel had lived in Los Angeles for his entire life, most of that outside the domes. He didn't need a singular cause to explain what the city had become. Everything magnificent that died left both carcasses and ghosts behind.

He set up in the Santa Monica station for the afternoon. It was already busy, so busy he didn't notice when Winslow Poole appeared again. One moment he looked down to hand a popsicle to a kid; the next he looked up and the man was there, a little ways down the platform, standing by a pillar. Staring at Daniel again. Daniel stared right back. Gave Winslow Poole a little nod, both acknowledgment and invitation, but the man kept his distance.

Daniel kept an eye on him through the day. After a while his itchy nervousness faded. The man wasn't hurting anybody. Daniel had work to do. A person could get used to anything.

Late in the afternoon, the station filled with schoolkids in stylish sneakers and prep school blazers. They passed through the Santa Monica station every day, traveling from their protected schools with green fields and trophy cases to their cool, clean homes behind high walls and locked gates.

"What'll you have?" Daniel asked as the kids lined up.

They were good kids, never gave him trouble. They made their purchases and drifted off to exits or trains. One of Daniel's regulars, a sometimes-collector with a shock of blue hair, stayed behind. Daniel didn't know his name, just had the kid saved in his phone as "Blue." The kids all called each other by goofy, ever-changing nicknames anyway—Plunk, Crunch, Grobb—and he couldn't keep track.

Thumbs tucked into the strap of his backpack, shoulders slumped in a slouch, Blue jerked his head toward Winslow Poole. "Is that guy a cop or something? He's staring at you."

"I don't think he's a cop."

Blue lowered his voice. "A rival?"

"I don't think he's that either," Daniel said. He unlatched the panel at the back of his cart and reached inside. "Don't worry about him."

He brought out the comics that had fallen through during the night. Three issues of *Dust City Detective*. The blue-haired kid was always eager to buy the comics. He liked the series so much Daniel sometimes wondered about the other kid, the one on the other side, and whether he had finished reading the issues he dropped from time to time.

Blue studied the cover of the top comic. A silhouetted person in a hat and long coat stood on a balcony, overlooking a nighttime city of bright lights and elegant skyscrapers.

"You ever think about it?" the kid said. "If this is what Mars would be like if things hadn't gone wrong?"

Fifty years ago, the first and only attempt at a Martian colony had failed, and humanity had stopped trying to live anywhere beyond Earth's orbit. But in *Dust City Detective*, the colony had survived its catastrophic first year, come through stronger and more resilient, and had grown into a thriving boomtown.

Maybe that's what happened in the other world. Nobody had ever dropped a convenient history book for Daniel to check. He could only put together so much from watches and jewelry. He mostly tried not to think about it.

He glanced across the platform. Winslow Poole was still there, watching. Daniel considered, for the first time, that he might be able to ask.

"There's a memorial thing this weekend," the kid was saying. "My parents say we have to go."

Daniel blinked. The kid had lost him. "Go where?"

"The fifty-year memorial." Blue tapped the comic book. "My great-granddad was one of the engineers. Not one of the ones who tried to be heroic till the end. He killed himself as soon as it started getting bad."

Daniel had no idea what to say to that. The film festival ads were still playing around the station. Like everybody else with crappy schooling and no personal connection, so much of what Daniel knew about the Martian colony came from Dimitriou's *The Wastes*. Whenever he heard the names of the people who had died, he pictured the actors' faces instead. Even now, decades later, Angelica Boucher was remembered for the film version of somebody else's tragedy even more than her own.

"You want all of them?" Daniel asked, with a nod at the comics.

The kid didn't haggle; he never did. It was his parents' money anyway.

Eventually the evening crowds drained away. Daniel packed up to go home. When the eastbound train arrived and the doors slid open, Daniel pushed his cart aboard.

Winslow Poole got onto the next car.

Got onto the next car, got off at the same station. He avoided meeting Daniel's eyes, but he followed Daniel out into the ruddy sunset, and he followed on the long uphill walk to Dimitriou's street. Daniel leaned forward to push the cart, its bell jingling with every step. A curtain twitched in the window of the once-green house on the corner. The woman who lived there was always watching. Daniel gave her a wave; she didn't wave back. They had only spoken a few times, right after Tiff took the job, when Daniel and his cart were an unfamiliar sight in the neighborhood.

Daniel reached Dimitriou's house just as Pilar was leaving. "There you are," she said. "I left your dinner—" She stopped when she spotted Winslow Poole. She tightened her grip on her saggy shoulder bag. "Who is that?"

"Don't worry about him," Daniel said.

He could see the moment she decided not to ask. Pilar never wanted to know. She'd lasted a long time in Dimitriou's employ by not asking.

She said, "Tiffany is giving Mr. Dimitriou his dinner now. The visitors exhausted him, so she's worked extra hard today. You can heat hers up when she's ready for it."

Daniel had forgotten about the visitors. Pilar was always saying things like that, giving Daniel instructions on how to be a better husband. He would have fixed Tiff's dinner for her anyway.

"Will do," Daniel said. "Have a good night."

Pilar crossed the road to give Winslow Poole a wide berth as she headed down to the station.

Daniel opened the garage and pushed his cart inside. He kept one eye on the driveway as he put everything away. He pocketed the wallet. The daylight was almost gone, and Winslow Poole was as muted as the twilight palm trees and spindly cacti.

Daniel stepped back outside, closed and locked the garage.

"Well, come on," he said.

He followed the brick path around to the back of the house. In the distance the city was growing darker, everything softened by the day's lingering haze. Daniel recalled the smell the campfires, the hum of generators, the crackle of jury-rigged wiring. He didn't miss the heat or the danger of being outside the domes. Tiff worried a lot less now. But there had been times when an odd kind of peace would come over the empty streets and crumbling buildings. It always happened at twilight, as the faintest breeze stirred the air, and he would look up and see one star, maybe two, only the brightest, and for a couple of minutes it wouldn't matter that the rest were hidden by haze and smoke and heat, because there was no dome overhead, only sky, so much sky, and he would hold tight to his cart, suddenly fearful, maybe hopeful, that he might float away.

Music drifted out of the house. The melancholy cello, the familiar score. The glass doors were open to the warm evening, and *Silver City*'s opening scene was on the screen.

Tiff stood beside Dimitriou, gently wiping his face and hands. She looked up and smiled. "Hey, honey. Pilar made us dinner."

"I saw her out front," Daniel said.

"She's trying out another of those soy-fruit hybrid products. It smells good, at least."

Tiff plucked the soiled napkin from Dimitriou's shirt and carefully set his hands on the arms of his chair. He let her do it, his twisted, scarred arms as limp as noodles. Sometimes he fought, but tonight he didn't seem to know Tiff was there. His eyes were fixed on the film. There were no holes opening in the screen yet, no lost items on the pillows beneath. Tiff had wrapped a blanket over Dimitriou's legs, in spite of the warmth of the day. It would slow him down if he tried to go for the screen again.

Tiff picked up Dimitriou's plate and turned toward Daniel. Her smile dropped.

"Danny," she said.

Daniel looked back to find Winslow Poole just a couple of feet behind him. The man looked even rougher up close. There was a raggedness to his breath that Daniel recognized: that was the wheeze of somebody who had breathed the air outside the domes too long without a mask.

Daniel took the wallet out of his pocket. "This is his, but until now he's kept his distance."

For a long moment Tiff only stared. Then she asked, "Has he said anything?"

"Not a word."

Tiff stepped back a little to stand behind Dimitriou's chair. Daniel moved to join her. The three of them waited in a tight little tableau, like a family portrait, while Winslow Poole finally came inside. His eyes widened when he saw the movie on the screen. He approached the screen quickly, almost frantically, and raised his hands.

"Wait, you can't—!" Tiff said, but she stopped when Daniel touched her hand. "He can't," she said, more quietly. "We don't know what will happen."

Of course they had wondered if people could come through, if they would be burned or distorted. Daniel tried not to think about it, the same way he tried not to think about leaving the domes anymore. But in that moment, as the train crossed the screen, Daniel wanted to know. He very much wanted to believe Winslow Poole could go home again.

Winslow Poole did not touch the screen. For a few minutes he stood between the projector and the screen, the movie playing partially across the back of his sweatshirt. After a while he lowered his hands and sank to the floor. Now the projected film touched only the top of his head. His shoulders trembled.

The screen remained whole. They could never predict when the holes would appear. Daniel looked down: Dimitriou had shifted his gaze. He was watching Winslow Poole with the most alert and curious expression Daniel had ever seen on him.

"What should we do?" Tiff whispered.

Standing before the open doorway, with the city and its scattered specks of firelight beyond, her forehead creased with worry, her shoulders round with exhaustion, Tiff was as beautiful as she had ever been. Daniel took her hand. He had no answer for her. In the film the train cars blurring together in lines of light and darkness. Indistinct figures in the distance raised their hands to point. Soon the music would stop. Daniel held his breath and waited for the sky to break open.

Alice Street

Paul Cornell

Alice Street

From Wikipedia, the free encyclopedia.

> This article is about the actress. For the adult film actress see *Alice Street Theater*. For those of the same or similar name see *Alice Street (disambiguation)*.

Alice Pleasance Street (born Alice Key, November 11th, 1949) is an American actress. She is known especially for her role as Dorothy Gale in *Wizards* (1986).

Other notable roles include Alice Liddle in *The Looking Glass War* (1984) and Patricia in *Brimstone and Treacle* (1982).

    Contents
    1 Early life
    2 Career
    3 Personal life
    4 Filmography

Paul Cornell

Early life

Street was born in New York City. Her mother, Rosemary Woodhouse, was a nightclub singer, a *Playboy* centerfold (Miss October 1957) and, it is claimed [citation needed] a prostitute, serving such clients as John F. Kennedy. The identity of her father remains unknown. Street herself claims to know his identity, and to have spoken to him on the telephone, but she has never publicly revealed his name. Street began acting at the age of six, having been 'taken in by' and 'looked after at' the Line and Square Loft theater company while her mother was out working. Her first role was as the baby in a burlesque comedy routine with Artie Muller, who was barracked by her mother, in the audience with a date, until she realised who his partner was. Street refers to herself as 'self-educated' but graduated from Bates High School in 1967.

Career

In her early teens, Street started taking leading roles at the Line and Square Loft, including Daisy Buchanan in *The Great Gatsby*. 'I was far too young,' she said, 'but when these people are presented to you, at that age, what can you do but inhabit them?' She was seen by theatrical agent Elijah Barnhart playing Sally Bowles in *Cabaret*, a role that Street herself had rewritten to portray Bowles as a male transvestite [citation needed]. Barnhart signed her to his Enchant agency, and she left the Line and Square Loft that same day, leading to her understudy having to finish the run of the play, a move which is still regarded with bitterness by her former colleagues [citation needed]. Under Barnhart, Street was to accept a series of roles on the Broadway stage which were to make her name in legitimate theater, including Rosaline in *Romeo and Juliet*, Dulcinea in *Don Quixote*, Violenta in *All's Well That Ends Well* and Mrs Churchill in *Emma*. But Street became tired of the hours and the 'endless repetition' of theatrical production, and increasingly sought a move into film. 'A film is one performance,' she said, 'there forever, the definitive stamp of you. It's made up of a lot of different yous, from different takes, but that's just the magic that makes the whole person. It's not like being onstage, when you've got your innards hanging out night after night.' She had a small part as Cocktail Waitress in *The Godfather Part II* (1974), but it was to be her role as Amelia in *Eraserhead* (1977) that was to be her big break. Director David Lynch called her 'the brightest thing I've ever seen in my life, my morning star' and was to feature her in small roles in every one of his theatrical movies (except, for reasons unknown, *Twin Peaks: Fire Walk with Me* (1992), up to and including *Mulholland Drive* (2001).

It was through Lynch that Street met Richard Loncraine, who was to cast her in *Brimstone and Treacle*, in a last-minute switch which left the actress originally cast in the part, whose identity he has never revealed, ready to sue the production company, finally settling out of court [citation needed]. It was Diane Lane [citation needed]. Street used the paycheck from the movie to set up her own production company, Venus Horizons, and was able to find financing from various out-of-Hollywood sources, said to include former Ugandan dictator Idi Amin [citation needed] to begin production on *The Looking Glass War*, originally conceived as an adaptation of the John Le Carre novel of the same name, but the end product being so far removed from the book that Le Carre, at the premiere, was moved to remark that he'd 'quite like to make a film called that too'. Director Antony Fortune had previously only made short art films such as *The Downcast of the First Aviator* (1978) and took a highly sidelong approach to the subject matter, using only some character names and changing the genre, setting and plot. Street herself appeared in the small but pivotal role of Alice Liddle, who, in fragmentary scenes, seems to be attempting to push herself through a mirror, severely injuring herself in the process. Those scenes, filmed without the use of special effects, earned the film its 18 certificate, and that only after numerous cuts requested by the British Board of Film Censors, edits which Street fought to the point where it looked unlikely that the film would gain a UK release. She later said of the project that it had been 'a terrible, failed experiment, proof that you can only take these things so far'. Fortune has never commented in public about the movie, having walked out of the premiere and used the red carpet and velvet ropes outside to symbolically seal off the Odeon Leicester Square, saying that 'what's in there should stay in there'. Venus Horizons made no more films, but in recent years *The Looking Glass War* has gained a cult following, playing every week to audiences bringing their own costumes and props in the Crescent Cinema in New York's Greenwich Village.

There is no doubt the film caused a lull in Street's career, and director Jeannot Szwarc had to fight Warner Brothers to cast her as Dorothy in his sequel to *The Wizard of Oz* (1939). But the role was to bring both of them lasting success, and Street her only Academy Award nomination. *Variety* said: 'Alice Street brings a startling strength to the role of grown-up Kansas farm owner Gale, initially turning down Major Thomas Newton's (Nick Nolte) request to join his unit of Marines in tracking down the source of mysterious whirlwinds that are destroying property and carrying off people, but finally giving in when the disappearance of a little girl brings to the surface her own repressed childhood experiences.' The decision to frame the sequel as a 'war movie, when the first picture was a dream' was controversial, and Street's support for Oliver Stone's script was crucial in achieving the director's vision. 'It was holding back the first sighting of the Munchkins,' she said, 'that was the biggest fight. But you had to get the audience to a point where they genuinely feared what they were going to see. That's what drags them in, that's what connects them to a grander reality.' During the production, she became close friends with Lance Henriksen (The Tin Man), but relations between her and the Cowardly Lion (Robin Williams) were famously sour, leading to much of his part being left on the cutting room floor [citation needed]. Street's final confrontation with the Wicked Witches of the East, North and South (Cher, Kathleen Turner and Brigitte Nielsen), and her delivery of the line 'get away from her, you witches', has since formed part of a permanent art exhibition on the sixth floor of the south tower of the World Trade Center, with the scene repeated every six minutes.

After completion of the film, Street turned her attention to charity work, becoming famous more as a spokeswoman for various ecological and heritage causes, and appearing only in occasional guest appearances as herself in movies like Woody Allen's *Celebrity* (1998), as well as continuing what she referred to as her 'deal' with Lynch. Her uncredited appearance on *Star Trek: The Next Generation* in heavy alien make-up as the Tark Ambassador, in the episode 'Lost and Heading Home' (1987) was interrupted by a coast-to-coast pirate broadcast, as an unidentified male dressed in silver robes and wearing what seemed to be a goat's head appeared onscreen for thirty seconds, yelling about 'not letting it out'.

Many *Trek* fans only got to see Street's brief cameo on the video release of the episode [citation needed]. Her appearance in the *Moonlighting* episode 'Hex and the Single Maddie' (1988), as Maddie Hayes' (Sigourney Weaver) ditzy elder sister Samantha went without such hitches and earned her only Emmy nomination. Viewer interest in a return for the character was scuppered by reported on set tension between Street and Weaver, possibly owing to Street's brief dating of co-star Bruce Willis [citation needed].

Street's final credit was, of course, *Mulholland Drive*. She was only supposed to appear in the small part of a waitress (the part she plays in the released version), but, as a documentary team filming the shoot reported, she was invited to do more and more, until one of the major cast members, who is still unknown, was written out to be replaced by her. But whichever part this was to be has never been revealed, as Street vanished from her trailer one evening towards the end of a shooting day. 'It was almost between frames,' Lynch said at the time. 'She was there and then she was gone. I just hope she's happy now.'

Personal life

Speculation as to the reasons behind Street's disappearance has characterised everything written (and now filmed, with James Cameron's *The Street Story* due in 2026) about Street's personal life. She never married, and was always, perhaps too predictably for it to be true, reported as dating the leading man of whatever production she was in at the time. The LAPD investigation into her disappearance is ongoing. Her friends have occasionally spoken in the media at their annoyance with Lynch continuing to employ, in small parts, a different, much younger, actress by the name of Alice Street. The battle within Equity to secure the name for one or the other performer is itself the subject of a book, Jon Ronson's *Street Names* (2020). Her mother having died when Street was eighteen, no other family has ever come forward, or been spoken of by the actress, with the exception of her unidentified father, still seemingly estranged from her at the time of her disappearance. Sightings of Street are frequent, both in Los Angeles and onscreen, as Street fans insist she has been seen in the background of such shows as *Fringe*, *American Horror*

Story, and *How I Met Your Mother*. On a number of occasions, these internet speculations have been denied by the studios involved, but this is increasingly infrequent, a supposed Street appearance adding ratings numbers [citation needed]. The closest Street came to autobiography was a long interview in the New York Times in 1982, in which she describes her 'never-ending search for a return to something which I can barely describe. "Haven't I done enough?" I always ask. But then the answer comes: "enough for what?"'

Filmography

Year	Title
1974	The Godfather Part II
1977	Eraserhead
1980	The Elephant Man
1982	Brimstone and Treacle
1984	Dune
	The Looking Glass War
1986	Wizards
	Blue Velvet
1990	Wild at Heart
1997	Lost Highway
1998	Celebrity
2001	Mulholland Drive

The Companionship of Lighthouses

Lizbeth Myles

ISEABAIL LAY IN the shadow of the lighthouse and stared up at a clear night. An unnatural storm approached, summoned with anger and hate. She didn't know how long it would be until she saw the stars again.

The first glimmer of familiar constellations twinkled down at her. She didn't know their names, she was no sailor, but she made up her own: the gannet, the kraken, the eagle.

The wind picked up. Squawks of indignant gulls peeled through the air, offering their warnings of the impending storm. Rugged waves smashed against the cliff face with a rare ferocity. And Iseabail was afraid. She was always afraid of the storms. Every instinct told her to dive, deeper and deeper, and swim until the water was still and calm and safe. But she knew her instincts were wrong. The lighthouse would stand no matter the fury of the ocean or sky.

Iseabail ascended its winding staircase. Her hand trailed against the cool curve of the bricks, marvelling at how were able to stand, century after century, indomitable.

The stairs ended at the gallery room. For this vantage point she often spotted minke whales or bottle-nose dolphins playing amongst the roiling waves. Not today. They'd sensed the storm too, and fled. Now, there was only the endless grey ocean.

She pulled open the ceiling hatch and climbed into the lanthorn room. This high up, and with only polished glass protecting her form the elements, the wind was a feral howl. She checked the oil levels in the lanthorn and the wicks she'd trimmed that morning. She lit the lamp, and she returned to the gallery deck where she snuggled down in a nest of blankets near the windows. From dusk to dawn, she would tend the light and watch the sea.

In the past week, Iseabail had spotted three Breteyne heavy frigates and two ships-of-the-line on the horizon, heading north-west. Most likely, they were on their way to the Gulf of Corryvrecken, to retaliate against the kelpie clans for attacks on shipping lines. The storm was the kelpies' doing, and it would not end until the battle was won, or lost.

For three days, she tended the lanthorn at night, then slept for a few hours in the morning before she prepared for the next watch. Outside, the storm screamed in wind and rain. Thunder rocked the sky and lightning gave her staccato images of the roiling sea. Even in her dreams, she heard the tempest.

On the fourth evening, she spotted a ship too close to the island. It was a small vessel. A corvette. Its mizzenmast had splintered, and the mainsail was torn. It listed into the wind, which pulled it further onto the rocks. The lanthorn had not gone out, they'd seen her warning, but something had gone terribly wrong.

She grabbed a coat and hat and fled down the spiral staircase. Outside, ice cold wind slammed into her face, heavy drops of rain pelted her coat. She yanked the hat down over her ears and ran for the beach.

It was impossible. She couldn't do this. The ship was lost. This was futile. Yet she still kept moving.

She dragged the rowboat over the shingle beach and shoved it out into the water. The waves slapped against its sides as icy sea water sank through her boots. She clambered aboard and began to row with short, sharp strokes. As she rounded the cliff face, the force of the storm winds struck her. The little boat rocked alarmingly, and she clung desperately to the oars, and kept rowing.

She closed her eyes, and listened to the waves. There was always a safe route, and she knew how to listen for clues.

When she opened her eyes, she saw debris in the water. Barrels and broken planks, but the ship had vanished beneath the waves. She saw no sign of survivors. She couldn't even see any bodies. If there was someone there, screaming out for help, how would she hear them above the shriek of the wind. What had she been thinking?

Her self-recrimination was rebuked by a muted shout. She looked desperately across the water and shouted back, her voice weak, her lips numb.

Another shout.

Her eyes fell on a wooden crate, bobbing violently. A body lay upon it, one hand raised weakly.

Her fingers were thick and clumsy with cold, but she rowed.

It was a man in a Bretagne navy uniform, ghost pale, but very much alive. He raised his head at her approach and awkwardly grabbed for the side of the rowboat. She lifted an oar and jabbed it at his fingers. He shot her a look of betrayal that she found almost comical.

"The prow," she shouted, though the wind snatched at her words. "Climb over the prow unless you want us both in the sea."

He heard her and moved. She reached down to help pull him aboard, shocked at how cold he felt even against her own chilled skin.

"He fell," gasped the man, collapsing back, eyes half-closed. "A moment ago. He slipped into the water. But he was alive. Please. He was alive."

It took a moment to realise what he asked of her. He couldn't know what he said. Delirium from the cold.

"Please…"

She looked at the grey water. It seethed as though it knew what she contemplated. But if it had only been seconds…

Before she could think about it too much, she stripped off her coat and boots and dived in. Her breath was knocked out of her as the cold stung like needles against her skin. She missed how warm it used to feel, how safe and coddled she was even in the Arctic seas.

Her vision was reduced to a few feet, but she knew the currents of this sea intimately. She guessed the direction the sailor would be pulled in as he sank. The frigid water stole away every morsel of her body's warmth as she swam deeper. Her throat burned, and she couldn't survive the cold for long.

As she was about to turn back, her fingers brushed against something solid. She grabbed at it. An arm. She clasped her fingers around the wrist and tugged. There was no response.

She swam around so she could hold him beneath his arms, but before she could swim up, he was yanked from her grasp. She twisted round, swimming deeper, and reached out to the sinking body. Something else got there first. It lunged out to snatch his ankle and pulled him into the darkness.

There was nothing else she could do. She kicked out to begin her ascent.

She broke the surface and took her first breath; salty air had never tasted so sweet. For a moment, she was terrified her boat had been tossed away by the storm, or the rescued mariner had taken it into his addled head to row off. But no, there it was, not a dozen feet from where she'd emerged. Relief was enough to will her limbs on and drag herself aboard.

By the time they reached the beach, the man was unconscious. The cold would kill him if she didn't get him inside and warmed up, but she hadn't the strength carry him to the lighthouse.

She grabbed his shoulders and shook him as hard as she could.

"Get up." She tried to shout but it came out a hoarse croak. "If you want to live, you have got to get up."

No response. Helplessness crawled over her as she shook him again. "Wake up, Captain. That's an order."

The rank did something, ignited some strength within him that allowed his eyes to half-open and his muscles to move. She wanted to sob as she pulled his arm over her shoulders and supported his weight as best she could. Her teeth chattered as they stumbled their way across the slippery rock, back to the lighthouse.

As soon as they were inside, Iseabail let him slide to the floor. His eyes were closed again. She lit a fire in the stove, generous with how much wood she used, before she turned her attention back to him.

She checked his breathing, weak but steady, then began to remove his outer clothing. It was a more difficult task than she expected. Her muscles protested her every movement, but she'd be damned if she rescued a man from the sea only to have him die on her floor.

The embroidered blue coat, now so sodden it looked black, was first to go. Then torn stockings, a long-sleeved shirt that she tore off in frustration. Propriety melded with her own exhaustion: she couldn't bring herself to strip a strange man naked so that would have to do.

She put a pillow under his head and patted him dry, then dragged out blankets from storage and tucked them around him. She'd have moved him to the bed if she could, but it was three floors up.

She'd been so focussed, she'd forgotten she still wore her own soaked clothes. With slow, heavy steps, she climbed to the bedroom, where she changed into a fresh woollen dress and threw a red shawl over her shoulders. Her skin prickled in pain as it began to warm.

She eyed her bed longingly, but there was work to be done. She needed to tend to the lanthorn. One ship had fallen to the storm under her watch. She had to do what she could to stop it happening again.

It was a long night. Each time lightning struck, she was afraid she'd see another ship on the rocks. Every hour or so, she'd return to the kitchen to check on the mariner, afraid she'd find him dead.

Eventually dawn came, and Iseabail extinguished the lanthorn. Her limbs ached with exhaustion. She would eat, check on him one more time, and then she would sleep at last.

The wood in the stove was cinders, and her guest was still alive and unmoving. She lit a fresh fire to heat a pan of water, stirred in oats, and boiled it into porridge. There was no aroma, the only flavour would be a pinch of salt, but this was when he woke.

He sat up and stared at her. She offered a cautious smile.

"I'm not a captain," he said, as though imparting this information to her was the most important thing in the world.

"That's all right," she said. "Would you like some porridge?"

He nodded, then twisted around in his blankets like a fish caught in a net. Finally, he made it to his feet.

"Have a seat," she said.

Opposite the little stove was a small table with two chairs. She'd only ever sat in one of them. That was the one he chose.

"Thank you." He rested his arms on the table, shoulders hunched. She brought him a bowl of steaming porridge and a spoon.

"How do you feel?"

He picked up the spoon and stirred the porridge. "Better than being dead." He took a nibble, then ate with the enthusiasm of a starving man.

She stayed by the stove as she ate her own helping. "I'm Iseabail," she offered.

"Lieutenant Daniel Gurrans," he said. "Where am I?"

"My lighthouse."

He frowned. "Your lighthouse?" In Breteyne it was the navy that maintained the lighthouses. It was not such a formal an arrangement north of the border.

"It was abandoned before I came here."

"You live in an abandoned lighthouse?"

Her eyes narrowed. "No, I am the lighthouse keeper of a formally abandoned lighthouse. The lanthorn is lit every night. You must have seen it before…before your ship went down."

Daniel winced and closed his eyes.

"I'm sorry," she said.

"We were withdrawing from Corryvrecken," he said quietly. "The ship was damaged. We couldn't navigate in the storm, couldn't fight the winds." He straightened his spine and rolled back his shoulders. "I need to report our loss to the Admiralty."

"We're a long way from the mainland."

"Any ships in port?"

"There's no port. It's a small island. There's just the lighthouse. Just me."

Daniel raised his eyebrows. "I see. Well, I'd want fairer winds before putting to sea anyway."

"There's a supply boat every few months. But perhaps your people will come for you before then."

He managed a wan smile. "Perhaps."

༄

It was unsettling not to be alone. It helped that Daniel didn't talk much. He was courteous, unassuming, and helpful. As the storm raged beyond the walls, he would clean pots and sweep the stairs and rest, at her insistence.

One afternoon, when he felt stronger, he joined her in the lanthorn room. She felt a wave of pleasure at how his eyes widened. There was something breathtaking, powerful, about being surrounded by only the sea, and towering over it. She liked being reminded of that.

"Where did it happen?" he asked. Iseabail pointed towards the rocks, invisible beneath the waves. He gazed out in that direction for a while and his gaze went distant. After a few minutes, he said, "I never thanked you." He turned to face her. "Thank you. You saved my life."

"You're welcome." She glanced away, uncomfortable with his gravitas.

By the next morning, the storm had eased. Rain ceased to make war against the land, and retreated to a heavy drizzle. The winds had dulled, and even the sky seemed lighter. Iseabail pulled on her coat and hat, plunged her hands in her pockets and walked down to the beach.

Slate-grey waves advanced and withdrew across smooth pebbles. They washed up driftwood and seaweed and empty, broken shells. There were no bodies. There were never going to be any bodies.

The memory of how Daniel's poor comrade had been wrenched into the darkness gnawed at her. She should have known she was not alone beneath the waves. She should have been faster, stronger. She could have been, if only…

She jerked round with a gasp as something touched her shoulder. It was only him.

"I didn't mean to startle you," he said.

Iseabail shrugged. "Lost in thought."

It was the first time she'd seen him properly in his coat and boots. His hat and sword had been lost to the sea, but there was enough of the uniform left to make it clear he belonged somewhere else.

"I was worried," he said.

"I don't like being cooped up inside. I missed the waves. They're never gentle, even in the best weather, but they're soothing."

They walked companionably along the shoreline. It was cold, but it was a good cold, fresh and reviving, with a bracing bite that reminded her she was alive.

"I've been thinking about that night," Daniel said. "It's been such a jumble. I'd forgotten I wasn't alone. That Jenkins was with me. That he let go." He gave her a severe look. "You dived in after him."

"So I did."

"Why?"

"You asked me to."

He snorted. "I was delirious. It was a mad thing to ask of anyone."

She remembered his face, and the wide, pleading eyes. "It didn't feel like that at the time."

"You wouldn't have done if you thought it futile."

They reached the end of the beach and turned back. Daniel stayed on her left side, shielding her from the worst of the wind. "I suppose not," she said.

He waited as though he expected her to say more, but she remained silent. The waves surged, splashing sea water across their feet.

He looked up and down the shore, then said, "I'd have thought…"

"Yes?"

He shook his head. "Nothing."

No bodies, no wreckage. Of course he'd noticed.

～

Sound carried easily in the lighthouse. While Iseabail cleaned the glass panes in the lanthorn room, she heard rummaging below. Cupboards opened, pots lids lifted, hampers pulled to the floor and lifted back up with a grunt.

She descended, and made sure her footsteps clanged against the metal stairs. By the time she reached the kitchen he sat on his chair, playing solitaire with a pack of yellowed, dog-eared cards.

She looked around the room. Her things were out of place. A pot handle pointed in the wrong direction, a corner of blanket poking out of a hamper, her shell collection imperfectly positioned on the shelves.

When she turned to Daniel, he met her gaze unflinchingly.

"What were you looking for?" she asked.

His eyes flickered as he decided whether or not to lie. He cleared his throat. "Why did you make that dive?"

It sounded too much like an accusation and anger flared. "To try and save your friend. Why else?"

"Where's your coat?"

She glanced at the hook by the door.

"Not that one."

"Then which?"

"Your seal skin."

She stared at him for a long moment. He didn't look away. A very different flavour of exhaustion washed over her. She hugged herself with her arms, as though that could drive away the chill of her memories.

"Gone."

Daniel reached for a sword that wasn't there and she laughed, sharp and bitter. "Are we now enemies?" she asked.

"You're a selkie," he said. He couldn't keep the fear from his voice, and she felt a swell of pity.

"Yes." She stepped towards him, slow and cautious, as though he were a wounded animal. "And you've slept in my home, you've eaten my food."

"Some sort of spell."

"No! No, you fool, there's no spell, no trick. I saved your life." She wanted to stamp her food like a child.

"The sea was red with blood at Corryvrecken," he snarled. "I saw men dragged into the water and torn apart."

"Breteyne education must be poor indeed if your people don't know the difference between kelpie and selkie. How dare you judge me by anything but my own actions?"

He looked away, his face suddenly flushed with shame. His shoulders slumped; his anger melted away.

"I'm sorry," he said, as he rubbed his hands over his face. He sagged back into his chair. "You're right."

"I'll make soup, and we'll eat. Then you can ask your questions."

⁂

"Where is your seal skin?" There was no anger now, only curiosity, and she couldn't judge him for that.

In fits and starts, she told him her story. She told him about the young, arrogant fisherman who'd caught her in his old net and refused to let her go until she handed over her coat. How he'd hidden it from her and kept her, called her wife, and promised he would only keep her a year. If she wanted to leave after that, she could.

He had lied. And one day, when he left for town, she'd torn his cottage apart looking for her seal skin. When she couldn't find it, she burnt his fishing boat.

After he returned, he revealed her seal skin's hiding place. And then he threw it into the hearth and made her watch until only ashes remained.

"What did you do then?" Daniel asked gently.

"What do you think I did? I drowned him."

When she closed her eyes, she saw the fisherman's mouth gasp open, desperate for air that he would never taste. She saw his body twitch and jerk until it would never move again. She saw him sink into the depths of the ocean, swallowed by the abyssal darkness and icy cold.

Daniel was a military man, but this was murder. She knew the difference between soldiery and a planned, brutal killing of a man who had no weapon greater than a fishing pole. And his terrified, bulging eyes haunted her, no matter how certain she was that he deserved his fate.

She didn't wait to hear Daniel's judgement, didn't even look at him once she'd finished her tale, but retreated to the lanthorn room. There was always more work to be done.

***

The salty air was still, and a pale sun peeked out behind soft, grey clouds. The storm was over. For once, Daniel was awake before her. From the gallery deck she saw him on the cliff top where he sat looking towards Corryvrecken.

After she ate breakfast, she went out to join him.

"Who won?" he asked.

"I don't know."

"The Admiralty will know the *Boreas* never reached port. They might send rescue ships now." He didn't sound hopeful. The *Boreas* wouldn't be the only ship lost as it withdrew from the battle. A single corvette would not be a priority.

"You'll reach home eventually."

He grunted but said nothing. She took a piece of salt cod, wrapped in a strip of linen, from her pocket and left it at his side.

***

The beach was not empty.

Iseabail watched from the gallery room, anger igniting in her chest, as kelpies emerged from the ocean. They advanced across the shingle, shedding their equine forms. The humanoid shapes they took were repellent and beautiful, with mottled grey-blue skin and gem blue eyes. They smiled sharp, knowing smiles as they looked up at the lighthouse.

The door slammed open and Iseabail swept towards them, her coat snapping in the wind.

The kelpies stopped at the edge of the beach and waited for her. They trilled amongst themselves, and their sharp smiles twisted into hunger as she approached.

"You're not welcome here," she said.

The kelpies fell silent. One, tall and lean, inclined his head to her. In respect, or a contemptuous mockery of it.

"We'll leave, but only with the human." There was a low, sibilant quality to his speech that reminded her of waves in a brisk summer wind.

"No."

The kelpie tilted his head and looked behind her. "Perhaps he'll give us a different answer."

"Daniel," she murmured as he stood next to her. "I told you to stay inside."

"I may not be a captain, but neither are you." He smiled with a confidence she didn't believe he felt. But she could see the energy in him, stirred by the appearance of his enemies.

"Come to us," the kelpie said to him. "Let us see you gasp and writhe beneath the waves. Come to us and we shall spare the cast-out selkie."

"You've no claim on me," she spat.

"You're a thief. Return what you stole, or suffer. We'll not ask again."

Daniel touched her arm gently. "I won't let them hurt you. I'll go." She shook her head and grasped his wrist. His pulse was strong and steady beneath her fingers. He would leave, but it would not be like this.

"I pulled him from the sea," she said, sweeping her gaze over the kelpies. "I laid my hands on him before any of you."

"We offered the ship to the sea. We claimed all that was aboard."

His words gave her pause. He wouldn't lie directly, not to her, not to a selkie, even if she was an outcast. But he had not told the whole truth.

"The *Boreas* ran aground," said Iseabail, raising her voice to carry over the wind. "You did not touch it. It ran aground and it was the rocks that tore into the hull. And then you surrounded it like carrion. You were weak. Cowardly."

The kelpies exchanged harsh, discordant trills between them. Elegant smiles turned into thin lips drawn over jagged teeth. Pretty blue eyes darkened with suspicion as they looked from one companion to another. Not all of them had been there as the Boreas was lost. And a selkie would no more lie to them than they would to her.

She took Daniel's arm in hers and turned back to the lighthouse. "Walk," she whispered. "Do not look back."

There was nothing more expensive in the lighthouse than the contents of Iseabail's tea chest. She set water to boil and measured out three teaspoons of leaves for her teapot.

Daniel sat at the little table and watched her. After a while he said, "That's twice I owe you my life."

"No one's keeping a ledger." She poured the water into the teapot and turned over an egg timer. Five minutes and it would be perfect.

"No?" He stood and closed the distance between them. Gently he raised her head to look her in the eyes. "Are you sure?"

She tried to speak but it came out as a choked sob. He wrapped his arms around her, and she buried her face in his coat. Silent, salty tears flowed, and she forget the tea, forget everything except the steady, unyielding warmth that held her close.

Iseabail straightened out a corner of the blanket, then rolled on her side to watch Daniel as he watched the sky.

"Don't ask me to leave," she said.

His lips quirked in a brief, gentle smile. "Why shouldn't I?"

"I don't belong on the land, and I can't return to the sea." She curled into his side. "What better place for me than my lighthouse?"

His hand brushed lightly over hers and he nodded.

And they lay on the grass in the shadow of the lighthouse and waited for the stars to appear.

A Species Called Hope

Ai Jiang

(CW: Death, Burial, Brief Graphic Imagery, Brief Violence)

MY CREATOR WAS cruel, in the human sense, when she whispered her last goodbye. She understood the mission she had programmed into me, to restore humanity, yet her final words were "There is no hope."

∽

Rough terrains from the destruction of the Solar Age scratch at my mesh wheels, debris infiltrating the interior through the miniscule gaps. The persistent tinkle bombards my sensory input. Though irritation gnaws, it is slight. Pieces of Edinburgh crumble as I roll forth. It was once a most beautiful city with the most gruesome of pasts. I wish I were there to witness it whole.

The Great Flood has long since swallowed countries, taking with it all bodies of water, leaving behind rubble and earth's cracked soil. Perhaps I could say that it also swallowed my birthplace, my creator's home, thus, also my home. I suppose this is what humans might describe as the feeling of loss—a strange melancholic thrum. Though for me, it is but a fabrication learned by my system. At least, that is what I believe.

Rain is sparse, if any, though from my analysis, the mountains are recovering the quickest. Layers upon layers seeming to rise several inches if not more each day. The peaks, once still below the clouds, seem to reach towards the atmosphere in hopes of breaching its boundaries, in hopes of escaping what fate rests for these giants unmythical remaining on earth.

The small drones I have dispatched have caught sight of several living species darting among the shadows between the Three Sisters regrown—though now it is more like Three Sisters along with several newborn siblings surrounding—and somehow, I feel less alone. This finding may well be considered the "hope" my creator thought lost. I must increase my travelling speed as my system detected several species in the area, one of which is invasive and seems to be quickly ravaging the area. My creator had whispered, that was also how earth came to pass. I never understood her meaning. Regardless, if "hope" for humanity is indeed where I suspect, indeed among these darting shadows, I must protect it at all cost.

At 18km/hr, it will take me approximately ten hours to arrive at the mountains, though with the rough terrains and now inexistent roads, it will likely take closer to fifteen. At this moment, I wish my creator equipped me with the speed capabilities of race cars and rockets I have witnessed when they still existed.

I was not made to wander rough earth terrains, though I believe my creator should have been wiser to have this forethought, even if I was created solely for the Mars New Planet mission. But from my accumulated data, I understand humans can be rather scatter-minded during disaster.

I arrive near the Three Sisters almost by my exact predicted time, less two or three seconds, settling myself a kilometer from its base, analyzing the rumpled terrain for the best path forth.

There is none.

A notification arrives from my dispatched drones: the species closest to humankind is nearby. My name appears as a banner across my sight— what my creator had renamed me upon my return to earth.

New Earth Rover.

My system focuses on a darting shadow northeast of my position, and I follow the tracker to the base of one sister, stopping to observe at the mouth shrouded in shadow. I should not feel fear, but I am hesitant to leave the cloudy light and move into the darkness between two mountains.

A being approaches.

I know not what the true meaning of excitement is, but upon seeing the creature, its human-like features, there is a jolt that rushes along my circuitry, like what my creator has described as adrenaline. A strange feeling, though not unwelcomed. Pop-up images of previous human ancestors litter the peripheral of my processing screen. I run an analysis and find there is an 85.6% match. Certainly, this is "hope." And a part of me wishes that perhaps I might find the shadow of my creator in the faces of new humanity.

I approach the primate without hesitation and pull up a formulation chart for humanity restoration, filtering out the failures throughout historical records—wars, political upheaval, chemical disasters—and pinpointing only the successes and desirable human behaviours and ecologically beneficial innovations—solar power, organic development, forest restoration. I think of my creator's last moments, her desperation, her insistent optimism that hope would prevail, until that was taken away from her within seconds by hands belonging none other than to the very species, *her* species, that she was trying to save.

A warning flashes.

Invasive species. Incompatible with mission.

This cannot be. I process the data again and again, searching for errors, then realizing there could have been none since I recoded after my creator's death. I halt, allowing the distance between the primate and me to grow. For now, I save them as "HS.2".

Upon re-entering the shadows between two sisters, HS.2 tumbles towards its kind. Small groups scattered every few meters, hovering over carcasses. Upon closer observation, I began to understand what renders HS.2 an invasive species.

Venom drips, unhalting, from the tips of sharp fangs with foaming lips peeled back. Not just the carcasses, but the surrounding grounds bruise a deep purple and blue, tainted soils, eaten grass, irreplaceable. At times, they begin attacking, devouring, each other. Yet they seem to populate much quicker than the rate at which they destroyed their own kind. If the HS.2 are left further unattended, it would not be a Solar Age next, but a Toxin Age—not unlike what humans had seen as a result of chemical plants, factories, and improperly disposed biomatter.

However, conflict brews within when I realize how ill-equipped I am, regardless of my knowledge access, for such a situation. Everything in my system matches this species with humans. Yet, to ensure HS.2 survive and evolve into new humans would mean to cause irreparable damage to earth. To eliminate them would likely delay the restoration of humanity, perhaps even indefinitely. And I would then fail in the sole purpose of my existence. None of the other species in the area, from what the drones had gathered, would be near in their similarity percentage compared to HS.2.

Above, I detect a new species and begin to find commonalities with what had previously existed. There is not one clear ancestor, but this new species has the skin of trees, the slender arms and legs of bats connected by a thick membrane, its shape wing-like. Its eyes protrude from its sockets, resembling the crawling creatures found in old human horror films. I save them as "UI."

I move closer to HS.2, and my first instinct is to protect, regardless of their status as an invasive species. The UI is likely a predator given its two-fingered and 6-toed claws, larger than the blade of scythes and similar in shape. I only have five of my fifteen drones left undamaged, but it seems I may have to sacrifice another to save my creator's hope.

I take aim at the UI and prepare to fire, then stop.

A handful of other UIs land close to the first, still high above the HS.2, though not enough to outnumber the HS.2. The UIs' looming presence eludes a menacing aura. I hold fire. It would be far too dangerous to cause alarm when there are now twelve to my five. The HS.2 may see me as an enemy as well. I will have to pick off the UI one by one as they depart.

The UI unhinge their narrow jaws, mouth stretched wide like cranes—teethless, tongueless. No sounds leave, at least not what I can detect, even though their throats quiver as though wailing. Then they dive like eagles, but with all limbs spread rather than tucked, the membrane wings allowing, surprisingly, for both speed and grace and a strange gentleness.

With each meter in their descent, I recall fragments of human histories—of war, of violence, of bloodshed, of injustice, of cruel survival. The HS.2 scatter, fleeing from the carcasses with falling trails of venom spotting unmarked earth, green turns to purple blue then dissolves, leaving bald patches. But rather than hunting, the UI land gingerly next to the carcasses, uncaring of how the venom eats at the surface of their claws and feet. Then, they bow their heads, short, round ears folding, with their beaks almost but not completely touching the dead—their dead.

That is when I notice their claws, though steeply curved, are dull.

Then, soundless, with a tap, a prod, against the living bodies of their companions, their family, they begin to dig. They make no noise even when the venom almost exposes the bones of their fingers and toes, eats through their claws. A strange custom to leave the dead where they had passed rather than burying them elsewhere. Images of burial rites, of funerals and wakes, of mourning and grief, of offerings and burnt symbolic wealth, flood me.

When the hole is deep enough for the carcass, only then do the UI stop. Together, they place the body within the pit, scatter what appear to be seeds of various kinds: trees, edible plants, fruits. Then they complete their burial and begin on the next, then the next, then the next. And from their lips pour liquid, drenching the ground they re-soiled—one that nurtures rather than burns.

The shadows of the HS.2s slink nearby, waiting to return, waiting to attack. Unflinching, the UI continue their task. Caring for the dead seems to be their only priority, as though to ensure rebirth. How much have they restored with their claws and beaks among the trees and life on the Three Sisters? How much land has been repaired with their liquid, by their respect for the living and the dead and the strength of their desire to heal rather than destroy?

My creator was the same.

I reformulate my plan and program my drones to follow the HS.2, the invaders—to target while they are struggling against each other. And as the UI complete their last burial, my observations begin to populate the data file I have allotted to this new species.

I rename them "Hope."

Then, I rename myself.

Acknowledgments

THIS TREMENDOUS ANTHOLOGY arose from the dreams of its editors, Jendia Gammon and Gareth L. Powell, but it is made possible by many generous supporters and friends.

We of course thank our wonderful authors for their marvelous story contributions: Adrian Tchaikovsky, Ai Jiang, Alice James, Antony Johnston, Cynthia Pelayo, D.K. Stone, David Quantick, Dennis K. Crosby, Eugen Bacon, Gemma Amor, Greg van Eekhout, Helen Glynn Jones, J.L. Worrad, John Wiswell, Jonathan L. Howard, Kali Wallace, KC Grifant, Khan Wong, Laurel Hightower, Lizbeth Myles, Mya Duong, Paul Cornell, Pedro Iniguez, Peter McLean, Ren Hutchings, Renan Bernardo, Sarah L. Miles, Stark Holborn, and T.L. Huchu.

Thank you to Niall C. Grant for the gorgeous cover art, and for Dash Creative, LLC for completed cover layout.

Thank you to Scarlett R. Algee for proof edits and interior layout.

We approached the fundraising for *Of Shadows, Stars, and Sabers* via both Ko-Fi and Indiegogo. Many contributors chose to remain anonymous, and we thank each one of you for your support. We also thank our named supporters: Kelly A. Varner, Flamebait, Kenya Winn, Dean Powell, Harvey Hamer, Rebecca Powell, Steve Taylor-Bryant, Fredrik Adolfsson, Jean-Paul L. Garnier, Lucien Telford, Allen Born, Gary J. Mack, Jason Pyrz, David J. Williams, Allen V. Cheesman, Bogdan Orlic, Nick Larmour, Stephen Crawford, Colette Reap, Roger Alix-Gaudreau, Dave Bradley, Ashley Capes, Ciaran Sundstrem, Deborah A. Levinson, Andy Tinkham, Banu, Benedict Molefe Jones, Michael J. Crawford, Owais Chaudhri, Gryftkin, Jack Fennell, Martin Trotter, Seras Routhier, Pat Mrizek, KariLikeSafari, Mike Mallow, Rich T., Stephen McGowan, Ruetha, Gavin Sheedy, Steve Taylor-Bryant, Rebecca, lsmick,

Acknowledgments

Sharie Hyder, Stephen Tanner, Chris, Cosplayer Parent, Martyn R. Winters, Mr. Melski, Graham Moonie-Dalton, Laura (1), Casey Adams Stark, Jordan King, Nick Codignotto, Laura (2), David Perlmutter, George Sirois, Fionna O'Sullivan, karterkn_north, Paul Moss, Steve Adkins, Ed Campodonico, Kyddryn, Leslie, Offer Kuban, Nicole Beste, Gloria Thomas, LadyDuckOfDoom, Mark Nicholson, Audry T, Kactus, Glori Medina, Paula Gutterud, Kristi Majni, Jonny Nexus, maphia, Jo, Alan, Jim Lehane, Steve Burnett, Zoe Kavadas, Tom McKearney, Ben Sundman, Lonnie, Kate, Devestave, Shelagh, Penfold, Ashur, Juli Rew, Anthony, Laura Madeleine, JCG, Jason Short, Andres Kabel, Urban Protagonist, Lynn H., Maxpocalypse, Sarah Grey, KaHicky, Science-Fiction Al, Greg Mendell, Clive Stone, Lyn, Em, Tim Kirk, Julianna, Brad, eMSig70, Dave M. Jones, Michael Mulhern, Dominique Knobben, huxbear, Keith Berry, Tal S, Richard Sands, Randall Reimers, Ruth, J. M. Le Cornu, George Poles, Jotham Austin, David Soponski, Stephen G Moss, Katherine Franklin, Bryan Ingram, Ripley M, A.J. English, Ian Warner, Julian White, Sophie Simpson, Mike Brooks, Kayla Severson, Dr. Rasa & Jaq Greenspon, Meghan Crockett, Carrie Ancell, Jamie Snowdon, Akira Keith, Matthew C. Brown, Phil Jimmieson, Tim Stretton, J. Kangas, Kristin Pratt, and Jelleke Vanooteghem.

Publication Credits

"The Shadow Eater of Órino-Rin" by Eugen Bacon. Copyright© 2024 Eugen Bacon. Original to this anthology.

"Morgen's Cottage" by Helen Glynn Jones. Copyright © 2024 Helen Glynn Jones. Original to this anthology.

"Underland" by Gemma Amor. Copyright © 2024 Gemma Amor. Original to this anthology.

"Existence: A Thought Experiment" by Greg van Eekhout. Copyright © 2024 Greg van Eekhout. Original to this anthology.

"Sing Yourself Back to Sleep" by Laurel Hightower. Copyright © 2024 Laurel Hightower. Original to this anthology.

"The Magic Wood" by Jonathan L. Howard. Copyright © 2024 Jonathan L. Howard. Original to this anthology.

"The Dreambug Infestation of Half Moon Oaks" by KC Grifant. Copyright © 2024 KC Grifant. Original to this anthology.

"Cruel Machinations" by Pedro Iniguez. Copyright © 2024 Pedro Iniguez. Original to this anthology.

Publication Credits

"The Fire Tower" by D.K. Stone. Copyright © 2024 D.K. Stone. Original to this anthology.

"Last Gasp" by Stark Holborn. Copyright © 2024 Stark Holborn. Original to this anthology.

"Unremarkable" by Alice James. Copyright © 2024 Alice James. Original to this anthology.

"Who's Afraid of Little Old Me?" by Sarah L. Miles. Copyright © 2024 Sarah L. Miles. Original to this anthology.

"A Hundred Thousand Eyes Gaze Upon the Core of You" by Khan Wong. Copyright © 2024 Khan Wong. Original to this anthology.

"Donhagore" by T.L. Huchu. Copyright © 2024 T.L. Huchu. Original to this anthology.

"Grey" by Ren Hutchings. Copyright © 2024 Ren Hutchings. Original to this anthology.

"Holy Fools" by Adrian Tchaikovsky. Copyright © 2024 Adrian Tchaikovsky. Original to this anthology.

"Hunger and the Lady" by Peter McLean. Copyright © 2019 Peter McLean. First published in *Grimdark Magazine* #18, January 2019. Reprinted by permission of Adrian Collins.

"His Lord Recalcitrant" by J.L. Worrad. Copyright © 2024 J.L. Worrad. Original to this anthology.

"Shadow Wraith" by Dennis K. Crosby. Copyright © 2024 Dennis K. Crosby. Original to this anthology.

Publication Credits

"The Bike" by Mya Duong. Copyright © 2024 Mya Duong. Original to this anthology.

"An Asexual Succubus" by John Wiswell. © 2024 John Wiswell. Original to this anthology.

"To the Rescue" by David Quantick. Copyright © 2024 David Quantick. Original to this anthology.

"Wish You Were Here" by Renan Bernardo. Copyright © 2024 Renan Bernardo. Original to this anthology.

"Long Last Alice" by Cynthia Pelayo. Copyright © 2024 Cynthia Pelayo. Original to this anthology.

"Outrider" by Antony Johnston. Copyright © 2024 Antony Johnston. Original to this anthology.

"Glitter Town" by Kali Wallace. Copyright © 2024 Kali Wallace. Original to this anthology.

"Alice Street" by Paul Cornell. Copyright © 2024 Paul Cornell. Original to this anthology.

"The Companionship of Lighthouses" by Lizbeth Myles. Copyright © 2024 Lizbeth Myles. Original to this anthology.

"A Species Called Hope" by Ai Jiang. Copyright © 2024 Ai Jiang. Original to this anthology.

About the Authors

Adrian Tchaikovsky
Adrian Tchaikovsky is a Hugo, Arthur C. Clarke, BSFA, Sidewise, and British Fantasy Award-winning science fiction and fantasy author. He is known for a wide variety of work including the *Children of Time*, *Final Architecture*, *Dogs of War*, *Tyrant Philosophers* and *Shadows of the Apt* series, as well as standalone books such as *Elder Race*, *Doors of Eden*, *Spiderlight* and many others. Overall he has over 50 novels and novellas in print as well as a variety of short fiction. Learn more about Adrian from his website https://adriantchaikovsky.com.

Ai Jiang (江艾)
Ai Jiang (江艾) is a Chinese-Canadian author and winner of the Bram Stoker®, Nebula, and Ignyte Awards. She has also been nominated for the Hugo and Astounding Awards and is a Locus and BSFA Award finalist. An immigrant from Shanghu, Changle, Fujian, Ai currently lives in Toronto, Ontario. Her work can be found in many speculative fiction publications, including *F&SF*, *The Dark*, *Uncanny*, *The Masters Review*, and many more. Ai is a prolific writer of both short and long fiction. Her books *Linghun* and *I AM AI* continue to garner recognition. Her novella *A Palace Near the Wind* publishes in 2025 via Titan Books. Learn more about Ai from her website: https://aijiang.ca/.

Alice James
Alice James—self-described as a science fiction and fantasy novelist, cat wrangler, and plant killer—is based in Oxford, England. Her paranormal romances, *The Lavington Windsor Mysteries*, star an amateur necromancer who helps solve murders by raising the dead to find out who killed them. She has had short stories published in *Andromeda Spaceways* and *Indie Bites*.

Alice lives in an 18th century chapel with four cats and a lot of wine. Learn more about Alice on her website: https://www.alicejames.co.uk/.

Antony Johnston

Antony Johnston is one of the most versatile writers of the modern era. The Charlize Theron movie *Atomic Blonde* was based on his graphic novel. His murder mystery *The Dog Sitter Detective* won the Barker Book Award for fiction. Learn more about this entertaining series on its dedicated website. The latest installment, *The Dog Sitter Detective Plays Dead*, is up for preorder. Antony's *Brigitte Sharp* spy thrillers are in development for TV. And his productivity guide *The Organised Writer* has helped authors all over the world take control of their workload. Antony is a celebrated video games writer, with genre-defining titles including *Dead Space*, *Shadow of Mordor*, and *Resident Evil Village* to his credit. Having also consulted on *Silent Hill Ascension*, he is the only writer in the world to have worked on all of the 'big three' horror gaming franchises.

His immense body of work also includes Marvel superheroes such as *Daredevil*, *Wolverine*, and *Shang-Chi*; the *Alex Rider* graphic novels; the post-apocalypse epic *Wasteland*; and more. He wrote and directed the sci-fi film *Crossover Point*, made entirely in quarantine during the coronavirus pandemic. Read more about Antony on his website: https://antonyjohnston.com/.

Cynthia Pelayo

Cynthia Pelayo is a Bram Stoker Award® winning and International Latino Book Award winning author and poet. Pelayo writes fairy tales that blend genre and explore concepts of grief, mourning, and cycles of violence. She is the author of *Loteria*, *Santa Muerte*, *The Missing*, *Poems of My Night*, *Into the Forest and All the Way Through*, *Children of Chicago*, *Crime Scene*, *The Shoemaker's Magician*, as well as dozens of standalone short stories and poems. Her latest novel, *Forgotten Sisters**, is now available from Thomas and Mercer and is an adaptation of Hans Christian Andersen's "The Little Mermaid." A new novel, *Vanishing Daughters*, arrives in 2025. Learn more about Cynthia on her website: https://cinapelayo.com/.

D.K. Stone

D.K. Stone is a Canadaian bestselling multi-genre author who has written both for adults and teens. *Switchback* (via Macmillan) (written as Danika Stone) was selected as the "Best YA Books of 2019", and her thriller, *Edge of Wild* (Stonehouse, 2016) was selected as part of *Chapters* "Our

Favourite Canadian Fiction." She was Writer in Residence for the Lethbridge Public Library, and has led numerous writing workshops. Learn more about D.K. from her website: https://danikastone.com/.

David Quantick
David Quantick was born in the North and raised in the Southwest. His novels include *All My Colors*, *Night Train* and *Ricky's Hand*. David also has also written movies (*Book of Love*) and for TV shows, including *Veep* (for which he won an Emmy Award) and *Avenue 5*. You can see more of his film and television work on his IMDB page: https://www.imdb.com/name/nm0702880/.

Dennis K. Crosby
Dennis K. Crosby is the multi award-winning author of the bestselling Kassidy Simmons Series (*Death's Legacy*; *Death's Debt*; *Death's Despair*). Since 2020, he has published three urban fantasy novels and numerous short stories. Learn more about Dennis on his website: http://www.denniskcrosby.com/.

Eugen Bacon
Eugen (*Yu-gin*) Bacon is an African Australian author. She's a British Fantasy and Foreword Indies Award winner, a twice World Fantasy Award finalist, and a finalist in other awards, including the Shirley Jackson, Philip K. Dick Award, as well as the Nommo Awards for speculative fiction by Africans. Eugen was announced in the honor list of the Otherwise Fellowships for "doing exciting work in gender and speculative fiction." *Danged Black Thing* made the Otherwise Award Honor List as a "sharp collection of Afro-Surrealist work." Stars and Sabers Publishing is also publishing her Sauútiverse novella, *The Nga'phandileh Whisperer*, in 2025. Read more about Eugen on her website: https://eugenbacon.com/.

Gemma Amor
Gemma Amor is a Bram Stoker® and British Fantasy Award nominated author, voice actor and illustrator based in Bristol, in the UK. She self-published her debut short story collection *Cruel Works of Nature* in 2018, and went on to release *Dear Laura*, *Grief Is a False God*, *White Pines*, *Girl on Fire*, *These Wounds We Make*, *We Are Wolves* And *Six Rooms* before signing her first traditional publishing deal for her novel *Full Immersion*, published by Angry Robot books in 2022. Gemma illustrates her own works and also provides original, hand-painted artwork for book covers on

commission. Gemma is the co-creator of horror-comedy podcast *Calling Darkness*, starring Kate Siegel, and her stories feature many times on popular horror anthology shows *The NoSleep Podcast* (including a six-part adaptation of *Dear Laura*), *Shadows at the Door*, *Creepy*, and *The Grey Rooms*. Read more about Gemma on her website: https://gemmaamorauthor.com/.

Greg van Eekhout
Greg van Eekhout is the author of four fantasy novels for adults and eight fantasy and science fiction novels for middle-grade readers, as well as officially licensed *Star Wars* fiction and dozens of short stories. His novel, *Weird Kid*, won the California Independent Booksellers Alliance's Golden Poppy Award for best middle-grade novel. Greg's book *The Ghost Job* was also an Andre Norton Nebula Award finalist! Other works of his have been finalists for the Nebula Award, Andre Norton Award, and Locus Award, and were listed by the New York Public Library among the best 100 books for children. Greg lives in San Diego. Learn more about Greg from his website: https://www.writingandsnacks.com/.

Helen Glynn Jones
Helen Glynn Jones writes fantasy and romantasy, as well as romance novels under the pen name Isadora Love. Helen made her traditional debut in 2024 with the novel, *The Last Raven*, billed as *"True Blood* meets *Twilight,"* publishing via One More Chapter/HarperCollins. Learn more about Helen at her website: https://journeytoambeth.com/.

J.L. Worrad
J.L. Worrad lives in Leicester, England, and has for almost all his life. He has a degree in classical studies from Lampeter University, Wales. He has found this invaluable to his growth as a science fiction and fantasy writer in that he soon discovered how varied and peculiar human cultures can be. He is the author of the fantasy novels *Pennyblade* and *The Keep Within*, published by Titan Books, and *Feral Space*, a space opera in two parts, published by Castrum Press. Find out more on J.L.'s website: https://jamesworrad.com/.

John Wiswell
John Wiswell is an ace/aro author who lives where New York keeps all its trees. He won the Nebula Award for Best Short Story for "Open House on Haunted Hill," the Locus Award for Best Novelette for "That Story

Isn't the Story," and has been a finalist for the Hugo, British Fantasy, and World Fantasy Awards. His short fiction has been translated into ten languages. His debut novel, *Someone You Can Build a Nest In*, released from DAW Books in April 2024. Find out more about John on his website: https://johnwiswell.blogspot.com/.

Jonathan L. Howard

Jonathan L. Howard is a game designer, scriptwriter, and a veteran of the computer games industry since the early 1990s, with titles such as the *Broken Sword* series to his credit. After publishing two short stories featuring Johannes Cabal ("Johannes Cabal and the Blustery Day" and "Exeunt Demon King") in H. P. Lovecraft's *Magazine of Horror*, *Johannes Cabal the Necromancer* was published in 2009 as his first novel. Since then there have been numerous sequels. He has also written *Carter & Lovecraft*, another series of novels. Find out more on Jonathan's website: http://www.jonathanlhoward.com/.

Kali Wallace

Kali Wallace is a Philip K. Dick Award-winning science fiction, fantasy, and horror author and geophysicist. She writes novels for adults, teens, and children, as well as a number of short stories and essays. Her science fiction horror-thriller *Dead Space* won the 2022 Philip K. Dick Award. She is also the author of the sci-fi horror *Salvation Day*, young adult novels *Shallow Graves* and *The Memory Trees* and the children's fantasy novels *The Secrets of Underhill* and *City of Islands*. Her short fiction has appeared in *Clarkesworld*, *F&SF*, *Asimov's*, *Lightspeed*, and Tor.com. She lives in the Pacific Northwest. Learn more about Kali on her website: https://www.kaliwallace.com/.

KC Grifant

KC Grifant is an award-winning writer based in Southern California who creates internationally published horror, fantasy, science fiction, and weird west stories. Many of her short stories have appeared in podcasts, magazines, games, and Stoker-nominated anthologies. Her weird western novel, *Melinda West: Monster Gunslinger* (Brigids Gate Press, 2023), described as a blend of *Bonnie & Clyde* meets *The Witcher* and *Supernatural*, is the first in a series. The second novel, *Melinda West and the Gremlin Queen*, will release in 2025. She is also author of the short story collection *Shrouded Horror: Tales of the Uncanny* (Dragon's Roost Press, 2024) and co-creator of the *Monster Gunslingers* card game. Learn more about KC from her website: https://scifiwri.com/.

Khan Wong

Khan Wong is a Lambda Award finalist speculative fiction author. Khan's background includes nonprofit arts administration, arts funding, playing the cello, firedancing, hula hooping, and poetry. His debut novel, *The Circus Infinite* (Angry Robot Books, 2022) was longlisted for the BSFA Best Novel and was a finalist for a Lambda Award. His second novel, *Down in the Sea of Angels*, publishes via Angry Robot Books in 2025. Learn more about Khan from his website: https://www.khanwong.com/.

Laurel Hightower

Laurel Hightower is the Bram Stoker®-nominated author of *Whispers in the Dark*, *Crossroads*, *Below*, *Every Woman Knows This*, *Silent Key*, *Spirit Coven*, and *The Day of the Door*, and has more than a dozen short fiction stories in print. Learn more about Laurel on her website: https://laurelhightower.com/.

Lizbeth Myles

Lizbeth Myles is a Scottish writer and podcaster. She frequently writes audio drama for *Big Finish*, and has contributed to their *Doctor Who*, *Blake's 7*, and *Survivor* ranges. Her story, "Peake Season," was a Scribe Award nominee. She's a three-time Hugo Award finalist, and has written for *SFX*, *Uncanny*, and *Doctor Who Magazine*. She can be heard on Hugo Award-nominated *Verity!* podcast, *Hammer House of Podcast*, and the ENNIE Award winning *How We Roll* podcast. Learn more on Lizbeth's website: https://lmmyles.com/.

Mya Duong

Mya Duong is the fantasy author of the *Mindful Things* series, a poet, and a healthcare worker. Mya Duong (in English pronounced Mia Dwong; in Vietnamese, Duong pronounced yuung or zuung) grew up in Wisconsin, then moved to California. She has been working in healthcare for 25 years. She writes in her free time, and currently lives in the San Diego area with her husband and two dogs. Learn more about Mya on her website: https://www.myaduong.com/.

Paul Cornell

Paul Cornell has written episodes of *Elementary*, *Doctor Who* ("Father's Day" and "Human Nature"), *Primeval*, *Robin Hood* and many other TV series, including his own children's show, *Wavelength*. He's worked for every major comics company, including his creator-owned series *I Walk With Monsters* for The Vault, *The Modern Frankenstein* for Magma, *Saucer Country* for Vertigo and *This Damned Band* for Dark Horse, and runs for Marvel and DC on *Batman and Robin*, *Wolverine* and *Young Avengers*. He's the writer of the *Lychford* rural fantasy novellas from Tor.com Publishing. He's won the BSFA Award for his short fiction, an Eagle Award for his comics, a Hugo Award for his podcast and shares in a Writer's Guild Award for his *Doctor Who* and the Grand Prix Nova and Scribe awards for the audio series Tom Clancy's *Splinter Cell: Firewall*. He's the co-host of *Hammer House of Podcast*. His latest book is the SF novella *Rosebud*, his latest graphic novel is Hugo-nominated *The Witches of World War II* for TKO and his latest comic series is *Con and On* for Ahoy. Learn more about Paul on his website: https://www.paulcornell.com/.

Pedro Iniguez

Pedro Iniguez is a horror and science-fiction writer from Los Angeles, California. A Rhysling Award finalist and Best of the Net and Pushcart Prize-nominated author, Pedro's poetry collection *Mexicans on the Moon: Speculative Poetry from a Possible Future* is out now from Space Cowboy Books. His horror fiction collection, *Fever Dreams of a Parasite*, is slated for a 2025 release from publisher Raw Dog Screaming Press. And Pedro's *Echoes and Embers: Speculative Stories* is the first solo author work publishing via Stars and Sabers Publishing. Learn more about Pedro from his website: https://pedroiniguezauthor.com/.

Peter McLean

Peter McLean was born near London in 1972, the son of a bank manager and an English teacher. He went to school in the shadow of Norwich Cathedral where he spent most of his time making up stories. He has since grown up a bit, if not a lot, and spent 25 years working in corporate IT. He is married to Diane and is still making up stories. Peter is the author of the War for the Rose Throne series, beginning with *Priest of Bones*. Learn more about Peter on his website: https://talonwraith.com/.

About the Authors

Ren Hutchings
Ren Hutchings is a speculative fiction writer, writing mentor, and lifelong SFF fan currently living in London, UK. Ren is the author of time travel space opera *Under Fortunate Stars* (Solaris, 2022) as well as the upcoming *An Unbreakable World* (Solaris, 2025) and *The Legend Liminal* (Stars and Sabers, 2025). Ren loves weird mysteries, pop science, elaborate book playlists, and pondering about alternate universes. Most of what she writes involves space, time, and/or uncanny liminal places. Read more about Ren on her website: https://www.renhutchings.com/.

Renan Bernardo
Renan is a 2023 Nebula Finalist, an Ignyte Finalist, a 2022 Utopian Award nominee, and a Locus-recommended author. He's also a SFWA member. His work has been published in English, Portuguese, German, Japanese, and Italian. Renan's collection of solarpunk/climate fiction stories, *Different Kinds of Defiance*, was published in 2024 by Android Press. Learn more about Renan from his website: www.renanbernardo.com.

Sarah L. Miles
Sarah L. Miles is a writer of prose and comics. She is also a comics journalist and book reviewer, and works in a comics and gaming shop. Sarah is also a competitive strongwoman, and enjoys tabletop gaming and Lego building, renovating furniture and painting things any color but white or cream. She lives on the south coast of England with her partner, and an ever-expanding collection of houseplants and books. Find Sarah L. Miles across social media as @iamgiantwoman and read more about her on her website: https://sarahlmiles.com/.

Stark Holborn
Stark's fiction has been nominated for the British Fantasy Awards, the BSFA Awards, and the New Media Writing Prize. Stark also works as a games writer on TIGA-award winning games projects, and is currently lead writer on SF detective game *Shadows of Doubt* and a contributing writer on cyberpunk slice of life sim *Nivalis*. Learn more about Stark on her website: https://starkholborn.com/.

T.L. Huchu
T.L. Huchu is a Nommo Award and Hurston/Wright Legacy Award-winning author. His work has appeared in *Lightspeed*, *Interzone*, *Analog Science Fiction & Fact*, *The Year's Best Science Fiction and Fantasy 2021*, *Ellery*

Queen Mystery Magazine, *Mystery Weekly*, *The Year's Best Crime and Mystery Stories 2016*, and elsewhere. He is the winner of a Hurston/Wright Legacy Award (2023), Alex Award (2022), the Children's Africana Book Award (2021), a Nommo Award for African SFF (2022, 2017), and has been shortlisted for the Caine Prize (2014) and the Grand prix de l'Imaginaire (2019). The Edinburgh Nights series now includes four books, with the latest, *The Legacy of Arniston House*, arriving late 2024. Follow him on Instagram: https://www.instagram.com/tendaihuchu/.

About the Editors

JENDIA GAMMON is a Nebula and BSFA Awards finalist author of fantasy, science fiction, and horror novels and short stories. She became a finalist for a 2024 Nebula Award (for *The Inn at the Amethyst Lantern*, as J. Dianne Dotson) and two 2024 BSFA Awards (as both Jendia Gammon and J. Dianne Dotson). She was also longlisted for the Lodestar Award and for two British Fantasy Awards. Jendia writes compelling characters within rich world-building. Jendia's campy horror novel, *Doomflower*, publishes in April 8, 2025 via Encyclopocalypse Publications. Her first thriller novel, with horror and sci-fi elements, *Atacama*, publishes May 13, 2025, via Sley House Publishing. She has eight books arriving in 2025 and beyond. Learn more about Jendia on her website, jendiagammon.com.

About the Editors

GARETH L. POWELL writes across multiple genres, including science fiction, horror and thriller, and his books feature relatable characters in extraordinary situations. He is the author of 20 published books, and is probably best known for The Embers of War trilogy, The Continuance Series, The Ack-Ack Macaque trilogy, *Light Chaser* (written with Peter F. Hamilton), and *About Writing*, his guide for aspiring authors. He has twice won the British Science Fiction Association Award for Best Novel and has been a finalist for the Locus Award, the British Fantasy Award, the Seiun Award, and the Canopus Award. Learn more about Gareth on his website, garethlpowell.com.

Upcoming Releases from Stars and Sabers Publishing

For 2025:

June 10—First Themed Anthology—*Of Enchantment, Enigma, and the Infinite*—a magic-themed anthology

July 15—*Echoes and Embers: Speculative Stories* by Pedro Iniguez

September 2—*The Nga'phandileh Whisperer* by Eugen Bacon

September 30—*The Legend Liminal* by Ren Hutchings

October 14—Second Themed Anthology—*Of Dread, Decay, and Doom*—a horror-themed anthology

For 2026:

February 3—*Shoeshine Boy & Cigarette Girl* by P.A. Cornell

March 10—*Imagine a Friend* by David Quantick

Learn more at starsandsabers.com.